THE
DEAD
WON'T
TELL

S. K. WATERS

THE
DEAD
WON'T
TELL

CamCat
Books

CamCat Publishing, LLC
Ft. Collins, Colorado 80524
camcatpublishing.com

Hardcover ISBN 9780744306019
Paperback ISBN 9780744306033
Large-Print Paperback ISBN 9780744306040
eBook ISBN 9780744306057
Audiobook ISBN 9780744306149

Library of Congress Control Number: 2022933558

Book and cover design by Maryann Appel

5   3   1   2   4

Camryn & Cathryn

PROLOGUE

July 25, 1969, 12:41 a.m., Hunts Landing

A crid sulfur from the fireworks faded with the nighttime breeze. Dr. Theodore Wexler held up his glass—red flashes from the police cars on the Quad pulsed chestnut in the bourbon. *Pulse. Pulse.* The cadence matched his heartbeat, steadier now, settled after this disrupted day of jubilee.

"Damn."

Fourteen hours ago, Armstrong, Aldrin, and Collins had splashed down into the tranquil waters of the Pacific, and the town had erupted in celebration. Engineers from Hunts Landing College—a small school on the Tennessee River—were instrumental in getting those men home safely. Their success ensured prestige and rewards. Theodore, the college president, had spent his day dreaming of accolades and endowments.

Now, however, his thoughts simmered.

Pulse. Pulse.

Wexler House stood elevated above the Quad. From the French doors of his study, he could inspect every corner of the common. He sipped seventeen-year-old Very Old Fitzgerald. The bourbon had been a reward, purchased three years ago when the college won the NASA contract, saved for today and stored in a particular nook in the cellar. Wexler had intended it for tonight's party.

Instead, only after the guests left, and he could brood in peace, did he send Cyrus to fetch the Fitzgerald. Now the bottle sat half empty.

Earlier, there'd been some fracas on the Quad. He'd observed the squad cars arrive with disinterest. If the incident involved any students, campus police would handle the situation. He would deal with the aftermath in the morning. No, his thoughts returned to the thick manila envelope on his desk, its contents strewn on his blotter.

Oblivious to the fiery liquid trickling down his throat, he sipped and contemplated. The implications of those papers tumbled through his thoughts as if he stood in the shadows of a snow-covered mountain, unable to escape the avalanche hurtling toward him. Yes, avalanche. The appropriate metaphor. The contents of the envelope could bury the college.

"Damn and damn again."

Like a chess player, he considered his first move, his second move, then a third, before discarding them all as futile and unlikely to save the school from exposure. Glass empty, he refilled it, three fingers' worth. His sister Nevelyn, who'd taken over management of the household (and of Theodore as well, if he would be truthful) after Theodore had been widowed, would disapprove. At the moment, though, he didn't care a bit what Nevelyn thought. He turned back to the open doors. There were more red lights now, from more squad cars than the campus police had in its fleet. Someone must have called in the town cops. With a scowl, he downed his drink. Allowing himself one final "Damn!", he swept the cursed papers into his desk drawer, and went out through the French doors.

CHAPTER ONE

Wednesday, March 11, 2015, 8:59 a.m., The Hunts Landing Times

Abbie Adams's loose fist hovered inches away from the engraved nickel nameplate reading *Sylvia Van Cleave*, and she wondered again if last night's nightmare, where Sylvia fired her, was coming true.

A summons from the editor of *The Hunts Landing Times* was rare. The last time, a reader had disputed a Sunday feature on worker conditions at the town's old cotton mills, calling the article an utter disparagement of her dear granddaddy Puckett, one of the town's more infamous mill owners.

Abbie had done the research on the piece for Will Irestone, the paper's primary reporter, and although she had double-checked every fact, the Pucketts had persuaded the paper to amend the article with more favorable language.

In Hunts Landing the memory of old money ran long, and its advertising dollars stretched far.

She gripped the strap of her shoulder bag, inhaled, and knocked.

At the terse "Come in!", she pushed open the door. Stacks of storage boxes littered the floor, Post-it notes covered the windows, and whiteboards crammed with scribbles dominated the walls. The cluttered office satisfied Abbie's sense of Woodward and Bernstein.

Sylvia Van Cleave's fingers flew over her keyboard. Her linen suit and silk blouse were crisp and professional, her hair was pulled back into a loose French braid, and the reading glasses perched on the tip of her nose only added to her flair. She extended a hand to the only empty chair but didn't stop typing with the other. One finger poised over the return key for a moment before she pressed it. "Abbie!" the editor smiled. "Thanks for coming in. We're in crisis mode today."

Part of the knot in Abbie's stomach loosened. At least Sylvia hadn't led with *You're fired.*

Sylvia fished a brown file folder from the messy pile on her desk. "Will crashed his Jeep into a cement truck last night."

Abbie gasped. "Is he alright?"

"On the one hand, yes," Sylvia said. "A mild concussion and a broken nose from the airbag. The bad part is that the truck crushed his leg. He needs a complete hardware reconstruction. Dammit," Sylvia shook her head. "There's no story in Hunts Landing worth speeding in the rain, but that's exactly what he did last night. No more marathons for Will, and that's going to really piss him off. After he's stabilized, he'll go into surgery."

Abbie realized she didn't know much about his private life, only that he was a bachelor. "Is anyone with him?"

"His sister is on her way." Sylvia handed her the folder. "I've farmed out his other assignments, but this one requires your touch. We're starting a new series for the Sunday edition. The history of Hunts Landing. Events that may have gone unreported or were reported only scantily. Will has begun the first piece, but it's not finished, and we've already sold the advertising. Waiting for his return isn't an option. Good news for you: you get the byline."

A byline!

Writing credentials were currency in this business.

Terrible that the opportunity came only because of Will's injuries, but gee, *a byline. By Abbie Adams.*

Sylvia motioned toward the folder. "This first story is an unsolved murder from 1969. Campus police found the body of a young Black woman, Rosalie DuFrayne, near the river. Cause of death: blunt force trauma. The police investigation was . . . half-hearted. Even this newspaper didn't seem to care much about the story. You'll find the reporter's notes and an unpublished article draft."

"Why unpublished?"

"No idea. Caleb Jackson covered the murder, but he died in 1989. His editor, Ozzie Etherington, passed four years ago. We can't ask them." She leaned forward. "There are two interesting angles to this story. The first one is the date. July 24, 1969. Do you remember the significance?"

"Of course," Abbie said. Anyone who'd grown up in Hunts Landing knew about the day the astronauts came back from the moon. Hunts Landing scientists had built the rocket systems that carried the Apollo crew into space, and the town still beamed with pride. July 24th was a day of celebration, starting with a parade and ending with parties that lasted all night long.

"That night," Sylvia continued, "there was a party on the college Quad, next to the river. Two hundred yards away, someone brutally killed Rosalie DuFrayne."

Abbie opened the file and found a photograph on top, a yearbook photo perhaps. Rosalie DuFrayne had been a looker, with light brown skin and bright eyes. "The police didn't do much of an investigation?"

"Next to none. That should be high on your list. Racism might have been one of the reasons why the authorities didn't sufficiently investigate the murder and why the paper's coverage was, well, let's say 'anemic.' I believe that's the aspect that Will was exploring."

Only because he didn't grow up here, Abbie thought. As a historian with an addiction for the truth, she wanted to dive right into any and every angle of the story, but as a resident of Hunts Landing, warning-bells pealed in her head. Perhaps forty-five years put enough time and distance between the present and the racial turbulence of the past. Or did it?

Given the viral nature of stories exposing potential racism, she wondered why the paper wanted to touch the topic now. Especially after the Puckett fiasco. "Don't you think this is a little risky for the paper?"

"It's part of the history of Hunts Landing," Sylvia said. "The murder of a Black girl that the police barely investigated and this very paper ignored? That's a story."

Abbie leafed through the folder. "You mentioned two interesting angles?"

"A more human aspect of the case. The victim's mother, Miss Etta DuFrayne, was the Wexler family cook. Rosalie worked with her mother at the Wexlers' party the night she died."

Abbie felt the blood drain from her face. "She worked for the Wexlers."

"Yes."

"And this is the first story in the series?"

"Yes."

"Why?"

"Funny thing about family-owned papers," Sylvia said. "They get to stick their hands in the editorial side of the house. The owners asked for *this* story."

"Did you know it was Dr. Wexler who shot down my thesis?" Abbie swallowed the sudden trickle of bile she tasted at the back of her throat.

The editor hesitated. "Yes, I knew. But your Dr. Wexler was only nineteen at the time of the murder. Miss Etta worked for his father,

Dr. *Theodore* Wexler. The question is, can *you* be objective about that family?"

"I don't know!" Abbie blurted before she could stop herself. She wanted this assignment, wanted the byline.

Sylvia took a seat on the armrest of the only other chair. "The board wants this series to tell the untold history of Hunts Landing, and the Wexlers are news in this town. I can't farm this out to someone who doesn't know the place. I need *you*. You're trained as a historian. Objectivity has been *ingrained* in you. Stick to the facts. What happened the night of July 24, 1969? Why didn't the police investigate thoroughly? Why did the paper ignore the story? How were the Wexlers involved? I smell something funny here, and the Wexlers are in the middle of it." Sylvia glanced at her watch. "I've got another meeting. Your article is due next Wednesday—legal will have to review this—and I need artwork by next Thursday. We print next Sunday."

All Abbie had to do to get the byline was go buy a jumbo bottle of Pepto Bismol to quench the nausea in her gut. After all these years, the Wexler name could still turn her stomach upside down. She tucked the file folder into her satchel. "Any tips on where to start?"

"Go talk to Will at the hospital. Room 227."

"He's about to go into surgery. They won't let me in."

Sylvia stood in dismissal. "Tell them you're Will's baby sister."

Wednesday, March 11, 7:37 a.m., Santa Monica, CA

Joss Freeman didn't know which crisis he should tackle first: his missing cat, his fiancée's empty closet, or the fallout from the phone call he'd just finished. Lincoln's missing pet carrier combined with the tangled mess of empty wire hangers only partially explained the cat's disappearance. Harriet loathed the long-haired Persian. Joss had never persuaded her to even pet the animal, let alone attempt to coax Lincoln into a pet carrier he had no intention of getting into. So why would she take him? And why had she left with no phone call, no note?

It wasn't the first time he'd missed a flight home.

Joss left two voicemails. Harriet would return the calls when she was good and ready. He opened the sliding glass door to the balcony. A few blocks away, the Pacific sparkled, a view that usually soothed him. Not today. Not when his career hung by a thread. The third crisis.

Shows got canceled all the time, but none whose hosts had as many social media followers as Joss did. At this moment, the news was going viral on Twitter and Instagram. #AmericasStories canceled. What will @JossFreemanHistorian do next? #IsHistoryDead? And some idiot would certainly post some Photoshopped meme of him in a gruesome state of demise.

The channel had called while his plane was in midair, and he hadn't returned the call until he'd landed and was far enough away from LAX that he could drive on autopilot. Stuck in gridlock, he'd been prisoner to the words coming through his car's speakers. "Shift in programming. *America's Stories* doesn't fit into the new concept."

The ocean was far enough that he could smell the salt in the air but couldn't quite make out the whitecaps on the water. *What to do next.*

He'd never been one to kowtow to the network establishment, which was why he'd been so unsuccessful yesterday. The six-hour flight to New York. The four-hour wait in the lobby of National Media Corporation's headquarters. The scant five minutes during which he attempted to enthrall programming executives with the reasons they should renew *America's Stories*.

Facts had always been his friend. The data was irrefutable. He'd never lost an advertiser. He had more social media followers and friends than all the other series on NMC combined. He couldn't define his ideal viewer because he didn't have one. Retired grandmothers commented on his posts as often as the high school girls suddenly acing history.

Joss loved being able to transform the dull, dusty names and dates from history books into vibrant stories that educated and entertained. His viewership reflected that.

His numbers were better than any other NMC series. Yet, those programming executives delivered the rebuke in seemingly innocent words: America's Stories *doesn't fit into the new concept.*

Joss didn't know what that meant. He didn't have many appealing options. He could pitch to one of the big networks, or he could go the indie route. Either option would compel him to spend more time on the business end of things and less time creating, and, well, creating was the fun part. None of his choices tickled his fancy. His doorbell chimed, and he buzzed in whoever it was without checking. Harriet, maybe? His heart leaped at the possibility.

Instead, Ursula Quinville swept in, a short dynamo with a backpack slung over her shoulder, sunglasses on her head, and readers tucked into her cleavage. "What the hell did you say in New York?" she breathed.

Ursula, his brilliant but excitable producer from the Bahamas, never wasted time on silly things like 'How was your flight?' At the moment, Joss didn't know if he appreciated that characteristic. "All I did was pitch them the profile for a new series. *America's Stories II: 500 Years of Amazing Tales.*"

"And all they did was cancel your old one! Zeesh, Joss, how many times to I have to tell you to leave this stuff to me?" She flung her backpack down onto his sofa. A shoulder strap snagged her readers, which tumbled under the coffee table. "I mean, what were you thinking? To appeal to that fraction of the audience that still thinks all true American history begins with Columbus?"

Joss thought it best not to mention the spectacles. "It's the same problem historians always have with pre-Columbian events. There's no documentation we can refer to."

"Oh, shut up. You hypothesize on camera all the time. You're the king of *what if.*" Ursula plopped herself onto the sofa next to her knapsack and dug for her phone. "We've got one chance to fix this," she said, and felt beneath her throat for her readers. "Aw, dammit."

Joss knelt and reached for the missing glasses. "How do we fix it?"

"How do we . . . ?" Her head trembled with the effort at self-control, and Joss could have sworn her jaw was about to become detached from the rest of her face. She pointed a single finger at him, once, hard. "*We* do nothing. *You* will do whatever the new director of programming wants you to do. Which is . . ."—she used the same finger to swipe on her phone—"a treatment on missing treasures from the Civil War."

Joss stifled his groan. "C'mon, anything but the Civil War."

"Civil War, Joss. Missing treasures. The new guy's named Kenetsky and according to his Twitter account he's a buff. You pitch him a week from Friday."

The countdown timer ticked in the back of his head. *Nine days times twenty-four hours a day . . .* "What am I supposed to come up with in a week?"

"You've gotta dazzle him. Any ideas?"

Too many, not necessarily good ideas, ricocheted through his skull like pinballs run amok. "I need more than twelve seconds."

"Don't take too many. You've only got nine days." She picked up her backpack and slung it over her shoulder. "Call me later." With a kiss on his cheek, she left.

Joss locked the door behind her. *Something new? In nine days?* Did Kenetsky have any idea what he was asking? It took *weeks* of planning, research, prep, and shooting to develop a documentary. The pinballs were heading toward Tilt.

He knew next to nothing about the Civil War, other than that it was an overplayed subject in the documentary universe.

He didn't have time to do a 101 course on the topic.

What about Abbie Adams?

When they were undergraduates, Joss had shared a house with Abbie and four other students who were at school on athletic scholarships. He and Abbie were the sole academics in the house, spending endless late nights with boxed wine and arguing the finer points of history. During those early years after graduation, they'd remained fairly close. Close enough to manage cross-country visits, although once she'd had her kids, those trips were harder on her. He'd stood in for her husband, Zach, deployed in Iraq, at her daughter's christening.

The Abbie he'd known in college, assiduously passionate about everything historical, who fleshed out multiple research topics before selecting one, just for fun, might be the person Joss needed. He wasn't ashamed to admit that, more than once, he'd taken one of Abbie's rejects to use for his own assignment. Joss was good at telling the story. In fact, he wasn't just good, he was great at it. But finding the story to tell, that's where Abbie shined. Of course.

Abbie was what he needed now. She'd help him come up with something sexy enough for Kenetsky. He activated his headset. "Siri, call Abbie Adams."

Wednesday, 9:49 a.m., Hunts Landing Medical Center

He looks terrible, Abbie thought.

Will Irestone reminded Abbie of a really young Denzel Washington. He was a big guy, who'd played football for Auburn. Today, he looked like the entire offensive line had piled onto him. He sported a swollen and taped nose, a black eye, and a large bandage on his forehead. Butterfly bandages crisscrossed his face. His left arm was in a cast, and the sheer number of machines surrounding him took Abbie's breath away.

Abbie stepped closer to the bed and whispered, "Will."

His one undamaged eye opened. "Hey, sunshine." His voice was low, raspy, and he spoke slower than he usually did. He winked at her, then winced.

"Quit that. What did you do to yourself?" Abbie pulled the single chair closer to his bedside.

"Hit a cement truck. Don't recommend it." The hint of a grin at the corner of his mouth belied the serious surgery that was only hours away. "I don't know how much time we have before they come get me, so let's talk." His phone, nestled in his right hand, buzzed. He ignored it.

"Does the truck look as bad?"

"The truck didn't get a morphine drip. I'll be alright. Focus on the story. It's a big break for you. Byline, Abbie Adams. You got the folder?"

Abbie pulled it from her bag.

"Caleb Jackson was the reporter in '69. That there is his file. I didn't get to dig too deep, but here's what I found out. Take notes."

She had already pulled a notepad and pen out of her bag. "Ready."

"I'm going to record us, 'cause I'm gonna talk fast." He swiped with one good thumb twice, then placed the phone on the bed near the edge. "Rosalie DuFrayne, student at Hunts Landing College, found dead by the river the morning of July 25, 1969." He paused and caught his breath. "Hunts Landing PD in charge. The paper assigns Caleb Jackson to the story. Caleb does his thing, writes a good article, about fifteen column inches. He submits it to his editor. You see some stapled pages in there?"

Two double-spaced typed pages were paper-clipped to a black-and-white photo. Abbie carefully held up the fragile pages, crinkly sheets of old-fashioned typing paper with preprinted margins and blue pencil marks.

"Reporters used to peck out their stories on that kind of paper. That was Caleb's original article. It was good enough for a blue-pencil edit. But that's not the version that made the paper. The clippings are in the file. That's it, that's the one."

Abbie held a half-page of yellowed newsprint, with a small article circled in ink. Only two column inches. She read aloud. "Campus police found the body of a Black woman Friday morning in the woods west of Hunts Landing College. Hunts Landing police are treating this case as a homicide." She shook her head slightly. "This is it?"

"Yup. Now, read Caleb's original." He winced again at some pain in his bruised body.

Abbie wondered if the morphine was working. She read again, this time from the typewritten pages.

Campus police found the body of twenty-year-old Rosalie DuFrayne of Hunts Landing early Friday morning in the woods southwest of the campus. "Right now, we're beginning our investigation, and we will not speculate prematurely," Police Chief Kenneth Farrow told reporters. Witnesses last saw Ms. DuFrayne leave the home of Dr. Theodore Wexler, president of Hunts Landing College, where she spent the evening as a domestic. Dr. Wexler's party celebrated the safe return of NASA astronauts from the moon. The Wexler family is not commenting.

Abbie stopped speaking, scanning ahead to the second page. "It's an entire page on Wexler and his party and the school. Nothing more on Rosalie until the end. 'Funeral arrangements to be announced tomorrow.' Is it wrong to say that this is fluff?"

"Exactly what I thought," Will said. "But a lot of fluff about the Wexlers. Now, Caleb left some handwritten notes in the file, legal-size page."

Abbie found the page ripped from a legal pad, covered with doodles and scribbles. Some notes were easy to decipher—Rosalie was the daughter of Wexler's cook who lived on such-and-such a street, the investigating officer was Officer Turner. A drawing on the bottom perplexed her, though, a pencil sketch with the name Dr. Theodore Wexler underneath, and the words respect for family, stand down next to his ear. Someone had underlined the words *respect* and *stand down*, twice. Abbie couldn't tell if the drawing resembled Old Dr. Wexler or not, but she liked Caleb Jackson's depiction of a lit pipe and smoke swirling around Wexler's head.

"Respect for the family?"

"Here's what I think. The police didn't have much to go on at first, so Caleb follows his nose to the Wexlers. Writes his piece and submits. Ozzie edits, which would only happen if the story were going to press. Then someone, I don't know who, maybe Ozzie, tells Caleb to back off. What gets printed instead isn't even two column inches. That's enough to make my nose itch."

Abbie thought for a second. "And now, forty-six years later, the board is pushing for this story."

Will shifted his position, causing his IV tube to swing and eliciting a groan. "I don't know the reasons behind their thinking, but I'll tell you this. Anytime a reporter is asked to back off, it's bad news. No idea why the board wants to open that can of worms."

A nurse in pink scrubs entered and propped the door open with a rubber wedge. "They'll be coming for you in a minute, Mr. Irestone." She left, and Will's gaze followed her out.

"Think she'd date me?"

"You've got other things to worry about," Abbie said. Even banged up as he was, Will was still trying to tell jokes.

"And so do you. Listen, the police never caught Rosalie's killer, so don't go down any rabbit holes. The case is over forty years old. Some people, you're just not going to find, you understand? Start with background. Try to track down her family, her friends, her schoolmates. She was a Black girl in a predominantly white private school in the deep South in 1969—how'd she manage that? Did she have a boyfriend?"

Two orderlies with a gurney entered the hospital room, and Will stopped. He swiped his phone two more times. "I sent you the recording."

Abbie gathered her things and squeezed his good hand. "Good luck."

"No need to wish you luck," he almost smiled. "You've got this."

Abbie had missed two texts from her teenagers.

Fourteen-year-old Martha's volleyball practice with her travel club had been extended; the girls had gotten trounced in a scrimmage Monday night, and there was a big tournament next weekend. Sixteen-year-old George was catching a ride home from school with Pudge, who'd passed his driver's test last week. At least she wouldn't have to interrupt her afternoon to pick up her kids.

She started to text George back when her phone chimed *Twinkle twinkle little star*. The ring-tone was Abbie's joke on her old college roommate, Joss Freeman, who thought himself a TV star.

Twinkle twinkle . . .

She answered. "Hey."

"Darling, I need you."

His story tumbled out in a frantic rush. His series had gotten the axe. He needed help. He knew next to nothing about the Civil War. He only had nine days.

"Whoa, Joss, hold on. My expertise was eighteenth century, not nineteenth. Pre-Revolution. You've got the wrong war."

"Don't you have some leftover paper from Northwestern? Just to point me in the right direction?"

Joss-the-TV-star lived in a very different world from Joss-the-history-student, although student Joss was never much good at coming up with his own research topics; he'd preferred taking Abbie's fleshed-out rejects.

Dang it.

Despite *The Times* assignment, she couldn't turn him away. Joss had held baby Martha at her christening while Zach was in Iraq. The kids called him Uncle Joss. He was family.

Abbie exhaled. Her grad school papers were up in the attic, collecting dust, along with the lifetime work of her parents. She wondered if one of those boxes held material sexy enough for a television show. "Tell you what. Give me until tonight, I'll see what I can find."

"I'll call you in two hours. Catch you later—"

"Wait, Joss!" Abbie gripped the phone hard, as if that would prevent his *click*.

CHAPTER TWO

Wednesday, 10:31 a.m., Abbie's House

Joss's problem would not stop Abbie from diving into the Rosalie DuFrayne case first. She entered her house from the garage door into the kitchen. Bright morning sunshine on the white cabinets, buttercup-yellow walls, and pale gray granite countertops welcomed her. For years, Abbie's mother had pleaded for the update to get rid of the 1970s linoleum and olive-colored appliances. Mathias Adams ultimately assented, and the contractors completed the remodel in December 1998. Two weeks before Christmas. Two weeks before a drunk driver on Andrew Jackson Parkway claimed the lives of Elsa and Mathias Adams.

This would always be her Momma's kitchen. Abbie hadn't changed a single thing.

Benjamin Franklin, the family dog, whined. "Alright," she soothed. He trotted ahead to the glass doors separating the kitchen from the enclosed sunporch. She let the mutt out, then carried the file to the dining room.

During grad school, Abbie had confiscated the dining room. The antique table, a ten-seater, was long enough to accommodate the many books and journals that accompanied a historian's work. She displayed her mother's porcelain behind the curved glass doors of the china cabinet, while the antique Georgian sideboard held her printer and office paraphernalia. Whiteboards dominated both walls, usually full of Post-its, research scribbles, and the occasional odd note from the kids. The family survived on whatever freelance work Abbie could get.

Today, the boards were mostly empty.

She pushed the silk flower centerpiece down to the end and sat. Will should be in surgery by now. And, because of a cement truck, she was going to earn her first journalism byline. That she'd been published before, in academic journals, was of little consequence; more people probably read *The Times* Sunday edition than *Southeastern Annals of History*.

Abbie pulled out the contents of the folder.

Topmost, the black-and-white photo of Rosalie DuFrayne, the lovely girl's eyes staring up at her. Rose touchups indicated a yearbook or perhaps a graduation picture. The face, serious at the urging of some unknown photographer, was unaware of the horrific fate that awaited her. She put the photo to the side and picked up the next one.

At the sunporch door, Benny scratched to be let back in—she opened the door without taking her eye off the picture of three smiling Black women, Rosalie in the center. All three girls wore sensible skirts and blouses and carried loose-leaf notebooks, but their smiles were carefree. On the back of the photo, she found a potential caption, handwritten in pencil: Rosalie DuFrayne (center) with fellow students Cleta Blakebill and Bernice Strong, May 1969.

She trusted Caleb Jackson's instincts. It would make an excellent picture for the story.

Abbie uncapped a blue dry-erase marker and began a to-do list, starting with the names Cleta Blakebill and Bernice Strong.

Next, she scrutinized Caleb Jackson's handwritten notes for anything she'd missed before. *Officer Turner*. Wait . . . could that be Jethro Turner? Hunts Landing wasn't that big forty years ago. There couldn't have been more than one cop named Turner on the force. Abbie hurried to her bedroom, to the hope chest at the foot of her bed. In a cardboard shoebox, she found her mother's address book, an old-fashioned one with a floral cover. With haste, she flipped through the pages and found *Jethro Turner* on the third page of *T*'s. "Gotcha." Now Abbie recalled a tall, skinny, red-headed cop who came to barbecues. "Thank you, Momma." She kissed the address book and returned to the dining room. To her list, she added *Jethro Turner*.

Two yellowing articles remained in the folder. Rosalie's obituary read:

"May 12, 1949 – July 24, 1969. Rosalie DuFrayne, 20, passed away Thursday. Ms. DuFrayne, a member of the New South Baptist Church, is survived by her mother, Miss Etta DuFrayne of Hunts Landing, and an aunt, Eugenia DuFrayne, of St. Louis. Services will be private."

On the margin of the obituary was a note written in pen, burial at church.

No mention of a father, and Rosalie's mother was referred to as "Miss." How difficult that must have been for Miss Etta, raising a child all by herself. The challenges of single parenting were all too familiar to Abbie. The last document was a full-page newspaper story covering the college's involvement in a NASA investigation of fraud. Finger following the text, she read the article.

September 8, 1971 – Hunts Landing. A grand jury indicted Dr. Quentin McCain on thirty-two counts of fraud in connection with the widening grant scandal at Hunts Landing College.

Hunts Landing was old enough for its share of scandals and juicy stories, but this one eluded Abbie's memory. She scanned the clipping as the back of her mind churned over the best way to dig up this dirt. No mention of Rosalie's name, no note in Jackson's sloppy hand, no apparent reason for Jackson to include it in his file. What was the connection between Rosalie and a scandal which hit the news two years after her death?

Or was it a misfiled piece of meaningless paper?

Abbie considered the fragile documents spread out on the table.

At the start of any project, she always copied and taped research materials to a whiteboard to allow for an at-a-glance overview. Old habits, from years spent handling historical documents, guided her. She made color copies of the folder contents and taped the duplicates to the whiteboard, tucking the originals back into the folder. At the top center, she taped Rosalie DuFrayne's photo. Such a pretty girl.

The wall acutely illustrated how little she had to go on.

What was it that Will had said? *Get the background first.* She checked her phone, found his message in her email inbox, with the audio recording of their visit attached. She listened to the audio, taking notes as Will's hoarse drawl played. Friends. Classmates. Officer (Jethro?) Turner. Stand down.

Sylvia had said that after Rosalie's murder, the cops did little and the paper did less. Abbie wondered how much less. How did the coverage of Rosalie's murder compare to others at the time? She added to her list. Look up Times reports, other '69 murders.

Abbie found comfort in lists, and this one was just the beginning. She would start with Jethro Turner. The number in her mother's address book was no longer in service, but she lucked out with Hunts Landing's online phone directory.

"Hello?" His voice was gruffer than she remembered.

"Mr. Turner? This is Abbie Adams. Do you remember me? Elsa Adams' daughter?"

"Sure, I remember you. Always running around in pigtails. Call me Jethro. What can I do for you?"

She'd always called him Mr. Turner as a kid, had taught her kids to treat adults with the same respect, so she found it uncomfortable to 'call him Jethro'. "Well, I'm on assignment with *The Times*, re-searching a murder from 1969. Rosalie DuFrayne." She allowed him time to brush the cobwebs off his memories. "The information I have is that an Officer Turner was investigating. Was that you, by any chance?"

He was slow to respond, perhaps still brushing off those cobwebs. "Rosalie DuFrayne. Now that's a name I haven't heard in a year of Sundays. Yup, that was me. Why is the newspaper interested?"

Why, indeed? "It's the first story in a new series on the history of Hunts Landing."

"*This* is the first story?" He didn't wait for her answer. "What do you need from me?"

"I'd like to discuss the murder and the investigation. I wouldn't take too much of your time."

This time the uncomfortable pause was at least ten seconds long. "I'm sorry, Abbie. It's been too long. I really don't think I can help you."

The phone went silent.

Dang it. Abbie tossed her phone onto the table, a little harder than intended, then winced. Now was not the time to crack a phone.

Dang it.

Her first witness, and she'd blown it.

Think, Abbie, think. Maybe she'd been too pushy? Maybe she hadn't been pushy enough? Weren't reporters supposed to be pushy?

Her phone sounded with Joss's text tone.

Joss: Anything yet?

He'd keep bugging her until she'd found something for him. *Joss knows how to be pushy.* She stared up at the ceiling. Perhaps the sooner she got it over with, the easier it would be. And while she was dusting off old files, her mind could percolate on how to approach Jethro Turner.

Wednesday, 10:59 a.m., Abbie's Attic

Abbie inhaled the dusty, musty air of her attic with a smile. Immunity to the evils of dust is one characteristic a serious historian develops over time.

The Adams family archive.

For years, her parents had stored books, papers, and all the materials for their various research projects up here, and it was crammed with the stories of other families and other people, instead of documents and artifacts from her own family. With pride, she stood amid the collections of three historians, even if her own fleeting career had produced but a fraction of the history preserved in this room, paying a little tribute to the work and the lives contained within this space.

The attic ran the long length of the house. In the days before computers, historical research generated vast amounts of paper, and her pack-rat parents had squirreled away plenty. After their deaths, she had spent weeks sorting books, newspaper clippings, and endless reams of copy paper. Yes, she took care with the documents, but the grieving daughter had paid only the barest attention to their content.

She had archived her father's work on the northern side of the attic and her mother's on the southern side. Neither Mathias Adams nor Elsa Adams had specialized in the Civil War era, but both had taught classes, undergraduate and graduate.

At the far end, her own work lay in a sorry mess, thrown in a heap and covered by a marine tarp. Out of sight.

But the briefest glimpse of the marine tarp brought her back to the present. The sooner she dealt with the Joss situation, the sooner she could focus on Rosalie DuFrayne's murder. *Fine. Let's get this over with.*

Joss needed Civil War treasure. Abbie doubted either of her parents had been treasure hunters, but she methodically checked each box, as if looking at it for the first time. All those years ago, when she spent so much time with these boxes, she'd only thought to preserve her parents' work. She hadn't been concerned with cataloging the contents, sorting direct sources from second- and third-hand sources, like any well-trained historian would. Then, she'd only packed the documents carefully into file boxes and plastic tubs.

Any project which showed promise, she stacked carefully in the center of the room. She concentrated on the 1860s and 1870s. At the end, she found eight possible candidates. She stepped back and surveyed the pile. She should grab the projects and go back downstairs. But the marine tarp at the far end of the attic was like the island of the Sirens, calling her, beckoning her.

How many years had it been? Ten? Eleven? A decade's worth of dust and spider webs coated a blue plastic sheet, concealing the evidence of her failure. With Frank Wexler's face floating on the periphery of her consciousness, her feet moved of their own volition, unstoppable, to the end of the attic.

She lifted a corner of blue plastic a little, tugged some more, then yanked the damned thing away from the pile. Remembering.

Remembering how her whole body shook with the depth of her heartbreak. How in a flurry she'd torn down every scrap of research from the dining room, shoveled her books and notebooks and files and Zip-drive cassettes and index cards, carrying the fragments of her work in a frenzied repetition of stomps up the stairs to the attic, tossing them to the floor at the far end. Refuse. Garbage. How, for the briefest of moments, she'd considered taking gasoline and setting the whole thing ablaze. Up and down the stairs, past her children who'd trembled in the corner, witnesses to their mother's despair, their faces wet with silent tears. Into the garage, to the boat, to that damned fishing boat Zach deemed so important, but which only consumed most of the precious few hours they'd had left. How, strengthened by her fury, she'd ripped the marine tarp off the boat, tearing holes where ropes secured the plastic to the craft, back up the stairs, to toss the tarp over the pile of destroyed research.

The disheveled remnants of her doctoral research lay in a cluttered mound of debris six feet wide. Wispy spider webs crisscrossed the yellowed papers. Hesitantly, she knelt, ran her hand across the top of the pile, winced at the unexpected nick on her finger which drew blood. *Ouch!* How could she forget the framed picture of Dr. Frank Wexler and his graduate students from 2003, the one she'd kicked on that terrible day? Shards of glass from the broken frame remained in the pile.

Abbie threw the tarp back on the pile of papers, almost panting with the effort. Now was not the time to be distracted by her own past.

As historians, her parents had both been fanatical record keepers, in those heady days before everything was computerized and could be indexed and searched. In each of the boxes she'd selected, Abbie found the inventory her mother or father had prepared, a one- or two-page document outlining the history contained in the archive. She would scan these and email them to Joss. He could choose. Then she'd scan the rest of the materials and email him the lot.

Without a further glance at the tarp, Abbie headed for the stairs. She'd wasted enough precious time on her memories.

Wednesday, 11:09 a.m., Somewhere Over the Rockies

Landing a same-day ticket these days was next to impossible. Joss wound up swapping floor seats to Friday's Lakers game for a buddy ticket from Larry, his flight-attendant neighbor. Squeezed between a slumbering giant of a man in the window seat and a talkative Mrs.

Gunderson on the right, Joss brooded over his dilemma. He needed to dazzle this Kenetsky guy. He needed to find a Civil War treasure story no one else had done before.

Surely Abbie could dig something out of her attic.

Nine days times twenty-four hours a day times sixty minutes . . .

He couldn't brood much. Mrs. Gunderson's grandnephew was an artistic genius, and the lady had the photos on her phone to prove it.

When the plane landed in Dallas, he sprinted away from Mrs. Gunderson, determined to be the first on the standby list for the connecting flight to Hunts Landing. Only after he'd checked in and settled for the two-hour wait did he stop to breathe. And think.

So consumed with the show's cancellation, he had given little thought to Harriet's empty closet. That he was more concerned she'd packed cat food for Lincoln than whether she was all right spoke volumes about their relationship. Harriet had left before. She'd come back. He wondered, this time, if he even cared.

She'd thrown wet clay at his head during one argument. With the temperamental sculptress, when it was good, it was so good. When it was bad, it was, well . . . But for her to take Lincoln with her, that was below the belt.

Joss called her. The call went straight to voicemail. What could he say? *What have you done with my cat?* Instead, he was brief. "Honey, I'm flying to Hunts Landing to work with Abbie Adams. I'll call when I get there."

He wondered if he'd given Abbie enough time to dig through her stuff and find him a project. Probably not. He called anyway. This call also went straight to voicemail. Why were the women in his life ignoring him today?

Get your mind off Harriet. Joss pulled up a browser on his phone and started a search. *Civil war treasures. Ugh.* The top results were mindless websites published by enthusiasts and conspiracy-theorists. He needed to get to Hunts Landing.

The gate-clerk activated her microphone. "Flight three-twenty-two to Hunts Landing has been delayed."

Of course.

Wednesday, 12:27 p.m., Abbie's Dining Room

Fingers drummed on either side of her laptop. Her first day as a reporter had sucked so far, Abbie acknowledged. How could she get Jethro Turner to talk to her? Pushiness was not in her DNA. She was trained as a historian and made her living as a researcher. All of her subjects had either been long dead or existed only as static images on a screen. She wanted to call Will, ask for his advice, but it was too soon for him to be out of surgery, let alone recovery.

And Frank Wexler's involvement in this marred her first chance at a byline. Eleven years after he'd killed off her dreams, he was still affecting her life. It wasn't fair.

Abbie made some fresh coffee. While it brewed, she closed her eyes and inhaled, an exercise she'd learned in grief counseling after her husband Zach's death. Focused breathing helped, when her mind raced and her heart fluttered, when things seemed overwhelming.

Oh, who was she kidding? Breathing exercises wouldn't help today. She needed to talk things out. She grabbed her bag and keys. "Guard the fort, Benny."

Abbie's best friend from childhood, Loreen Oliver, owned a shop on the Square. Although she usually walked, Abbie drove. An uncomfortable urgency hit her. Besides, the sky had changed from blue to gray while she'd been in the house. March weather was so unpredictable in the Tennessee Valley.

Only a week to research and write this story. And, sometime within that week, she'd have to face Frank Wexler. *Sooner rather than later.* She parked in front of the shop. Loreen would settle her fraying nerves.

The Sommelier, Hunts Landing's only wine shop, was housed in a nineteenth-century Victorian townhouse. The retail space occupied the ground level. Loreen had spent a small fortune restoring the original flooring and woodwork, filling the rooms with artisan racks and oak tasting tables, giving the place a Napa Valley atmosphere. On the second floor, her private apartment reflected the house's history, full of antiques and overstuffed furniture. In the main showroom, Abbie found her friend setting up the day's samples. "I like."

Loreen's face brightened at sight of her. "Try this." She held out a plate with a thin slice of French baguette spread with a creamy cheese and topped with a sliver of pear. "This is a new Camembert we just got in. I poached the fruit with a brown sugar and a splash of sherry."

Abbie took a bite and closed her eyes in delight. "Oh gosh, this is good."

Loreen poured an inch of an amber liquid into a tasting glass and handed it to her friend. "Wash it down with this. Fantastic, right?"

"Isn't it a bit early?" She sipped anyway. "Oh, yeah." She moaned a foodie's moan of pleasure.

Loreen eyed her friend up and down. "You're dressed up. Tell me about it over here. I've got a new malbec from Argentina you've got to try." She led the way to a bar across of the room.

"You know I haven't had lunch yet."

At the tasting bar, Loreen busied herself opening a fresh bottle. "In some parts of Europe, they serve vino with breakfast. Don't be a snoot. So, what's wrong?"

The two women had first met on the playground when they were five years old. Susie Meeks, a girl with Dresden doll looks, had poked fun of the two little girls with unruly brown curls and freckles. In an instant, Abbie and Loreen joined forces. Abbie's mother would later tell the story of how the new friends had taken little Susie Meeks *out*. Since that day, Loreen had been Abbie's best friend, and could detect Abbie's mood with a single look.

"You heard about Will Irestone?"

"It was all the talk at Suzette's Bakery this morning," Loreen said. "What's Sylvia going to do without him?"

"She's divvied up his assignments, and I got one of them. A new feature series for the Sunday edition. The history of Hunts Landing. Sylvia feels it's in my bailiwick."

"That's fantastic! So why are you down?"

"Because I'm not sure I can do the assignment. On the other hand, I want, no, I *need* the byline."

Loreen sniffed. "And what makes you think you can't do it?"

Abbie briefly filled in her friend on the case and the lack of official interest in the story at the time. "But that's not the worst part."

"I give."

"The dead girl was connected to the Wexler family."

"Get outta town!" Loreen gulped from her wine glass. "Now that is interesting. So, what's the problem?"

Elbows on the bar, Abbie dropped her face into her hands. "I don't know how to interview witnesses."

"Oh, there's a simple solution to that." Loreen topped off Abbie's glass to near full.

"Which would be?"

"YouTube."

Oh, Loreen can fix me just right, so fast.

She'd been right to come here. But that wasn't the end of her problems. "Wait, there's more. I'm the reporter on this piece, not the researcher. I have to maintain objectivity, and I'm not sure I can do that with Frank Wexler."

"Why do you have to be objective? It's a historical piece, right? Didn't you always tell me how historians can't be objective because histories are always subject to the interpretations of the historian?"

Abbie shook her head. "No, I was quoting Nietzsche. 'There are no facts, only interpretations.' But isn't it weird that the paper asked me to explore the dead girl's connection to the Wexlers in particular? My impression was they *want* me to find dirt on the Wexlers."

"What's weird is that you aren't jumping at the chance to do it."

"Loreen—"

"You should pounce at the opportunity to get even with that sonofabitch."

"My beef," Abbie said, placing the snifter on the counter a little too hard, "is with Dr. Frank Wexler, not his parents, not his wife, not his kids. If I find any dirt, it could embarrass the entire family. Why would a newspaper want to put the Wexlers through that kind of humiliation? This doesn't pass the smell test."

Loreen pursed her lips. "What do you care? You'll get the hyline. Besides, just because you thought Dr. Wexler walked on water, doesn't mean other people did."

"I never thought . . ." Wisps of memory, of rushing to Loreen's house to tell her about her latest meeting with Frank Wexler, flitted through her mind. "Was I that pathetic?" Abbie asked.

Loreen reached for Abbie's hands. "Never pathetic. But you counted on Frank Wexler, and he let you down, for no other reason than he is a genuinely hateful man. So why you would jeopardize your career, and your livelihood, over some misplaced loyalty to that jackass is beyond me."

Abbie paled at the rebuke, but she saw the immediate flash of regret soften Loreen's eyes.

"Take the job," Loreen continued. "Get the byline. And for once in your life, screw Frank Wexler." She held up her glass. "Cheers."

"Cheers." Abbie took another bit of the poached pear delight. Part of it went down the wrong pipe. She started choking.

The front doorbell dinged.

Abbie coughed droplets of malbec into a bar napkin, and her eyes watered from the exertion.

"Let me help," a deep, masculine voice said.

Through tear-blurred eyes and a traitorous nose that threatened to sneeze Argentinian wine all over the bar, Abbie discovered a strange man holding a white handkerchief out to her. *What kind of man still carries a white handkerchief?*

She tossed the purple-spotted bar napkin aside and coughed into the snow-white linen.

"Geez, Abbie," Loreen said, coming around the bar. "People are gonna think you don't like my wine. Hi, Nick."

"Everything going okay in here?" the guy named Nick asked.

Abbie nodded with his handkerchief pressed to her mouth. One more cough. "I'm fine, thank you." She folded the cloth to hide her wine drops and hesitantly handed it back to him. "Thank you."

He took it with a smile. "You're welcome. Nick Preston."

The handshake was uncomfortable, considering her face was still a little red from the near-choking incident.

Loreen saved her. "Nick, let me introduce my oldest and dearest friend, Abbie Adams. Her mamma named her after the second first lady of the United States, 'though most of us never understood why. And this, pal of mine, is Detective Nick Preston, the newest addition to Hunts Landing's finest."

Nick was taller than most men she knew, with close-cropped dark hair and the teasing hint of a beard the boys at the high school only dreamed of cultivating. His eyes were the clearest gray she'd ever seen.

She could stare into those eyes all day.

Which was something she could ill afford to do. She needed to leave. "It's very nice to meet you, Nick. Sorry, Lo', gotta run." She kissed her friend's cheek.

Loreen frowned. "Abbie, where's your manners? Stay a bit."

Abbie recognized the cajoling lilt in Loreen's voice, the lilt that meant Loreen was up to something. She shouldered her bag, having no intention of playing into one of Loreen's schemes. "Can't. Deadline."

"So come back later for Wine Down Wednesday," Loreen pleaded.

"Not this week. Bye." Abbie headed toward the door.

"What about you, Nick?" Loreen said behind her. "You up for the games tonight?"

"I can't either," Nick said. "Taking my daughter out to celebrate. The volleyball club let her join the team as a trainer."

Abbie stopped and spun on her heel. "What? Hunts Landing Volleyball Club?"

Nick nodded.

"My Martha is on the team." Oh, how was she going to cope at all the tournaments and road trips and day-long stints in food tents with a parent who looked as scrumptious as Nick Preston? Abbie gave herself a mental shake. *Byline.* "I'm sure I'll be seeing you, Nick."

Once more, she tried to leave

"Hey." Nick met her at the door. "Can you recommend a restaurant a fourteen-year-old girl would like?"

She had to crane her neck a little to look into his face. Thankfully, the club volleyball season was almost over. "Mario's Pizza, other side of the Square. Be warned, though, the fourteen-year-old boys like it too."

Wednesday, 1:14 p.m., Dallas-Ft. Worth Airport

Every time Joss's phone buzzed, his heart leapt a little. All he needed was an affirmative from Abbie Adams, or an "I'm OK," from Harriet, to settle his nerves. Instead, he seemed doomed to disappointment and never ending robocalls.

As he stood in line at the Starbucks a few gates down from his next flight, he admitted that the copious amounts of coffee he'd consumed in the past twenty-four hours weren't helping his nerves a bit.

Joss's phone buzzed. Ursula. "Did you find out anything?" he breathed.

"I've got some intel on the competition. Eddie Udell is going with Custer's gold."

Figures. Eddie Udell was a viper who always picked the lowest hanging fruit. With General Custer as a topic, Udell would have ready access to hundreds of photos and artwork, the backbone of any historical documentary. Custer was a built-in viewer magnet. Kenetsky was a newcomer to the industry, one Udell could easily seduce with gold dust.

Why didn't you think of it first, you big dummy? "Any word on how he's going to pitch it?"

"No," Ursula admitted. "But if I know Eddie, he'll probably have a snazzy storyboard, and maybe a dramatization or two. Do you have your camera with you?"

Joss never travelled without his compact video equipment. One never knew when a good shot might appear. "Yeah."

"Call me when you've got a topic." She cut off the call.

He tucked the phone into his jacket pocket. Nine days to find some gold dust shinier than Custer's gold.

Eddie Udell had his topic and a full day's head start.

And Joss had zip.

CHAPTER THREE

Wednesday, 1:21 p.m., Abbie's Dining Room

A bble needed to take another stab at Jethro Turner. Loreen's wine was giving her courage. *Nothing to lose.*

She dialed.

He answered so quickly, she wondered if he'd been waiting for her call. "Abbie."

She caught herself before addressing him with the formal *Mr.*— after all, he'd told her to drop it. "Jethro. I was wondering . . . would you reconsider discussing the DuFrayne case?"

"I thought about it, Abbie, I did, and I still don't think any good is going to come of this story."

"How could a fresh look at a dark episode in the history of Hunts Landing not be good?" Abbie asked. "It's our home, for good or for bad, our story." He didn't answer right away, and she scrambled for another approach. *Pushy. Pushy.* "If not for the history, then would you do it to help the daughter of a friend, one who needs a break?" *Yeah, that really came out of your mouth, Abigail.*

"Well, I don't suppose you could do much harm now. Even if you played dirty pool with an old man."

An appropriate amount of guilt knocked on her head.

"Tell you what," Jethro said. "Down on the river, west side of the parkway, is Walker's Boat Launch. I'll meet you at two o'clock."

Wednesday, 1:59 p.m., Walker's Launch

The street originally called Andrew Jackson Road, later turned to Parkway, was named so by the town's founders in an attempt to curry favor with the newly elected President Jackson.

Abbie's first grade teacher had gone to great lengths to explain how General Jackson had, in 1813, retreated from Natchez in defeat, marching his battle-weary soldiers through the hamlet of Hunts Landing, where the villagers greeted the troops with cheers and refreshments. Abbie the historian knew better—Jackson's retreat was marked by Natchez Trace, far west of Hunts Landing. Still, the name stuck.

Abbie turned off the parkway at the foot of Memorial Bridge, onto the service road that ended at the boat launch. The parking lot was almost vacant, save for one Chevy Tahoe hitched to an empty trailer and a muddied green Ford F150 parked in the shade. She pulled up next to the pickup as Jethro Turner exited his vehicle.

The last time she'd seen him, in high school, he was still a Hunts Landing cop. Now retired, Jethro was both the same as she remembered and different. His lanky body seemed the same, if a little thicker around the middle, and the silver hair was new. His face had the freckled and leathery look of someone who spent a lot of time outdoors.

He extended a hand. "Little Abbie Adams. All grown up."

"Jethro." She shook his hand, the feeling of awkwardness fading as she recalled wearing his police hat on piggyback rides, thirty years ago.

Letting go of her hand, he got straight to his point. "Before we get started, why don't you tell me how you picked this case for your story?"

She bristled. "I didn't. The editor of *The Times* did."

Jethro studied her, arms crossed, face drawn. She wondered what he'd meant regarding the harm he thought she might cause. After another moment, he smiled. "All right, we'll start here." He cocked his head at the bridge. From their vantage point, she could see the paved pedestrian path from the boat launch eastward, under the bridge, toward the college on the other side. "In '69, all this was woods. Used to be part of the Meyers Plantation."

"But now it's Meyers Wildlife Refuge land, right?" The plantation used to take up most of the land west of what is now Andrew Jackson Parkway, but the family couldn't keep up with the property taxes, so they wound up selling a parcel to the Army, another parcel to the college, and donating the tracts closes to the river to the state as a wildlife refuge.

"Yup. Kids from the college used these woods to do whatever kids do. We didn't patrol the place regularly." He turned east. "Those tall buildings over there?"

"The river dorms?" The dormitories stood along the southern edge of the Quad, next to the Tennessee River.

"Those weren't there in '69. Some old oaks stood there, like the ones in the middle of the Quad now. That's important. Because that's where the party was."

Confused, Abbie turned to him. "I thought the party was at Wexler House?"

"Honey, the entire town was a party. We had a parade and fireworks. Chief Farrow called in the whole department. Yes, ma'am, Hunts Landing was one big celebration that day. America beat the Russians!"

"How did I not know that?" Abbie said, mostly to herself.

"No reason you would." Jethro's eyes hardened as he continued the story, the eyes of a veteran cop giving testimony. "Some parties were planned, but most just popped up. That's what we had on the Quad that night. The kids started gathering by the river a little after dark."

In Abbie's imagination, the River Dorms disappeared, replaced by black night sky and moonlight dancing off the water.

"What do you know about Rosalie?" Jethro asked.

"Very little. Rosalie DuFrayne, aged twenty, straight-A student. Occasionally worked parties at Wexler House, where her mother was the Wexlers' cook. That's really all."

"Right. Night of July twenty-fourth, Rosalie helped clean up after the party and left the house a little after eleven-thirty. She walked west—witnesses put her on the Quad. We figured she headed this way directly from the Wexlers."

He led her toward the trees bordering the lot. At first, Abbie thought they were heading straight into a clump of scrub brush, but a gap appeared, and he stepped onto a well-worn path. "Birders still come down here a lot," he said over his shoulder. "My wife belonged to the Hunts Landing Bird Society."

Abbie scrambled to remember the name. "How is LuAnn?"

"She passed a few years ago."

"I'm sorry. I didn't know." In a small town like Hunts Landing, it was near heresy to not know every family member of every friend and fourth cousin around. Abbie wanted to kick herself.

"We lost her to early-onset Alzheimer's, but she'd made her wishes clear. No fuss, no funeral, no obituary. Just me and the kids taking her ashes down to the ocean. 'Return me to the sea,' she'd told me. We honored her wishes. But I'll tell you this, she loved your momma's barbecues." He chuckled. "Elsa made a mean pork butt."

"You know, Momma never told me how she knew you."

He stopped to hold a wayward branch so she could pass. "In '76, dispatch sent me to your parents' house. Robbery. Crooks took a TV, a stereo, but all Elsa cared about was your grandmomma's pearls."

Abbie fingered her neck. "I wore them on my wedding day. Momma cried when she put them on me."

"Sounds like Elsa," Jethro continued. "It was a sloppy job, fingerprints all over the place, which was weird because the robber had brought gloves with him—we found them in the kitchen. I figured our guy might not be the sharpest tool in the shed, might try to pawn the stuff locally. Sure enough, I caught him with the pearls at Sweeney's Pawn Shop. Stupid redneck named Bubba."

"You've got to be kidding."

"I know. But Bubba was his given name. He got five years for that particular stunt. Well, we got the pearls back, and most of the other stuff. I carried the property back to your parents, and Elsa insisted I come back the next day for barbecue. Turns out, your momma served with LuAnn on some committee." They stepped out of the trees into a clearing. "It was a sad day when Elsa and Matt died. I probably should've checked up on you some more, and I'm sorry about that. But Lu was already ailing." His sigh was deep and long. "Anyway, I sure miss your momma's barbecue."

So do I, Abbie thought. She wondered about the other memories Jethro had of her parents, hundreds, surely, memories that she didn't share.

He quit talking for a moment, and Abbie surveyed her surroundings, pushing aside the sudden, achy pang Jethro's story triggered. The clearing, roughly oval, boasted fallen logs and boulders arranged in a circle around a central fire pit. The ashes in the pit were cold but recent. She peered south through the trees—despite the foliage, there was a decent view of the river below.

Her first crime scene. She clasped her hands behind her back to quell the fidgets and tried to soak in the ambiance.

S. K. Waters

"People still use this place," he said. "When I was still on the force, if we suspected something illegal was going on, we'd go ahead and make the arrest. Otherwise, we'd leave people alone. People are careful here. There isn't any trash." He looked around, perplexed. "Funny, the place doesn't look that much different from back then."

He strode over to a large log on the western side of the clearing. "This is about where we found her. Face down, her arms and legs were straight. He'd pressed her face into the sand. Completely unnatural position. A body wouldn't fall like that. The killer must've arranged her post-mortem."

Abbie gasped. "Is that normal?"

"No," Jethro said, "this guy was anything but normal. Now, we couldn't get any useful footprints, since it rained that night, but we think the victim came here down this path here," he pointed to another track Abbie hadn't noticed before, leading away from the river. "At the time, that path opened up behind the sorority houses on the Quad. Anyway, when it rains hard, footprints get blurred. There wasn't much we could tell from them. But there were two different size depressions on the path, and the length of the stride between the two sets told us something. The victim stood five foot two. Her killer was considerably taller, big feet." He stood, pointing to the river. "There were a mess of prints over by that other log, but they were so jumbled, and the rain did a job on them, so we couldn't ascertain if they belonged to the killer."

Abbie stepped closer to the log, but not all the way. It felt too much like stepping on Rosalie's grave. The hairs on the back of her neck rose. Did other people, people who used this place, the people who'd last burned a fire in that fire pit, know a young woman died a horrible death, just a few steps away. "Did she put up a struggle?"

"Couldn't say for sure. I think she entered the clearing, and the killer attacked from behind. There were foot impressions next to her,

40

down on the southern end of the clearing, and on two paths, the one we came in on, and the one leading north. There were none on the path over there to the west. That's important. Her killer left the scene on a path that led to the college. Or he swam away."

"In July? Wouldn't the snakes get him?" The Tennessee River teemed with copperheads and cottonmouths in the middle of summer.

"That's what I'm thinking."

Too many questions jumbled in her brain. She was going to forget to ask some. She should have prepared better and written them down. "Was she robbed?"

He stood, brushing the sand off his hands. "Nah, we found her purse next to her, opened, contents on the sand. There was cash and a bus ticket in it. This guy, he beat the back of her head to a bloody pulp and left her purse. More like a crime of passion than a robbery, that's what I said to myself at the time."

Abbie turned her eyes away to block the beginnings of a mental image, of Rosalie's battered body, face-down in the sand. Her stomach rumbled with the tinge of nausea. Who did she think she was, to be poking around some bloody murder as if she were Miss Marple?

An odd bit of color caught her eye on the other side of the log. It was a flower, a yellow lily, faded and browning at the petals' edges. "That's a bit out of place, you think?"

"Like I said, people still use this place."

They retraced their steps and left the clearing on the same path they came. "Do you think she knew her killer?"

"I don't know. Maybe if we'd gotten to finish the investigation . . ."

"Wait, what?"

He walked in silence for a moment. "The ABI—that's the Alabama Bureau of Investigation—took over. On July 23rd, two days before the murder, three prisoners escaped from the Mississippi State Pen. Walter Tennents, a hitman for the Klan, and two brothers doing life for murder. The Feds tracked them east. They killed an old woman and her dog over in Muscle Shoals, stole her car. Two days later, they killed a farmer and his family in West Georgia. Shot 'em all, then sat down and ate the family's supper. The Feds caught up with 'em north of Atlanta, there's a shootout, and the brothers bought it. So, the ABI figured it must've been the Tennents gang who killed Rosalie DuFrayne, as they worked their way east from Muscle Shoals."

Her jaw dropped. "Did you, I mean, do you think that's true? I mean, it sounds a little . . . too convenient."

Emerging from the woods, they now headed toward the pedestrian path on the far side of the parking lot. Jethro stuffed his hands in his pockets. "Let's just say that in '69, the ABI was focused on . . . well, in other directions. As for the Tennents, they were bloodthirsty enough. They hacked the old lady to death. They shot the farmer's family multiple times. They catch a Black girl alone in the woods, sure, they could've killed Rosalie. But at the other crime scenes, the gang took money, food, a car—things they needed to continue their run. Here, the killer or killers took nothing. Do I *think* they killed her? No. Besides, Tennents denied ever being in Hunts Landing."

"Is he still alive?"

He shook his head. "Died in prison, I want to say in '78."

Then why didn't the case go back to Hunts Landing?

On the other side of the bridge, he turned off the path, northeast, onto the Quad. In the eleven years since Abbie last walked the paths of the old campus, nothing much seemed to have changed. During the '80s, the Army sold a parcel of land to the college for expansion, and most of the science and technical and athletic facilities relocated to the 'New Campus.'

The 'Old Campus', the sixteen-acre rectangle that had made up the college in 1969, now contained the original classroom buildings and residential buildings. Tall, stately oak trees graced the middle of the Quad in an elegant regiment, providing shade for the clusters of students studying for midterms beneath them.

Jethro stopped in front of the middle dorm, pointing toward the oaks. "In '69, those trees extended to the river's edge. The April '74 tornado took out the trees closest to the river. The storm tore those oaks up by their roots, clearing the way for those dormitories."

"The River Dorms." Loreen had spent her freshman year in the center dorm, Abbie remembered, and stayed long enough to realize that communal living wasn't for her.

"Yes. Keep in mind, though, in '69, the trees still stood. July 24th, parties sprung up all up and down that side of the common." He extended his hand west. "And at some point, the frats carried all their kegs down to the river for one big party. The chief ordered extra patrols on foot to keep an eye on things." He winked at her. "You ever party hearty at school?"

"Not really my kind of scene," Abbie admitted.

"Good girl."

Even though she hadn't been a huge partyer, she could imagine boys rolling kegs down the footpaths. "How many people?" she asked.

"A couple of hundred. Most of the college. Faculty too. We hung back because of the faculty. Me and my partner, Dan O'Leary, we patrolled the east side. I'd made sergeant in '68, but that night the chief called all hands on deck, so I patrolled on foot instead of in a car. We were there in case of trouble. The kids mostly behaved themselves."

He paused, a sad smile suddenly clouding his face. "Sorry. The memories. A good buddy, Dan. Killed in 'Nam in '71. Anyway, on the other side of the college buildings, a couple of blocks over, Mill Town, was a bunch of run-down cottages. Poor neighborhood, mostly Black families. Now, they're all fixed up as expensive bungalows, but at the time most of the calls HLPD responded to came from Mill Town."

"My dentist's office is over there," Abbie said, wondering if statistics would support Jethro's memory of Mill Town as a crime-infested Black neighborhood or if this was merely a lingering stereotype.

"Oh, Mill Town is fashionable now, but in '69? Shoot. All night long, sirens went off a few blocks over yonder. So, that night, we kept to the east side of the Quad, in case trouble spilled in from over that way. You know what the Quad's like at night, right?"

Abbie nodded and stared across the Quad, remembering well the dim, yellow light cast by streetlamps onto the pathways. Enough light to see by to make your way, but not much more. "You couldn't have possibly seen everything going on."

"Yup. And the haze that night was as thick as LuAnn's gumbo. Damned poor visibility. About midnight, the party wound down. Girls who lived in the dorms or the sorority houses, the ones with curfews, went home. Possibly thirty or forty remained down by the river, most of 'em boys from the college."

He gestured toward Barton's Chapel on the southeast corner of the Quad. "A little after midnight, out of nowhere, all hell breaks loose by the riverbank. Me and Dan, we didn't see the kids from Mill Town coming 'round the chapel, it was so dark. All Black kids. All the college boys at the bonfire were white. Both sides'd been drinking. Not sure who started the brawl, the Black kids blamed the whites, the white kids blamed the Blacks. Somebody threw a punch, and that was all she wrote."

Abbie sucked in her breath. "Really? I've always heard that the college was pretty integrated by then."

"To a certain extent, it was," Jethro said. "But these weren't Black boys from the college; they were Black boys from Mill Town. By the time we reached 'em, some of the boys had already run off, and we rounded up those who had stayed behind. We handed the college boys over to the campus cops, took the Mill Town boys down to the lockup. Let 'em sleep off their booze, took statements, booked 'em, let them go. If every person who got a little rowdy that night got thrown in jail, half of Hunts Landing woulda been behind bars."

Abbie closed her eyes, and for the briefest moment, she could imagine the brawl, piles of young men, fists flying, blood from broken noses spurting, silhouetted against the flames of a bonfire, made fuzzy by the steamy July air. "This is terrific background," she said. Great stuff she could write up for the article.

"Not just background. The coroner put the victim's death sometime around midnight. Now, Rosalie DuFrayne left Wexler House a little after eleven thirty. I figure she walked straight to that clearing in the woods. After she arrives, she's killed. The killer leaves the scene, either via the north path or the east one. Either way, he comes out in the southwest corner or further north but still on the west side, with everybody's attention focused on a bunch of brawling kids in the southeast corner of the Quad. Twelve cops on the scene, and the killer probably walked right past us."

The walk back to the boat launch was quiet. With every step, Abbie couldn't help but wonder: Had Rosalie placed her foot here? Was she following the path of a ghost? What had Rosalie been feeling, thinking, walking through these woods by herself, at night, down a path that was eerily unsettling on a March afternoon.

They reached the cars. "Before you go." He reached into his pickup, retrieved a manila envelope. "My notes. You need anything else, you call me." He gave her a one-armed hug. "You're as pretty as your momma."

His grin made her smile back. "Thank you."

"Always seemed a shame that we gave up on Rosalie DuFrayne."

An annoying question popped into the front of her head, one that had little to do with her story. Or, rather, had everything to do with it. "Jethro, you're my first live witness."

"Oh?" He grinned, spread his arms wide. "Do I get a prize?"

She smiled despite herself. "It's just that, first interview and all. How'd I do?"

Jethro stared at the river for a few moments. Abbie wondered if she'd done that badly. Finally, he answered. "You didn't come prepared with questions, which is almost okay 'cause when law enforcement arrives on a crime scene, we don't have a lot of questions, either. But that meant that I drove the interview, not you. I told you what I wanted to tell you. Now, I can promise you, I didn't hold anything back." He paused. "Others may."

Abbie considered this guidance. Books, journals, documents, were so different, so impersonal, never demanding of questions, always ready to reveal their facts, their secrets. All she'd ever had to do was read. But this was different. Real people were so different. "Gotcha."

"I was a friendly," Jethro continued. "Not all of your witnesses are gonna be friendly. Most are gonna lie, or at least try to hide something. You drive the interview with the questions you need answered. And don't trust anything anybody says until you verify it."

Questions, lies, trust, verify. Mental notes on the whiteboard of her mind. "Well, let me try this question. Who do *you* think killed her?" Abbie asked.

"On the record?"

"No, just for me."

He leaned one hip back against the pickup. "I think Rosalie knew her killer. No robbery, no sign of sexual assault, yet somebody bashed that girl's head in. Somebody mad enough to kill her and leave her with her face pushed in the sand. I think that in the moments before she died, she looked into the eyes of her killer, and she knew. She feared her killer. That bus ticket in her purse? One-way ticket on the 2:10 a.m. to St. Louis. On the night she died, Rosalie DuFrayne was headed out of town."

Wednesday, 3:03 p.m., Starbucks

Abbie decided to beat the afterschool rush for Starbucks and headed straight there after leaving Jethro, but the line was still long and snaked around the building. She shifted into park and pulled her notebook out of her purse. Tennent's gang. ABI. Frat party. St. Louis. Jethro had made the need for questions, and more questions, clear.

St. Louis. Rosalie DuFrayne's obituary mentioned an aunt in St. Louis. Had she been going to see her aunt the day after the murder? Why would she, in the middle of summer term?

The line crept slowly. Abbie took the opportunity to pull out the contents of the envelope Jethro Turner had given her. His notes surprised her, the words printed in a meticulous hand on sheets of lined paper ripped from a spiral pocket notebook. Nothing in the pages referred to the murder, the inquiries related only to the brawl on campus.

A typewritten page grabbed her interest. The alphabetized list, over thirty names, bore the designation *HLPD* or *CPD* beside each name, half of the entries checked off with blue ink. It was Jethro's interview roster, the one he'd been working through when the ABI halted his investigation.

Handwritten asterisks stood out next to the names Cyrus Porter and Isaac Leon Moore. The HLPD by Cyrus Porter's name was crossed out, replaced by CPD.

HLPD stood for Hunts Landing Police Department; likewise, CPD likely stood for Campus Police Department. Only one way to confirm. Abbie searched through her recent calls on her phone and swiped to dial.

The call went straight to voicemail. She texted.

Abbie: Why asterisks by Cyrus Porter and Isaac Moore?
Jethro: Porter one of the Black students. We handed him to CPD. Moore was his buddy. Both closest to woods.
Abbie: Did you suspect them?

Minutes passed with no reply, but at least the line picked up. Abbie placed her iced-coffee order at the kiosk.

One of the Black students. It was a discomforting way to put things. When she'd been a grad student at the college, the school was well integrated, but in 1969? And what about the town? Abbie did not know what things were like in Hunts Landing at the end of the sixties. She wasn't familiar enough with the Civil Rights era, and Sylvia had specifically asked questions about race. Abbie frowned. Eighteenth-century, easy peasy. In the twenty-first century, she was out of her depth.

She hadn't even been *born* when Rosalie DuFrayne died. *Gee whiz.*

She needed to get her bearings on the Hunts Landing of 1969. If *anyone* would know what the town was like in 1969, it would be her mother's old friend Madeleine. In the genuine spirit of the 1960s, Madeleine Winthrop-Rutledge, of the Hunts Landing Winthrops, bucked her family's expectations of being a debutante and marrying into another of Hunts Landing's older families. Instead, she graduated with a degree in journalism. Though *The Times* was compelled to give her a job, they relegated her to the women's section until Watergate happened and Peter Rutledge arrived as the new editor. Madeleine and Peter married the day after Richard Nixon resigned, and she remained a feature reporter for the paper until Peter's death in 2002. Now she served as the director of the Hunts Landing Historical Society.

And Abbie was only few blocks away from the society's office.

Minutes later, she pulled the handle of the office's glass door. The society was housed in a storefront off the Square, close enough to still be near the center of town and far enough for the cheaper rent. Madeleine's face broke into a huge smile when Abbie entered. The retired reporter wore white jeans, a lime-green cardigan that landed just past her hips, and bright orange sneakers. Auburn curls streaked with grey were held back with silverish combs. She threw her arms out. "Abbie, darlin'! What's new and exciting?"

What to tell her first? That she had a chance for her first byline? That she was looking at a murder that was never properly investigated because the police back then didn't care enough about a Black murder victim? That she was going to have to summon up all her courage and call Frank Wexler? She had so much to tell, she was surprised to hear the words that stumbled out of her mouth. "I met a man."

"Really?"

And the words kept coming. "He's a cop, new in town. His daughter plays volleyball with Martha. He's got the most amazing gray eyes."

"Forget the eyes. How's his butt?" Madeleine asked. Her eyes twinkled with mischievous humor.

"You seriously asked me that question?"

"Butts are important. Where'd you meet him?"

"The Sommelier."

"And when are you going to see him again?"

"I'm not sure I will." But Abbie knew, in a town like Hunts Landing, it would be impossible to not to run into Nick. "That's not why I'm here, though," Abbie said. She gave Madeleine a rundown of *The Times* assignment. "Sylvia wants me to write a story, write about the Wexler family, write about a time I know nothing about. I'm scrambling."

"And here I am, asking all the questions," Madeleine said. She pulled her spectacles off. "I've got one more. This might be none of my business, but did you agree to do this to get back at Frank Wexler?"

No use trying to fool Madeleine. "I'd like to say it's all about the byline, but I'd be lying. Part of me wants to watch him squirm. But another part of me doesn't want to go anywhere near that angle of the story."

"Why on earth not?"

Abbie sighed and ran her hand through her hair. The apprehension had been brewing all day. "No matter my feelings about Dr. Wexler, his wife and his kids have done nothing to me . . ."

"And you think Grace Wexler's going to be embarrassed?"

Abbie nodded to herself. "Something like that."

"That's the silliest thing I ever heard come out of your mouth. Grace Wexler isn't the saint you think she is. If you ask me, getting a little ruffled by a piece in a local paper is probably just desserts."

"Possibly. But I need to talk to Frank, and soon."

"What I wouldn't give to be a fly on the wall for that one. Make sure you keep that little pistol of yours handy."

Abbie's "little pistol" was a Glock 17 she kept hidden in her bedroom. "Now you're giving me bad ideas."

"In this case, it might be justifiable. Where are you going to start?"

"It turns out the investigating officer was Jethro Turner. He showed me the crime scene."

"That old coot? I don't think I've seen him since LuAnn passed."

"See, I didn't know that before. I didn't know she'd passed. That's precisely why I need your help. You know everybody. I don't know what Hunts Landing was like in 1969. Can you help me?"

Madeleine checked her watch. "I'm tied up with museum business right now, but come back in the morning. I'll see what I can dig up."

Abbie's text tone sounded as she left the society's office.

Jethro: Also, Porter worked the Wexler party. Old Doc W. vouched for him personally.

CHAPTER FOUR

Wednesday, 3:46 p.m., Abbie's Kitchen

The sound of a car door slamming alerted Abbie that George was home. Lanky, awkward while his body got used to growth spurts, George nonetheless entered the house with a flourish; he dropped his backpack on the floor, greeted Benny, opened the refrigerator door, and asked his mother, "Can I take the car tonight?" all in one fluid motion.

Maybe it was time to reinstate family game night, Abbie mused. But not tonight. She really needed to work on her assignment. "Sure. Where're you going?"

"Study group at Pudge's."

"Studying? Not Minecraft, right?"

"Nope, Minecraft's gonna be here Friday night."

"Son, why do you make plans without . . ." With a purse of her lips, she nixed the thought. A houseful of teenagers trumped worrying about where her children were when they were gone—although teenage visitors consumed massive quantities of chips and soda.

Cha-ching! Unabashed, George checked out her phone on the counter. "Sylvia says, 'Will's in recovery, looking good.' Is Mr. Will sick?" He had Zach's cerulean blue eyes, only darker, and her own unruly caramel curls. She watched those eyes widen as he was reminded about the frailty of human life. A reminder he surely didn't need. An errant lock seemed to pop out of place. She longed to tuck it back into place.

"He had emergency surgery this morning." She filled him in on what she knew.

"Wow, so you're getting his assignment. That's cool, Mom. Does that mean I get to buy the next *Zombie Slashers* game?"

And he came up with that question without skipping a beat. Abbie wondered which parent George had inherited that talent from. "What's the rating on the game?"

"Mature seventeen."

"Then, nope."

"I'm almost seventeen."

"In six months. Talk to me then."

He sulked for a moment, Zach's sulk, the one other people thought was deep contemplation but was actually a well-disguised brood. It didn't last long—it never did—just long enough for him to pour himself a glass of milk. "But the game doesn't have any sex, just a lot of violence."

"Mmm. Exactly the kind of educational entertainment I want you exposed to."

George opened his mouth to protest, then shrugged. Abbie knew that shrug. He would try again later.

He headed upstairs but stopped, his attention drawn to Rosalie's picture taped to the dining room wall. "Is this her?"

"Yup. Meet Rosalie DuFrayne. Murdered the night the astronauts came home from the moon." Thankfully, there were no graphic photos of a dead body on the wall.

"Was it a racial thing?" George asked, his voice raised in curiosity.

"What makes you ask that?"

"During Black History Month, we did a unit on the Civil Rights era in Hunts Landing. Mrs. Zanier said there were problems after Dr. King's assassination. But she never mentioned this."

Funny how George zoomed in on the racial angle, as Sylvia had. Why had she resisted the notion, given how little she knew about the case? She needed to get her blinders off. "The school probably frowns on teaching murders to high schoolers."

"We learned about the Sixteenth Street Baptist Church bombing down in Birmingham, but not about a murder right here?"

Damned if I know, Abbie thought, *but it's a good question.* Why *wasn't* the killing of a Black girl in 1969 taught? Probably for the same reasons the newspaper didn't give it much coverage, and Chief Farrow gladly handed the case over to the ABI. Rosalie's picture stared at her.

Tracking down her family and friends was going to be her next step. Maybe friends first, as the murder happened just off campus and so other students would likely have more information. The two girls from the photograph, Cleta Blakebill and Bernice Strong. And the Black student that Jethro had arrested, Cyrus Porter. He worked at Wexler House the same night as Rosalie. How many Black students could there have been at the private college in 1969? Then there was the aunt in St. Louis.

"Hey," she stopped him from heading up the stairs. "Good thinking. Take the car tonight."

Wednesday, 5:41 p.m., Abbie's Kitchen

Cell phone plastered to her ear, Abbie rummaged in the freezer, looking for anything she could assemble into a meal. "Loreen, I can't go out tonight."

"Well, I don't think you should stay home."

If Loreen had her way, Abbie would be bar-hopping every night. Abbie would rather stay home in her pajamas. "But . . . aha! Goulash." She pulled out a plastic tub of frozen stew. "I really need to start on *The Times* assignment, and I didn't get the chance to tell you, but Joss called today and he's in a crisis—"

"Joss Freeman might be cuter than a baby bunny, but he's *always* in a crisis."

"This time it's serious." She recapped Joss's current predicament while retrieving frozen vegetables. "It's not my problem, but I can't leave him hanging. He needs help with the research. I dug through my parents' stuff and picked out a few possibilities for him. Once he chooses his topic, I need to scan and send the materials to him so he can get started. And Martha has volleyball practice tonight. So I can't go play in your shop with you. Besides, the weather's gonna be lousy. Nobody's gonna be there."

"Nick Preston will be there. He called and told me after you left. Something about late practice?"

Nick Preston. Thinking about Hunts Landing's newest detective was a distraction she didn't need. "Can't do it, Lo'. Good luck tonight."

Abbie put a pasta pot in the sink. Through the arched opening to the dining room, Zach smiled at her from their wedding portrait. His blue eyes twinkled as she filled the pot with water.

The day they met, those eyes had weakened her knees and caused her to drop her camera bag. Each night, his eyes were the last things she saw—he would kiss her eyes closed before wrapping her up in his arms.

Then came his first deployment, and he was far away. Research and young George filled her days. During the daily emails and those oh-so-few phone calls, she wasted so much time talking about people who'd been dead for two-and-a-half centuries. Zach's return was her liberation. He kept the baby while she spent hours in the library.

"Mom."

She never dreamed he'd sign up for another tour. Obsessed with her research, she hadn't noticed his growing restlessness.

"I'm going back," Zach had said. "We ship out in two weeks." At that moment, his beautiful eyes had lacked luster.

"Mom?"

She'd been mad at him and stayed mad at him until he left and then it was too late, because he was an ocean away. No more phone calls, only a few terse emails. And then the horrible afternoon when Major Winters brought the news, so sorry, an insurgent attack, Zach's unit in the crossfire. His eyes, now closed forever.

"MOM!" Martha dropped her backpack and rushed into the kitchen. Only then did Abbie realize the pasta pot was full, and the sink too. Water splashed on the floor. Her daughter turned off the faucet.

"What're you doing, Mom?" Careful not to spill any water, Martha lifted the overfull pot. The sink began to drain.

Abbie retrieved a mop from the pantry. "Lost in thought, I guess." *More like guilt.*

Martha eyed her critically. At fourteen, she'd inherited her father's lean height and her mother's eyes. "Okay. A new girl started school this week. Isabella. She's having a sleepover Friday. Can I go?"

The doorbell rang. Abbie leaned the mop against the counter. The new girl had to be Nick's daughter. She played dumb. "Parents going to be present?"

"She lives with her dad."

"That's not an answer, Martha," she said over her shoulder on the way to answer the door.

"I'm sure he's going to be there."

"All right." The doorbell rang again as she reached for the doorknob. Abbie swung open the door.

Joss Freeman stood on her doorstep.

"Golly, what're you doing here?"

He didn't get to answer because Martha squealed, "Uncle Joss!"

Abbie was forced to wait for a response. Within seconds, her kids and Benny surrounded Joss, each demanding his immediate attention. She'd wait. It wasn't every day a couple of teenagers from Hunts Landing entertained a TV celebrity on their family room floor and got a chance to post photos on Snapchat.

He ruffled Benny's fur one last time and crossed the room in two long strides. Even without pancake makeup, the TV historian appeared as delicious in person as he did on the screen. With looks reminding her of a young Robert Redford and a grin to match the older one, small wonder he earned the highest ratings on the channel.

"Abs . . ." His arms wrapped around her in a tight hug, lifting her off the floor.

She repeated her question with a laugh. "What are you doing here?"

"I caught the first flight out. I figure, how can I research the Civil War from Santa Monica?"

There was something in his eye, something wary, something she couldn't quite put a finger on. That, too, could wait. "Why didn't you tell me you were coming?"

"You would've tried to talk me out of it. Don't worry, I won't be any trouble. Got a reservation at the Hunts Landing Inn." Benny whined at his feet, and Joss scratched the dog's ears again.

George said, "Why can't he stay here? In the spare bedroom over the garage?"

"Please, Mom!" Martha added, her eyes glued on their guest.

Joss waved a hand in denial. "The Inn will be fine."

Her Southern, mother-of-two-who-must-set-a-good-example sensibilities battled with her instincts. She and Joss had shared a house for three years. They could do so again. The single mother of two had long since stopped caring about what the neighbors truly thought. "Nonsense. My parents' students used to crash here all the time.

Not as sweet a setup as a hotel with room service, but probably more comfortable."

His green eyes twinkled. "I hoped you would say that."

Wednesday, 7:51 p.m., Abbie's Attic

After dinner, Joss followed Abbie upstairs to the attic, both carrying their wineglasses. In the rafters, bare light fixtures with high-wattage bulbs provided enough illumination for easy reading.

He took a moment to appreciate how she'd organized the materials. When Elsa and Matt Adams died, he'd been out of the country and missed the funerals. It had taken him a couple of weeks to get to Hunts Landing, only to find Abbie deep in grief, unable to cope with the multitude of bankers' boxes containing the remnants of her parents' campus offices. Joss had helped her carry the boxes up here before his return to California.

His eyes settled on the neat row of boxes she'd lined up for him on the middle of the floor. "Are these the top hits?"

"Yes," Abbie said. "But first, what's going on with Harriet?"

Damn, but she had the nose of a bloodhound. "What makes you think anything's going wrong with Harriet?"

"Stop it, you big fibber. Last season we worked long distance, and we FaceTimed. So, why are you here?"

Joss sipped his wine. He'd forgotten how easily she could read him, although to admit, back in college he could read her expressions just as easily. "This is indeed marvelous. Where'd you land this?"

"Loreen's. Quit stalling."

Joss downed the rest of his glass. "Harriet's not taking the situation well. I'm supposed to be the steady one, the one who brings home the bacon. She's the one who gets to play with clay all day and not worry about how groceries get in the fridge. Get it? She freaked out, packed her stuff and left."

"Mmm." Abbie bent down to take the lid off the first of the archive boxes.

"What?" Joss asked.

"What do you mean?"

"That 'mmm'."

Abbie shrugged. "I just always thought that Harriet made 'temperamental artists' look like day-old puppies."

"Wait, wha . . . why didn't you ever tell me?"

"Would it have made a difference?"

"Truth?" he asked.

"Always."

"Not sure. Regardless, I've got to make this pitch work. And I have only nine days to make it happen. Else, I think . . . I lose . . . Harriet . . ." For a few seconds, the memory of his empty apartment squeezed his heart, and it hurt. Bad. He shook himself, like Benny often did. "Enough. You okay? You didn't look too good when I got here."

He watched her as, this time, she was the one to sip. Was she avoiding his question? Twenty-something Abbie Adams wouldn't have been able to exhibit any restraint. When she answered, there was a slight fatigue in her eyes.

"The job for *The Times*. I can get my first byline," Abbie said. "But the story . . . It's about a local murder from 1969. The victim had an association with Dr. Frank Wexler, my faculty advisor for my Ph.D. work. The paper specifically asked for me to investigate the connection."

"Ouch."

"Yeah. I would be Dr. Abigail Adams, right this minute, if not for Dr. Frank Wexler. Instead, I'm . . ." Abbie shivered, crossed her arms.

It wasn't quite pain on her face, more of a sad recognition of the shiny object she'd chased most of her life and would never get now. "You know, you never told me what happened with your orals."

"Didn't I?" She eased herself to the floor and crossed her legs. "Short version, 1763, the Great Lakes Native American tribes revolted against British forts. Eleven of them were captured, and the soldiers slaughtered. But at Detroit, the commandant, Henry Gladwin, had an informant, and could save the fort."

He mirrored her movements and eased himself to the floor opposite her. "Sounds like a good topic for a documentary."

"Nah." She sipped. "No drama, really. Instead of a rout, it turned into a boring siege. But for the rest of his life, Gladwin refused to give up the name of his informant. That's the big mystery, a mystery that historians debated for over a century afterward." Wine finished, she placed the glass on the floor next to her. "In an archive in the UK, I found the correspondence between Gladwin and one of his childhood friends, a Lady Sarah Winthrop, who was pestering him for information on the informant. The last letter suggested Gladwin revealed the name to Lady Sarah."

"Still think it'd make a good documentary. So, what was the problem?"

Abbie shrugged, noncommittal, but he knew better. "Two of the letters were missing. The one where, I presume, Lady Sarah insisted on knowing the informant's name. And the one where Gladwin answered her. I extrapolated, examined the likely suspects, and presented my theory. Dr. Wexler," her chest heaved with a deep inhale, "felt the evidence was incomplete and didn't support my conclusions."

"Geez, Abbie! The record is *never* complete, especially before the nineteenth century." Joss fell backwards, oblivious to the dust on the floor, and flopped his arms over his head. "I mean, historians are always bridging the gap, always doing exactly what you did." Joss couldn't believe her trusted advisor had done that to her. Harder to believe was that the school administration had let him get away with it. *Wexler is truly a monster.*

Abbie took his glass and finished it. "Cheers."

He righted himself, reached for her empty hand, and squeezed it. "I'm so sorry."

Abbie squeezed his hand back. "The materials for the topics I picked out for you are here on the floor." She rose and pulled a folding chair out from the corner and placed it in the center of the room. "If you really don't like any of these, Momma's wall is on this side, Daddy's wall is opposite."

Joss stood with hands on hips and assessed the archive. "Do you think they'd mind?"

"Mind? They'd probably get a kick out of their work being on TV." She turned to head back downstairs. "Shout if you need anything."

"Hey, Abs?"

She stopped at the top of the stairs.

"Do *you* mind?"

A flat smile creased her mouth. "No. It'll be like school all over again." She paused, foot poised to take the next step down. "Harriet's not good enough for you, Joss. Never was. Wish you'd get that through your thick skull."

Wednesday, 9:13 p.m., Abbie's Dining Room

Abbie carried a fresh mug of chamomile tea to the dining room and took a chair opposite the Rosalie wall. From the photo, Rosalie DuFrayne's brown eyes smiled at her. She shouldn't be smiling, Abbie thought. She'd been brutally murdered. Shouldn't Rosalie's face be angry? Piercing?

Relentless in a pursuit of justice?

Don't go down that rabbit hole, Abbie.

Start with Rosalie's friends, her schoolmates, the people around her, Will had said. The people around her. Aside from the list of people in her notes, names without faces, people who might be dead or untraceable, Abbie knew of one witness who knew Rosalie and was alive, living a few blocks away. Frank Wexler.

Able to avoid thinking about him for most of the day, Abbie now found Dr. Wexler dominated her thoughts, as if he stood in her dining room, right next to Rosalie, smirking his smirk—

Enough.

Time for professionalism, following the leads she was given, wherever they led. But Frank Wexler wasn't an option; he was an imperative. And she shouldn't delay in contacting him any longer.

She opened her email app before she could change her mind. His email address was easy to remember, despite the passage of time since she'd last used it.

Her fingers typed the subject line quickly. Rosalie DuFrayne.

Her left ring finger hit the Tab key twice. Then her fingers froze, hovering over the keyboard.

To Frank Wexler, she owed nothing. No matter where her inquiries took her, if Frank Wexler got dirtied, so be it. But to Grace Wexler, she owed some consideration. Unlike other faculty wives, Grace had always treated her husband's students like family. And she'd been one of the first to call Abbie after Elsa and Matt Adams were killed. Abbie imagined Grace on a Sunday morning, a few weeks from now, opening the paper to read all about how the Wexler name was associated with an unsolved murder. The image jostled Abbie right outside of her comfort zone. She typed.

The Times has hired me to write an article on the Rosalie DuFrayne murder in July 1969. Miss DuFrayne was last seen at your home the night she died. I'd like to interview you at your earliest convenience.

She hit *Send.* For the next couple of hours, she Googled the names from her whiteboard. Cleta Blakebill. Bernice Strong. Cyrus Porter.

Isaac Leon Moore. Either nothing came up for a particular name, or hundreds of results came up. She had to find out more about these people before she could refine her searches.

Abbie closed the laptop and yawned. Her eyes were so strained, her eyeballs felt fuzzy. She let Benny out and headed upstairs with a fresh mug of tea.

Joss, sitting cross-legged, smiled and accepted the mug. "Gonna stay up here, okay?"

"No worries. There are clean linens in the garage apartment."

He raised the mug in salute.

One floor down, she checked on the kids. Martha slept buried under covers. Abbie followed the sound of soft snores to find her daughter's head and kissed it. The glow from the streetlamp outside filtered through partly closed blinds, leaving stripes of light and shadow on the bed.

Through the window, the street was empty, as it should be. Sometimes, kids from the college parked across from the house, causing a commotion late at night, but tonight, everything was quiet. George slept on his stomach with arms and legs askew, one arm hooked around a pillow.

Careful not to disturb the teenager's sleep-through-a-hurricane slumber, she kissed his damp curls.

In her own bed, with Benny sprawled on the other half, she lay with her eyes half-closed, the television tuned to *The Tonight Show* with the volume down. Jimmy Fallon was singing karaoke with some young actor she didn't recognize.

Her eyes fluttered shut. On the bedside table, her phone buzzed.

Dr. Wexler: 1 p.m.—my office.

She sat upright, staring at the phone.

"When did *he* start texting?"

Thursday, 1:27 a.m., Abbie's Attic

Joss should have been exhausted, but after a couple of red-eye flights coast to coast, he wasn't sure which time zone his body was in.

Abbie'd gone through the trouble of opening each box stored in this attic and pulling out anything that contained Civil War references. He'd given each box its due but, after a couple of hours, slumped in defeat. The elder Adamses, may they rest in peace, were pure academics. Their materials were dry. The paradox the TV historian had to grapple with was that while actual history might be incredibly rich with detail, most of it was too dull for the average viewer. Joss had no doubt that if either Elsa or Matthias Adams had been alive, they could point him in the right direction. But they weren't alive, and it was evident that during their careers, they'd never been interested in treasure-hunting.

It was Thursday now. *Eight days, times twenty-four hours a day, times sixty minutes . . .*

He stood, stretched, and ruffled his hair. He'd been so certain that he could find the answer to his problem in this room. He paused.

Where was Abbie's work now? She'd been a history student for, what, nine years? The shelves in the attic were clearly labeled with the work of Elsa Adams or Mathias Adams. Surely Abbie hadn't thrown away her own stuff?

Scanning the room, at the end opposite the stairs, under a dormer and out of the cast of the fluorescent light bulbs, Joss noticed a blue tarp in the corner, conspicuously haphazard in a room that was otherwise neat and orderly. He paused before lifting the corner—the battle between shame at snooping and increased curiosity was brief. Curiosity won. He pulled back the plastic.

It was the culmination of Abbie's doctoral work, alright.

Her name was on every folder and CD. Covered in standard blue cardboard, her thesis, *The Identity of Henry Gladwin's Informant,*

Revisited, by Abigail Adams, lay top and center. He reached to take it from the pile and nicked himself on a shard of glass.

Joss sucked on his pinky to stop the bleeding. *Abbie, Abbie, Abbie.* How shattered she must have been over her failure, smashed like whatever piece of glass he'd cut himself on. She hadn't been able to throw her work away, but neither could she look at it long enough to put it away safely in a box, like she'd so lovingly done with her parents' work. She'd just chucked it into a corner and thrown some plastic on it. He hadn't been a good friend to her then, had moved on to his own career, unaware of the depth of her disappointment.

Joss picked up the thesis carefully and shook it to ensure there were no more pieces of glass. He'd do a little light reading with this Gladwin dude, get some shut-eye, and try to figure out his next step.

Dehydrated from so many flights in such a short period of time, he headed to the kitchen to grab a bottle of water. On his way through the dining room, he stopped short. Abbie had erased one of her whiteboards, had written Joss's name across the top. He grinned, fatigue creeping up his spine.

On the other board were Abbie's notes in her meticulously neat hand. Two notes from the kids, in decidedly sloppier hands, letting Abbie know about tomorrow's activities. Volleyball until 6:30. Study group at library.

Joss uncapped a marker and wrote his own note. Struck out. J.

Thursday, 7:55 a.m., the Square at Hunts Landing

Abbie let George take the car to get both him and Martha to school, so she had a few extra minutes, enough time to hit Suzette's Bakery, a tiny place on the Square. A Creole pastry chef from New Orleans with a German husband, Suzette saluted both cultures by arranging pralines and bread pudding dripping in whiskey sauce next to decadent German chocolate cake. Crème brûlée adorned the same shelf as glazed *Lebkuchen*. When she was little, Daddy would bring her to Suzette's on Saturday mornings. The pretext had always been to give Momma some time to herself, but the reality had been to score some *Lebkuchen* fresh out of the oven.

In anticipation of hot cookies, perhaps a beignet or two, Abbie rushed through the front door—and straight into Detective Nick Preston.

"Oh! Nick. Hi. Sorry." *Could she be anymore clumsy?*

"Abbie." His gaze fell on his slightly crushed white bakery bag. "At least I wasn't carrying coffee."

"Is it ruined?"

"Just a little squashed." He smiled at her. "I'm relieving a stakeout team. Smushed donuts will have to do." His wink did something unaccountable and uncomfortable with her insides, as did the thought of Nick on a stakeout.

"Let me get you some fresh ones," she offered.

"Don't worry about it. Missed you at Wine Down Wednesday."

"I had to work."

"Listen, would you like to—" His cell phone rang. He glanced at the number, and the smile disappeared from his face. "Got to go, Abbie."

She admired his retreat, cell phone pinned to his ear, long strides taking him to a black Range Rover parked only a few spaces down from Suzette's. Abbie willed her stomach to settle.

Behind the counter, the bakery owner grinned at Abbie. "Now that's one fine addition to Hunts Landing," Suzette said after the door was safely closed behind Nick.

"Mmm."

"I think he likes you." Suzette didn't bother taking Abbie's order, instead reaching into the below-counter fridge for milk. She was surprisingly thin for someone who dealt with pounds of sugar every day. Her dirty blonde hair, as always, was tightly plaited in a long braid that ended halfway down her back, topped by the ever-present baker's hat.

"Maybe." But Abbie had no intention of discussing the myriad of mixed feelings Nick Preston aroused. "Hey, when did y'all come to Hunts Landing?"

Suzette poured the milk into a frothing cup and stuck it under the steam wand of the commercial cappuccino machine behind the counter. "You mean, come back."

"I thought you were from New Orleans?"

"Raised there, but born here. We came back when my granddaddy died and left Mother this building. That would have been, oh, 1972. I'd just finished cooking school." Suzette turned her attention to the cappuccino machine to finish Abbie's latte. She handed the drink over the counter with a still-warm *Lebkuchen* wrapped in a napkin and winked.

Abbie sniffed at the cookie in appreciation and restrained herself from cramming it into her mouth. "Shame. About three years too late." At Suzette's raised eyebrow, Abbie told her about *The Times* assignment.

"Well, I can't really help you with anything before '72, but Rosalie's mother, Miss Etta, that had to be the Miss Etta from Calvary Baptist."

"Not so sure," Abbie said. "The obituary said Rosalie and Etta were members of New South Baptist. That's gotta be out in the county, right? Oh, and I need some beignets too, please."

Suzette opened a new bakery bag with a practiced flick of her fingers. "Oh, *ma petite*, the '74 storms destroyed New South Baptist. The congregation rebuilt as Calvary Baptist, right down there on Maple Street."

Yet another hometown factoid of which she'd been completely unaware.

"There could only be one Miss Etta, you understand," Suzette continued while she fished the choicest beignets from the display case. "What a wonderful woman. The two of us, we did up all the baked goods for the Harvest Festival each year, right up until she died. Never knew she lost a daughter. How horrible for her. Now, I didn't know Rosalie, but there were enough people in this town who adored Miss Etta. I would ask around at the church, if I were you. Somebody there surely remembers them."

Abbie thanked Suzette and headed out the door. Mentally, she kicked herself. New South Baptist should have been her first question, and she might have learned the story behind Calvary Baptist. As a historian, she knew church records were often the only records left about a person's life. She Googled the number as she walked toward Madeleine's office and hit Dial.

"Calvary Baptist Church, this is Reverend Fisher speaking." The booming voice reverberated, and she imagined a linebacker on the other end of the line.

She quickly explained the reason for her call.

"1969?" the minister asked. "That's a bit before my time, I'm afraid. I've only been in town for a couple of years now."

"Her obituary says she's buried at your church. I'm looking for background information on her, nothing personal. Do you think I could look at the church records?"

"Hmmm. Normally, I would say that our records are confidential. I guess I would need to check with the family. Did you say DuFrayne?"

"Yes, sir," she said. "As far as I know, she doesn't have any living family. The only relative was her mother, and she passed a few years after her." It was only a little fib. She didn't yet know if Rosalie's aunt was alive or dead. Still, she kicked herself for not staying up a few more minutes last night and running a search on Eugenia DuFrayne.

"All right, miss. We'll check around, and I'll call you back."

She thanked him and hung up. A new preacher was bad luck for her. He wouldn't know the families of his congregation all that well. What did she think he would say, *Come on down and snoop around in our archives*?

There had to be another way to get to Miss Etta's part of the story.

CHAPTER FIVE

Thursday, 8:07 a.m., Hunts Landing Historical Society

A bbie stacked two latte cups, gripped the bakery bag with her pinkie, and opened the glass door with her free hand.

Madeleine emerged from a back room. "Darlin'! And you brought coffee, bless you."

Abbie held up the white bag from Suzette's. "And breakfast."

"Sweet girl . . ." The older woman burrowed her nose into the bag. "Want one?"

"All yours."

"If you insist. Fill me in." Powdered sugar dusted her nose as she bit into a square pastry. "Oh, this is fabulous. I didn't ask you yesterday, but how are those babies of yours? Doing alright?"

Abbie grinned. "Yes, ma'am."

"Good. I haven't seen them in ages. You bring them around to see me, you hear? Oh, what am I saying, I've got two perfectly good legs; I can come by and see them myself. So, have you made any headway since yesterday?"

"Well, I wrote up the crime scene down by the river last night. What a sad place to die, but pretty at the same time. I think I should go take some pictures, check the place out at night, view the clearing through Rosalie's eyes."

Madeleine waggled a finger and licked the powdery sugar off her lips. "Now, don't go down to the river by yourself. Those wetlands aren't safe after dark."

"Kids hanging out?"

"Snakes, too. Copperheads, mostly. Since we're speaking of snakes, when are you going to meet with Wexler?" She bit into another beignet.

"This afternoon."

"Call me afterwards." Madeleine wiped her lips. "I've dug up some stuff for you."

On a table next to the window were some documents in protective cellophane wrappers. Madeleine pulled the first one out and laid it flat. "This is a map of town from 1971. Not too different from 1969."

Abbie loved old maps, and this one was no different. The map was slightly yellowed, a foldable map printed by the Chamber of Commerce. Blue lines marked the streets, green filled in the natural spaces. Square ads for local merchants lined the margins. "Let's trace Rosalie's steps."

"Right," Madeleine said, and pointed to a street northeast of the Square. "The DuFraynes lived here."

Madeleine's finger rested on a neighborhood called the Mill Heights, a cluster of well-groomed garden cottages shaded by big, leafy trees. Mill Heights, north of Mill Town, was where the mill managers and their families lived, whereas mill workers were housed in Mill Town. Part of Abbie's research that had landed her in so much trouble with the Pucketts was the comparison between the two neighborhoods. Abbie often walked Benny in Mill Heights, past driveways full of Mercedes and Lexus SUVs. "How on earth could a cook afford a house in Mill Heights?"

"I presume old Theodore paid Miss Etta well," Madeleine said.

That makes little sense. Abbie tucked the thought away for later. She imagined a reproduction of this map in the paper, a red arrow tracing Rosalie's steps that fateful night. "Okay, we know she left for the Wexlers in the afternoon."

Madeleine's finger traced the shortest route to Wexler House. On the map, the house took up an oversized patch, bigger than the surrounding properties, with the big house on the northeast corner, the smaller carriage house opposite.

From past visits as a student, Abbie recalled broad steps to the front door guarded by concrete lions, and a veranda out back that overlooked the Quad. The property was at least an acre, a monstrosity in the small town. "It's even big on paper."

"Did you ever attend any Wexler parties?" Madeleine asked.

"Too many. I'm not one for schmoozing, and there was always too much of it at Dr. Wexler's parties."

"His father's parties were schmooze-fests, too. The one that night in 1969 was a doozy! I missed it, of course. I'd already returned to Vassar. However, my parents went. Momma told me over two hundred people showed up. Theodore Wexler celebrated with *gusto*."

"So, I've heard," Abbie said.

"I recollect Momma telling me how Ms. Wexler—we're speaking of *Nevelyn* Wexler, Frank's aunt, never married—came to live with the family after Frank's mother passed. Nevelyn wanted to serve roast beef, but Miss Etta couldn't get any. None! All the markets completely sold out, no beef or chicken or ribs to be found within miles. So, Miss Etta sent the boys across the river to all the fishing shacks, and they bought up all the catfish they could, and she fried fifty pounds of it for the party. Momma said it was the best catfish she'd ever eaten."

Abbie tilted her head. "Okay, she was a splendid cook. Doesn't explain why Wexler paid her so much."

"Who can ever explain why any Wexler does anything?"

Indeed. "Okay. Rosalie left Wexler House around eleven-thirty. Witnesses said she didn't go toward her home, or toward the bus station, but headed west."

"Why would she head to the bus station?" Madeleine asked.

"She had a ticket in her purse for St. Louis that night. Her obituary said she had an aunt in St. Louis. I guess she was visiting her aunt. But you'd think she would go home and change first, pick up her luggage, right? Instead, she went west."

"You've got to find that out, find out why that girl went straight to the river," Madeleine said.

Abbie put her own finger on the map and slid it left. Following a straight line left/west led directly to the artist's depiction of the woods of Meyer's Plantation.

"Let's look at this one." Madeleine pulled out a second map. "I do believe old Theodore had this one commissioned."

This was a hand-drawn map of the campus, the lines in sepia ink. Some features, the river and the woods, were filled with watercolor. The artist detailed the trees and paths of the Quad, and the buildings were three-dimensional with their names carefully lettered. On the east side, Donahue Hall, Meyers Hall, the stately Ellesby Hall, and the southernmost one, Barton's Chapel. On the west stood miniature Victorian-styled houses marked by tiny Greek letters, with fluffy woods behind them.

Maddie poked the northwest corner of the map. "From here, your Rosalie could go two ways down to the river. She could walk down the sidewalk on the Quad, or she could enter the woods here, and use the woodland paths."

"Jethro's notes show that people saw her here along the north end, but nothing about anyone seeing her on the Quad itself."

Madeleine thought for a moment. "I don't think she went down the Quad, and here's why." Her finger slid down to the tiny houses. "In

'69, sororities occupied these first two houses here. Miss Violet lived in the third house. The administration worried about women being housed in such proximity to men, so they set up Miss Violet to act as blocker. Miss Violet terrified my friends, I can tell you. Only met her once, and that was enough. The woman was built like a linebacker and had eyes better than a barn owl. She missed nothing. She would have spotted Rosalie."

If Maddie was right, and Rosalie couldn't have gone down the Quad without being seen by Miss Violet, the girl had to have taken the woodland path to get to the river.

"Once you have a better idea of what you need, I can pull more documents from the Society's archives. What else can I tell you?"

Abbie asked the uneasy question. "Is it possible that this was a murder nobody wanted to talk about because it had racist undertones? And is it possible that the police back then, heck, the whole town wasn't color-blind? Sylvia thinks so."

"*Racist* undertones?" The ex-reporter took some time to respond. "I don't have an appropriate answer for you, darlin'. Chief Farrow could be as much a good old boy as you'd ever find in this town. If he tried to protect some white man, hey, possible, but you said the ABI took over the case. Out of Farrow's hands." Madeleine took off her readers and cleaned them with the corner of her shirt. "Now, as for the paper, there was a lot of news going on in the world!"

"Putting a man on the moon was big news," Abbie agreed. Perhaps she should visit the newspaper archives. The building was only a couple of blocks away.

Madeleine huffed. "Not only did America just put a man on the moon, *we beat the Russians to it*. You're way too young to have experienced what it felt like to be afraid of the Russians. You never practiced duck-and-cover in your classroom. And in 1969, the Vietnam War raged white-hot. Also, the week before, at least I think it was the week before, Ted Kennedy killed Mary

Jo Kopechne at Chappaquiddick. There was more news than *The Times* had ink to print. But that's just my opinion. What are you going to do next?"

Her next step was exactly the question bouncing around Abbie's head. "Try to find her friends."

"When you do, you ask them why Rosalie was headed to St. Louis to see her aunt, and why she needed to go down to the river before she left."

Abbie replaced the maps in their cellophane wrappings, careful with their fragile edges. "Thanks so much, Maddie." She slung her purse over her shoulder.

"Are you going to tell me about that mysterious rental car in your driveway?" Madeleine asked with a single raised brow.

Nothing gets past her. "It's Joss Freeman, from college."

"The cute one from the TV?"

"He certainly thinks of himself as cute. He's here to do some research for his show. Needs a topic. Last night, he camped out in the attic with my parent's boxes but, according to the note he left me, he struck out." Abbie briefly explained Joss's dilemma.

"Well, why don't you send the boy down here and we'll see if we can dig anything up together?" Madeleine winked. "It'll give the old biddies from the Ladies' Society something to sink their teeth into."

Thursday, 8:33 a.m., the Guest Room Over the Garage

Buzz. Buzz.

Lincoln was running toward him, his grey coat sleek, feline claws scratching the sidewalk of the Santa Monica pier. "Save me, Joss!" the cat screeched.

Buzz. Buzz.

A block away, a lone figure in painter's overalls and sleeveless t-shirt, her hair carelessly shoved into a baseball cap, reached into a bucket. "Get back here, you miserable creature!" She threw, hard, like a major-league pitcher. A brown clump of wet clay just missed Lincoln's tail.

Buzz. Buzz.

Joss knelt. "C'mon, buddy!" The clay bombs kept coming, faster and faster, Lincoln had to dodge one, then the other. Another bomb whizzed past Joss's ear. Lincoln was feet away . . .

Buzz. Buzz.

Joss opened one eye. Daylight peeked through the slats of the blinds near his bed. *Where am I?* Oh yeah, Hunts Landing. Abbie's house. Garage apartment.

He found his phone by following the vibrations.

Abbie: Meet me at the Historical Society. 171 French Street. Behind the old courthouse.

If texts had voices, this text would be one of the annoying Siri ones. It took a couple of heartbeats to clear the jetlag before his eyes focused again. *Historical Society.* Had she found something?

Thursday, 8:47 a.m., The Hunts Landing Times

Abbie left the Historical Society and walked the three blocks to *The Times's* building. She loved walking through town in the early spring. The mingling of late viburnum and early lilac tantalized her senses. The perfumed air cleared her mind and allowed her to think.

Growing up in Hunts Landing, she'd never considered the place as having a racial history. The town was an anomaly in the deep South. Since the sixties, as the engineers and scientists supporting NASA and the Depot and the defense contractors moved in, the population became more and more diverse and cosmopolitan. Hate crimes were almost unthinkable in the Hunts Landing of 2015. But what about in 1969? The paper had devoted two column-inches to the DuFrayne murder. Had *The Times* treated other crimes the same way? The paper's archives might hold the answer.

On her last assignment, the paper had been in the middle of a project to digitize back issues, but it was incomplete at the time. Abbie, familiar with microfiche machines and old documents, had spent so many hours in the archive room that Will Irestone took to calling it 'Abbie's Dungeon.'

Inside *The Time's* newsroom, she found Sylvia with a group monitoring the weather reports on the big screens. The red-colored wedges on the weather map promised more afternoon storms, quite common this time of year, but Abbie guessed the staff was a little on edge after Will's accident. Abbie tried to slip around the group to the newspaper morgue when Sylvia waved her over. "Morning. What's going on?"

"Headed to the dungeon," Abbie said.

"Whatcha looking for?"

"I want to check on other murders reported on by this paper, especially Black victims," Abbie said. "Plus, full issues from July and August 1969. What else was going on in town that might have drawn attention and prompted more coverage than this murder?"

"Good thinking. And your timing is perfect." Sylvia opened her portfolio. "We've got a new intern who's driving me nuts. Takes a two-hour project and finishes it in ten minutes. I'm running out of stuff to keep her occupied. I'll send her downstairs."

"What's the news on Will?"

Sylvia grinned. "He's as loopy as Cheerios with all the meds he's on. But he's well-guarded. His sister is like a gargoyle and won't let any of us in to see him."

"None of us?"

"Not even me, his boss."

Abbie wondered if she had the guts to try and sneak around Will's guardian-sister.

Stuffed into the basement of *The Times* building, the morgue's air bordered on the humid side, threatening over a century's worth of yellowed newsprint stored there. Numbered boxes of back issues lined wooden shelves, and dusty racks of cassette boxes flanked the aging microfiche machine.

Sylvia's promised intern descended the morgue's wooden stairs with a clack of high heels and an eager "Hello!" A pretty girl, she had a pert nose and thick blonde hair, the kind only the young could cultivate. "I'm Whitney."

In a light-gray suit, Whitney was overdressed for *The Times*, a college student trying to impress. Abbie smiled in response, remembering her own first business suit and how hard she'd tried to leave her mark. It took Abbie only a minute to explain what she wanted, and the girl was at the shelves before she'd finished speaking. A small cloud of dust followed the first microfiche box Whitney pulled, and she absentmindedly wiped the dust on her skirt. Abbie liked her immediately.

"So, do you want photocopies or scans?" Whitney asked.

Thursday, 9:14 a.m., the Square

Joss opted to walk into the town center instead of driving. Following the step-by-step directions from his map app, the cool spring air slowly giving way to the warmth of the sunshine and the hypnotic scent of early blooms tantalizing his nostrils, Joss's step was the lightest since he'd left for New York.

Hope kindled and grew with every passing moment. As Joss turned the corner near the historical society's office, he saw Abbie approaching him from the opposite direction. They met midway up the block.

"Be warned," Abbie said. "Maddie's a character."

Understatement, Abs, Joss thought after the introductions. But he liked Madeleine's orange sneakers.

Madeleine offered them seats in the conference room, where memorabilia of Hunts Landing cluttered the walls. "Abbie told me a little of your problem, Joss. Civil War treasure, hmmm?"

"Not my choice, I assure you," Joss said.

"Looks like both of you are working on projects that aren't of your choosing." The older woman smirked. "I'll help if I can. Your problem, Joss, is that the Civil War barely touched north Alabama, not like it did Tennessee."

As airy and light as he'd felt minutes before, Joss felt hope sinking. *Eight days times twenty-four hours a day times . . .*

"But I remembered something," Madeleine continued. "Not a lot of fact, more a legend. It was, oh, 1981, and I was a reporter for *The Times*. I was still doing mostly fluff pieces, and my assignment that week was to cover an open house at the Grover mansion. You know the place, Abbie?"

Abbie nodded, but scrunched her brows, a gesture Joss recognized as Abbie trying to remember something. "One of the first houses, right?"

"Um hmm," Madeleine nodded. "Joss, Hunts Landing was incorporated in 1831, a source of particular pride to the residents. For the hundred and fiftieth anniversary, the Ladies' Society arranged an open house tour of some of the first homes built in town."

"I remember that now," Abbie said. "We all had to draw posters for school."

"It was a big deal in Hunts Landing, I can tell you," Madeleine said. "My assignment was the Grover place. Now, Ezekiel Grover was the town doctor in the 1830s when he built the house. Every few years the Grovers would have another child, or two, or four, and Ezekiel would add onto the house, until it became the monstrosity it is today."

"The house is shaped funny," Abbie added. "Not square, or rectangular. More like an *L*."

"Right. It really is an ugly old thing, and beautiful at the same time, the way an old building can be beautiful. I interviewed the current owner, Mrs. Chenoweth, and she showed me the front stairs. Gorgeous set of stairs, crafted by hand with carved walnut banisters. But off-center, because with the additions, the center hall wasn't exactly in the center of the house any longer."

Joss resisted the urge to drum his fingers on the clean conference table.

"That's when she told me," Madeleine continued. "Mrs. Chenoweth pointed to the stairs and said, 'That's where the Yankees rode their horses up the stairs, looking for the gold.'"

Abbie inhaled sharply, and the hairs on the back of Joss's neck bristled. *Finally, something.* "Go on."

"Remember," Madeleine wagged a finger, "this was Mrs. Chenoweth's story, in her words. By the 1860s, Ezekiel Grover was an illustrious town father. People listened to him. Now, the story went, after the Battle of Shiloh in 1862, General Grant sent forces southeast to get control of the railways between Memphis and north Georgia. The depot here in Hunts Landing was a strategic point on that railway. News of the southern defeat at Shiloh raced across the Tennessee Valley fast. People were terrified with a Union army in their midst. So, Ezekiel Grover convinced some of the shop owners on the Square to hide their valuables with him. But, according to Mrs. Chenoweth, somebody talked. When the Union troops got here, they looted his pharmacy on the Square, then went to the Grover's home, looking for the gold."

"Did they find any?"

"Well, that's the magic question, isn't it?" Madeleine cocked her head. "I didn't write any of it up, this wasn't all that long after *Roots*, and the paper was avoiding stories from that time like the plague. But if you need a Civil War gold story, one that hasn't been told before, Grover's gold is as good a place as any to start."

—— ·· ——

Thursday, 10:39 a.m., South of Hunts Landing

Hunts Landing copy center didn't have equipment large enough for the maps, so Abbie drove to the large office supply store a few miles up the interstate.

The minutes were counting down toward her meeting with Wexler. *Meeting? Confrontation? Showdown?* The console clock's minute digit updated itself with disconcerting frequency.

Seventy-nine minutes left. Seventy-eight minutes left.

Abbie parked and carried the cellophane-protected maps into the store.

The kid behind the counter—*kid*, because he didn't look much older than George—seemed too young to have any respect for archival documents, so she only let him take one map at first, and scrutinized his every movement. He fed the Hunts Landing map into the oversized scanner with care, his hands ready in case of a jam. Abbie tilted her head in acknowledgement. So much for her preconceptions of the young.

While the scanner's computer processed the first map, Abbie pulled the campus map out of its sleeve and laid it flat on the counter. It really was a work of art, and she wondered how Theodore Wexler had come to part with it. Of course, the family probably had donated the map to the Historical Society after his death. She'd have to ask Madeleine.

Tiny watercolor strokes tinted the trees next to the river at the south end of the Quad, trees that were no longer there. Instead of the straight concrete sidewalk that now flanked the river, a squiggly, dashed line marked a footpath from the trees of Meyers Plantation to the campus. Had this been where Rosalie's killer exited the woods?

Opposite that footpath, on the southeast corner of the Quad, stood a little square building with a minuscule cross on top. Barton's Chapel. Jethro'd said that the boys from Mill Town had come 'round Barton's Chapel. Barton's Chapel, the trees where a party turned into a brawl. Everyone's attention on the east side of the map. Nobody looking at the footpath.

Twelve cops on the scene, and the killer probably walked right past us.

If that were the case, why wouldn't the killer or killers have taken the safer, more hidden path north, under the cover of the trees, behind the Greek houses? Why risk coming out on the Quad at all?

Luke—Abbie noticed his name tag now, instead of just his babyish face—returned with the first map and her copy. "Did you want me to roll this up for you?" he asked.

At least he's polite. "No, thanks, let's keep them flat." She slid the campus map across the counter, returned the original Hunts Landing map to its sleeve, and studied the copy.

Hunts Landing of 1969. Drawn to scale, with the lack of personality municipal maps often revealed. An inset showed the town's location within the county, hugging the Tennessee River to the south. Back then, Hunts Landing was only accessible by county roads; Andrew Jackson Road, running north/south, and County Road 62, running east/west.

The ABI figured it must've been the Tennents gang who killed Rosalie DuFrayne, as they worked their way east from Muscle Shoals.

County Road 62, miles north of Hunts Landing, wasn't a major thoroughfare any longer, used mainly by farm vehicles and strawberry pickers in the spring. Elsa and Matthias Adams had taken their little Abbie strawberry picking each June, and Abbie had taken her own kids two or three times as well.

There's something wrong with this, Abbie thought, but whatever that something was, it whisked away as soon as she focused on it.

"Okay, Ms. Adams," Luke approached with her second copy, "I need your email address so I can send the digital files."

Abbie wrapped up the transaction and headed to her car. She laid the maps flat on the cargo mat and started the engine. *Thirty-six minutes.* Enough time to drop the original maps back at the Historical Society, drive to campus, and sit in the parking lot for a few minutes, coming up with the questions she needed to ask Frank Wexler.

Thursday, 10:52 a.m., Grover House

Abbie was right, Joss thought. The place was really ugly.

And Madeleine was right, too, because there was a beauty about the house he couldn't quite put his finger on.

From Elm Street, the house presented as a typical antebellum manse, two-story brick, with cream-colored columns and floor-to-ceiling windows. A large, white wooden sign was planted next to the street. *Harmon Auction House. Auction next Saturday!* Sadly, the yard was in a desperate state of neglect, the concrete slabs of the walkway buckled and broken.

What a shame. With a little love, this place could be magnificent.

Joss walked around the corner to the side of the house and immediately saw what Abbie had meant. With each addition the nineteenth-century Grovers made to the house, they'd used a different color of brick, still reddish but giving the house a distorted look. The additions stretched backwards from the east side of the house in a long structure, giving the home that L-shape. Several of the windows bore cracks and holes reinforced with cardboard and duct tape. There was a patch of cheap and weathered aluminum siding at the northern part of the house, the look of an inexpensively enclosed porch. It appeared that the Grovers weren't the only family to blithely add onto what was once a magnificent building.

What a shame, he thought again. *The old girl has good bones.* Bones, Joss was certain, built by slave labor, given that the original structure was built in the 1830s.

A bucket propped open the door to the ad hoc porch, and he watched as a steady stream of people, college kids, he guessed, five or six of them, left the building carrying cardboard boxes. They tucked some boxes into the back of a black pickup parked in the driveway with *Harmon Auction House* painted on the door. Otherwise, most boxes were tossed into a construction dumpster parked on what might have been the last patch of decent grass on the property. Joss watched them for a few minutes.

What the heck.

He followed one kid into the house.

The floor was littered with debris. Piles of old newspapers and *National Geographic* magazines were stacked underneath the porch windows. Broken dinnerware and moth-eaten linens cluttered the path before him. He made his way toward the front of the house, not really noticed by anyone.

Through a room that had been carpeted with what was once orange shag, Joss found himself in the original center hall of the house. Inside the front door, the ceiling had collapsed, revealing thick iron piping. Boxes of water-damaged junk were piled beneath the break.

Joss shook his head with a sigh and turned.

Ah, the famous staircase.

It was, indeed, magnificent. The craftsmanship was something he hadn't ever seen except, perhaps, in Monticello or Mount Vernon. The carvings on the balustrade were smooth, the finish polished with age and use. Joss reached out to touch the bannister and gave it a slight nudge. The railing held solid. The skill of the slaves who'd constructed these stairs, stairs that didn't budge after almost two-hundred years, took his breath away, and saddened him at the same time.

"This is going to be what sells this house," a voice said behind him.

Joss turned and faced a burly man with a short-trimmed beard and a *Harmon Auction House* t-shirt.

The man extended his hand. "Wayne Harmon."

"Joss Freeman." The handshake was firm, friendly, the handshake of a man used to selling to other people.

"Are you interested? The auction is a week from Saturday."

No need to tell him I'm on a treasure hunt. "My interest is historical. I'm a documentarian. We're considering doing a piece on some of the more unknown antebellum homes." *Not too far from the truth.*

Wayne nodded with a closed-mouth smile. "I thought I'd recognized you. The wife loves your stuff. I don't mind taking a break. How can I help?"

Joss spread his arms at the trash all over the floor. "What happened here?"

"Family feud." Wayne pointed up to the busted ceiling. "The Chenoweth estate used to own this property. Parents died, eleven years ago, intestate, no will. Kids fought for years over the house, stopped paying the property taxes. Last winter, they stopped paying the utilities bill. First big freeze, pipes burst." He motioned to a room off the hall. "Let me show you around."

Wayne led them into a room full of clothes racks and more piles of newspapers, and what must have been at one time a truly magnificent fireplace. He pointed to the front windows. Stained and torn wallpaper hung in strips from the walls, and underneath the windows the floorboards buckled. "The water damage extended to the entire front of the house. It's a pity, too, because we can't save those floorboards, and they're original."

"Did the family really live like this?" Joss couldn't believe the amount of clutter.

"Oh, while the kids fought, they invited every member of the extended family to use this place as the Chenoweth family storage unit. Some rooms upstairs were four-feet high with junk. Now, the county has repossessed the property, and nobody wanted their stuff."

Joss walked over to the fireplace and nudged a pile of newspapers with his toe. "And these?"

Wayne joined him, running his hand over the hand-carved mantel with the care of one who truly appreciated fine workmanship. "Oh, the old couple never threw away a scrap of paper, not that I can tell. We found a box of check stubs from 1964. Can you imagine?"

Joss had heard of hoarders, of course, but had never seen the toll it took.

Wayne showed him the rest of the house, which had been sinfully neglected over the past decades. The Chenoweths had made many shoddy renovations with a mind to their modern sensibilities rather than the aesthetic beauty of the home. Somebody had installed a pink DIY bathroom counter in front of an upstairs window, blocking the lower fourth of the window. It was a downright shame.

It also meant that lacking a complete demolition of the interior of the house, Joss wouldn't be able to visualize the house as she was in 1862, when Union soldiers had come in search of the town's gold. Nor would he be able to film here, not in the home's current condition.

The tour ended at the top of the main staircase. "Ah," Joss said, "the Union troops rode their horses up these stairs."

"You know about that, huh?" Wayne asked, leading the way down.

"Oh, something I picked up at the Historical Society. That must have been Mrs. Chenoweth, then, who gave that tour?"

"That was a bit before we came to Hunts Landing, I'm afraid," Wayne shrugged.

"Is there a basement?" Joss asked. "Wouldn't a house in those days have a basement."

"Not much to see down there except a bunch of old boilers," Wayne said. "But, come along, I'll show you."

An easily missed door near the kitchen hid a narrow flight of wooden steps with a rickety railing. Joss gingerly followed the beam of Wayne's flashlight.

The ceiling was low, and they both had to stoop. The floor was dirt, coated with years of dust, and the walls were made of old, crumbled brick. Whoever bought the house would certainly have foundation work to do.

Six boilers lined one wall, each one more ancient than the next. Other than that, there was nothing to show the basement had ever been used by the family.

"Disappointed?" Wayne asked.

"A little," Joss admitted. He'd expected what? A full basement, complete with nooks and crannies where one could hide a hoard of gold? He'd been so eager to see the house he hadn't bothered with the most rudimentary research. *Idiot, you know better.*

"Come along," Wayne said, headed back toward the stairs. "I'll show you something really cool."

The detached garage was as full as the house, this time only with gardening tools and buckets of rusty nails. Wayne led the way around cluttered metal shelves to a tiny space with a metal dome and a single door bolted to the floor.

"What the heck is that?" Joss asked.

Wayne grinned. "Bomb shelter."

CHAPTER SIX

Thursday, 1:01 p.m., Hunts Landing College

Some students beat Abbie to Wexler's office, so she walked on past to a water fountain. How well she remembered the mad sprint up two flights of stairs to reach his office before Dr. Wexler did, because if a student didn't get in line before Wexler got to his door, he wouldn't get to see him.

Unmistakable footsteps echoed on the linoleum. Perhaps a little less brisk than during her graduate school days, but his stride was still unique, making the footstep of a loafer sound louder than a dress shoe. The professor's voice, softer in the hallway than in the lecture hall, but only by a little, welcomed the students. "Sorry, something's come up, no office hours today, email your questions, see you next Thursday."

Muffled concerns about the upcoming exam amid retreating footsteps wafted down the hall. Taking a moment, she inhaled a good, deep breath.

The door to the outer office stood open, but no lights illuminated the room. Wexler had walked straight past the wooden reception desk, through to his office, where only desk lamps shone. Striding through the outer room years after her last meeting here, Abbie navigated the darkness without bumping into anything.

Wexler's office presented a study in dichotomy, the left-hand side decorated with the trappings of a department head—the elaborate desk, the visitor's chairs. On the wall, framed awards and diplomas— the mementos of a long academic career. The right-hand side reflected Wexler's true personality—a conference table surrounded on three sides by overstuffed bookshelves, the table littered with stacks of term papers and ungraded exams. Wexler the department head worked on the left side of the room, Wexler the aging history professor worked on the right.

Today, he sat at the conference table, face illuminated by a reading lamp. It was truly amazing how someone could age and change so little. His graying hair, much whiter now, his khaki trousers, his reading glasses tucked into his shirt pocket, as always. The way he crossed his legs, right ankle resting on his left knee, and interlocked hands behind his head, a pose impossible for her to forget. The amused teacher, he assumed this posture whenever preparing to listen to a student's argument.

The same posture he assumed with her now.

"Dr. Wexler." She lowered herself into the seat across from him.

"Abbie!" The perfunctory smile showing no teeth did little to soothe her nerves. "You're looking well."

She nodded, unsure what to say next. The dread in her gut clashed with the familiarity of her surroundings and disrupted her balance. As a graduate student, she spent many happy hours in this room, so many happy hours, until the heartbreaking last day. Today, her shattered equilibrium unbalanced her.

"Grace and I read about Zach. We should've sent our condolences. I'm sorry, Abbie."

Yes, you should have. "Thank you."

"Kids ok?"

"They're good." She would not share her personal life with Frank Wexler. Not now, after all this time.

He pursed his lips, a gesture Abbie recognized, one he used when considering his next point in the debate. "Well. Your email said you'd like to talk about Rosalie DuFrayne."

The tightness in her throat eased. Today, she was acting as a reporter, not as his groveling graduate student eager for his praise. She would lead the questioning, not Frank Wexler. *Stick to your questions, Abbie.* "*The Times* hired me to research the murder of Rosalie DuFrayne. How well did you know her?"

A moment or two passed as he considered his response. "Rosalie DuFrayne was the daughter of my family's cook. Her murder was a tragedy." He closed his mouth, sighed, opened his mouth again. "No one in the family has ever publicly commented on the event, and we don't intend to begin now."

She should have expected he'd be pigheaded. "On the evening of July 24th, 1969, Rosalie was part of the help at a party at your home. What did she do there?"

"I assume this is on the record?"

"Of course," Abbie said.

"Then I repeat myself. The family will not comment on this event."

"What if it were off the record?"

"My answer would be the same."

Keep asking the questions. "When was the last time you saw Rosalie DuFrayne?"

Was that annoyance in his eye? The way his gaze narrowed, just slightly, like when a student didn't quite follow a lecture. The mischievous child within her hoped he was annoyed.

"One last time, the family will not comment on this event."

Golly, he was a stubborn cuss. "Why on earth did you agree to see me if you weren't going to answer my questions?" Abbie asked.

Almost imperceptibly, the narrowed gaze widened. "I wanted to see you. I wanted to see how you are."

He'd never given a moment's thought to how she'd fared after his treachery, Abbie was certain, and she'd be damned if she was going to fall for his spurious concern. "In that case, Dr. Wexler, we have little to discuss." Abbie reached for her bag and stood.

"Why this story, Abbie?"

His question stopped her. "*The Times* is doing a series on the history of Hunts Landing and hired me to research the DuFrayne murder."

He looked sincerely puzzled. "Hunts Landing is full of history. The town is over two-hundred years old. Why *this* story?"

"I didn't pick it," she replied, unwittingly defending herself. "I'm simply doing the research." There was absolutely no reason on Earth she should tell him about her byline.

Again, Wexler pursed his lips. "Unable to find honest work as a proper historian, I suppose?"

"The honest work is researching the story and presenting the facts I find. All part of the history of Hunts Landing."

"This so-called story, this research of yours, this work isn't history."

Abbie bristled. "I work for *The Times,* and I'm a researcher for *America's Stories* on *The NMC Channel.*" *Okay, maybe only the one time. He doesn't need to know.*

"Cable television! Call this the work of a real historian? You might as well argue those idiots who dress up in Civil War costumes and parade around shooting cap guns at each other are historians. Don't you remember what being a historian means? To perform meticulous research and present your work for analysis and review by your peers? That's what a historian does. Who is reviewing your work now? Huh? I'm disappointed in you, Abbie."

She couldn't believe her ears. "You're . . . disappointed? In me?"

"Your mother, God rest her soul, would never have tried to parade comic book research as history."

Any other day, tears would blur her vision, but not today. "You disdain these research jobs I'm forced to take? Whose fault is this? Whose? My research was impeccable and sailed through the review committee. Did they think my research incomplete? No! Dr. Frank Wexler was the only faculty member to find my work flawed."

He brought his hands down to his knees. "Your research, yes, impeccable. Except for the Gladwin letters. Without those, the entire work, collectively, was incomplete." His voice resumed the steady, seductive tone that kept his students enthralled. "You didn't defend your theories. You jumped to conclusions you couldn't justify."

He was baiting her, entrapping her, trying to force her to re-argue and defend her work again. A repeat of her oral examination, to an audience of one.

No way. Take control back, Abbie.

Abbie shook her head. "I'm not here as your student, Dr. Wexler. I am here to seek the truth about what happened in 1969. A young woman was *murdered*, a woman connected to your household. Don't you care? Don't you want justice for Rosalie DuFrayne?"

"You aren't seeking justice," he said. "You make your living by seeking sensation. Whatever will sell a newspaper. Or pull in ratings for a TV show. Rosalie's dead, Miss Etta is dead. Who's going to get justice now? Let this go."

"No." In her entire experience with Frank Wexler, Abbie didn't think she'd ever acted against his wishes. "The story of Rosalie DuFrayne is going to be told, and I'm going to tell it. The historical record for her is a hole waiting to be filled. And if setting the record straight isn't the job for a living historian, well, by God, I'm glad you made sure I'm not one of those." Abbie shouldered her bag, ready to leave, this time for good.

"If you proceed," Wexler said, his words stopping her, "I'll be forced to pursue a legal remedy."

"Ha!" Did he really just threaten her?

It was too much. "Go ahead. The paper has lawyers." She leaned forward. "You can't hurt me anymore."

Thursday, 1:36 p.m., Hunts Landing Historical Society

"Geez, Maddie, what did I think would happen?" Seated across from Madeleine's desk, she dragged her hands through her hair while Madeleine poured some bourbon into a paper cup. "The man lounged at that damned table, calling my work cheap. He told me—" She downed the bourbon in one gulp, not noticing the burning in her throat, or remembering that she didn't particularly like bourbon. Her anger at Frank Wexler had diluted the feelings of inadequacy he invoked, but now, safe with Madeleine, those feelings burst through. "He said Momma would be disappointed in me, that working for a TV show, or a newspaper, wasn't worthy of a historian, that the quality of my work wouldn't have met Momma's standards."

"Don't listen to him." Madeleine blinked three times. "This is 2015, missy! You're eleven years older, and you live in the real world, a world where dental bills and car repairs and groceries trump the world where Frank Wexler can sink a career over a few two-hundred-year-old letters that probably fell to bits a hundred years ago. Believe you me, darlin', your mother would find no fault with what you're doing. If circumstances lead you to work for a TV show or a newspaper or the damned grocery store to put food on the table for your kids, that's what you do, Frank Wexler be damned. Your momma lived in the real world. If she had lost her opportunity to research and teach, she'd have been the first one waiting tables at Dixie's Diner if doing so meant getting money for your ballet lessons."

Madeleine wrinkled her nose and poured a bourbon for herself. "What's Frank Wexler ever done except publish a few books nobody ever bothers to read, except for the students who have to read them for his classes? He never did a damned thing on his own—his daddy got him out of combat in Vietnam, and his wife married him for money he never inherited. His aunt's the only one with any social standing left in Hunts Landing."

Abbie raised her paper cup. "Miss Nevelyn. Gracious lady."

"Talent certainly skipped a generation in that family." Madeleine touched her cup to Abbie's. "Jumped from Old Dr. Wexler right over Frank down to his kids." She thumped her fist on the desk. "Don't you ever tell me again Frank Wexler made you feel small. He's a wormy little pissant cuss who needs to lord it over his students because the department head of a small college is all he'll ever be."

"I've never seen you lose your temper before," Abbie said. "And I've known you since I was four."

"Good Southern women do not lose their temper. Damned good thing no one ever accused me of being one." As Abbie had done, Madeleine drank her bourbon all at once. "Lord, how I hated watching him reduce you to something less than our Abbie. And Grace Wexler, well, they're two of a kind. Now, you take another minute to lick your wounds, then you get after this story. He gave you a 'no comment.' Print that and move on."

Getting dressed down by Madeleine was exactly what she needed. Her anxiety shrunk and cooled. Or maybe that was the bourbon working. Abbie didn't know and didn't care.

"Why do you dislike Grace so much?" Abbie asked.

"I don't much care for fakes and phonies," Madeleine said. "Never could stand for them. Not too many other ladies in town do either. That woman's been hankering to get into the Ladies' Society for years, but try as she might, she'll never get in. Thought if she married into the Wexler family, we'd roll out the red carpet and crown her Queen of Hunts Landing. Things just don't work that way." Madeleine shrugged. "I suppose it wasn't easy for her. She lost her momma kinda young, if I recall. Small wonder she and Frank hooked up." Her face flushed from the bourbon, Madeleine leaned forward. "When I heard there was a strange car in your driveway last night, I thought it might have been your sexy new cop."

Abbie started to tell Madeleine about how she crashed into Nick Preston a couple of hours ago, when she suddenly realized what Madeleine had said a minute ago. "Frank didn't inherit his father's estate?"

Madeleine leaned back in her chair, cradling the empty paper cup. "Old Theodore didn't leave Frank a dime. All the money went to Nevelyn, with the caveat that Frank and Grace and the children could live in Wexler house until Frank died. Now, I believe, Nevelyn's will leaves everything to the children, but that's maybe just gossip. I couldn't tell you for sure. Grace has been living in that big house all these years, playing lady of the manor, but the only money she's ever had was from Frank's teacher's salary. Wouldn't that twist your panties?"

How horrible it must be, living that kind of lie.

At least in Abbie's memory, Grace had always lived up to her name, the gracious lady of the manor. All these years, Abbie had thought Frank Wexler had all the family money, living as a liberal arts professor because he could.

"So, Abigail Adams, what are you going to do? Are you going to let Frank Wexler knock you down all over again?"

The image of Frank Wexler, his right ankle resting on his left knee, that supercilious smirk of his as he coolly repeated *the family will not comment,* floated before her eyes.

That same unbearable smirk.

She wanted to take a giant eraser and rub at the image of his face until the smirk vanished and all that remained was a fleshy nothingness. "To hell with his 'no comment,' Maddie. I'm going to find out what happened to Rosalie DuFrayne."

Thursday, 2:11 p.m., the Square

On Revere Street, food trucks parked across from *The Times* offices. Joss texted Abbie, asking for an introduction, and grabbed some late lunch while he waited.

During all his previous visits to Hunts Landing combined, he'd never seen as much of the town as he had this morning. People *walked*, not in a hurry, but still with destination obviously in mind. Some stopped to talk to a friend. He heard laughter on either side of him, and people smiled at him sitting on the bench outside the hardware store as they passed him on the sidewalk.

It was definitely a different sort of pace from what he was accustomed to.

The sun disappeared behind some light gray clouds, and the door to the hardware store opened with a tinkle of a bell. An older man with a blue apron and hair sprouting out of his ears took a few steps out of the door, put his hands on his hips, and sniffed. "Smells like weather comin'."

Joss peered up at him. "Weather has a smell?"

The man returned his look and chuckled. "Y'all ain't from around here, are ya?"

Joss shook his head.

"Well, y'all be careful now this afternoon. Storms comin' in. Don't need no Weather Channel to tell me, either. It's in the air." He sniffed again. "Y'all have a good day." With another tinkle of the bell, the blue-aproned man retreated into the store.

Joss did his own sniffing and couldn't smell a thing except for the remains of his tuna melt.

Buzz. Buzz. He fished his phone out of his pocket.

Abbie: Go ahead, ask for Sylvia.

With one last look at the sky, Joss tossed his lunch into the nearest trashcan and hurried inside.

A moderately tall, slim woman in a chic pant suit greeted him. She immediately extended her hand. "You must be Joss Freeman, Abbie's friend. I'm Sylvia Van Cleave."

Joss shook her hand, a little disappointed that the editor hadn't recognized him.

She wiggled her fingers and turned. "Follow me." The hallway was short, opening up into the open space of the newsroom. "Abbie told me you have a show on NMC? Apologies, I'm not one for history. If it hasn't happened in the past twenty-four hours, I'm not interested." She strode with authority down a center aisle between desks, Joss a step behind her.

Sylvia stopped at a door with a nameplate *Morgue*. "Whitney's waiting on you. She's a little dynamo, she'll help you out."

Stepping gingerly down dimly lit stairs, Joss paused half-way to let his eyes adjust to the gloom. Taking the remaining steps, the archive's mustiness reached his nostrils and triggered memories. Once *America's Stories* had become a hit, Joss could afford to hire researchers, but in those early years, he'd had to do all the dusty work himself.

The intern, Whitney, waited for him in the middle of the morgue. Like Sylvia, she wore a smart pantsuit, and her long blonde hair was gathered into a single ponytail. Her eyes widened as he said, "Hi."

Ah, he knew that look, the wide eyes, the raised eyebrows, the smile that was too hesitant at first, then too broad.

Whitney was a fan.

He allowed himself a moment to wonder if she followed him on Twitter, then extended his hand. "Joss Freeman."

That seemed to shake her out of the over-broad smile. "Mr. Freeman, I'm Whitney."

"Call me Joss, please."

She hesitated, licked her lips, then nodded. "Of course. Mr. Joss, Ms. Sylvia said you wanted help with the Grover House?"

He explained the article Madeleine had written in the eighties. "I need background on the house, back to the 1830s."

Whitney looked around at the shelves. "This archive only goes back to the turn of the twentieth century. But I might have some luck at the campus library." She turned back to him and smiled again, a genuine one this time, eyes shiny with a challenge. "Anything else?"

Joss started to say *no*, then changed his mind. "Yeah. Anything you can find on bomb shelters."

Thursday, 2:47 p.m., Nevelyn Wexler's Cottage

The bourbon she had gulped down in Madeleine's office was enough to simmer her blood. Frank Wexler be damned! *The family will not comment on this event.* The pompous, arrogant ass, speaking for every Wexler as if he were the great lord of some great family on some great estate.

Well, thanks to Madeleine, she now knew that while he might live in Wexler House, the Wexler dynasty had passed right over him.

There was more than one Wexler alive and living in Hunts Landing now who had been there in 1969.

Did she dare?

No, Abbie, he probably picked up the phone and called his wife right after she stormed out of his office.

But . . .

Would Nevelyn Wexler, Frank's aunt, speak to her?

Nevelyn Wexler was a classy lady. Abbie doubted the woman would slam the door in Abbie's face.

And besides, Will wouldn't let the notion of a slammed door stop him.

Abbie made her choice in a split second, gripped her shoulder bag, and headed toward Wexler House. Nevelyn Wexler lived in a renovated carriage house on the northeastern corner of the Wexler property, a cottage that had its own garden gate and walkway to the street, facing away from the big house. Nevelyn had hosted Frank's students once, so Abbie knew that the white double doors on the exterior were original, but the interior and roof had been newly replaced for the older woman's comfort. The windows were spotless, and window boxes containing purple and pink flowers adorned the small building.

Nevelyn answered the door a full minute after Abbie knocked. "Abigail Adams! You sweet girl, come in, come in." Nevelyn walked with the aid of an aluminum walker with tennis balls at the bottom of each leg and a bicycle basket strapped to the front. Abbie followed her into a large room with an open floor plan, where strategically placed furniture broke the space into a living area, a dining area, and a kitchen. The western wall, where on the outside of the building the original carriage doors remained, had been sheet-rocked, painted, and was now decorated with many framed photographs and a walnut curio cabinet. The southwestern corner was walled up, concealing Miss Wexler's bedroom.

Nevelyn led them to the kitchen area and eased herself into a chair. "In my day, we would never dream of hosting company in the kitchen, but these days the extra steps aren't worth it. Sit down, please."

Abbie smiled and dropped her bag to the floor. "Thank you for seeing me, Miss Wexler."

"You call me Nevelyn, just like you always have."

"I wasn't sure if you would see me."

"Oh, because of the ruckus you've caused up at the big house?" Nevelyn chuckled. "Being summoned to a family meeting was the most fun I've had in years. Grace certainly has her pantyhose all tied up in knots. Worried you'll besmirch the family name." Nevelyn peered over her glasses. "Is that what you're intending to do?"

"Ma'am, my only intent is to write a newspaper article," Abbie said.

Nevelyn stared at her intently, and Abbie got the funny feeling that her visit wasn't exactly unexpected.

"Good. Frank and Grace might not approve, but I don't suppose that anything I could possibly tell you can cause any harm, not after all these years. So, what can I tell you?"

Abbie had been running on adrenaline since leaving Madeleine's office, and for the second time in as many days found herself unprepared with good questions. "Well, first, will you go on the record?"

Nevelyn pursed her lips. "Well, unfortunately no. As much as I don't appreciate my nephew trying to tell me who I can or can't speak to, I don't really know anything worth going on the record for. We threw a party for a hundred and fifty guests or so. Rosalie worked at the party. I was very busy being a hostess that night; I can't really recall seeing Rosalie that much. I don't know what time she left the house. I didn't see her leave. The next day, the police came to tell us that her body had been found down by the river."

The older woman wasn't telling her much, but she'd opened the door to Abbie and invited her in. Abbie decided not to press the issue, at least not until she had more information. She could always come back. "Perhaps my coming here was a little premature."

Nevelyn placed her hand on the table between them. "Forgive me for not being more gracious. And this is for you, not for your story. You see, that murder, the wicked brutality of it, changed this town, the university, the family forever. That's why Frank doesn't want to comment."

"It changed *your* family? With all due respect, I think the family most affected was Rosalie's. Seems the Wexlers have survived all these years just fine."

"You're right, of course. Forgive my thoughtless comment. Nothing compares to the pain of losing a child." Nevelyn paused, looking at Abbie as if she was searching for a signal to proceed. "A murder that close, of someone you know, it affects you, even those seemingly unaffected. We were never the same after that."

———————

Thursday, 4:10 p.m., the Sunporch

When Abbie returned to the house, George had already come home from school, and Joss was pacing outside with his cellphone pressed to his ear. She carried the map copies into the dining room and spread them on the table. Both maps made for good artwork. Sylvia always wanted artwork. The more the better, so she could pick which images to print and which to post for the online version of the story.

A thick envelope with the pre-printed address of *The Times* was on her laptop. Inside were a stack of microfilm printouts, the inverted white-print against a black background difficult to read, unless, of course, one had a background in archival documents. Whitney must have given the envelope to Joss.

Abbie made a pot of jasmine tea and took the clippings out to the sunporch. She pulled out a set of pages held together by a binder clip—photocopies of back issues for the week before and after the murder. A Post-it affixed to the July twenty-sixth issue marked Caleb Jackson's two-column inches. A second yellow square stuck out from the July twenty-seventh issue, next to Rosalie's obituary. Whitney had left a handwritten note on the Post-it. Scanned through the next six months. No other mention of DuFrayne.

Nothing after the obituary? That didn't make sense. The ABI might have taken over the case, but it had been in Hunts Landing PD's hands for at least a few days. Surely a dead body in town merited some coverage.

Respect for the family, stand down. The words printed next to Jackson's pencil sketch of Theodore Wexler. Had Old Dr. Wexler asked Jackson to back off the story? Why? To protect the family from scandal? Hunts Landing was an old town, and the Wexlers were one of the oldest families. Wexler's standing in town had been so closely tied to the college that any whiff of scandal could be devastating.

A second set of paper-clipped article copies bore another message. *Five other murders in Hunts Landing 1968–1970.* That *The Times* heavily covered those crimes was clear, given the thickness of the stack. Clearly the paper had not paid adequate attention to the DuFrayne murder. Not by a long shot.

"Hey Mom?" George called from the kitchen. "Uncle Joss says he's gonna cook tonight, so I'm taking him to Publix, okay?"

They left, and the house settled to a quiet before she thought to ask George if he had his homework done. Memories of college meals made her wonder exactly what atrocity Joss was planning on serving them.

Abbie put aside the newspapers and went to stand before her whiteboard. Her photos of Rosalie and her friends were taped to the top. Erasable markers lay unopened on the marker tray. She picked a blue one and wrote What I Know.

Underneath, she wrote her confirmed facts. Rosalie killed evening July 24. Miss Etta, Wexlers' well-paid cook. Party at Wexler House. Miss Etta + 50 lbs Catfish. Party at river. St. Louis bus ticket. Not a robbery. ABI takeover. The Times *squashed the story.* That last bit was more conclusion than fact, but she included it on her list, anyway.

She'd only been at this for a day and was disappointed in how little she knew.

On the other side of the board, she wrote What I don't, and sighed. This list was definitely going to be longer.

She retraced her steps, starting with Caleb Jackson's file. He'd included the grant scandal article for a reason, and the *why* was a big unknown. Had he intentionally included the article, or was it a misfiled clipping? Three years after Rosalie's death? She wrote Caleb Jackson and **grant scandal**. Next to the word **scandal**, she printed a capital **M** with a circle around it. Maddie might know something about the scandal.

Rosalie had a one-way bus ticket in her purse. Why St. Louis? Her aunt? Why would she leave in the middle of summer term? Abbie added **St. Louis** to the right side of the board.

In his notes, Jethro had singled out two names—Cyrus Porter and Isaac Leon Moore, the two brawlers closest to the woods. She didn't have any sort of lead on either name. Maybe Jethro could help? **Porter** and **Moore** joined the list, and she put Jethro's name next to them.

Bernice Strong and Cleta Blakebill, Rosalie's friends, at least friendly enough to pose for a photograph with Rosalie. So far, no luck in locating either. After writing those names on the whiteboard, she stepped back, scanned the board for other unanswered questions.

Of course, there were the two from the maps.

Killer(s)—woods—Quad?

Escaped prisoners—Tennents gang—travel time to Hunts Landing?

She stopped and looked at the entire board again. She'd be working extra this weekend. Luckily for her, George was going to be at robotics club, and Martha had a volleyball training camp. The only child she would have to deal with was Joss.

At least he was housebroken.

Chirp chirp chirp. She swiped to answer the call. "This is Abbie."

"Miss Adams, this is Honoria Leonard, Reverend Fisher's secretary. We've got some of the information you requested."

Thursday, 4:17 p.m., Calvary Baptist Church

The church itself sat on a large property north of the Square. The threat of an afternoon storm had passed without a drop, and now spring sunshine beamed. Behind the building, the parking spaces were empty, save for two spots near a one-story outbuilding. The church office, Abbie guessed. She went inside.

The name on the first nameplate read *Honoria Leonard*, and the lady herself, dressed as if ready for Sunday service, greeted her. "Miss Adams. Welcome."

Abbie shook her extended hand. "Yes, ma'am."

"So glad you could come in. Please sit," Mrs. Leonard said, and took her own seat with a practiced smoothing of her skirt. "I was only a little girl when Rosalie died, but we all heard the story, the kind your momma tells you to keep you out of places she didn't want you to go. 'Course, I knew Rosalie's momma, Miss Etta. Everyone did."

"I'm learning," Abbie said. "Can you tell me anything about her?"

"Did you know she kept the fixins' for cakes in barrels under her kitchen worktable? Big old wooden barrels, the old-fashioned type, full of flour and sugar. If you got sick, Miss Etta made you a cake. Birthday, anniversary, baby got born, somebody died, somebody got married, someone else got divorced, well, somebody got a cake. And she never forgot what cake you liked once she made it for you."

Abbie recorded the anecdote in her notebook.

"She also taught art at bible camp every summer."

"*Really?*" No one thus far had mentioned this aspect of Miss Etta. How interesting.

"Hmm. I remember drawing, and clay and watercolors. 'Course, I can't draw a straight line. But Miss Etta would say, 'Sweetness . . .'— she called every kid *Sweetness*, even the troublemakers—she'd say, 'Sweetness, the Lord loves crooked lines, that's why the trees are all different shapes.'"

Smiling at the memory, Mrs. Leonard opened a water-stained manila folder on her desk. "Most of the church records didn't survive the '74 storms, but I managed to find the family file. The DuFraynes joined New South Baptist in '52 after they moved here from

New Orleans." She pronounced the name of the city like a native. *N'Orleans.* "Rosalie sang in the choir and worked with the youth groups right up until she died. She was buried in the cemetery out back on July 28th in '69. Afterwards, Miss Etta organized all our picnics and parties, any event needing food." The church secretary lowered her voice. "Although I wouldn't say so to the other ladies around here, I don't think we've had a decent batch of fried chicken since Miss Etta passed."

Abbie couldn't help herself, she liked Mrs. Leonard. "Your secret is safe." *Questions, Jethro said, don't forget your questions.* "Any other family listed? I know of Miss Etta's sister in St. Louis, but perhaps she had some family in town?"

"All I see here is Eugenia DuFrayne, St. Louis," Mrs. Leonard said.

"So, Miss Etta was on her own after Rosalie passed? Was she close with anyone? Rosalie's father, perhaps?"

"I don't know about Rosalie's father. I don't recall that she had any, what do the kids call them, BFFs? She was kind of, well, everywhere and nowhere. How do I explain this?" Mrs. Leonard pressed her lips together and *humphed.* "Miss Etta was sort of a permanent fixture here. I can't recall a church function or wedding or funeral that she missed. But at the same time, and I'm guessing here, I think that, after Rosalie, she just found it hard to let other people in."

This aspect of Miss Etta, too, Abbie found relatable. She would have locked herself up in her bedroom and never come out after her parents and Zach died. Only Loreen and two young kids had kept her from becoming a recluse.

"How about when Miss Etta passed?"

The older woman leaned back in her chair. "It was a terrible winter, January '88. Snow and ice here in Hunts Landing, do you remember?"

Abbie nodded. "Four inches of snow, and not a single plow in the county. Lots of fun for us kids."

"My kids had fun, too," Mrs. Leonard said. "Now, Reverend Martin, our pastor, he'd been calling around, checking on our older parishioners, or those who lived alone like Miss Etta, and, well, she didn't answer her phone. So, he goes around to check in on her, 'cause he heard another storm coming. She always left her back door unlocked, in case someone was hungry, they could come right into her kitchen and get something to eat. He found her in the little room where she painted, paintbrush still in her hand. Doctor said she didn't suffer. Heart attack. Took her real quick."

A blessing for that poor woman, Abbie thought. "I wonder if any of her work is still around."

"My grandmother might have had a painting. I'll have to ask my mother."

Abbie closed her notebook. "Is Miss Etta buried out here too?"

"Yes. I'll take you to them."

Abbie followed the woman out the door, toward the cemetery behind the parking lot.

Chirp chirp chirp.

"Excuse me." Abbie answered the call. "This is Abbie."

There was silence on the other end of the line.

"Hello?" Abbie waited a few more seconds, but no one answered. She tapped *End.* "I hate those robocallers, don't you?"

"Absolutely, especially the ones who call at dinnertime." Mrs. Leonard walked and spoke with the practiced ease of a tour guide. "Now, I don't recollect Rosalie's funeral, I was a little 'un back then, but I recall Miss Etta's. Seemed like half of Hunts Landing showed up. The entire congregation, Black and white. The First Episcopal Church down the street offered up their hall for us to use, and even that building couldn't hold all the people."

"Do you remember if any family attended Miss Etta's funeral?" Abbie asked. "I'm trying to track down Rosalie's aunt, Eugenia DuFrayne, from St. Louis."

"Not that I recall."

"How about Rosalie's friends? Cleta Blakebill? Bernice Strong?"

"I'm sorry, but no." Mrs. Leonard headed for a shady spot under an enormous oak tree.

"Anyone else with a connection to the family? How about Isaac Leon Moore? Cyrus Porter?"

Mrs. Leonard stopped. "Cyrus? Of course, I should have thought of him, don't know why he didn't come to mind. He worked with Miss Etta up at Wexler House. Oh, Cyrus! He was everything a girl could want in a guy. All of us girls thought so. 'Course, he wasn't interested in any of us, just my cousin Lucretia. Only had eyes for her. He married her the day after he graduated college."

A break! "Do they still live around here?" Abbie asked.

"They sure do. I'll call him, ask him to get in touch with you." Mrs. Leonard turned and walked under the tree. "I'm sure he'll talk to you. Here they are."

Rosalie DuFrayne's wide marble headstone held a simple inscription. *Rosalie DuFrayne, born July 3, 1949, died July 24, 1969. Beloved daughter.* With her Nikon, Abbie snapped a few pictures. Miss Etta's stone, smaller but a little more elaborate than Rosalie's, bore a similar inscription. *Etta DuFrayne, born November 13, 1931, died January 30, 1988. Beloved mother and friend to all.* The Nikon's shutter clicked with each shot. With an eye toward pictures for Sylvia, she scanned the other nearby monuments. The DuFraynes' markers stood out—they were larger, and clearly costlier than the ones surrounding them.

Beloved mother and friend. Not wife. Zach's stone read, *Beloved husband,* as did her father's. And her mother's read, *Beloved wife.* Would she ever find out about Rosalie's father? *Some people, you're just not going to find,* Will had advised. And did it matter for a story on Rosalie's murder?

Perhaps, perhaps not.

"Do you have any idea who paid for the plot?" Abbie asked. "And the headstones?"

"Well, I'm not sure. I didn't find any mention in the family's file. Most of the financial records from those years will be in the basement archives."

Somebody laid out big bucks for these nice headstones. Abbie knew from personal experience that fine marble stones were expensive. "Do you think the Reverend would allow me to snoop around?"

"Oh dear, I don't know. People are funny about records these days, but I suppose they have to be. I'll ask him. And I'm so glad that someone is taking an interest in Miss Etta and Rosalie. About time somebody looked into that girl's murder. The police sure didn't do anything."

CHAPTER SEVEN

Thursday, 6:03 p.m., Abbie's Kitchen

Joss was getting his ingredients ready when Abbie entered the kitchen with her bag in one hand and a bottle of wine in the other.

Behind her, Martha, laden with schoolbooks and her volleyball gear, mumbled, "Hi, Uncle Joss," before trudging up the stairs.

"She isn't normally that grumpy, is she?" Joss asked. He took the bottle from Abbie's hand and tucked it into the fridge.

"The coach is really wearing these girls out, but she'll be fine after a shower," Abbie said. She surveyed the cluttered counter with narrowed eyes. "Is this one of your Spam Specials?"

"Ah, no faith, no faith at all."

"Any progress on your project?"

"I've got plenty to share."

"Give me a few." She left him in the kitchen and headed toward her own laptop to download the photos from the graveyard at Cavalry Baptist. The pictures themselves were disappointing. She hadn't accounted for the bright afternoon light that caused dark shadows crisscrossed with bright patches. She couldn't clearly make out the words on the tombstones. *I'll have to do these over.* Abbie printed them out anyway and taped them to her whiteboard.

In the kitchen, Joss had lined up his mixing bowls and cutting boards. He handed her a glass of something red and proceeded to zest a lemon.

"Where did you get this?" Abbie asked. It wasn't the wine she'd brought.

"Not Loreen's, that I can tell you."

"Don't let her hear you say that, and you'd better hide the bottle." The wine was wonderful, crisp with a nice finish. "We might need another one of these before the week is out." Joss's hand moved the lemon so quickly against the rasp, Abbie was certain he'd scrape off skin any second. "Are you sure you know what you're doing?"

"Relax, Miz Adams, all is in hand." He waved the lemon at her. "Meatballs à la Joss is on the menu tonight."

"Meatballs à la . . . made from real meat, right? Not Spam?"

"No Spam." He dumped a container of ricotta cheese in a bowl and reached for some eggs. "So, what do you know about the Grover House?"

"Not all that much," Abbie said, fascinated as he cracked eggs one-handed. *When had he learned to cook?* "I shared what I know this morning. My people have only been here since the sixties. Not all that long in this town. But I seem to remember going to school with one of the Grovers. Quiet girl. Loreen would probably know more. Her family's been here since it was Cherokee territory."

"Then I'll have to have a chat with Miss Loreen." Joss stopped whipping his batter. "Did you know there's a bonafide bomb shelter under the driveway?"

Abbie was so glad she'd swallowed her wine. No need to repeat yesterday's purple choking incident with Nick. "What?"

With a silicon spoon, Joss dropped globs of batter into hot oil. "An honest-to-goodness steel bomb shelter, eighteen steep steps down from a door in the garage. Complete with—" he quickly found the photo on his phone—"U.S. Government-issued canned emergency drinking water."

"That's incredible." Who would've thought such a thing possible in little Hunts Landing? "I bet the kids would love to see this."

"It really was pretty cool," Joss said. "The thing is like a can on its side. Rounded walls, I mean. There were some rusty bunks, and the cans of water." He fussed with his fry pot, flipping things over with a fork. "And one little itty bitty air vent. I mean, nothing to stop radiation from trickling down that vent, right? I guess they didn't know any better in the fifties."

Her mouth watered, the aroma in the kitchen was so scrumptious. "You've dated this already?"

"According to a guy who's selling some on eBay, those cans of water date from the '50s." He grabbed a plate lined with paper towels and started pulling round balls out of the oil.

"Those don't look like meatballs, Joss."

"Ahh, Miz Adams, these are the appetizer. Fritters à la Joss." A sprinkle of powdered sugar later, and he held the plate beneath her nose.

She bit into a still-warm fritter and groaned as the sensation of warm cheese and lemon worked its way down to her toes. "Sounds like you have an impressive start to your story . . . not that . . . mmmm . . . not that bomb shelters have anything to do with . . . oh my gosh . . . civil war treasures . . . good golly, when did you learn to do this? And you did it without a cookbook."

"Unlike historical trivia, my dear Abigail, outstanding recipes are the one thing a good cook should commit to memory." He winked and went to wash his hands. "I think I can earn my keep around here."

Benny growled just before the doorbell rang. "Easy, boy." Abbie went to answer the door. "Whitney?"

The girl stood on her porch, clutching a bunch of printouts. "Hi, Miss Abbie. I have some of the things that Mr. Joss asked for."

"Well, come on in." *She sends stuff for me with Joss, but hand-delivers directly to him? Zeesh!*

Joss met them in the living room, wearing one of Abbie's flour-smeared aprons. "Oh, Whitney, you didn't have to go to all of this trouble."

"Oh, it wasn't any trouble at all," Whitney gushed. "Like I told you, the paper's archives only go back to the early 1900s, but I pulled everything I found." She handed him the printouts. "Next, I tried the campus library, but that historical section goes back only to the Reconstruction, probably because that's when the school was built. So, I went to the courthouse and . . ." she sucked in some air, ". . . and sweet-talked my way into their records room and found the deeds to Grover House." With a triumphant smile, she opened her purse and retrieved a small object. A USB drive. "They let me use their scanner."

Joss flashed Whitney his TV smile, the one plastered all over his social media.

Abbie turned her head to roll her eyes. This was only day one of Joss's visit.

Thursday, 7:57 p.m., the War Room

It was so easy to fall into old habits. After dinner, with the kids upstairs studying or showering or doing whatever teenagers do on Thursday nights, Abbie and Joss worked quietly in the dining room, each tapping away on their own laptop. George had dubbed the room the 'War Room.' So much like those endless study nights back at school. Abbie was sure that if she closed her eyes, she could smell the horrific wine and excellent pizza that had been their diets.

She had a lead on Cyrus Porter, thanks to Mrs. Leonard. Now she needed to find the two other people she was certain knew Rosalie—

Bernice Strong and Cleta Blakebill—and the guy who'd been arrested with Cyrus, Isaac Leon Moore.

Logging into Newspapers.com, she searched for the names. Twenty fruitless minutes later, she got a hit, a wedding announcement from 1999.

The bride's father, Samuel Kellerman, and her mother, Bernice Strong, both live in Phoenix, Arizona. In the accompanying photo, a young Black bride wore a white fluffy bridal gown. Not positive proof that the mother of the bride was the same Bernice Strong she sought, but it was a possibility.

The online directory for Phoenix contained four listings for B. Strong. It wasn't too late to make phone calls, she hoped. The first number went straight to voicemail. She explained the purpose of her call, ending with, "If I've reached the right lady, please call me back." She repeated the message with the second and fourth numbers. A guy named Brian, number three on the list, couldn't get to the phone right now but was just dying to talk to her. Abbie didn't leave a message.

Some people, you're just not going to find, Will had said.

She tried one more name on Newspapers.com: Eugenia DuFrayne, St. Louis. It only took two clicks to find the obituary. April 14, 1979. Miss Eugenia DuFrayne lost her battle with cancer. She is survived by her sister, Miss Etta DuFrayne, of Hunts Landing. Her only son, Reginald DuFrayne, died serving his country in Vietnam. Services will be held on April 17th at New First Baptist Church.

The entire family was gone. And Miss Etta, she'd had to bury not only her daughter but her sister as well. Abbie's heart ached for the depth of Miss Etta's grief and loneliness. At least Abbie had had Loreen to keep her from sinking into darkness, but Miss Etta had everyone and no one, at the same time.

And neither could she ask Miss Eugenia why her niece had been coming to see her. Abbie stretched and scratched that spot between her shoulder blades she could barely reach. What did she know for sure, that she could capture for the article? She wrote up the descriptions of the crime scene and Rosalie's grave—only a couple of paragraphs, and none of them a good start to a feature piece. Two days in, and she didn't have much.

There were so many loose ends on the case. She stared at her whiteboard. Why had Rosalie DuFrayne been headed to see her aunt in St. Louis the night she died? What did her friends Cleta Blakebill and Bernice Strong have to say about Rosalie and her life? Why had Caleb Jackson included an article on a NASA scandal in his file?

She re-read from the copy of *The Times's* article . . .

September 18, 1971 — Hunts Landing. A grand jury indicted Dr. Quentin McCain on thirty-two counts of fraud in connection with the widening grant scandal at Hunts Landing College.

McCain, Dean of the School of Engineering, is accused of falsifying test data on grant applications made to NASA between 1964 and 1966. NASA funded research grants to the college for the development of electronic guidance systems. The amount of grant money awarded to the college is in the tens of millions of dollars.

Dr. McCain remains in Hunts Landing while on bail and vows to mount a vigorous defense and clear his name.

Abbie logged back online. McCain went on trial in 1973, and the jury convicted him in less than four hours. The judge sentenced him to twelve years. The same grand jury that indicted McCain cleared the college and Dr. Theodore Wexler of any wrongdoing.

McCain died in prison of lung cancer two years into his sentence.

Newspapers from Washington, D.C., New York, and Houston all provided extensive coverage of the Hunts Landing College grant scandal.

Not a single article mentioned Rosalie DuFrayne.

Her phone rang with her generic ringtone. Joss didn't look up from his laptop. She swiped to answer. "This is Abbie."

"Ms. Adams? This is Cyrus Porter. I understand you've been trying to reach me."

After agreeing to meet Cyrus Porter at Starbucks in the morning, Abbie spent the next couple of hours jotting down and revising questions.

You drive the interview, Jethro had said.

Only after she was satisfied did she head upstairs to check on her kids.

George had finished brushing his teeth. "It's fun, Mom, having Uncle Joss here. And him being a TV star and all."

"Star, maybe not. Personality, definitely." She winked. "But don't tell him I said so."

Martha lay asleep with her social studies book open. Abbie closed the book and turned off the light. As she passed the window, she surveyed the street, as usual.

A black SUV was parked across from the house, a few doors down. She could only see the front of it, a neighbor's tree blocking her view. The built-in radar all mothers possess kicked in, and the hairs on the back of her neck rose.

She closed the blinds.

Downstairs, Joss pecked at his laptop. She let Benny out the back door. Curious, Abbie went to the front of the house and checked the street through the blinds.

The SUV was gone.

Thursday, 10:31 p.m., the War Room

Joss spent the evening across from Abbie typing up notes, earbuds firmly in place, listening to a playlist that was probably too loud and energetic for this time of night and not caring a bit.

Whitney's USB drive showed she'd done a good job with the public records. Deeds, wills, and codicils allowed him to trace the line of owners of the Grover House from the time the family sold the place in the thirties to the time the Chenoweths bought it in the fifties. The house had changed hands several times over the course of twenty years, but of course there had been the Depression, then World War II, so Joss wasn't surprised.

He called it a night when Abbie did, not wanting to disturb the household, taking his laptop and clippings up to the garage apartment. Both exhausted and wide-awake, his body had not yet adjusted to his new time zone. A couple of more hours of digging, and he'd be ready for sleep.

Joss flipped through the printouts Whitney had brought, looking for the one article he'd hoped she'd found. There it was, in the middle of the pile, the piece Madeleine had written. The former reporter had been accurate in her assessment of her work: 'fluff' didn't begin to describe it. The only interesting line was the quote from Mrs. Chenoweth. *And the Yankees, they were so mad, they rode their horses right into the house, right up these beautiful stairs.*

The most interesting part of the stapled pages was the last one, which was not part of the original article. Instead, it was a letter to the editor, complaining about Madeleine Rutledge-Winthrop's article.

When will this newspaper stop glossing over the events of the War of Northern Aggression as if they never happened? It is well known that other families' homes were destroyed during the Sack of Hunts Landing, destroyed completely, unlike the Grovers who only had to endure a little manure in the upstairs hallway . . .

"Hah! The War of Northern Aggression. Who fired on Sumter?" His eyes scanned the letter again. "The Sack of Hunts Landing?" Joss flipped open his laptop and typed as quickly as he could into the Google search bar.

The obscure historical references didn't show up until the third screenful of search results, but then, there it was. A page buried on the state's Historical Society site.

Madeleine hadn't called the incident the Sack of Hunts Landing, probably because Mrs. Chenoweth hadn't, but some graduate students from Auburn University had, back in the twenties. Their paper confirmed some of Madeleine's facts, that the town was a strategic depot on the railroad, that the Union forces had occupied the town, and the destruction of stores on the Square during the Union withdrawal. All good stuff he could use. There were at least five to six minutes of screen time in this material. His imagination already in overdrive, snippets of potential monologue came so fast he could barely type fast enough to capture them all. *As Confederate troops advanced on the small river town of Hunts Landing, the occupying Union forces laid a path of destruction in their wake . . .*

Oh, yes, good stuff.

But in the forty-two pages of text, there was no mention of gold in Grover House.

The bibliography was six pages long, full of citations to primary sources, letters, diary entries. Yet, despite a sudden and unreasonable hope that the webpage would include links to the sources, there were none.

Joss shut down his computer, ready for bed. Outside, thunder rumbled. He wasn't used to this ever-changing weather. In Southern California, it was mostly sunny, not too hot, and dry. Too dry.

As he snuggled his head down into his pillow and sleep approached, the myriad of facts cluttering his mind dropped out, one by one, until only two facts remained.

The Union troops had destroyed multiple homes during the Sack of Hunts Landing.

The Union troops had spared the Grover House.

Why else, he yawned, *unless the troops were looking for something?*

Friday, 6:26 a.m., the Guest Room Over the Garage

The clamor of migrating geese yanked Joss out of a horrible dream. Harriet had hurled clay at him again, with a catapult; this time, she got his nose.

He bolted awake, disoriented, belatedly remembering he was in Hunts Landing when one goose shrieked. Was something wrong with Abbie? The kids? In the dark and unfamiliar room, he stubbed two toes before reaching the door. He pulled on a Northwestern sweatshirt while taking the steps down two at a time.

"Abbie?"

Six teenaged girls crowded around the remains of blueberry muffins, and they were all talking and texting at the same time. Martha smiled at him from the middle of the pack.

"Morning, Martha," he said. "I'm gonna start calling you 'Rabbit'."

"Why?"

"Because you multiplied overnight."

The other girls giggled, eyes opened wide as they took in the celebrity with messy hair. Martha, having had him in the house two whole nights already, played it cool. "We have jump training this morning. Mom's taking us to the gym."

"Mom also wants you to hurry up and finish," Abbie said from behind him. She handed him a cup of steaming coffee and leaned close to him. "Do you want me to tell you how bad you look?"

He shook his head. "Uh uh." The steam from the coffee probably wasn't helping his hair, either.

"Mr. Freeman?" one of Martha's friends asked. "Can I take a selfie with you?"

Abbie answered for him. "You don't get to take a selfie with a TV star before he's had his shower."

The other girls giggled and texted some more.

Abbie scooped her keys off the counter. "Girls, let's go." To Joss, she said, "Jump training is a half-hour away, so I've got to stay with them. I'll be back around lunch."

For the second morning in a row, the silence following the departure of Abbie and kids was deafening.

He poured his second cup of coffee and took Benny outside to the patio. Next Thursday afternoon, he would have to fly to LA to pitch the new series. *Six days times twenty-four hours a day times . . .*

Benny didn't seem to mind the spring chill. The mutt scampered around the backyard, right up to the split-rail fence but no further, almost humanly methodical in his inspection of the yard. *Ignore the names she calls you, Benny my friend, you're a great guard dog.*

What should be his next step? That the Sack of Hunts Landing was far more extensive than Madeleine had possibly known, or at least communicated, was evident by the Auburn paper. The paper supported the letter to the editor, which claimed Union forces destroyed many homes on that fateful day in 1862. The paper did not mention Grover House, Union horses on anyone's stairs, or some Hunts Landing treasure.

That didn't mean it didn't happen, though. The original house still stood. The Union troops didn't burn that one down.

In the 1830s, Mr. Grover had been the town's doctor. Joss could make a historian's leap—just a little one, not like the one that sank Abbie's career, and he still failed to see the justice in that situation—and assume that Grover was also the town's apothecary. The Union soldiers had raided his surgery before heading toward his house.

From his time munching on his tuna melt yesterday, he knew that there was only one pharmacy on the Square. Hunts Landing Drugs.

Yes, that would be his next step.

He whistled for Benny without knowing if the dog would listen to him or not, but whistling had sometimes worked for Lincoln, so it was worth a shot.

Benny shot across the yard at a full gallop. Joss opened the screen door with a smile. "You're a great dog, pal. No matter what Abbie says."

Friday, 8:07 a.m., Hunts Landing Drugs

The walk to the Square helped clear the fatigue fog from Joss's brain, more effectively than two cups of coffee and a hot shower had. Leaves and fallen petals littered the sidewalks, remnants of last night's spring storm. There were still plenty of blossoms on the trees, pretty ones. Joss had no earthly idea what any of these trees were called, but they were pretty.

The drugstore sat at the southwest corner of the Square, a two-story building that was narrow and long, stretching back from the front half a block. After Grover's initial construction in the 1830s, someone had added a classical facade with creamy limestone blocks and a pediment to the front of the building. *Looks more like a bank than a pharmacy,* Joss thought.

A bell above the door tinkled as he entered, like the one he'd heard at the hardware store, and he couldn't decide if having a bell was a city hall mandate or a quaint peculiarity of small-town shops.

Inside, the expected aisles of metal shelving crammed full with sundries from toothpaste to cough syrup were accompanied by a surprise: an old-fashioned soda fountain behind a counter running the length of the store. Swivel stools bolted to the floor completed the look. Joss hadn't seen one of these since he was a kid. Midway down the center aisle, an older man with close-cropped gray hair and a long, thin nose was stocking the shampoo shelves. Joss guessed him to be in his late fifties.

"Excuse me," Joss said. "I'm looking for . . ." *What was the word?* ". . . the proprietor."

"That would be me. What can I do for you, son?"

The *son* did it. Over sixty, for sure. Not likely to be a fan. Joss pulled a business card out of his wallet, the one without all of his links to social media, and handed it over. He explained his purpose without mentioning the Grover gold, while the man with the name tag *Rufus* stared at his card.

"So, you see, er, Mr. Rufus, I'm trying to fit as many of the nine-teenth-century buildings into the script as I can, and this building is a crown jewel on the Square." Joss flashed his TV smile, but Rufus wasn't looking at him yet. "I'd love to film this place."

Rufus peered at him over the thick-rimmed glasses perched on the end of that long nose. "I'm sorry to tell you, Mr. Freeman, but I don't think it would be *appropriate*, you understand, for my customers to see their local drugstore on the TV. It's a matter of trust, of course, my customers expect a certain amount of *discretion* from their druggist."

It had been a long time since Joss had scouted locations himself. Even so, he couldn't recall a historical property owner who didn't leap at the chance to show off his property on TV. "How about a tour, then? I find these old buildings fascinating."

With a squish of that long nose, Rufus shook his head. "Sorry, son, don't think it's a good idea. You have a good day now." With a dismissive nod, Rufus turned back to the boxes of shampoo.

Joss left the drugstore with his mouth slack, his mind scrambling to make sense of Rufus and his refusal.

A little bit of the fatigue fog crept back in. Joss rubbed his eyes with the butt of his palms. He looked around the Square, searching for what? Inspiration? His hands slid down his face, fingers coming to rest on his jaw.

Ah, a familiar name. The Sommelier. Would Loreen be open now? If memory served, Loreen lived above the shop. Would she answer the door? There was only one way to find out.

Not only was she up, but the front door was propped open. He knocked on the doorjamb anyway and stepped inside. The Napa Valley atmosphere Loreen had created in the shop appealed to his Californian senses. He inhaled deeply, the mixed aromas of wine, cheese, and spring flowers from the open door tantalized.

"Well, don't you look like something the cat drug in," Loreen said from a doorway to the back of her shop.

"My cat wouldn't bother dragging me anywhere right now," Joss admitted.

"Have a seat. I'll get coffee."

He slung his body onto a stool while she disappeared into the back, returning a few moments later with a coffeepot and mugs.

"So whatcha been up to this fine mornin'?"

The coffee was fresh, black, and good. "I've been running into brick walls, my friend."

Loreen leaned back against the far counter. "Tell all to your favorite wine peddler."

He did, or at least tried to.

Half-way through the story, Loreen interrupted with a disgusted, "Oh, dang that man." She banged her coffee cup with a splash and pulled out a rag to clean up the spill. "I swear, Rufus is more stubborn than the mules his daddy used to raise." Spill cleaned, she picked her cell phone up, swiped, and tapped a number. "And his daddy was one of the sweetest men in the world, don't know where this persnicketiness of Rufus came from . . . Rufus! Mornin'! . . . yes, yes, fine day."

Loreen picked up her rag and wiped at a furious pace, though the coffee spill was long gone. "Listen, a friend of mine popped in to visit you . . . yes, Joss Freeman . . . well, he makes documentaries . . . no . . . no . . . no, he's not weird, he's just jet-lagged . . . would you mind showing him . . . Rufus, you know darn well that there ain't nobody gonna walk into that store on a Monday morning that's gonna fuss about you givin' a stranger a tour . . . you know, I got a case of that Madeira your momma likes so much, why don't we bring you over a bottle? . . . Thank you, Rufus."

She hung up, shaking her head. "Rufus is a widower, lives with his momma. Maybe that's where the persnicketiness comes from." She untied her apron and reached for a paper shopping bag from under the counter. "Let's go."

Out on the sidewalk, Joss took two quick strides before Loreen stopped him. "Hold up. Let's take our time."

Time was something he didn't have a lot of. *Six days times . . .* Still, Loreen was hand-walking him into the building where Dr. Grover had built his practice in the 1830s. He could slow down.

He matched his pace to hers, which was slower than a casual stroll. "Why so slow?"

"Rufus probably needs time to, um, clean up a bit upstairs," Loreen said without further explanation.

This time, upon entering the drugstore, Rufus greeted them with a broad smile. "Of course, young fella, you should've told me you were a friend of Miz Loreen here. Come along, come along." He turned and motioned for them to follow. Rufus's thin arms pointed to the walls on either side of them. "I bought into this place in the '80s and never changed much. I think the last renovation was after the second World War, when the previous owner installed the soda fountain for the GIs on the Depot."

Rufus led them behind the pharmacy counter toward the back of the store where, tucked between stacks of boxes of inventory, was a narrow staircase up. "I think it's fair to say that not much remains of the original layout on the ground floor, but up here may be different.

Come along, come along." He trudged up the stairs, and Joss let Loreen go up before him.

Upstairs, a wide landing led to four rooms. "Go on, go on, look around," Rufus offered.

If this had been Dr. Grover's surgery, Joss mused, it made sense for there to be rooms for recuperating patients. Three of the rooms were cluttered with boxes and dusty storage bins. The fourth held a daybed, a table, a recliner, an older model television, and a modern air cleaner, the tall kind that rotated left to right and blew out clean, cool air.

Unfortunately for Rufus, the cleaner wasn't quite up to the job. Some smells, no matter how faint, could trigger the strongest memories.

Brow raised, Joss looked at Loreen. She raised a brow and pressed her lips tight against a ghost of a smile.

"Mr. Rufus, if we get the go-ahead with the project, do you think I could come back and film here? At no cost to you, of course, the production company will pay for prepping the site for filming."

"Well," Rufus said, scratching his chin. "I don't see why not. Might be fun."

"Hey, Rufus," Loreen said, before Joss could come up with a snarky response. "You remember Mrs. Chenoweth? At Grover House? She told this story, how after the Yankees trashed this building, they rode their horses up the staircase at Grover House."

With a chuckle, Rufus shook his head. "Sure, I heard that story. Grover's Gold. Is that what y'all are looking for? Shoot, you aren't going to find it here. Been in this place over thirty years, never found so much as an Indian head nickel. But if you want to know about Civil War gold, you go see Amos Underwood at his antique shop over on Jefferson. If anybody knows anything about the treasures of this town, it'll be Amos."

Outside, Joss couldn't hold his question in any longer. "Loreen, upstairs . . ."

"Yep."

"I didn't know pot was legal in Alabama."

"It isn't," Loreen laughed. "But I'm sure Rufus would argue he uses it for medicinal purposes only, and I'm not sure Judge Mackey would necessarily disagree, if you catch my meaning." She looked at his face and laughed again. "Oh, owning a wine store in a small town is like being a bartender. I hear a lot. Speaking of which, I've got to get back to the shop. Amos's place is over yonder," she pointed toward a side street that ended on the Square. "Tell Abbie I'll bring dinner tonight."

CHAPTER EIGHT

Friday, 9:01 a.m., Starbucks

Cyrus Porter greeted Abbie from a table in the corner of the coffee shop. Tall, thin, with close-cropped graying hair, he wore khakis and a green golf sweater. She tried to imagine him as a young man in 1969, a scrawny kid without a single white follicle.

He bought coffees and settled in a chair across from her. While he took a cautious sip, he eyed her in a way that disconcerted Abbie, as if she were the one being interviewed. "Are you going to record me?" He didn't ask for her press credentials, for which Abbie was glad, because Sylvia had never gotten around to giving her any.

She nodded. She launched the record app on her phone and placed it on the table between them.

"Ask away, Ms. Adams."

"Abbie, please." She'd worked on her questions for Cyrus last night, and for once felt prepared. This was going to be a cool, professional interview. "You lived in Hunts Landing in 1969?"

"Born and bred. Didn't leave until 1971, when my number came up."

"Vietnam?"

"A year in the jungle, yes. Then back here in 1972."

"Thank you for your service," Abbie said softly with a pang. Had anyone ever thanked Zach, before he was killed?

Cyrus acknowledged her with a slight bow of his head.

"And after 1972?"

"Six years of schooling, thanks to a scholarship and the G.I. Bill. Got my masters here. Went to work for Boeing in Seattle, oh, the summer of '77. When me and the missus retired, we came back here."

"Great. In 1969, July the twenty-fourth, you were here in Hunts Landing, the night there were parties all over town. I've discovered that you attended two of those parties."

"I wouldn't say I attended the parties. One party I worked. The other, I crashed."

She wished she were recording video, to capture every expression that crossed his face, the amusement over the memory of a crashed party. "Why don't we start with the Wexler party?"

"Abbie, since I talked to you, all I can think about is that night. Some parts are as clear as yesterday. Other parts are a blank. All these blotchy scenes, like watching one of those old movies at the Palladium when I was a kid. The film would jam the projector and melt. Old Marvin would splice the film and start up the projector, but he'd always lose a few seconds of the movie. Thinking about that night reminded me of those spliced films. A scene here clipped short, jump to another scene there, then another. Cary Grant leaning down to kiss Ingrid Bergman and the film burning before he reached her. I'm sorry. Forty-six years is a long time, but I'm trying to remember. For Rosalie."

"Did you know her well?"

"Rosalie? Not best-friend well, but well enough. Our families went to the same church, and Rosalie, Bernice, Cleta and I were the first Black students at the college."

"I didn't know y'all were the first."

"Private school? Nobody could afford it. Dr. Wexler funded scholarships for us. I'm talking Dr. Theodore Wexler, not Frank."

His phone buzzed with an incoming text, and he fingered a quick reply before turning back to her.

"So you went to school with Bernice Strong and Cleta Blakebill, too." With rapid swipes, Abbie found the picture of the three women on her phone and passed him the device.

His face broke into a toothy grin. "Hey, I took this, with Cleta's Instamatic. Send this to me, would you?" He handed her back the phone.

"Sure," Abbie said, working the phone. "Tell me about Rosalie."

"Rosalie." He rubbed his palms over his knees. "Good person. Dedicated to her studies. Today, I would call her *focused* more than *driven*. Gave plenty of her free time to the kids at the church, not that she had a lot of free time."

Abbie nodded and checked her list. "The party at the Wexlers. How'd you land the job?"

He checked his phone to make sure he received the picture. "Lord Almighty, those were pretty girls. Now, Dr. Wexler, he was a *good* man, got us part-time jobs during the school year, helped us find summer work. In those days, the Wexlers entertained a lot, and Dr. Wexler always offered the work to us. Good money, under the table, a way of getting us some extra cash. Rosalie and Cleta and me, a few kids from church, worked the big party."

Yeah, great guy, hired them to work as staff.

Cyrus sipped his coffee. "At first, I answered the door and helped the guests with their coats—go figure, right? End of July, hot as anything, and those crazy people showed up in mink coats. After everyone arrived, I kept an eye on the kids serving drinks and fetched people for Dr. Wexler."

"You fetched people?"

"He held some private meetings in his study. For a couple of hours. Department heads, NASA folks, the Mayor or some other politician wanting to connect themselves to the college. Whoever he wanted to meet, I fetched them."

"Odd way to put things."

"Well, maybe, but it's the way he put it. 'Cyrus, go on and fetch me so-and-so.' Now, Abbie, if you think I'm going to bad-talk Dr. Wexler, you're much mistaken. Theodore Wexler did more for the Black students at this school than any dean since. The man gave me the opportunity to earn my education."

That she didn't think much of either of the Wexler men, she kept to herself. "Back to the party. What do you remember?"

Cyrus blew on the foam of his cappuccino. "Guess I got to the house right around lunchtime. Helped set up the tables and chairs, moved all of Miss Nevelyn's heirloom china safe upstairs. The guests started arriving around four-thirty. Didn't see Rosalie before then because she helped her mother in the kitchen. And I didn't run into her much during the night, either. Dr. Wexler paid me to stay near his study, so I did."

"And he had a lot of meetings," Abbie said. The unexpected insight into the inner workings of Wexler House during a party captivated her.

"It was a big night for the school. Now, Dr. Wexler, he loved this expensive Kentucky bourbon he kept locked up in the cellar. Sent me down a couple of times for a fresh bottle. Lots of toasts in the study that night. One or two arguments, but nothing unusual. One of the deans, though, really got into it with Dr. Wexler."

"Which dean was that?"

"Dr. Quentin McCain of the School of Engineering. I studied with him for one semester. A real self-righteous son-of-a . . ." He caught himself. "Sorry, Ms. Abbie. McCain came down hard on us, the Black students. Didn't share Wexler's embrace of integration."

Abbie's pulse quickened. *McCain, from the grant scandal.* "So, Dr. McCain and Dr. Wexler, they argued?"

"You really think this pertains to Rosalie?"

"I don't know," Abbie admitted. "But since working at Wexler House is among the last things Rosalie did before she died, anything out of the ordinary at that party interests me."

"She also worked part time in the engineering school office."

"She worked for Dr. McCain?"

"A few hours a week. Old Dr. Wexler got her the job."

Really? Maybe there was a connection with the grant scandal after all. "What did she do?"

Cyrus scratched the back of his neck. "Can't help you there. Didn't have much cause to be in that building, at least not in '69. I didn't elect engineering until I got back from Vietnam. You know, you thanked me before, and I don't usually get many thanks, except on Veteran's Day and the Fourth of July. Did you serve?"

"No. My husband."

"Afghanistan?"

"Iraq." The story got the teensiest bit easier to tell each time. "Killed by a roadside bomb in Anbar Province."

Leaning forward, he grasped one of her hands. "Mrs. Adams, let me thank you for *your* service and sacrifice."

Her service and sacrifice.

This kind stranger was the first person to ever express appreciation, and the feeling humbled her.

"Thank you. Actually, Adams is my maiden name. Zach was so certain I would become a famous historian like my parents; he wanted me to keep their name and the family academic tradition alive. My kids are Youngbloods, his name."

"Historians? Your parents?"

"Yes. Right here in Hunts Landing."

"Your mother? Dr. Elsa Adams?"

"Yes," she smiled.

"Well, small world. I took History I with your mother! The only teacher I ever had who made history fun. How is she?"

The smile faded. "Momma and Daddy . . . they died in a car wreck on Andrew Jackson Parkway, fifteen years ago."

Cyrus shook his head and squeezed her hand. "I'm so sorry for your loss, Abbie. I liked your mother very much." After another squeeze, he leaned back, swirled his coffee for a moment. "I want you to understand something about Theodore Wexler. Close to Christmas in '70, he had himself a slight heart attack. Not as big as the one that wound up killing him, but serious enough to keep him in the hospital over the holidays. His secretary didn't want to trouble him, so she kept a whole bunch of scholarship paperwork on his desk, waiting for his signature. My paperwork was in that pile. The papers weren't signed in time. Come January, my number came up, and I headed to Ft. Bragg a couple of weeks after New Year's, 1971. Understand, Dr. Wexler was *furious* about the mix-up. He wrote me over in Vietnam, told me he tried everything he could to keep me stateside."

"But what could he do? You'd been drafted."

"The man's reach was longer than you'd think. But, by the time he was well enough to do anything about anything, I was in Laos."

"You must have been angry," Abbie said.

"Mostly, what I was, was grateful. Grateful to be alive and in one piece. When I got back in '72, he sent his driver to pick me up from my Momma's house. Took me straight to Dr. Wexler's office. When I entered, the old man stood up. He needed a cane to do that much, but he shook my hand and he poured me a glass of Very Old Fitzgerald. These days, a bottle of that stuff costs three hundred dollars. After the drink, he thanked me for my service."

"As he should have," Abbie said.

"Well, Americans didn't exactly welcome back vets with open arms. Now, I loved that man for what he did for me, but it was, shall we say, *disconcerting* to be in his office that day. I just wanted to shed the uniform and get on with my life." He pressed his lips together into a tight line.

Don't push it, Abbie.

Vietnam has nothing to do with Rosalie.

"And you went back to school?"

Cyrus nodded. "He told me that day, 'Time to get back to school, Cyrus. Finish that degree.' Dr. Wexler made sure my scholarship money waited for me, and he encouraged me to pursue engineering, mostly because my math and science grades impressed him. And that's what I wound up doing. Got my Master's in Aerospace Engineering in 1976. All thanks to Dr. Theodore Wexler." In a silent salute, Cyrus raised his cup to the heavens.

Abbie gave him a moment. "So, what happened between Wexler and McCain?"

Cyrus nodded. "About nine o'clock, Dr. Wexler asked me to go fetch McCain. A bit later, when the fireworks over the river started, McCain bursts out of the study, cussing Dr. Wexler and demanding his coat. So, I go to tell Mrs. McCain her husband wanted to leave, and when we got back to the foyer, the S.O.B. was already gone. Jerk left his wife at the party."

"Anything else happen, out of the ordinary?" Abbie asked.

"Not that I can recall."

"How about the other Wexlers? Frank and Miss Nevelyn?"

"I can't tell you much about Miss Nevelyn, except she kept rushing back and forth to the kitchen, not that Miss Etta needed checking up on. Miss Nevelyn kept a little bottle of brandy in the pantry, you know what I mean?" Cyrus winked.

"So, with her going back and forth to the kitchen, Miss Nevelyn was near Rosalie all night?"

"As far as I can remember."

"And Frank?"

"Frank, he and his friends spent their evening on the lower patio. Rosalie might have brought them drinks. But they left during the fireworks, I watched them."

Abbie scribbled in her notebook. *Where did Frank go? And who did he go with?* "And Rosalie was still at Wexler House?"

"Yes. The party broke up around ten-thirty. After the last of the guests left, Miss Etta fed us leftovers. There was a large bonfire burning on the south end of the Quad, down by the river. Lots of laughing and music. Creedence Clearwater Revival. Sounded like a great party from where we sat, but it was a party for whites." His shoulders sagged with the memory, the confident ex-engineer replaced by the poor Black kid who knew his place in 1969.

"And Rosalie was still at the house?"

"Until almost eleven," Cyrus said. "That's when Miss Etta told us, the help, that we could go home. But before I left, I checked in on Dr. Wexler—he asked me to fetch him another bottle of the Very Old Fitzgerald from the cellar, a special one he kept hidden away. Something was on his mind, for sure, because he was alone with a fifty-year-old bourbon and a bunch of files from his office on his desk. So, I got him the bottle, said goodnight, and left with the girls."

"You and Rosalie and Cleta?"

"Umm hmm. We stopped a couple of blocks away. The girls should've walked home together. I didn't pay attention, and I should've, but I only waved 'cause I was so tired and I still had a term paper to finish for my summer class. That was the last time I saw Rosalie."

"They didn't walk home together, though," Abbie said. "Rosalie headed west, toward the woods. Alone."

"I found out later. What kind of shit of a man am I, not to walk those girls home? Excuse my language, Abbie." Cyrus pulled a white handkerchief from his pocket and wiped his forehead. "Amazing, how the memories can get to you. Clear as yesterday." He downed the last of his coffee and stood. "We've been sitting here a while. I'm going to get us some refills." He hadn't asked Abbie if she wanted another.

Cyrus returned with two paper cups of coffee and napkins.

"About the second party," Abbie asked. "The one down by the river."

"Now, I lived in the Mill District, behind the new River Walk. The closer I got to home, the louder the music from the Quad, Creedence and The Animals and The Byrds. Fantastic music, not as good as Motown, though. Anyhow, the party got pretty loud. But I hurried on home."

Cyrus didn't drink his coffee, just held the cup with both hands, as if he were gleaning some warmth for his fingers. "Two blocks behind Barton's Chapel, I turned the corner and found trouble. Bunch of the brothers there, mad because of the heat and nobody owned an air conditioner, and these white kids partying near midnight on a Thursday. But the brothers drank a bunch too, and when you mix too much booze and too much heat with a bunch of white boys and a bunch of Black men, trouble follows."

She couldn't help herself, despite her earlier misgivings about racial questions. "Didn't you say the campus was pretty integrated at the time?"

"Yes, but we're talking about the Mill District, not the college. On that side of the property, they'd built a twelve-foot-high fence, between the college and town. No other fences like that on campus. Dr. Wexler controlled things on campus, but off campus, we lived in a very segregated world."

Abbie shook her head. "Sounds like a powder-keg."

"Ready to blow," Cyrus nodded. "With this loud white boys' party, tempers flared. One of the brothers, Ollis Hutch, he egged the brothers on, telling everybody we needed to go to the Quad and stop the party. I waved those guys off. All I wanted was my bed. But then, up comes my buddy Leon—"

"Leon Moore? Isaac Leon Moore?" This was the man from Jethro's notes, the one with an asterisk like Cyrus.

"We just called him Leon. He runs up to me, says, 'C'mon, man! We going to the college boys' party!' High on something and raring for a fight. I tried to convince him to come on home with me—I had two bottles of Budweiser in my icebox—because nothing but *trouble* waited for us on the Quad. But Leon, he's street smart, not book smart, and he was high and hot and pissed off. Nobody in the Mill District cared about Neil and Buzz. Ollis shouted at the brothers, urging them on, and Leon followed Ollis."

He rocked slightly.

Abbie felt the urge to touch his arm, to comfort, but didn't want to interrupt his memory.

"Maybe if Leon hadn't pestered me, I would've gone on home. Instead, idiot me, I let him drag me along. It's not easy for me to admit I fell to peer pressure, but I did. They cut a hole with wire cutters through the chain link. They ran to the chapel. Nobody thought anything through, though, and those white boys outnumbered us. The way Ollis stopped cold in his tracks, I believe he might have left, but then those damned fools played 'Fortunate Son' by Creedence. You know it?"

Abbie chuckled. "Momma was kind of a hippie."

"Now Ollis, his brother's number had just come up, and to Ollis, every one of those white boys was a 'senator's son.' He screamed out, 'Let's get 'em!' Off they went. Leon, too. And me, the fool, followed.

"We came out onto the Quad. The brothers hollered, then the white boys hollered, and then we all jumped into one big pile of bodies and punches. Some guy clocked me twice in the gut and once in the face before I caught sight of Leon, wrestling down this big old boy, James something, linebacker for the football team and as dumb as a stump. James elbowed my kidney when I went to pull him off Leon, but somehow, I tripped him up and kicked him a couple of times near his . . . um . . . his private parts, enough so he would let go of him, because Leon's lip bled like a stuck pig."

This guy can tell a story. Abbie was carried along, willing him not to stop. "Was he badly hurt?"

"Blood kept pouring out of his mouth. We kinda crawled away. I pulled Leon up off the ground and got his right arm around my shoulder." Cyrus paused, and when he spoke, his cadence changed— now he chose his words with care. "I looked up and coming at me is Frank Wexler."

"Frank Wexler, there, at the fight?" *So Frank went down to the party at the river.*

"Yes, with one of his buddies, David Breckenridge. One of McCain's students. I took the guy's jacket at the Wexler party."

"Frank was definitely down at the river?"

"Getting his butt whooped like the rest of us," Cyrus said. "He didn't hold up his own very well, though, if you know what I mean. Blood all over his shirt, a shiner that was going to be purple in the morning. David held Frank Wexler like I held Leon, as if I looked into a mirror, except the mirror turned the skins from white to black."

"Frank was injured?"

"Yeah, he was pretty beat up. Now, I knew I should get Frank and take him on home, but I couldn't leave Leon bleeding in the dirt. In the meantime, those other boys are still fighting all around us. Breckenridge says to me, 'I'll get him home. You take care of yours.' He'd recognized me, too. Next, he and Frank break away from the crowd and head toward Wexler House."

His chest heaved as he caught his breath, and Abbie needed to gulp air herself. Not a single diary entry, letter, eyewitness account she had ever read during all her scholastic research equaled her visceral response to listening to this story. His eyes were wide, and his chin trembled, for this painful memory wounded him anew. Her heart ached for him.

He exhaled a last, deep breath before continuing. "I dragged him toward the chapel, away from the fight, but the cops showed up, lots of police cars with lights flashing in the parking lot behind the chapel. They cuffed me and Leon, threw us in the back of some redneck's pickup. Hunts Landing didn't keep a patrol wagon at the time. So, at two o'clock in the morning, I'm in the lockup downtown with Leon and Ollis and all the other brothers. Campus cop comes and springs me, says Dr. Wexler vouched for me. Takes me straight home. Not a thing I could do for Leon at that hour. So, I popped the cap off one of those two Budweisers, drank the bottle down in one swallow, and went to bed."

He waggled his empty coffee cup with a wry smile and winked. "Kinda wish this was the other one of those Budweisers. Damn! Amazing how much you remember once you start thinking about it." He stopped talking.

"They say Rosalie died around midnight . . ." Abbie prompted.

"Right," Cyrus said. "Midnight, I was on the Quad, brawling with a bunch of drunk boys and every single one of us should've known better, and while I punched on that boy James, somebody else crushed Rosalie's head, only a couple of hundred yards away. Makes me sick to my stomach." Cyrus closed his eyes, rubbed his brow, and grimaced, the 1969 wound bleeding fresh.

Abbie gave him a moment. "Are you sure that Frank Wexler was in that brawl?"

Cyrus pulled his hand away from his face. "Don't see how he could've been beat up like that if he wasn't. Wait, you don't think . . . ?"

"Let's say I've spoken to him. He won't comment on that night."

Cyrus thought for a moment. "No. Rosalie was a little slip of a thing. No way she could have put that kind of hurt on Frank, not the hurt I saw. Let me tell you something else. Next morning, one of Miss Etta's little friends from church comes knocking on my door. Break of dawn. Frank Wexler got himself a concussion, a bad one, the kind where you vomit all over your mother's antique rugs. The doctor ordered him to bed. Nevelyn Wexler asked me to stay with him, so I stayed in the room, helped the boy to the restroom when he needed to go, sat with him while he slept and worked on my paper the rest of the time. A little while later, the police came to tell Miss Etta somebody had found Rosalie."

Abbie's heart leaped into her throat as she imagined getting a knock on the door, some acne-pocked cop who stank of stale cigars coming to tell her George or Martha were dead. "How horrible."

"A person can die, Abbie, can go and die without the body knowing it's dead. That's what happened to Miss Etta. That poor woman just dropped to the floor when the cop said they found Rosalie. Dr. Wexler and Miss Nevelyn held her up, but I think, for a second, her heart just stopped. When it started pumping again, it wasn't the same heart. Her heart beat only for the sole purpose of pumping blood, because it couldn't beat for Rosalie anymore. The big old heart who loved everybody died that day. Good God, whoever killed Rosalie, he really killed two people."

Cyrus stopped talking. His gaze lay some place over her left shoulder, and not a place in the current day. Lost in his memories, he ignored the single tear rolling down his cheek. "She brought me a cake when I came back from 'Nam. Coconut cake, a big fluffy white one. Miss Etta toasted the coconut to a golden brown, crunchy and sweet. My Lucretia tried one time to make me coconut cake like Miss Etta's. Not even close." The white handkerchief came out again, wiped the single tear away. "What else can I tell you, Abbie?"

She swallowed her own emotions, caught up in his story, and ran a shaky finger down her notes. "Was there anyone else at the party with a connection to Rosalie?"

"No, I don't think so. We were the help."

Abbie nodded, scribbled some notes. "Do you remember anything else?"

"Just one thing. I'm not sure if this is important. My memory," he touched his forehead, "it's like the film strip broke again. Little snippets. Well, that night . . . nobody was where they were supposed to be. On the Quad, I mean. Crazy thing, you know, I'm not sure if this is a real memory, but I remember a white lady running around the Quad in her underwear."

Friday, 9:22 a.m., Hunts Landing Antiques

The shop occupied half a block on a side street off the Square. Rusty wrought-iron furniture and a 1930s mahogany dresser flanked the glass doors. Inside, labyrinthine aisles snaked through the store, displays of people's castoffs piled high on either side. Every inch of wallspace was covered with the obligatory dusty still-lifes, portraits and prints. Joss didn't recognize any at a quick glance, which was to be expected in a small-town shop.

There was never a straight path from the front door to the register in an antique store, Joss knew from the innumerable shopping trips his mother had dragged him on. Antique dealers wanted you to stroll past their treasures, in hopes you'd find something intriguing along the way.

Despite his historical background, Joss preferred the minimalist décor of his condo to rooms filled to the brim with bric-à-brac.

Toward the center of the store, in a square made of glass display cases, he found Amos Underwood talking to a customer. Joss took the opportunity to examine the closest display. There were some cloisonné pieces his mother would have liked back in the day, but since her move to Florida, she'd downsized a lot.

Amos finished with the other customer and came round to face Joss. "Can I interest you in something for the missus?"

"Not exactly." Joss handed him a business card. "I'm Joss—"

"Ah, I know who you are," Amos said. "Rufus called. Said Loreen'd have my hide if I didn't talk to you. Don't know why he was fretting, though. Always happy to talk shop." Amos glanced around the store. A few other customers were browsing. He lowered his voice. "Tell you what, why don't you head on back to my office while I get somebody to watch the register?"

Amos's office was exactly as Joss expected, messy and crammed full of papers and old furniture. A brass statue of Venus de Milo partially obscured a fat computer monitor on an antique roll-top desk. The room smelled like the store outside, of age and dust and old memories.

There was Amos's swivel office chair, also a relic, with cracked leather. A stack of file folders eight inches high occupied the only other seat in the room. Joss picked up the folders and, unable to find a spot to put them, sat and placed them at his feet.

Amos entered a moment later and shut the door behind him. He dropped his body into the swivel chair, which creaked in response. "Best we discuss Civil War treasures out of earshot, no need for all of Hunts Landing to know what you're doing here. Oh, don't you worry none, Rufus won't breathe a word, he's not the kind. 'Sides, he's too afraid of Loreen."

"And you aren't afraid of Loreen?"

"I have a healthy respect for her ability to land some good wine," Amos admitted. "But if word gets out, well, I have a cousin, down in Decatur, old place. Some rumor on some website started, said there was treasure in Decatur, and his house was the likeliest spot. Treasure hunters came during the night, dug up his yard, broke a basement window and dug in the basement. Now, if treasure hunters were to come to Hunts Landing, don't get me wrong, it'd probably be great for business, but I'd hate to think what may happen to my neighbor's homes, you understand? So, keep it on the quiet side."

Joss nodded. "I've got no problems with that."

"Good. Now, Joss. You're looking for Civil War treasure, in Hunts Landing. I don't think you're gonna find anything. Plenty searched, back in the day, during Reconstruction when there was nothing to eat, and people burned their Confederate money to stay warm."

"During the Sack of Hunts Landing, the Union troops thought there was gold hidden here," Joss said.

"Oh, you heard that story, huh? It's not something they teach in school in this town, not an episode of our history that we're particularly proud of." Amos scratched his head, thoughtful. "It's the kinda story you don't hear much about unless an old-timer is telling it, and in a place like mine, the old-timers talk."

His own people had spread westward with each generation, New York, Pittsburgh, Omaha, never in one place longer than a couple of decades. The idea of having roots, and memories, that extended over a century was an unknown to Joss, though for years he'd studied people and places with longer memories than Hunts Landing. "Well, no one seems to dispute that Dr. Grover collected the town's gold." Joss explained his theory of how the Union soldiers had spared the Grover House in the belief that gold was hidden inside. "Why else would the troops target that house?"

"That's the part that doesn't make much sense to me," Amos said. "I don't think Grover would ever have hidden valuables in the house itself. Too easy to find. Same thing for the yard. How do you hide dirt that's recently been turned over? In my mind, if it were me, it would have been the basement."

Joss shook his head. "I've been down there. There's nothing except a bunch of boilers and a 1950s bomb shelter."

"Shoot, too many owners over the years, I suppose, and none with any respect for the house. My gran's house was over there on that side of town, not too far from Grover House. Now, her basement was a fun place for a ten-year-old. Ahh, maybe my memories of Gran's place are getting in the way. Shame, 'cause if I had some treasure, that's where I would have stuck it."

Joss leaned his elbows on his knees. "Still, a box of gold coins shouldn't have been that hard to hide in a basement."

"What makes you think the treasure was in coin?"

Joss thought for a moment, trying to remember who he'd learned that notable fact from. "I guess I assumed—"

"That's probably where I can help you, friend. Antebellum families didn't just measure their wealth in gold coin. There was silver coin, and then, well, silverware itself. Heavy stuff, the real thing, no plate. Had a few pieces from an estate down in Montgomery last year, they sold before I could get the price tags on them. What I'm saying is, don't just look for coin."

CHAPTER NINE

Friday, 10:45 a.m., Sally's Catfish and Barbecue

A bbie shoved the gear shift into *park* and drummed her fingers on the steering wheel. Sally's was the kind of place where you wanted to linger and enjoy your food at one of the picnic tables underneath a tin roof, where old-fashioned fans mounted in the corners provided a cool breeze in the summer, and where the tea was always sweet, cold, and served with extra lemon. Which was why Abbie could never understand why the line at the drive-thru was always so long. But, then again, she was one of the customers waiting in the drive-thru.

As was the jerk in the muddied-up SUV behind, so close on her taillights she could see the reflection off his grill in her rear-view mirror. Spring turkey season was right around the corner, and brought out the worst of the hunters, Abbie felt. This one had probably skipped work to set up his hunting hide, and now was hungry.

After she'd ordered two grilled catfish platters with salads, she called Will Irestone's cell and immediately got his voicemail greeting.

Rats. She really wanted to pick his brain about Cyrus Porter. The line moved one car forward. She called the hospital and asked to be connected to his room. The phone rang six or seven times before she hung up.

Two more cars made it past the cashier's window. Abbie called Sylvia.

"Hey, Abbie." Sylvia's voice, usually sultry, sputtered with breaths, as if she'd rushed to answer the phone. "Whatcha need?"

"Do you have any news on Will?" Abbie asked. "I can't seem to reach him."

"That's his sister Delores playing traffic guard. She's got his cell and unplugged the room phone. She let me talk to him on her cell phone for one minute this morning, not fifty-nine seconds, not sixty-one seconds. Sixty seconds exactly. And I'm his boss. The good news is that he's awake and speaking, but he's kind of doped up."

Will didn't seem to be the kind of man that enjoyed being fussed over, not from what Abbie knew of him. "Do you think she'd let me speak to him at all?"

"You can try." Sylvia gave her a phone number, which Abbie jotted down on the back of a pharmacy receipt. "Do you have anything to report?"

"I've spoken to the investigating officer and a witness who was with Rosalie for much of the night." Abbie reached cashier's window. She recounted the interviews while paying for her lunch.

"So, Frank Wexler doesn't want to talk. Not surprised. I wouldn't trust anything he said, anyway. Do you have alibis for the Wexlers yet?"

"Cyrus Porter puts Frank Wexler at the fight by the river. And he said when he left Wexler House, he'd just fetched a fresh bottle of bourbon for Old Dr. Wexler." Abbie pulled up to the serving window, and reached out to grab her sack of food.

"And that other fella with Porter?"

"I'm still trying to track him down," Abbie said.

"You get him to confirm Cyrus's story," Sylvia said. "I'd go after the Tennents gang next. And that article from Caleb Jackson's folder. There's gotta be some reason why he saved it."

Friday, 5:24 p.m., the War Room

In the lull between the end of the work week and the official start of the weekend, Joss pecked at his keyboard, headset firmly affixed to his ears, and the kids upstairs played their music at a more subdued level than usual. Abbie took the opportunity to write up her notes on Cyrus Porter.

The difference between reading hundred-year-old written accounts and talking to a living witness was still taking her breath away. While Jethro Turner had also been a witness, his testimony was more detached, a cop who was more a bystander than a participant. Cyrus Porter was in the house with Rosalie DuFrayne, had been one of the last people to see her alive. His self-disgust about not walking the girls home was palpable, as was the pain in his memory of seeing Miss Etta collapse. She replayed his words. *Good God, whoever killed Rosalie, he really killed two people.* His words brought a lump to her throat. And she hadn't even known these people.

Cyrus's alibi for Frank Wexler clenched her stomach. Oh, there was that part of her that had wanted to find Frank Wexler guilty of something related to the DuFrayne case, an ugly part that disdained objectivity and sought revenge, a part which shamed her. Abbie allowed herself a couple of minutes to mentally lock that part of her in a box and throw away the key.

And Cyrus had known Bernice Strong and Cleta Blakebill . . . *Dammit, Abbie, why didn't you ask him for contact info?* She'd been so wrapped up in his story, and making sure she'd crossed off certain questions on her list, she'd completely neglected to make the obvious follow-up inquiry. *Dammit.* It was only five-thirty. Too early for dinner. She swiped to place the call.

After a few rings, Cyrus's voicemail picked up, and she was forced to leave a message.

Joss was now making a lot of noise in the kitchen. She closed her laptop and gathered up the articles Whitney had prepared for her.

In the kitchen, Joss had pulled a clay baker from the oven.

"That smells *heavenly*," Abbie sighed.

Joss placed a tray of baguette slices into the oven. "Roasted garlic spreads like softened butter."

"Remember, Loreen's bringing supper."

"This is an appetizer."

"I love the way you de-frag your brain." At the kitchen counter, Abbie leafed through the printouts of the newspaper from that fateful week in July 1969.

Joss busied himself with a bottle opener. "Don't you think you can quit long enough to eat?"

"*Au contraire.* Too much to do. Here's the police register from July 24, 1969. Somebody stole a car from the parking lot by the South Gate to the Depot. That was the night Rosalie DuFrayne was murdered. Suppose her killer used the woods as cover, he would have come out into the open right outside that very gate. Maybe he got himself a getaway car."

"Why head toward the campus at all? Why not escape to the west?" He poured a glass and handed it to her.

"Maybe. But the ground to the west is swampy."

"You're speculating a lot."

She sipped her wine. "I prefer to call it 'filling in the blanks.'"

He pulled the toasted baguette slices from the oven and tried to remove them to a cooling rack, burning his fingers. "Ow!"

"Tray's hot," she cautioned.

A knock at the sunporch door interrupted her thoughts.

"Hey, Momma Abbie." Olivia, one of Martha's friends, let herself into the house, carrying a backpack and a sleeping bag.

"Hey, girl. Come in and meet my friend Mr. Freeman."

Olivia shook his hand with a smile, revealing a full rack of braces. "So, you're the TV star?"

He tilted his head and flashed the grin that kept him on the home page of the network's website. "Sure am. Want an autograph?"

"Not really. But nice to meet you." The teenager took the stairs two at a time.

His grin slid off his face, and she stifled a laugh. "Don't get upset. Unless you're a Japanese cartoon character with special ninja powers, these girls aren't going to be interested in you."

"Ninja?" he asked, mouth slack.

"*Anime*. Japanese cartoons. All the craze with middle school girls."

"Too bad for middle school boys."

"Hello!" Loreen called from the screen door.

"This place is like Grand Central Station," he said, holding the door for Loreen. "I smell Chinese."

"General Tso's chicken, pad thai with tofu, and Abbie's favorite coconut soup, from that new place on the Square, Pan Asian Delights."

"Whadja bring me?" He kissed Loreen's cheek as he took some bags out of her hands.

"Mongolian beef. Let's eat outside."

Abbie had a mouth full of pad thai when Olivia and Martha came downstairs with backpacks and sleeping bags and headed for the backdoor. "Wait, girls!"

"Can't, Mom, Isabella's dad's here."

"What?"

"He's giving us a ride," Martha said. The girls rushed through the door.

"Wait!" She washed the food down with a gulp of Beaujolais, spilling some on her jeans. *Of course.*

The Range Rover idled at the foot of her driveway. Nick pushed his sunglasses up with a grin. "Come to wish me luck?"

"You're gonna need plenty with those girls."

"Easy as pie." He winked. "We're talking pizza, Dr. Pepper, and something called *anime.*"

"I fear for you, Grasshopper." She leaned into the car and waved to the girls. "Y'all have fun tonight." She turned to Nick. "You, too."

"I've been told that I'm barred from the family room during the *anime* marathon."

He really had no idea what he was getting himself into, Abbie thought. "Get used to the notion. They're *fourteen.*"

Loreen pounced when Abbie returned to the sunporch. "Was that tall-dark-and-handsome-and-please-oh-please-arrest-me?"

"Sure was." She filled her glass and downed half in a single gulp. She managed ever more complete sentences each time she saw Nick Preston, but her heart still raced. Each time.

"The single parent gods are smiling down on you, I think. Joss, tell her."

Joss scooped some more General Tso's chicken on to his plate. "Tell her what?"

"How she needs to date, starting with that scrumptious hunk of a cop."

"Well," he said, "I didn't follow you to the garden gate to ogle at said hunk of a cop, and so I can't really confirm how scrumptious he is."

Abbie saluted Joss. "Let's forget Nick Preston for tonight." She definitely didn't need Loreen's romantic speculations. The cop did something to Abbie's equilibrium that she didn't need right now. "Heard you helped Joss get into Rufus's this morning."

"He's such a flippin' grouch, it's a wonder I still do business with him, but I'm too lazy to drive someplace else when I can walk to Rufus's."

"Did you tell Joss about Rufus's little habit?" Abbie's eyes twinkled.

"Oh," Joss said, "I sussed that out by myself. But he did send me on to Amos Underwood."

"Ha!" Abbie laughed. "Amos has had a crush on Loreen since, what, fifth grade?"

"It was sixth, I believe," Loreen shrugged.

Joss's recollection of his morning's adventures had both Abbie and Loreen laughing out loud in his face. This was the kind of Friday night she remembered from undergrad, except both the food and the wine were better now.

"I don't know if I'll ever figure out this town," Joss said. "Apparently, you can smell the weather, the local pharmacist smokes pot, and the antiques guy has bootleg records he's labeled as 'vintage.'"

"And that's only one side of the Square," Abbie said, wiping tears away with her napkin. "I'm sorry, Joss, you're just not used to small towns. Did Amos give you any leads?"

"He did. Amos advised me to look for silver, not gold. Search for *Civil War treasure* and all you get are treasure hunters and conspiracy theorists. But search for how Southerners hid their valuables, and you hit the jackpot. Most of the wealthier families converted their gold coin for Confederate currency early in the war, giving the South the cash it needed. But silver, in particular family silver, well that was generally held back, and the smarter families found very creative ways to hide it. I could do an entire episode on that subject alone. More wine?" Joss poured the last of the bottle into each woman's glass, then headed to the kitchen for a fresh one.

Abbie kept one eye on Joss. "You still think he's cuter than a baby bunny?" she asked in a low voice.

"Funnier, perhaps. Definitely nerdier." Loreen gathered empty dishes. "C'mon, it's getting chilly."

Inside the house, they settled in the living room. "So, how's your murder going, Abs?" Joss asked.

Abbie's retelling of Cyrus Porter's story was definitely more somber than Joss's tale had been.

"That could be your article right there," Loreen said.

"No," Abbie denied. "There's more to the Rosalie story than Cyrus Porter, I can feel it in my bones."

"Then what's your next step?" Joss stretched his long legs out before him.

That question had been on her mind all evening. "Until I can track down Rosalie's other friends, I've got to go back to Caleb Jackson's folder."

"Wait," Loreen sat up straight. "*Caleb* Jackson? Unless I'm mistaken, and there couldn't have been two Caleb Jackson's in Hunts Landing, that might be my mother's second cousin. Mother was a Jackson."

"You knew him?" Abbie didn't remember a cousin Caleb at Loreen's house.

"Only from family reunions," Loreen replied. "If he's the fella I'm thinking of, he drank too many beers on his bass boat one night, oh, twenty-something years ago, and fell overboard upstream of Meyer's Dam. I can ask Mother."

Abbie opened her mouth to ask another question about Caleb Jackson.

Chirp chirp chirp.

She held up a hand in apology, swiped the phone to answer the call. "This is Abbie."

"Eleven teenage girls are watching Japanese cartoons in my living room, and they only let me in if I bring them pizza or Doritos," the deep voice said.

She hustled out the sunporch door. "How did you get my number?"

"Bribed your daughter with a Dr. Pepper."

"You shouldn't be teaching them criminal tactics."

"Last resort. You didn't call me. I left my card for you at Loreen's."

She glanced at Loreen's back through the sunporch window. "I've been busy."

"So, I guessed," Nick said. "Otherwise, you would've called me by now. Or at least, texted."

It had been over twenty years since the last time she called a man. "I would only do that to ask you procedural questions."

"Like what?"

Think, Abbie, think! "Like, how long does the coroner keep a body after determining the cause of death?"

"Wow. I think that's a first date question."

"And I need to know what the answer would have been in 1969."

"Since you gave me homework, I'll tell you over dinner. Tomorrow night."

His smoky voice, almost a caress, caused her to blush. "I'm busy tomorrow."

"No, you aren't."

"Huh?"

"You'd be surprised how much information I can pry out of a kid with an extra slice of pepperoni pizza."

"Not fair."

"Fair no, resourceful yes. Seven o'clock?"

Rosalie . . . the byline . . . Frank Wexler. I've spent three days already, I'm running out of time. "I'd love to, but I really can't . . ."

Loreen snatched the phone out of her hand and danced out of reach. "Nick? Loreen. She'll be ready."

Loreen said goodbye and tossed Abbie her phone back. Next to her, Joss stood as her co-conspirator.

"You eavesdropped?" Abbie accused.

"I was making sure you didn't blow a potential date by being stupid." Loreen tapped on Joss's shoulder. "He agrees."

"He can speak for himself." Abbie turned an angry eye on him.

Joss held up both hands in surrender. "You were quick to tell me I looked like shit this morning, so let me return the favor. Get away from Rosalie, get away from your computer. Before you start looking as bad as I did."

A couple hours and a couple of bottles of wine later, both were forgiven.

Loreen called it a night. "Big day tomorrow. 'Nite," Loreen kissed Abbie. "'Nite, sugar." She kissed Joss's cheek and left through the sunporch door.

He leaned back and tipped his head. "She called me *sugar.*"

"Only because she thinks you're spoken for. Otherwise, she'd play hard to get." Abbie picked up wine glasses. "I'm gonna check on the boys."

George and his buddy Pudge lay sprawled on the floor, fingers flying across their laptops. On the TV screen, Abbie recognized a Minecraft character, armed with a shield and a glowing sword, entering a familiar forest.

"Aren't those the woods where I always die?" Abbie asked.

"If you go into Mystic Forest without a Zen charm, like this loser over here, well, duh, you're gonna die." George nudged his friend.

"Who's a loser?" Pudge shot back. "There goes your car." On the television screen, an armored car in the center of the forest burned.

Abbie smiled, the smile of knowing that her kids were all tucked down for the night. "Don't stay up too late, robotics tomorrow."

Out of habit, she checked Martha's room. The blinds were open again. She went to close them and spotted a dark SUV parked across the street. *Wait . . . could it? The same one from last night?*

She raced down the stairs, skipping some steps. As she passed the switch, she tripped the hall light off and peered through the wooden slats.

"What's the matter?" Joss said behind her.

She pointed to the car. "Across the street, the SUV. That side is no parking at night."

"Maybe your neighbor has company."

Goosebumps crawled up Abbie's arms. "It was parked in the same spot last night, too."

The headlights of a passing car illuminated the SUV, and her breath caught as she noticed a silhouette inside the vehicle.

Joss was out the front door before she could stop him, and he reached the curb as the SUV peeled away. He stood in the street, watching until the vehicle turned the corner and disappeared. *Joss, come back inside, please!* He took his time walking back to the house, his eye watching the street for the SUV's return.

"Tennessee plates, couldn't make out any numbers. Probably nothing."

He was probably right, but Abbie shivered, nonetheless. She crossed her arms tight so he wouldn't notice her trembling.

Joss's eye was still on the empty street. "Probably nothing," he repeated. "Still, where's Benny? I think I'll take him for a walk."

CHAPTER TEN

Saturday, 7:31 a.m., the War Room

Fragrant steam rose from her mug of Earl Grey tea. Abbie leaned over the vapors, inhaling the spicy aroma, willing the caffeine to be transferred by osmosis so she needn't spend the energy to lift the mug. Her plan wasn't working.

Joss whistled while he poured coffee.

"How many bottles did y'all open last night?" Abbie asked.

"Too many, I think. Didn't you sleep?"

"Not well." She shook her head. "Got to wake up. Too much to do today." From the smudges under his eyes, she guessed he hadn't slept well, either.

He inspected her refrigerator with a frown. "How do you keep two teenagers fed with what's in here?"

"Groceries are on the to-do list today."

"Let me be a good houseguest and go to the store for you," he offered. "Where's your list?"

She pointed to the bulletin board behind him.

"Okay, I'll go. One less thing to worry about before your date tonight."

Abbie'd almost forgotten. She winced. "How did I let Loreen talk me into going out with Nick Preston? It's seventh grade all over again."

He aimed his gaze outside. "I don't think there's any way to stop that lady once she's got her mind set on something," he said. "Speaking of which . . ."

"Mornin'!" Loreen swept in, carrying a garment bag and a sack from Suzette's.

"What's that?" Abbie asked.

"Clothes, silly! I'm not gonna let you wait until five minutes before Nick Preston shows up before you dig something out of your closet. I'm going to pick out the perfect outfit for you. This," she waved the garment bag, "is Plan B."

"You get me a dinner date and dress me?" Abbie moaned. "Maybe you should go on the date for me too."

"No way you're ducking out of this!" Loreen said, returning from the bedroom with a couple of hangers. She held up one sweater against Abbie, and then a different blouse, then shook her head. "We're going to need Plan B."

Joss licked the powdered sugar around his mouth. "What are these things?"

"Best beignets in the Tennessee Valley." she said as she poured herself some coffee.

Chirp chirp chirp. "Who on earth would call me this early?" Abbie asked.

"Seriously, Abs, this house is so busy, you should charge admission," Joss said.

The caller ID seemed familiar.

"This is Abbie."

"Ms. Adams? This is Bernice Strong."

How does the woman survive without earphones? Joss seriously considered adding earphones to his shopping list as Abbie retreated to the war room, phone pressed to her ear.

Loreen sighed and carried her Plan B garment bag to Abbie's bedroom. "I swear," she said upon her return to the kitchen, "one of these days I'm going to empty out her closet and take it all down to the Goodwill. That'll make her go clothes shopping."

Considering Abbie had spent her years at Northwestern in leggings, sweatshirts, and sneakers, Joss seriously doubted it.

"So, what are you going to do today? Go look for people's family silver?"

Joss popped another beignet into his mouth and chewed while he considered his options. "I guess I'm going to try to track down the families who might have entrusted their treasure to Dr. Grover." He told her about the Auburn University paper. "They listed MacKenzies, Lawlors, and Kincaids."

Loreen thought for a moment. "Well, I don't know of any MacKenzies or Lawlors, but I can ask Mother, she might know. Or Madeleine might know. Now, Miss Kincaid, I *think* her family has been in town a long while. She's a widow with too many cats, if you catch my meaning. Loves Prosecco. She lives over in the Cottage District. Wanna take a walk?"

Abbie rushed to the war room as she tapped to put the call on speaker.

"I'm sorry I took so long to get back to you," Bernice said. "My daughter and I just got back from an Alaskan cruise. I've got to say, your message caught me by surprise. *Rosalie DuFrayne.* Good Lord, forty-six years. How can I help?"

The woman's voice was sweet, lyrical. Abbie imagined her in choir robes on Sunday.

She flipped on her MacBook. "Yes, ma'am." Two clicks, and she was recording. "You went to school with Rosalie?"

"Yes, we were both on the Wexler scholarship. Only back then nobody called it that. Dr. Theodore Wexler paid our tuition out of his pocket. I think the family only established the scholarship after he died. The entire application process is formal now, but in 1967 I simply wrote an essay about what I wanted to do with my education, and then I interviewed with Dr. Wexler."

"That confirms what I've already learned, that Old Dr. Wexler funded your education." It was a delicious little tidbit for the story. "What was he like?"

"Oh, he took a great interest in us. Six of us, all together, me and Rosalie, Cleta Blakebill, Lawrence, I want to say Johnson, Davis, and I don't remember Davis's last name, and Cyrus Porter. Lawrence and Davis didn't survive the first year's final exams. And Cyrus didn't graduate with Cleta and me. He served in Vietnam for a year."

"It must have been quite a novel experience, going to an all-white school."

No response, and Abbie wondered if she'd offended her, gone too far, too soon. But, finally, an answer. "Well, I don't mind telling, we were scared at first. Alabama was still very much George Wallace's state. Lots of white folks in Hunts Landing didn't want us on campus. So, yes, we were scared."

"Was Rosalie scared? Considering her mother worked for the Wexlers?"

Bernice chuckled. "Rosalie? Always thought she was kinda fearless, at least off campus. But on campus, she was more . . . subdued. Well, one had to be; it didn't do to draw unwarranted attention to yourself."

"And off-campus?"

"Oh, she was lively, bubbly even, quick with a joke and quicker with a laugh. Had a crush on Sidney Poitier, heck, who didn't in those days. But anytime there was a Sidney Poitier movie playing at the Palladium, she'd drag me and Cleta with her to go see it. I think the last one we saw was *For Love of Ivy*. Had to be, the Mr. Tibbs one didn't come out until much later."

Abbie scrolled through her interview notes with Cyrus Porter. "I've got a quote from Cyrus. 'Dr. Wexler controlled things on campus, but off campus, we lived in a very segregated world.'"

"That's how I remember it," Bernice said.

"So, was it like that on campus? What was it like showing up at Hunts Landing College?"

"Well, like I said, it was scary walking onto campus, but it was like Cyrus said, Dr. Wexler controlled the college. We couldn't live on campus, but he paid for our meal plans. Our first day, in 1967, all six of us met at the cafeteria in Lyndon Hall for lunch, and Dr. Wexler, he brought us in and introduced us to all the lunch ladies, making sure they understood we could eat with the white students."

That Old Dr. Wexler had needed to smooth the way with the lunch ladies so Rosalie DuFrayne and her friends could eat in the cafeteria irked. "Didn't that make you angry?"

Bernice laughed. "Oh, Miss Adams, that's just the way it was."

"Was the lunchroom itself segregated?"

"Not exactly," Bernice sighed. "That first day, we sat off in a corner by ourselves. I think Cyrus fretted the most. He kept looking around like he expected trouble. Barely ate. After a few minutes, two white boys come over. Cyrus got to his feet in a heartbeat. Now one of them, Frank Wexler, was Dr. Wexler's son, introduced himself and his friend David, and they shook all our hands. Then they sat down to eat with us. Some of their friends joined them. Soon enough, the table filled up, and no one cared that we sat with them."

"Frank Wexler, a nice guy?" Now, Abbie couldn't keep still.

She stood quickly with the phone and started pacing around the table. "That doesn't quite jibe with the Frank Wexler I know." *Dang, I probably should not have disclosed that bit of information.* "I should have told you, I studied under Dr. Frank Wexler."

"Well, Miss Adams, I can't speak for the sort of person Frank Wexler is now. The boy I met that first day, he was nice enough. The Wexlers, Frank and Dr. Wexler both, they did what they could to help us be accepted on campus. I mean, Hunts Landing College was officially integrated, but in truth, it was anything but color-blind."

Abbie wasn't ready to give Frank Wexler that kind of credit. He'd probably felt obligated to be friendly to Rosalie, to the daughter of his family's cook, or perhaps his father insisted he do so. "Did you see much of Frank Wexler on campus after that?"

"Very little. I studied accounting, and I think he was in the sciences."

Abbie was on her second lap around the table. "And Rosalie? Do you think she saw much of Frank Wexler?"

"Oh, I couldn't say. I saw Rosalie most days on campus, but Cleta knew her better, I think. Cleta stayed with Miss Etta and Rosalie freshman year. Sophomore year, Cleta and I got a place with two of Dr. Wexler's freshmen. Four women and one bathroom. Can you imagine?"

You should try two teenagers when the hot water goes out. "I've had no luck locating Cleta."

"That's a shame," Bernice said. "You should speak to her."

Abbie was almost out of questions. "The night she died, Rosalie had a bus ticket to St. Louis, I think to see her aunt. Any idea why? Summer term wasn't over yet."

There was a pause on the other end. "No, I can't think of why. Rosalie was so focused on her studies. 'Course, it's been a long time."

"Did she have a fella?" It was a question that had been percolating in Abbie's mind. *What was it they always said on the TV cop shows, that the boyfriend/husband is always the primary suspect?*

Bernice sighed. "Can't say for sure, Ms. Adams. But, spring of '69, Rosalie, she seemed happier than usual. I thought, back then, Rosie's got herself a fella, but now that you ask, I can't figure where she found the time. She carried a full course load and worked part time. She practically lived in Ellesby Hall, where her job was."

Abbie couldn't imagine Loreen being able to hide a boyfriend from her. "So, what does your gut tell you?"

Bernice thought for a moment. "If she went out, it was with Cleta and me. On campus she was always with us or Cyrus, or in Ellesby Hall with those engineers, and those fellas all had girlfriends. So, I think, no."

Abbie had crossed off the last question on her list. "Mrs. Strong, thank you. This has been very helpful."

"You write up a good story about Rosalie."

"Do you have an address or phone number for Cleta?"

"Well, after school, she joined the Peace Corps. Went somewhere in Southeast Asia. I don't remember. Seems she came back, though, I remember getting a wedding notice. Let me do some digging. You'll want to talk to Cleta."

Saturday, 8:11 a.m., the Cottage District

With Benny in tow, they stopped first at The Sommelier. Loreen selected a bottle of Prosecco from the back of the chiller. "Never hurts," she said.

Hunts Landing on a Saturday was slower, and yet faster, than a weekday, Joss mused. People weren't busy hustling to work, but many were out in their yards, mowing lawns, laying down mulch. Shrubs and trees alike were in full flowering glory, plants that Joss couldn't name, more luscious and verdant than what he was accustomed to in southern California. The Cottage District was aptly named, with smaller, more compact homes. The lawns were smaller than in the Garden District where Abbie lived, but no less vibrant with foliage and color.

Hunts Landing residents took obvious pride in their gardens. "This reminds me of the Cotswalds in the UK," Joss said.

"I've never been," Loreen replied.

"To England?"

"Out of the country," she said. "Wait, no, we had a school trip in eleventh grade to Quebec. A bunch of kids took French for the first time that year just so they could get on that trip." She smiled at the memory. "Me and Abbie, we got into our share of scrapes on that trip." They turned a corner, and Benny growled. "And here we are."

Joss grabbed hold of Benny's collar and petted him to calm him down. "Easy boy."

Miss Kincaid's yard was as immaculately trimmed as her neighbors, with pink flowering shrubs on either side of her front porch, where three cats lazed in the morning sun. Early tulips—at least Joss knew what tulips looked like—were lined up in front of the shrubs, adding additional splashes of color. Miss Kincaid herself, at least Joss guessed it was Miss Kincaid, was kneeling at her tulips, wearing denim overalls and a floppy gardening hat protecting her face against the sunshine.

"Yoo hoo!" Loreen called. "Miss Kincaid!"

Miss Kincaid looked over her shoulder and slowly got to her feet. Joss guessed she was in her late sixties or early seventies. Of course, he hadn't done so well so far at guessing ages in Hunts Landing. And the floppy hat hadn't done its job; her nose and cheeks were a splotchy red.

"Loreen Oliver. Well, well. How's your momma?" The woman came to a stop on the other side of the garden gate but after eyeing Benny eyeing her cats, didn't invite them in.

"Momma's fine, thank you, I'll be sure to tell her you asked after her." Loreen's hand extended to Joss. "This is my friend, Joss Freeman."

"Pleasure," Joss said, flashing the best smile he could muster.

"Huh." Miss Kincaid peered at him through thick spectacles. "You ain't from around here, are ya?"

Joss opened his mouth, but Loreen beat him to it. "Joss is a friend of Abbie Adams's, Miss Kincaid. He's from California."

"Huh." The older woman tipped her hat back a bit. "That explains it."

What 'it' was, Joss wasn't about to ask. "I'm a documentarian, Miss Kincaid."

"A docu-whut?" Over her shoulder, the cats had suddenly noticed Benny, and the dog growled in the back of his throat. Joss rubbed Benny's neck with his thumb.

"He makes TV shows about history, Miss Kincaid," Loreen offered.

"Bah," Miss Kincaid huffed. "What's the point? Life's in the here and now, my papaw used to say, meant for livin', not for looking backwards like a screech owl."

"I'm more interested in the pre-Civil War homes," Joss said. "Like the one that's up for auction, Grover House."

"Ain't talkin' to nobody about that cursed house." With that, she spun on her heel and stormed back to her gardening.

"Miss Kincaid, wait, please!" Loreen called, and raised the shopping bag from The Sommelier. "I brought you a new prosecco we got in."

That stopped the older woman, who returned and took the bag Loreen offered. She peered inside. Satisfied, she appeared to accept the bribe. "What do ya wanna know?"

"Why does Grover House upset you, Miss Kincaid?" Joss asked. "It's just a house."

Miss Kincaid screwed her lips tight. "There's a curse on that house, for sure, and anybody dumb enough to buy that heap o' bricks is just lookin' for trouble."

"A curse?" Both he and Loreen echoed.

"Sure enough. My papaw cursed that house and every Grover in it, and look what's happened. No more Grovers around here, house went from one lazy good-for-nuthin' family to the next, and now it's empty, nothin' left except for the ghosts."

"But why on earth would your papaw curse Grover House?" Loreen asked.

"'Cause Harold Grover was a no-good low-down cheat who stole from everybody, most particular my papaw. Left my family dirt poor after the crash. Papaw had nothin', 'cept what he could grow in his own dirt. But then old Harold got caught with his hand in the church roof fund. Stealing from your neighbors is one thing, but stealing from a church, that was too much for even this town. Papaw was there when they carried Harold off to jail, and then he went 'round to Grover House and put the curse down." Miss Kincaid's chest heaved with the telling of the story. She raised the bag. "Thank you kindly, Loreen Oliver. You be sure to give my best to your momma."

The old woman turned and carried the bag inside her house, cats following her.

"Should have warned you," Loreen said. "Sorry."

"No worries," Joss said. "But we learned plenty." He tugged softly on Benny's leash, and they turned to go.

"And what would that be?"

"Papaw Kincaid didn't know where the town treasure was. But it looks like he thought Harold Grover did."

Saturday, 9:08 a.m., the War Room

Abbie drank another cup of tea before she typed up her notes on Bernice Strong. Until, and if, Bernice came through with a phone number for Cleta Blakebill, she needed to explore other avenues. The Tennents gang was next on her list.

She Googled until her phone sounded with the *woo woo woo* of a police siren. Jethro. Just the person she needed. "Hey, great timing. Did you know the Library of Congress posted three hundred and eighty-seven maps of the Tennessee Valley from the 1860s, but not a single one from the 1960s?"

"No," Jethro replied.

"But I found a map on a website called *Everything You Ever Wanted to Know about Alabama.* The webmaster wants the Pope to beatify Bear Bryant."

"Auburn fans might object. Listen. I had a buddy of mine pull the blotter from July 1969. No reports of sexual assault. Doesn't mean there weren't any, only that in those days most sex crimes went unreported."

"Okay, makes sense." Abbie had to keep reminding herself of how different things were in 1969.

Jethro continued. "Then, this mornin', I wake up and remember somethin'. Morning after the fight, we were at the station filing our reports, and a patrolman told a story about drunk sorority girls. Otto Grunberg. He's retired, lives in town, spends his weekends playing the slots at Tunica. I called him, and he remembers picking up a girl runnin' around in her underwear. He dropped her off somewhere in the Garden District, not too far from your place. He didn't remember exactly where, though."

Abbie jotted notes. "I wonder if I'll be able to find her. Will Irestone warned me that there are some people I just won't find. Still," she pursed her lips, "it would be nice to talk to her, if for no other reason than to find out why she was in her underwear. Can I ask you something about the Tennents gang?"

"Happy to serve," Jethro said.

"It looks like the only direct road from Florence to Hunts Landing in 1969 was County Road 62. I remember my parents driving on that road when I was a kid, and I remember 62 being little more than a dirt road." Funny how the memories came flooding back, of lazy Sunday afternoon picnics and strawberry picking, all along County Road 62.

"It was a dirt road. Most of the way, until the late '70s."

She reached for a stack of printouts. "I found old newspaper clips on the Tennents gang. July twenty-third, they escaped from Mississippi State Penitentiary. They stole a green Ford pickup truck and headed east. Sometime on the morning of the twenty-fourth, they got to the old woman's farm in Muscle Shoals. A neighbor said he saw her, alive, getting eggs from the henhouse, just after dawn. Come dusk, the pastor rode his bicycle past the house and saw the green pickup. So, the gang is in Muscle Shoals at around eight o'clock the night of the twenty-fourth."

"That sounds about right," he agreed.

"So, how did three escaped convicts get from Muscle Shoals to Hunts Landing, over eighty miles, in less than four hours on a dirt road, and happen to stumble upon Rosalie DuFrayne in the woods?"

Jethro took some time to answer. "I told you, I don't believe they did."

Abbie had already made her calculations. "Surely, the ABI could do the math, too, so why would they insist the Tennents gang killed Rosalie?"

"Well, it didn't make much sense to me, either."

"Then why didn't Hunts Landing PD take the case back?" She ignored the alarm bells ringing in her brain. "Do you think it's because the victim was Black?"

"Now wait a daggum minute! Kenneth Farrow was a good man, a good man who spent the better part of his life protecting the citizens of Hunts Landing—"

She interrupted him before thinking. "And Rosalie DuFrayne was one of those citizens!"

"Dammit, girl, you don't have any idea what you're talking about."

"Then explain it to me."

"Doin' the right thing, Abbie, that's not always easy. And sometimes it's downright dangerous." He hung up.

Abbie stared at her now silent phone, jaw dropped. *I had to ask the question, had to. He was the one who told me to ask questions.* But she also wondered what kind of hornet's nest she'd stepped into.

Crap.

Saturday, 12:29 p.m., the War Room

Joss was on the phone with his producer, begging her to overnight him better camera equipment. "We won't be able to shoot it later, the house goes up for auction next week . . ."

Abbie had long ago learned how to tune out Joss's voice, and tune him out she did. She had to keep her focus. Five days left. She wrote a big "5" on her whiteboard and circled it twice. Focus.

Irksome details about the Rosalie case fluttered through her brain, a welcome distraction from the impending date, now only hours away, a date she could ill afford to go on. Jethro's hang-up still stung, and she didn't want to dwell on the memory. With rapid swipes of the whiteboard eraser, she wiped away her old notes and started her lists afresh.

What I know: Body @ river, party @ river, Cyrus P @ both, Frank W @ both—

Two men, in both places Rosalie had been at or near the night she died. Three men, if you counted Frank's friend David.

David B @ both—

If she were to believe Cyrus Porter, and her gut told her to do so, then the other Wexlers, Nevelyn and Old Theodore, had stayed at Wexler House, nursing their bourbon or brandy or whatever wealthy people drank on the sly.

Old Doc & Nevelyn @ W. H.

George came in from outside. "What's for dinner?"

"Steak à la Joss," their house guest answered, his phone call complete. "Your momma's got a date tonight."

Abbie glared at Joss, who remained blissfully unaware until George chuckled. "You're in for it now, Joss. She gave you *the look*."

He glanced up from the sink. "What'd I do?"

"I don't think you were supposed to tell me she's got a date." George burrowed his head into the refrigerator.

"Do you both realize I'm standing right here?" Abbie said. "And how was robotics?"

"Awesome. We got Wally the robot to climb a pole and drop a tennis ball into the basket. Two points." He opened a bottle of Gatorade. "So, do I get to check out this guy you're seeing tonight? See what time he's going to bring you home, and all that stuff?"

"Absolutely not."

"You take all the fun out of everything." George bounded up the stairs two at a time.

"See, he doesn't care," Joss said.

"You need to stay *very* quiet." Abbie moaned to herself. She should have rehearsed something to tell the kids. Why hadn't she thought of this before? What would they *think*?

"It's a dinner, Abs. Didn't Martha tell the guy you were free tonight?"

"Yeah, but—"

"No buts. They're the coolest kids I've ever met, and I live in LA. They love their momma. That they're so well behaved is unreal. They should break curfew or get caught watching inappropriate movies once in a while. I should probably teach them a few bad habits . . ."

"Don't you—"

There was a knock on the screen door. Jethro Turner stood on her porch.

Alone on the sunporch with Jethro, Abbie was unsure what to say to the man who'd hung up on her a little while ago.

Jethro, with his elbows on his knees, rubbed his hands together and peered at her. "If I squint a little, you look exactly like your momma. You even stick a pen in your hair, just like Elsa."

Abbie started to speak, but he cut her off. "No, darlin', let me say my piece. This house," he looked around, "it brings it all back. Your momma and daddy, you no taller than a strawberry runnin' around in pigtails. Elsa's pork butt and Matt's cold beer. There was a time when I ate at your momma's table regularly, when LuAnn and I were goin' through a spell."

"You'd go fishing with Daddy," Abbie recalled, the memory sharp. "And Momma'd fry up the catch."

Jethro nodded, his lips pursed. "They both of them were good friends with a willingness to listen and the wisdom not to say too much. And how do I repay their friendship? By ignorin' you? Widowed girl, raisin' two kids by herself, no family left to help. Makes me sick to my stomach. Abbie, I'm sorry, honey. I'm sorry I hung up on you."

Whatever she'd been expecting, it wasn't an apology, and her eyes widened. "I didn't mean to ruffle any feathers."

"Ruffle?"

"I think I didn't realize how sensitive folks in Hunts Landing are to suggestions of racism."

"Sensitive, hmm. That's puttin' it mildly."

Abbie leaned across the table and grasped his hand. "Jethro, I'm the one who's sorry. I'm used to the written word, things people put down on paper that came to me long after those people died. Pieces of paper, they're one-dimensional. Living, breathing, remembering, talking people, they're so different. I've been careless."

"Girl, I came here to apologize to you."

"I know. But this is new territory for me. I don't think I realized how sheltered I was. I mean, Momma and Daddy, our social lives revolved around the college. Academia. I didn't go to the public schools. My kids have more Black friends than I ever did. And I never gave that much thought. So I pushed, without really thinking about the words that came out of my mouth, and how they would affect you."

"Trust me, sir, she's more comfortable with people who've been dead for two hundred years," Joss announced, a dishtowel draped over his shoulder. He extended his hand. "Joss Freeman."

Abbie made the introductions. "Joss is staying in the room over the garage."

"Maybe you can teach her a thing or two about dealing with the living." Joss winked at her. "I'll leave you two . . ."

Jethro raised his hand. "No need to leave. Abbie asked me some questions earlier today. Questions I didn't wanna answer before. But I'm ready now, and there's nothin' I'm going to say you can't hear." Elbows back on knees, Jethro leaned forward. "You asked me if I thought Chief Farrow didn't take the case back from the ABI because the victim was Black. Well, when you asked me the question, well, *yes*, I got angry, I'm not ashamed to admit."

"Well, I pushed too hard," Abbie admitted. Joss took a seat next to her.

"Kenneth Farrow was a good man," Jethro continued, "born and raised here, always wanted to do his best for Hunts Landin'. There were still a lot of good old country boys in town back in '69, old-fashioned, set in their ways, and you can't forget the Klan. Farrow kept the Klan out of Hunts Landin'. That's important, 'cause twenty miles outside of town, county sheriffs had a whole different patch of problems."

"Were there any Black officers on the force then?"

"No, and not because Farrow wouldn't hire any. I think he would've. Jack Stove was our first one, 1971, if I recall. Now, it's different, of course."

"Okay," Abbie persisted, "but that doesn't explain why Chief Farrow didn't reopen the case."

"I thought about that a lot since this mornin'. This needs to be off the record. I don't want Farrow's name smeared in *The Times*, you understand?"

She nodded.

Jethro paused, as if he were deciding whether to trust her. "In '69, the city council appointed the Chief of Police. Keepin' your job meant keepin' the powers that be happy, and in '69, those powers sat in the hands of just a few. Mayor Tully, the mill families, some of the defense contractors, and Dr. Theodore Wexler."

"Do you think any of those men told Chief Farrow to back down?" She raised a finger, went to her dining room, and pulled down a piece of paper off her whiteboard. "Caleb Jackson, you remember him, the reporter? He saved this note." She read, "Respect for the family, stand down."

Jethro pulled reading glasses out of his shirt pocket and placed them on his nose with two hands before considering the doodle of Old Dr. Wexler. "The suggestion bein', Wexler asked the chief to back down off the investigation? Sure, the guy was powerful. Wexler came from old Hunts Landin' money, cotton and lumber, and he was the president of the college. You didn't ignore a man like Theodore Wexler. But why would he tap the brakes on a murder investigation of a student he sponsored at the school? Doesn't make a lick of sense." He handed her back the paper.

"Somebody told Jackson to stand down," she said. "The paper didn't print the article he wrote."

"And you think it was Theodore Wexler?" Jethro considered the idea. "You ask Frank Wexler?"

"'The family will not comment on Rosalie DuFrayne's murder.'" Abbie made air quotes with her fingers. "All we can print is that the family wouldn't go on the record." *Chirp chirp chirp.* Abbie glanced at the caller ID and jumped up, mumbling an "Excuse me." Cleta Blakebill was calling.

CHAPTER ELEVEN

Saturday, 1:07 p.m., the Sunporch

A bbie carried her phone back out where she'd left the men talking.

"Joss here has invited me for supper," Jethro said. "Can't wait to taste a steak cooked by a real-live TV star." He dropped his voice. "Plus, gives me a chance to look for this SUV y'all keep seein'."

Abbie squashed the sudden butterflies in her stomach. "Probably somebody who doesn't realize they can't park on that side of the street," she replied, staring at her phone.

"It scared you enough to send you running down the stairs," Joss reminded her.

"I'm not scared now," she said. "But I won't get in the way of two men and Steak à la Joss. Here, listen." She sat down between them. "That was Cleta Blakebill. She mostly confirmed things, and then she gets to this—" Abbie hit *play*.

Cleta Blakebill's voice came from the phone's speaker. ". . . of course, Rosalie looked ill from the moment she came into the kitchen.

We helped Miss Etta cook all afternoon, and I believe the heat got to her. Or maybe it was the catfish, we fried up so much that day."

"I heard that was all Miss Etta could get," said Abbie's voice.

"Well, I loved Miss Etta's catfish, but after fifty pounds, I didn't want to catch a whiff of another fish ever again. Anyhow, Miss Etta sent her home to cool off, but when Rosalie came back, she was still kinda green around the gills, and it was like she walked into a wall. Dropped this paper shopping bag she was carrying, and all these papers flew all over the floor. Now she got down on her knees, trying to pick up all the papers, but Miss Etta shooed her out, told her to get outside and start getting the drinks ready, and me and Miss Etta picked up all those papers."

"What sort of papers?" Abbie prompted in the recording.

"Oh, Miss Adams, we didn't read them! Mostly photostats, I think—do you remember photostats? The kind you got from a big Xerox machine, cost five cents a copy in the library and the copies always came out gray and fuzzy. Lots of photostats."

"What happened to the papers?" Abbie's phone voice encouraged.

"Well, she came back with a brown memo envelope," Cleta answered, "the old-fashioned kind with a string-tie. She stuffed those papers into the envelope and took it away with her."

Abbie stopped the recording. "I'm going to skip a bit. She worked the rest of the party with Rosalie." She clicked the track pad, and the recording picked up.

Cleta picked up her story. "I was by the window to Dr. Wexler's study, and I heard them argue clear as day, Dr. Wexler and Dr. McCain, though with river fireworks blasting away, I'm not sure anyone inside the house heard *those* fireworks, you catch my meaning?" Cleta chuckled at her own joke. "Then there was a bunch of slammed doors, and Dr. McCain stomped down the porch steps and took off out the gate toward the Quad. He didn't even stop to collect poor Mrs. McCain."

Abbie watched Jethro's face as Cleta spoke, looking for any change of expression, finding none. Had the local police continued looking into the case, they would have learned about the dramas at the Wexler party. As it stood, Jethro had never had the chance to consider any connections between the party and the murder.

On the recording, Cleta sneezed. "Excuse me. These darned allergies. Around eleven o'clock, the last of the guests were gone. Miss Etta sent us home. She told Rosalie to go on because she had some things to finish up in the kitchen. I guess that was the last time Miss Etta saw her daughter alive."

"Cyrus told me you all left together, but Rosalie went off by herself," Abbie's voice said.

"Right before midnight. Cyrus said goodnight to us on the corner, and I thought Rosalie and I would head home together. But Rosalie told me she had something to do. I wish to God I'd made her come home with me, good Lord, I prayed for forgiveness so many nights. I should have *made* her tell me where she was going, but I didn't." Cleta sighed with the memory.

"No, Miss Cleta, not your fault . . ." Abbie's voice soothed.

Cleta sniffled a few moments. "I'm sorry, Miss Adams."

"You don't need to be. Tell me . . . Rosalie's errand. Bernice thought maybe she had a fella on the side."

"Rosalie? Most of the young men at church asked her out at one time or another, but she kept her nose in her books. She studied and worked and was in her mother's house every evening when Miss Etta locked the doors."

Abbie stopped the playback. "What do you think, Jethro?"

The retired cop nodded. "Catfish did it to my LuAnn, too."

"For me, it was the detergent aisle at the supermarket," Abbie said.

"What're you talking about?" Joss asked.

Jethro laughed. "Bein' a bachelor and all, you wouldn't understand," Jethro said.

Abbie shook her head. "Silly TV star. There are times when certain odors can make a woman sick, or at least 'green around the gills.' On the night she died, I think Rosalie DuFrayne was pregnant."

Saturday, 5:57 p.m., Abbie's Bedroom

For the third time, Abbie considered backing out.

She'd loved Zach, buried him, mourned him. Somehow, she'd moved on to a life without the man she thought she would grow old with. Now, for the first time since he'd died, she readied her nerves to go out with someone else. Was her apprehension just a case of the jitters?

Or was she masking her sense of betrayal?

When Martha had come home from volleyball clinic earlier, she'd sent Abbie to shower. "Gee whiz, Mom, you're running out of time!"

"Wait! How was clinic?"

"*After* you shower," Martha said, with the same stern voice Abbie herself used when trying to induce a child to do what the child didn't want to do.

Now, showered, with hair flat-ironed by her daughter (Abbie had never flat-ironed her hair in her life, and wasn't sure if she liked the straight locks), makeup applied (mother and daughter barely spoke after the purple eyeshadow incident), and dressed in Loreen's outfit, Abbie felt like a carefully coiffed puppet. Her puppeteers huddled in the kitchen, preparing Steak à la Joss.

She wondered if she still had time to throw on blue jeans and pull her hair back into a ponytail.

The doorbell rang.

"I'll get it!" George shouted, and Abbie's heart leaped. At the sound of the *clack* and *swish* of the lock, she glanced in the mirror. *Oh, for crying out loud, it's only dinner!* She ran her fingers through her hair to muss the straightened strands up a bit.

That's more like it.

By the time she got to the kitchen, Joss and Nick were shaking hands.

"Martha said there was a TV star in the house," Nick said.

"Abbie was gracious enough to let me have the spare room while I'm in town."

Martha came in from the patio. "Hey, Mr. Preston!"

"Hey, Martha." He turned to Abbie, smiled, and cocked his head. "Hey, Abbie."

"Hi, Nick."

First date awkwardness, in front of her kids and Joss as witnesses, made her knees a little wobbly.

"Hullo!" Jethro called from the sunporch door. "I bring hothouse strawberries from the farm, ice cream from the grocery store, and . . ." he handed Joss a brown paper bag, "somethin' for the grownups."

"It'll be quite the party," Nick mused.

"Oh," Joss said, sounding a little exasperated, "it's been crazy like this all day."

Abbie kept introductions short. She kissed the kids good-night. "All four of you, behave."

She led Nick out through the dining room, where he stopped at the sight of the whiteboards. "What's this, a command center?"

"Something like that." Abbie pointed to Joss's wall. "On one side, the mystery of the Grover House treasure, that Joss is working on for his TV show." She tapped the other board with two fingers. "This side is my project for *The Times*. Rosalie DuFrayne, killed right here in Hunts Landing, July 24, 1969."

"Local murder?" Nick stepped closer to Rosalie's picture.

"Unsolved local murder."

"Pretty girl."

"I think so too. I've been lucky, been able to talk to people who knew her. Jethro, he was the investigating officer." Outside, Jethro waved his arms at the smoking grill.

"You need to tell me about it," Nick said, extending his hand. "Shall we?"

With a little trepidation, Abbie took it.

Their reservation was at The Cajun Asian, a new fusion restaurant on River Walk, a few steps east of the old campus. Three blocks of riverfront property boasted some of the finest and most diverse dining Hunts Landing offered, designed to cater to college kids and defense industry employees. It amused Abbie to think that in Cyrus Porter's day, people considered the rows of houses behind them to be slums. Nick had reserved an outside table next to the river.

Abbie had never eaten at any of the new restaurants before, so the views were as new to her as they were to Nick. They opted to share The Cajun Asian Special, a platter of boiled shrimp and crawfish, red potatoes, andouille sausage, and corn served with a Vietnamese garlic butter and a spicy Louisiana pepper sauce.

"Is it always so busy at your house?" Nick asked.

"Umm." She was unsure how to answer the question. Then she had to laugh. "Joss was right, it *has* been like Grand Central Station all day. Joss is here because he's working on the documentary. Jethro came to apologize for an argument we had this morning. Joss invited him over for steak." Talking about everyone else proved easier than talking about herself, and Nick seemed interested.

"Lucky break, Jethro being a friend of your mother's."

"I would've gotten nowhere fast without Jethro. He led me to Cyrus Porter, who not only worked at the same party as Rosalie, but was also at the fight down by the river." Abbie pointed to the three tall dorms. "Right over there. Somehow, he was in proximity to Rosalie all night long."

Nick flexed both eyebrows. "Sounds like your Mr. Porter could have been a prime suspect to me."

"No, Cyrus had an alibi. He was getting pummeled in the stomach in front of sixty witnesses at the precise moment when Rosalie was killed." Abbie stopped to taste some of the crawfish. "Oh, this is so good."

He grinned. "You're funny."

"I'm hungry," she said with a grin of her own. Surprisingly, she was hungry, despite the afternoon's nervous flutters in her stomach. *Was it uncool to eat on a first date?*

"You have a passion for this."

"I'm passionate about history, that's true," Abbie agreed. "But, over just a couple of days, Rosalie's story has become so much more to me. I lived and breathed historical subjects during eight years of college, but those people were long dead. I've *talked* to Rosalie's friends, something I never could before. You think Cyrus Porter's a prime suspect? I say, no way, because I talked to him. Rosalie was his *friend*."

"Friends kill each other," he said, serving himself more of the shellfish. "Brutus and Caesar."

"Ancient reference," Abbie said. "Anything more recent?"

"Um, nope."

"Sorry, old academic's habit. You know, you've had an unfair advantage. You had Martha all last night, got to pump her for all sorts of information."

"You can take Isabella all day tomorrow," Nick said.

"Why don't you just tell me?"

"Maybe I don't have very much to tell."

"Did you always want to be a cop?"

"No. I wanted to quarterback for the Broncos, but there were six, seven hundred guys better than me."

He winced, and she couldn't help but laugh. Nick was easy to talk to. She relaxed and settled into the moment.

An hour later, she'd learned he went to Penn State and married his college sweetheart, but there was trouble from the beginning when she landed a job with the State Department and started spending three of every four weeks abroad. Isabella was an unexpected but happy accident. His ex-wife opted to pursue her career over her marriage, and now he had custody and she had a Skype relationship with their daughter.

Expecting the conversation to turn to her own marriage, Abbie was grateful when it didn't. She didn't want to bring Zach to the table, not yet. Too soon.

Chirp chirp chirp. Abbie hesitated to pull her phone out.

"Go ahead," Nick said.

She smiled and looked at her phone. The number was vaguely familiar. *Oh, that call when I was with Mrs. Leonard at the cemetery.* She swiped to answer, "This is Abbie."

No one responded.

This time, she didn't wait. She ended the call. "Some telemarketer, I think. Sorry." She tapped the number in her recent calls list and then tapped *Block Caller.*

Nick paid the check, and they ventured onto River Walk. Her nerves fluttered anew.

"So, what do you want to do next?"

She had a sudden idea. "How'd you like to visit a crime scene?"

Saturday Evening, Who Knows When, the Sunporch

After dinner and ice cream, Martha headed to her room to get on her phone with her friends, but George and his buddy Pudge stayed downstairs with Joss and Jethro, listening to them tell stories, each trying to outdo the other.

Joss thought he had a winner with the time he'd finished shooting a scene when the set caught fire and burned around him while people shrieked and ran in terror. That the 'fire' was from a single candle that had toppled over, igniting a cardboard backdrop, and that the only person 'shrieking' had been Joss himself, well, nobody really needed to know.

Then Jethro countered with one of his own. "One time, Andrew Jackson Parkway northbound was blocked by this huge snappin' turtle. I mean, this sucker was almost two feet long from tooth to tail. So, my partner takes his nightstick, and kind of nudges the thing, tryin' to get it to move along. Quick as a wink, that turtle cranes his neck 'round and SNAP. He gotta hold on that nightstick and started waddlin' off the road."

"And what did you do, Mr. Jethro?" Pudge asked.

"Only thing I could do, considerin' the circumstances. I called it in." Jethro mimicked talking into a microphone. "Dispatch, this is unit eleven. Be warned that the suspect is now armed, on foot, and attemptin' to flee the scene."

The boys eyed Joss to see if he was going to try to top that story. "I give," Joss said, raising his hands. "You win."

Later, when the boys were safely upstairs with their video games, Jethro fetched the paper bag from the kitchen and pulled out a clear glass bottle with a brown wrapper.

"What's that?" Joss asked.

"This here, young fella, is the best darned 'shine in the county." Jethro poured while Joss watched, skeptical. "I used to bust this guy, back in the day, every few months or so. He'd just move the still to another part of the woods until I busted him again. Never turned him into the Feds, though, him being a preacher's kid." Jethro winked and lifted his glass. "This was Matt Adams's favorite. Best you don't sip it." He threw back his head and downed the shot, then let out a little cough.

Joss eyed his glass. Wasn't moonshine the equivalent of paint thinner? Still, no use letting the old man show him up. He downed the clear liquid and choked. "They made this out in the woods?"

"Naw," Jethro grinned. "Got this from Hunts Landin' Liquors. Just wanted to see if you'd drink it." Jethro pulled another bottle out of the bag, a green bottle of Remy Martin. "This was actually Matt's favorite. Why doncha find us some snifters and we can raise a toast in my friend's memory."

The moon was rising, full, shining her bright beams into the sunporch, and they enjoyed the brandy while Jethro told fishing stories. "Matt caught more rusty cans than he ever did fish, but he sure enjoyed being out on the river." Jethro fell silent for a moment. "Now, about y'alls black SUV." Jethro refilled their snifters before Joss could protest. "I don't think anythin's gonna happen tonight. This part of town hops a little on Saturday nights."

Indeed, now that Joss was paying attention, he could hear sounds of people around him, laughter, music, the hum of conversation, people venturing outdoors on this nice spring evening.

"But come tomorrow night, I'm gonna be watchin'."

———

"Are you sure you know where we're going?" Nick asked as they headed straight toward a looming wall of foliage.

"Sure. Jethro brought me here two days ago."

"Jethro brought you here in the daytime."

"Well, yes, but Rosalie was murdered at night." She reached the obscured entrance to the path. "I want to see what the place looks like, the way she saw it. We're lucky—there's a good moon tonight."

"So you're using me for my . . . protection skills?"

"Mostly for your ability to keep the snakes away." Abbie had no idea where this irresistible urge to tease him came from.

"Snakes!"

"I'm guessing they're gonna come after you and leave me alone." She disappeared into the brush.

"Abbie!"

She re-emerged with a grin. "Sorry, thought you were right behind me." She stretched out her hand.

Back on the path, the visibility amazed her. Moonlight filtering through the trees glistened against the sandy path, in contrast to the brush lining the trail. She could see quite well as they headed to the clearing. "Jethro told me people still use this place."

"People?"

"I think he meant 'lovers.' I don't think much illicit activity goes on here. The other day, the clearing was clean—no trash, not even a beer bottle."

Leaves rustled off to their left, and he froze. "What was that?" he whispered.

She didn't answer for a moment. "Sounded like a copperhead to me."

"Really?" Nick sidestepped off the path, away from the sound.

She burst into laughter.

"Oh, you're mean!"

"Sorry. Couldn't help myself. C'mon."

A few more steps, and they stood in the clearing.

By daylight, with sunlight filtered through the trees and casting shadows across the open glen, the spot was sleepy, lazy. The mottled light bespoke of long summer days spent swimming and fishing.

But at night, the clearing was hypnotic. The moon, now clearing the trees on the eastern side, shone with bright, milky beams. Leafy boughs shielded the ambient glow coming from the college, and she could see every log, every rock, with startling clarity, down to the silver reflections rippling on the river. Abbie gasped at the beauty of the place. "No wonder people come here." Poor Rosalie. "Jethro said the killer came in from this path and approached Rosalie from behind," she crossed to the fallen log, "striking her down. Rosalie fell, here." She pointed down, then halted her recitation.

On the old log lay a wilted yellow lily. Abbie picked up the blossom, rubbing the limp but still moist petals. The spicy scent of the flower was faint but detectable.

"What's with the flower?" he asked.

"I found one that was dried up here Thursday morning. Somebody put this flower here afterward."

"Well, Jethro told you people still use this place."

She nodded, unsettled. Some unknown person left flowers here, by the same gnarly knot on the log, likely right next to where Rosalie DuFrayne died. Twice in less than a week. "I wonder, no, that's crazy. But, maybe? Could someone be leaving these flowers here for Rosalie?"

Nick looked around the clearing. "After four decades? It's a stretch, I think. Besides, this seems as good a place for a romp in the woods as any. There's no telling who's used this place over the years."

Abbie nodded as she replaced the lily. Down in the sand, next to the log, lay an uneven contour roughly two feet long, a mere dip, dark in the shadow of the rising moon.

She gasped. For a moment, the impression shimmered like a growing pool of blood.

She looked up to find him watching her, the moonlight illuminating half his face. "You okay?"

She shook her head to clear it. The shadow was just that, a shadow. To convince herself, she knelt and swirled her hand through the sand. The sand was cool and dusty. Cool and dusty and dry. No blood.

"I guess I'm seeing ghosts." She smacked her hands clean and strode southward toward the river. "Jethro found indentations here, possibly from another person on the scene. But no drag marks. The murderer killed Rosalie by the log. He escaped by the path over there, east side of the clearing."

He came up behind her. She could feel his soft breath on her ear. His right arm wrapped around her back, right hand settled on her hip.

Abbie gulped essential air. "So, what do you think of the crime scene?"

"I think . . ." Nick turned her with his arm so that she was facing him. "I think you're neglecting the other exit routes, to the south and the west." His head, haloed by the moon behind him, dipped closer to her.

"Umm . . . south is the river . . ."

"He could have hidden a getaway boat . . . right . . . by . . . the water . . ." His head dropped lower.

"Fireworks barges on the river . . . too risky . . ."

His lips curled, just a little. "Then to the west."

She focused on his mouth, only inches away, and bit her lower lip. "West was depot land back then . . . fenced off right up to . . . the . . . water's edge . . ."

With a sparkle in his eye, Nick pulled his head back. He rested his other hand on Abbie's other hip, facing her squarely. "You want to know what I really think about your crime scene?"

Talking seemed easier than breathing, so Abbie answered. "Uh, huh."

"I think your Jethro is right, people use this place." He tilted his head a fraction of an inch. "I think it's a perfect place for a first kiss." Another fraction, a little closer. "I think that when I take you home tonight, George and Joss and Jethro and your ridiculous excuse of a guard dog are going to be waiting on that porch for us." Now his breath tickled her lips. "So I think I'd better get my goodnight kiss now." His upper lip hovered over hers with the barest touch.

Then his phone buzzed.

"This *isn't* happening," Nick muttered, stepping back from Abbie and fishing for his phone. "Preston."

Abbie settled down on a log while Nick responded to his caller with a series of "hmm's". He finished with an "I'm on my way," then grabbed Abbie's hand and pulled her up. "I need to get you home. Work."

Back at the car, he held the door open for her. She ducked to enter, but he grumbled something which sounded like "Oh, hell," and pulled her back out. His hands cupped her head, tilting her head, his lips covered hers in an assertive kiss that seemed to last for hours.

Sunday, 6:19 a.m., Abbie's Bedroom

A steady stream of texts woke Abbie from what had been a good dream.

Loreen: How did it go?

Loreen: Did you have a good time?

Loreen: I'm dying here, you gotta tell me what happened.

By the time she'd tapped out enough details to satisfy Loreen, Abbie'd forgotten what the dream was all about.

So much for sleeping in.

With the sounds of snoring drifting downstairs from the kids' rooms, and Joss not yet descended from the apartment over the garage, Abbie made coffee and followed Benny outside with her mug, her bathrobe loosely belted against the chill in the morning air.

Hunts Landing was due for another round of spring weather later in the week, but today dawned sunny. The grape hyacinth was just blooming; in a couple of days, the backyard would be awash in splashes of purple. Abbie's mother Elsa had held a superstitious abhorrence for any red flowers that Abbie herself had somehow inherited.

Even Valentine red roses were suspicious. Too much like the color of blood. Zach had planted a row of Abbie's favorite yellow roses along the back fence before his first deployment.

From her vantage point on one of the lounge chairs, Abbie could see new leaves sprouting on the rose bushes. Soon enough, the buds would appear.

They always reminded her of Zach.

Was it bad that she didn't feel guilty about her date with Nick Preston? She'd enjoyed her time with Nick last night, and she hadn't thought of Zach once. She certainly wasn't thinking about Zach when Nick had dropped that last-minute kiss on her lips. Didn't that make her a betrayer?

No. I've mourned him for ten years. Longer than I knew him. He'd want me to move on.

She barely had a moment to consider her conclusion. Joss emerged from the sunporch, hair tousled from sleep. Abbie wasted no time with pity. "What did y'all *do* last night?"

Joss waved his hand. "Not so loud." He dropped into the lounge chair next to her. "It started with moonshine that Jethro *said* was your daddy's favorite—"

"Daddy couldn't stand the stuff."

"—and ended with some brandy."

Had they been back at school, she might have been tempted to mess with his hangover, but instead she took pity on him. "I should get some food in you."

"No food, no." Joss's eyes were closed. "Top it off, I missed a call from Harriet."

In Abbie's opinion, that was probably good news, but to be fair, Joss looked miserable. "She'll call back. I'll make you some toast."

"No, no toast, well, maybe that cinnamon raisin . . ."

"You should go back to bed."

"Can't. Ursula wants an . . . update."

That decided it. She went inside to the kitchen and put some milk on the stove to warm. She pulled spices out of the cabinet, sprinkled a little of one, a dash of another, repeating the recipe from memory. This was Loreen's family hangover recipe.

Outside, she shoved the warm mug into Joss's hands.

"What is this?" He sniffed and groaned.

"You really don't want to know."

CHAPTER TWELVE

Sunday, 8:22 a.m., the War Room

Showered and dressed and refreshed by a new pot of coffee, Abbie settled in the war room to review her notes from the Cleta Blakebill interview. Rosalie's bundle of papers was a tantalizing tidbit. She'd brought papers to Wexler House and left without them. *Oh, golly. Cyrus.*

It had been an innocuous comment, so easily explained she'd dismissed it. Abbie pulled up the recording of Cyrus's interview and fast-forwarded to the right spot. *Something was on his mind, for sure, because he was alone, with a fifty-year-old bourbon and a bunch of files from his office on his desk.* Of course a college president would have files on his desk, she'd thought during the interview. No need to give that fact any importance.

Except, now, it was important, because Rosalie had brought a pile of papers to Wexler House and left without them.

Was it too much of a stretch to draw the line from the papers Rosalie had dropped in the kitchen to the papers on Wexler's desk?

Abbie stood to draw on her whiteboard when the doorbell rang. Nick Preston stood on her doorstep.

Abbie pulled the door open wider to let Nick in. "Hey!"

He entered the house with a grim expression she didn't like. "Is there someplace we can talk?"

The house was still quiet, but something in his face alarmed her. "Back here." She led him into the sunporch.

Nick took the seat she offered and leaned forward. "I'll get straight to it. Cyrus Porter was killed Friday, and his wife said the last time she heard from him was when he was meeting with you."

"Oh, good Lord!" Her stomach cramped as if from a suckerpunch. She sank into her seat, her knees weakened from the news.

He pulled a small notepad from his jacket pocket and flipped the cover open. "How well did you know Cyrus Porter?"

"Wait!" She held up her hand. "What happened to him?"

Nick tapped his notebook. "Looks like a robbery gone bad. Patrol found him a little after eight last night, shot in the head. His wallet is missing, but we found his phone under the seat. You called him yesterday."

"Y-yes, but he didn't answer."

"How well did you know the victim?"

This couldn't be happening. He was *questioning* her about a murder. Just last night . . . that wonderful kiss. This cold, expressionless man with his rapid-fire questions was a stranger. "We met Friday."

"Why'd you meet with him?"

"My assignment with *The Times*. He was close to the victim. I forgot to ask him a couple of things, so I called. The call went straight to voicemail."

"He was already dead," Nick said. "The coroner put the time of death Friday afternoon. Where'd you meet him?"

He was already dead when I called him. His phone rang, but he didn't hear it. He was dead. "Starbucks on University."

"What did you talk about?"

"Rosalie DuFrayne's murder. He gave me so much good information, and he was so sweet . . . sharing his memories." Abbie struggled to catch her breath.

"When did the meeting end?"

"Ten-forty-five, maybe."

While he peppered her with questions, his intent gaze never left her eyes. "Did you leave together?"

"No, he brought his car, I brought mine."

"We can verify that with security footage."

"Do you need to verify it?" Abbie asked, incredulous.

"As far as we know, you're the last person to see him alive. I think you'll want me to confirm that Porter was breathing when you left him. What did you do after your meeting?"

"Umm, I went to pick up lunch at Sally's Catfish. Then I came home."

"Can anyone verify that?"

"I can," Joss offered from the sunporch door.

"Mr. Freeman, this is a private discussion," Nick said.

Joss sat down next to her. "Abbie brought lunch a bit after eleven. Then we worked all afternoon."

Nick nodded as he made a note. "Did Porter tell you where he was going after the meeting?" he asked Abbie.

"No," she answered. "Maybe to play golf?"

"What was he wearing?"

"Khakis. A golf shirt, green."

"That matches what we found on the body." Nick examined his notebook. "One more thing. Do you own a gun?"

"Several. My husband, Zach, wanted me to be able to protect us while he was deployed." No need to mention her father's gun collection, locked safely away in the gun safe at the back of Zach's closet.

"Any that chamber thirty-two caliber rounds?"

Thankfully, she only had one. "Yes, a Beretta 81."

"Would you get it, please?"

"Sure." She kept an eye on him as she stood.

"Is this necessary?" Joss asked.

"It is, if we want to eliminate her as a suspect. Abbie is the last person we know to have seen the victim alive, and she owns a gun that shoots the same caliber that killed Cyrus Porter."

Abbie walked into the house, her steps a little shaky. Cyrus Porter killed? Thank goodness the kids were still in bed. She didn't think she could hide her face from them.

Opening the gun safe proved to be a challenge. Abbie's fingers shook enough to make inserting the key into the lock tricky. After she finally opened it, she dropped the Beretta, wrapped in oilcloth, into an old tote bag. Just in case. No need for the kids to see her carrying a firearm through the house.

Outside, she handed the bag to Nick, who pulled the oil cloth aside to check. "Lot of gun for a woman."

"I can handle it."

"I have to take it." Nick pulled a plastic evidence bag out of his pocket, bagged the firearm, then tucked it into a pocket inside his jacket, out of sight. "Is this your only thirty-two?"

"Yes." While she was grateful for his discretion, the feeling quickly faded, replaced by a mixture of hurt and anger that he could remotely consider her complicit in Cyrus Porter's death.

"Okay." Nick nodded with satisfaction. He stood. "Sorry to put you through the ringer." He looked a little guilty, like one of the kids when she caught them stealing cookies.

"Is that it?" She hoped she managed the same level of coldness that he'd given her throughout this surreal conversation.

"We can verify your story with security footage from Starbucks and Sally's. As long as the gun is clean, that should be the end of it.

But I'll need you to come down to the station some time tomorrow and sign an official statement. Like I said, we're likely looking at a robbery." He turned to go.

"Wait." Abbie crossed her arms and clenched them tight against her chest. "You asked me what we talked about, Cyrus and I. But you didn't ask the most important question. Cyrus and Rosalie worked the party at Wexler House in 1969. Yeah, *those* Wexlers, who still live right here in town. I'll bet you don't know where Frank Wexler was on Friday night."

Nick opened his mouth to say something, but nothing came out.

"Goodbye, lieutenant." Abbie couldn't close the door fast enough.

Sunday, 8:47 a.m., the Sunporch

Joss fussed around the coffee pot, keeping one eye on Abbie as she sat, quiet and motionless, on the sunporch. He carried a fresh cup out to her, placed it in front of her. She ignored it, ignored him, staring blankly at the hedge of budding roses along the back of her property.

She was hugging herself, shivering with the morning chill, or with the shock. He couldn't tell. In her bedroom, he found a cashmere shawl draped over an ottoman. He brought the shawl outside and draped it over her shoulders.

She brought a small fistful of the fabric to her nose. "This was my mother's. Sometimes, I imagine I can still smell her."

He gave her another half-minute. "You know, it's not the worst thing in the world. Your date got cut short because your boyfriend got called to the scene of a murder. Turns out, the victim was a man you met on Friday. Apparently, you're the last person to see him alive. Then, lover boy comes here and interrogates you like you're Al Capone. You know what?" Joss pursed his lips. "I got you beat."

"Huh?"

"I said, 'I got you beat.'"

She hugged herself and rocked a little. "I don't think so."

Joss sipped his coffee and smacked his lips. "My fiancée told me this morning that she's leaving me to go 'explore the outer reaches of her consciousness' at an artists' commune on the Baja Peninsula."

That seemed to shake Abbie awake. "No way!"

"She also asked me to loan her five grand for the move."

"Ouch."

"And she's taking Lincoln, our cat."

Abbie leaned back in her chair. "Okay, you've got me beat."

"Told'ja."

"Always thought you were more of a dog person."

"I am this week." Joss scratched Benny's scruff. "How many days do you have left?"

"Four. You?"

"Five."

"Then we need to get busy." Abbie stood and extended her hand. "But first, I need breakfast."

Sunday, 10:05 a.m., the Sunporch

Abbie felt the tight fist of dwindling time squeezing around her. Usually, Abbie enjoyed lazy Sunday mornings, letting her teenagers sleep in and lingering over a late brunch. Not today. She copped to what so many of her mom-friends secretly confessed to; texting children who were just upstairs.

Food in the microwave. Homework!

She scooped up her laptop and notebook and headed for the quiet of the sunporch. Now, without distraction, Abbie could dig back into

Cleta's interview. For Abbie, who'd experienced the abrupt and knee-buckling physical reaction to unpleasant odors while pregnant, Cleta's apparent ignorance of an obvious pregnancy symptom bordered on the ridiculous. Cleta had to be in her sixties. Surely she'd been around pregnant women in her life before?

Or maybe not. Still, it didn't hurt to be cautious. Abbie flipped open the lid of her laptop and composed several draft emails to Cleta, before settling on nonaccusatory language.

Abbie: Miss Cleta, your comments got me thinking. Any chance Rosalie could have been pregnant that night?

She'd gone from interviewing Cleta Blakebill to getting ready for her date with Nick. Had it really been less than a day? How quickly the deflation, from the romantic wonder of last night's kiss, her first grownup kiss in over ten years, to the disappointed puddle of this morning, with Nick's iciness.

She'd been silly, stupid even, to read so much into a simple kiss. When push came to shove, Nick stood ready to accuse. *He's just doing his job.* But this turn-around jarred her bones, the warmth in his eyes last night absolutely gone this morning. And after over ten years of, well, nothing, nobody, did she really need somebody in her life who was so quick to turn?

No. She didn't think so.

She'd managed fine, on her own, all these years. This kind of crap, well, she didn't need. Or want. Nick's attentiveness had been flattering, yes, but now that she'd seen the man who could consider her a murder suspect, there was no need to worry about how she'd deal with the future volleyball tournaments. She knew exactly how she was going to deal with Nick Preston in the future. At arm's length.

But he had brought her news of Cyrus Porter, and for the first time since Nick had left, she could think about that sweet man uninterrupted. Benny ignored her need for a few undisturbed moments; he jumped onto the sofa next to her and curled up protectively at her side. Abbie stroked his scruff absently, recalling her meeting with Cyrus. How angry he'd been with himself for not walking Rosalie and Cleta home that night. His smile over the picture of the three girls, of Rosalie and Cleta and Bernice. He'd taken the picture himself, and his grin had been broad with the memory. He'd so obviously cared for those young women.

And the two who were still alive had heard nothing about his death.

She didn't suppose it was her place, but Abbie was reasonably certain that no one else would think to call either Bernice or Cleta, and she hated the thought of them learning of Cyrus's death from an obituary. The clock on her computer read ten past eleven—church time on a Sunday morning. She typed out a quick email addressed to them both, and though she barely knew the women, and had only met Cyrus the one time, she fought some tears as she hit *Send*.

Benny pawed her once, twice. The dog always knew. She pushed the laptop aside, and he crawled up onto her lap, and she held him, and let some of her unshed tears fall, tears for Cyrus, a man she barely knew, tears for Rosalie, a woman she'd never met, tears for . . . what?

Stop it, Abbie.

"Enough, buddy." She squeezed Benny one last time, then gently urged him off her lap. He trotted off with only one backward glance.

Her thoughts roamed back to Cleta Blakebill, and Rosalie's strange comment, a comment made right after Quentin McCain had stormed out of Theodore Wexler's office. *Sometimes having two bosses can be a bad thing.*

Back on Wednesday, when Abbie had first read the grant scandal clipping in Caleb Jackson's file, there'd been nothing connecting the scandal with Rosalie DuFrayne. Now, thanks to Cleta, Abbie believed that Rosalie had worked under Quentin McCain at the Engineering School.

Not wanting to venture inside into the war room, she looked up the article from memory on Newspapers.com and scribbled notes.

Fraud. Falsified test data. NASA $$$. McCain convicted 1973. Died in prison 1975.

Abbie drummed her fingers on her laptop. Dr. Quentin McCain died in 1975, but did he have any surviving family? Would they talk to her? None of the articles mentioned his wife's name.

Abbie snapped her fingers. "Of course. Maddie."

Sunday, 10:03 a.m., Grover House

A long, hot shower and three Advils later, Joss was almost ready to face the day.

Five days times twenty-four hours . . .

Yesterday, he'd spent his productive hours prepping what he'd found so far for his pitch to Kenetsky. It was good, fascinating to a history buff. But no Civil War treasure. Yet. No wow-factor that would beat out the competition. To be fair to himself, he knew Eddie Udell's work—not as good as his own, but passable. With a story connected to General Custer, Udell had built in flair, even if all he could offer was gold dust, because no one had ever found a trace of Custer's gold, and Joss doubted anyone ever would. But, to build a story on a small town like Hunts Landing that most viewers had never heard of, well, Joss needed more than gold dust.

Ursula was overnighting higher-resolution video equipment to him. In the meantime, the cloud cover provided perfect lighting to shoot some preliminary video with his own camera. It was time to scout some locations. With any luck, the auction people would be at Grover House, hustling to finish the cleanup ahead of next Saturday's sale.

With his camera bag strapped on one shoulder, Joss took Benny for a stroll through the Garden District.

Grover House was quiet. There were no trucks in the driveway, no young people in auction t-shirts carrying boxes to the dumpster. From what Joss had seen on Thursday, those folks didn't have a moment to spare.

So where were they?

"You looking for somebody?" a voice said behind him.

Joss turned to find a man wearing a blue windbreaker and a Hunts Landing Volunteer Fire Department baseball cap. "Yes. The auction people. Thought they would be on the job today."

"Oh, they're probably at church. At least the Harmons will be. Don't know about those college kids, though. Ole Wayne'll probably be around later this afternoon." The man extended his hand. "I'm Harry Lawlor."

Benny let loose a belated bark. "Good guard dog," Joss said with a wince, and took the offered hand. "Joss Freeman."

Harry Lawlor showed no recognition at all. *Don't these people watch TV down here?,* Joss wondered.

"You thinking about buying the place, Mr. Freeman?"

"Joss, please, and no. I find old houses interesting. I'm a historian."

"Shame, 'cause if you were my neighbor, that guard dog of yours would certainly scare all the burglars away!" Harry laughed at his own joke. "Well, she's an old one, that's for sure. That's my place over there, catty-corner." Harry pointed to a neat home with red brick and white trim. "Not as old as this house, of course. My granddaddy told me that *his* great-granddaddy built our place during Reconstruction." Harry leaned in closer and lowered his voice. "Don't let on that I told you this, but apparently *that* particular Lawlor was a Yankee carpetbagger."

"So, the Lawlors weren't here during the *Union* occupation of the town?" Joss asked. *The Yankees are a baseball team.*

"Not as far as I know," Harry said. "It's a shame you couldn't ask old Mrs. Chenoweth. Used to own this house, but she passed, oh, it's going on twenty years now. That's why the place is up for auction; her kids couldn't stop fighting over the estate."

"I read an article on Mrs. Chenoweth," Joss said. "Something about an open-house in the '80s?"

"Oh, I remember that. It was a big deal around here. Mrs. Chenoweth, she was a nice lady, but she really wanted to show off her house. Did all this research into the Yankee occupation, because apparently the Yankees burned most of the houses around here, ours too, but left Grover House alone. I guess that's how the carpetbagger got a hold of the property, because the original house had burned to the ground."

Since the Federal troops had destroyed so many homes, it was common sense that people rebuilt in the ashes. Grover House might be the only antebellum home left in the vicinity.

Harry scratched his jaw. "Tell ya something interesting, since you're a historian and all. My granddaddy used to tell a story, about a tunnel between our place and this house that *his* granddaddy used when he was courting one of the Grover girls."

"A tunnel?" Joss's imagination began to run wild.

"It would have been before World War I, and who ever heard of tunnels in a town before, but granddaddy, well, he could spin a yarn as good as anybody. Between you and me and the wall, I didn't quite believe him, but that didn't stop me from taking a peek in the cellar every time we visited. In fact, I didn't trust a single word of his story until one big snowstorm when I was in high school. Four inches of snow, and it lay like a blanket. Except . . . ." Harry's hand drew an imaginary line from the corner of the Grover driveway, across the street, up to the curb in front of his home. "Snow covered everything except this clear strip diagonal across the street. Looked like it had been shoveled clean, but nobody in Hunts Landing owned a snow shovel in those days." Harry shoved his hands in his pockets, staring at the imaginary line, for a moment lost to his memory.

"How do you know that means a tunnel?" Joss asked.

"My granddaddy said the air in underground spaces stays warmer than the ground around it. So snow didn't stick." Harry nodded with conviction. "Yes, sir, I do believe he was telling the truth about that tunnel."

Sunday, 11:37 a.m., Abbie's House

Madeleine still hadn't called back. Shortly after Joss and Benny returned from their romp around the Garden District, Abbie's phone buzzed with an incoming text.

Madeleine: Sorry, on the golf course. Grant scandal? Be at your house in 45 minutes. Wanna hear about your date.

Abbie grabbed her gardening shears and headed outside. Some Southerners considered mint to be a vicious weed, quick to overpower any garden plot. Others lived happily with the fundamental wisdom that fresh mint is essential to those most glorious of Southern concoctions, the mint julep, and the Cuban *mojito*. Madeleine enjoyed both drinks, so Abbie headed to the far corner of the yard, where she grew the fragrant herb far from more delicate plants. Young shoots had sprung from last year's growth. She bent down and clipped. Beside her, a low canine whine. "Benny?" She put the shears into the small gardening basket along with the fresh-picked mint. His stiff tail and pricked ears alerted her. His stare focused on the hedge behind the yard.

"What do you see, boy?" Abbie herself noticed nothing but new leaves on an old hedge, but the hairs on the back of her neck stiffened. She peered over the hedge, into the alley, but it was empty as far as she could see. "Come on. Lady Madeleine comes to visit."

"The kids are so grown up. Good job. And this *mojito* is absolutely *delish*." Madeleine raised the glass and wriggled her toes in her sandals. "I think you need to tell me about your date first. Loreen told me he's just scrumptious in person."

Madeleine looked disappointed in Abbie's brief recap of her date. "Child, didn't we teach you better than to take a date to a crime scene? You might've gotten a better kiss than that. Do you like him, at least?"

Abbie ignored the question. She wasn't ready to discuss her irritation with being treated like a suspect. "What can you tell me about the grant scandal?"

"You keep dancing around the things you don't want to talk about. Fine. The NASA scandal. Hunts Landing College, a hundred and twenty years in the making with a sterling reputation, and there goes Quentin McCain, taking data, thinking he wouldn't get caught. Theodore Wexler spent every bit of political capital he possessed to keep the feds from closing down the place."

"Why did he need to fake the data?" Abbie asked. "The guidance systems worked. The news articles said so."

"Oh, you've lived in academia. Our little college competed with the big boys in those days, MIT, Stanford. All the schools fought for NASA dollars, but those other schools didn't have what we had."

Abbie knew well what Hunts Landing College had that other schools didn't. At the end of World War II, the US Army rounded up all the German rocket scientists that the Russians hadn't already rounded up and brought them here to Hunts Landing. Otto Von Braun led the team that got American astronauts on the moon. Anyone who'd grown up in this town knew the story. "But I still don't get why McCain thought he needed to fake data. I mean, the systems worked."

Madeleine squeezed her lime wedge into her drink. "Sure, those systems worked, but to get the funds to build the systems, McCain needed to prove to NASA that little itty bitty Hunts Landing offered the best engineering talent available. So he transformed two or three successful tests into twenty or thirty, and the school got the money."

Abbie had lived in academia and understood rivalries between small schools and large, and egotistical academics who thought they knew better. Like Frank Wexler. Was his father the same? Abbie wondered. "Didn't Wexler support McCain at all?"

"Testified against him at both the grand jury and the trial," Madeleine said. "Now, grand jury proceedings are secret, but our cleaning lady in those days sat on the grand jury. Poor dear, she was a terrible gossip, always sharing things she shouldn't, and she told me everything."

"So Theodore threw McCain under the bus."

"Ida McCain, that's Quentin's wife, never forgave Theodore, or any of the Wexlers. I think something snapped in her little head when Quentin died. You'd think she'd move away from Hunts Landing, but she didn't."

"She's still here?"

"Lives and breathes to stick it to the Wexlers. Ida blackballed Grace from the museum board last week."

"Really?" *This was too outrageous, even for Hunts Landing.* "Because of what Grace's father-in-law did?"

"Fifth year in a row." Madeleine shook her head. "Ida can carry a grudge like an Olympic torch bearer, and she's lugged this one around for forty years."

"Do you think she'll talk to me?"

"I think the only problem you'll encounter with Ida McCain is getting her to shut up." Madeleine held up her phone. "Siri, call Ida McCain."

CHAPTER THIRTEEN

Sunday, 12:33, the Cottage District

Abbie drove through the side streets of Hunts Landing, noticing the kids playing in the yards, people coming home from church, smelling the starts of the first barbecues of season, although, in reality, Hunts Landing people found a way to barbecue all year long. Plenty of SUVs, too.

It seemed that everyone in Hunts Landing owned a pickup truck, an SUV, or a minivan. She passed only one lime-green Toyota Prius. Most of the vehicles were muddy and dirty, because of the spring rains, and because the roads outside the city limits where unpaved and threw up chunks of mud with each passing yard.

Nothing special about that SUV, Abbie thought.

Ida McCain lived in the Cottage District north of the Square. "I've downsized," she explained, leading the way toward her patio. Abbie estimated her to be in her eighties, at least. A mix between Debbie Reynolds and Ellen Burstyn, Ida McCain must have been a knockout in 1969.

Ida's garden was bordered by just-budding blue hydrangeas. She poured two glasses of tea and plopped a lemon wedge into each glass. "Cheers!"

Abbie swallowed and almost choked. Mrs. McCain liked her iced tea *spiked.* "Wow!"

"Lemon Stoli." Ida downed half her glass. "Now. You want to discuss that dreadful Theodore Wexler."

"To be clear, I'm researching the murder of Rosalie DuFrayne."

"I remember that night. Dear Lord, do I remember that night." Ida's left eye was ticking. Abbie wondered if meeting Ida McCain was a good idea after all.

"I'm trying to see if there's a connection between the victim and the NASA grant scandal," Abbie explained.

"I'm not sure how the girl could possibly be connected," Ida said. "I mean, she only answered phones. However, Theodore had a soft spot for the girl. He made my Quentin take her on. Quentin didn't like it. Didn't like Theodore putting eyes into the department."

So, academic politics hadn't been constrained to the battle between the schools. The jealousies reigned within Hunts Landing College itself. "From what I read, Dr. Wexler didn't support your husband."

"Didn't *support?* Theodore Wexler as good as *killed* him. Theodore wanted the school to be *the* school associated with the Space program. He got what he wanted. Quentin handed Theodore success on a silver platter. Every news report about the Apollo mission named the college." Ida swirled her drink. "Money poured in like milk over corn flakes. Do you think they could have built the new campus and research facilities without the money raised by Quentin's work?"

Perhaps it was better to let Ida vent all her steam about Theodore Wexler first. "Before the scandal, did your husband consider Theodore Wexler a friend?"

Ida scoffed. "Good Lord, no! Quentin was merely an *employee* to Theodore. Quentin's brilliance couldn't be dismissed—only through his endless work, pushing the team as he did, was the guidance system finished on schedule. Some weeks, the team lived and slept in the lab, but did Theodore appreciate their dedication? Absolutely not! Theodore never thanked Quentin for the financial windfalls his efforts produced, but he was sure quick enough to get his picture taken with Buzz Aldrin in '71."

"Yet still your husband worked so hard—"

"Determination and *drive*, I tell you, and he *succeeded*." Ida McCain was adamant. "Wexler's party that night should have been Quentin's victory lap. Instead, that despicable excuse of a man ruined everything."

"I spoke to a couple of witnesses who say your husband and Old Dr. Wexler argued."

"Argued?" If Ida had any spit in her mouth, it would have wound up on Abbie. "More like a pistol whipping."

"What happened? Do you know?"

"Theodore summoned Quentin to his study. With the house full of guests and the entire town celebrating. Those ridiculous accusations. Quentin would stand for none of it. He left the party before Theodore spun any more of his lies."

Wexler's lies?

The image of Rosalie's papers flooded Abbie's mind. Cleta Blakebill had said that Rosalie had packed up those papers in an interoffice envelope and taken them away from the kitchen. Cleta hadn't seen them again, not when she and Rosalie and Cyrus had left Wexler House that night.

Abbie was convinced that Rosalie had given that envelope to Theodore Wexler. And that meant . . . "Mrs. McCain, the evidence presented during the trial . . ."

"Oh, posh, Abigail, those were falsified, and I know by whom. By Frank Wexler!"

"Frank Wexler? Professor of History?"

"Engineering student in '69, one of Quentin's. His father likely pressured Quentin to take him on. A sheer waste of time, because Frank Wexler never had the mettle to make a talented engineer."

Frank Wexler, an engineering student? Abbie doubted he'd used enough of his left-brain to have been successful, let along falsify any data, but why would Ida lie about something Abbie could so readily check? "I'm having trouble picturing Frank Wexler in engineering."

"Oh, he dropped out of the program as soon as he came back from Vietnam," Ida said. "Proves he had no intention of pursuing serious study. And he always loitered around the department between classes, even when he had no good reason to be in the building."

Abbie'd had no idea that Frank had served in Vietnam. Hunts Landing being so closely identified with the Depot, there was a large former-military population who'd retired here. Military service was a source of personal pride and distinction in Hunts Landing. Yet Abbie had had no idea he'd ever put on a uniform.

And Ida's suggestion that Frank Wexler could have fooled NASA reviewers wasn't making sense. To whose benefit would it have been? His father's? Abbie doubted that Theodore Wexler would have condoned such an act, as it would have been detrimental to the school. "Mrs. McCain, you're insinuating that an undergraduate student could create data that passed NASA's scrutiny—"

"Of *course* he was responsible," Ida McCain interrupted. "Frank Wexler falsified those test results and then gave them to his father and then that bastard Theodore Wexler handed them over to the prosecutor."

Oh gosh, I'd love to nail Frank Wexler for this, but it doesn't make sense. "Why would Frank do such a thing?"

"Theodore's jealousy of all the attention Quentin received. Many tried to recruit Quentin away, you see. All the big defense contractors, the major universities. They courted Quentin. We would have been . . . well, Theodore made sure the prosecutors indicted my husband on false charges and manufactured evidence. Then he testified against my man. What unspeakable malice, hidden from the world. I never dreamed Theodore capable of such rancor. Listening to him on the stand that day, so solid and so certain as he tore my husband to shreds with those lies. By God, I beheld the face of Evil that day." Ida gulped hungrily from her glass and poured herself another. Fat, salty tears trailed down her cheeks.

Abbie rummaged through her purse for tissues. "Mrs. McCain, I'm so sorry to keep coming back to this, but the night of the party, your husband left. Without you. Do you have any idea where he went?"

Ida wiped her tears with a delicate sweep of tissue against eyelash. "He went home, of course. Mayor Tully and his wife, Phoebe, were kind enough to give me a lift. I got home a little before one and found Quentin sound asleep on our couch. I'm afraid he'd been drinking. He never drank heavily, not before that night."

Sunday Afternoon, on the Side Streets of Hunts Landing

Abbie drove the short distance from the Cottage District back to the Garden District without noticing the street signs pass.

That Ida McCain was a bitter, bitter woman, one whose hatred for Theodore Wexler and, by extension, his son Frank Wexler, palpably tainted every memory. Abbie wasn't sure how much of what Ida had said she could trust.

However . . .

Ida suggested that Frank Wexler had loitered at the Engineering School office, where, according to Cleta Blakebill and Bernice Strong, Rosalie DuFrayne had worked seemingly endless hours. If Theodore suspected McCain in the first place, suspected something fishy, would he really insert two young kids into the Engineering School to spy for him—one, his son who couldn't be ignored, and another, a young Black woman who could easily be dismissed?

But Rosalie had brought a bunch of papers to Wexler House, papers she carried away with her in an envelope, perhaps the same papers Cyrus had seen on Old Dr. Wexler's blotter. And the description Cleta'd provided of the envelope, the old-fashioned kind, the kind with the cardboard circular tab and the string, exactly the type of interoffice memo the school had still relied on decades later when Abbie was a graduate student. Rosalie, being an employee of the school and also of Theodore Wexler's household staff, would know that plenty of those envelopes lay around the house. It was natural that Rosalie had gone and fetched an interoffice memo envelope to hold the papers she'd dropped in the kitchen when she'd gotten a whiff of fried catfish.

What if . . . what if Old Dr. Wexler sets up Frank and Rosalie in the Engineering school office. To keep their eyes on things. Frank, as a student, probably wouldn't have had any insight into the workings of the office, but Rosalie, as a student office-worker, would.

What if she found discrepancies, perhaps, in the documents she was asked to photostat? Nobody thought her a threat. Ida thought all she did was answer the phones. But Rosalie was smart. What if she kept copies and brought them to Wexler House the night of the party?

Abbie could visualize the halls of Wexler House, cleaned to a gleam for a party, people mulling about, and Rosalie, probably in uniform, carrying a handful of documents to Dr. Theodore Wexler's office . . .

On the night of Hunts Landings's moment of triumph, had Rosalie DuFrayne had the nerve to bring news that could topple that triumph?

It explained why the girl felt the need to leave town hours after the party at Wexler House.

Abbie's phone rang, and she finally realized the car was still running. She checked the number as she twisted the car key to the off position. *Will?* "Will, how are you?"

His voice was rumbly, as if he hadn't spoken regularly in a while. "My sister is a true jailor. One phone call. You're it. How's it going?"

As quickly as she could, omitting no pertinent facts, Abbie recounted what she'd found so far.

"I didn't think old Caleb Jackson would have left that clipping in his file without good reason," Will breathed. "And it's a good theory. You can connect the dots, from the Engineering School to Rosalie to Old Dr. Wexler to her needing to leave town. Doesn't explain why she was killed, though."

Abbie's subconscious had continued her line of reasoning, percolating ideas, which now bubbled to the surface. "I've got two witnesses who put Dr. McCain in a furious huff storming away toward the campus. Rosalie brought papers to Wexler House and left them there, Wexler and McCain had a terrible fight, McCain storms off. Later, McCain is indicted. If those papers were proof of McCain's crime, and Wexler confronted him with that proof, surely that's enough motive to kill Rosalie, the girl Wexler had planted in McCain's office?"

"But," Will breathed, and his breaths were audible, labored, "his wife said he was asleep on the couch when she got home."

"She didn't get home until hours later," Abbie reminded him. "It could explain why Rosalie was headed out of town, and why she had to die that night."

"It's an explanation," he agreed. "But there's another. You think she might have been pregnant, right? That's reason enough to leave town. And what about the father? He might have been upset enough to kill her."

Abbie considered that for a moment. "I do think she may have been pregnant, but I don't have any proof, just a hunch in my gut."

"I wouldn't dismiss your gut."

"A hunch in my gut doesn't explain why she had to leave that night," Abbie replied. The Sunday afternoon traffic was picking up a bit, folks getting home from after-church lunches. "And her friends insist all she did was study and work. She didn't have time for anyone on the side."

"Not on the side, perhaps. But what about Frank Wexler?" In the background, Abbie heard Will asking for a few more minutes. His sister, most likely. Will returned to the call. "I mean, Ida McCain puts him in the office all the time."

And as Miss Etta's daughter and herself as an employee, Rosalie would have been at Wexler House frequently. "I'd love to nail Frank Wexler with something, believe me, but merely being Rosalie's potential lover and hence the potential father of the potential baby doesn't give him a motive for killing her. Hide the relationship, yes, ask her to get an abortion, sure, but that's a far cry from murder. Plus, Cyrus Porter insisted that Frank Wexler was on the Quad while Rosalie was being murdered."

"Have you asked him?"

Abbie nodded. "Frank Wexler refuses to answer any questions regarding the Rosalie DuFrayne murder."

"Then," Will breathed, "you're asking the wrong question. Half a minute, sis! Go ask him what he was doing in the Engineering office all the time. Tell him McCain accused him of falsifying data. I bet you'll be surprised at his answer."

Sunday, 1:42 p.m., Close to Wexler House

Unsure of what to do next, Abbie pulled over a car length or two from the stop sign at Woodland and Franklin. She was only a few blocks away from Wexler House, a few blocks away from home. Unconsciously, she'd parked at roughly the midway point between.

Turn right at the stop sign, and she'd be on her way home. Go straight through the stop sign, and she would wind up at Wexler House.

Did she dare?

If old habits hadn't changed, Dr. Frank Wexler was spending his Sunday morning on his back patio with newspapers from New York and Chicago, a few academic journals, and a book or two, at a white cast-iron table overlooking the Quad. As one of Wexler's grad students, he had summoned her more than once to a Sunday morning meeting on his patio. Of course, in those days, Dr. Wexler had seemed larger than life, able to survey his domain from his elevated perch above the college commons. Now, he seemed to be a fragment of the man his father had been, the man who'd built Wexler House and the patio where Frank held court every Sunday.

Did she dare?

Before she could change her mind, Abbie started the car, shifted into gear, and drove through the stop sign.

She parked a little away from the house, a couple of cars from the driveway entrance, and grabbed her keys and phone. Her sneakers on the gravel driveway yielded a familiar crunch.

When she rounded the corner of the big house, she wasn't sure if she was surprised that Frank Wexler was there, at his white cast-iron table, or if she was disappointed. *People change, Dr. Wexler. Why haven't you?*

But there he was, with a thick newspaper in his fingers, the bridge of his nose visible above the top edge of the newsprint. True to form, he didn't stop reading as she drew closer, although Abbie didn't doubt he knew exactly who approached. She didn't give him much time to play his power game, but plopped herself into the seat across from him, turned toward the Quad, and breathed in the clean spring air. "I'd forgotten how lovely this view was."

On this lazy Sunday afternoon, the campus shone with tranquil beauty. The trees budded with young blooms and students, some studying under the mottled shade of spring trees, others doing the things that students do, occupying grassy patches between footpaths.

How many times had she also propped herself under a tree on the Quad, one eye on her book, the other on the house at the corner, where the Wexlers reigned?

"Abbie," Wexler said. He folded his newspaper as if with great reluctance, although Abbie doubted he was interested in much other than obituaries and the occasional historical human-interest story. "Can I interest you in some coffee?"

Abbie opted to play along with his politeness. He poured from a thermal carafe into an old-fashioned porcelain cup she recognized from grad school days.

His smile as he handed her the cup seemed almost genuine. "Have you made progress with your pet project?"

Fiddling with cream and sugar allowed Abbie to mask her irritation. "Quite a lot. It's amazing how many people in Hunts Landing still remember that night."

"The family is still not going to comment on Rosalie DuFrayne's murder," Wexler said, and lifted his own cup to his lips.

"I'm not here to get a comment on Rosalie," Abbie said with her own smile.

"Then to what do I owe the pleasure, Ms. Adams?"

"There was an odd newspaper clipping in Rosalie's file, and I couldn't figure out the connection at first, because it had absolutely nothing to do with Rosalie. The article was a story from 1971, two years after Rosalie died. It was about Dr. Quentin McCain, indicted for using false data to obtain NASA contracts for the school. Surely you remember the scandal?"

"I really can't tell you much," Wexler said. "I was in Vietnam when that scandal broke." There was the faintest hint of a smirk at the corner of his mouth.

"Yes, but did you know that Ida McCain accuses you of being the one who falsified the data in the first place? Surely, you'd like to comment on that?"

Wexler's laugh erupted from his belly, and he threw his head back. "Ida McCain! Well, that old biddy never ceases to amaze." He pulled a handkerchief to wipe laugh tears away from his eyes. "Sure, I'll comment on that."

Abbie pulled her phone out of her pocket and placed it on the table between them. "May I?"

"Of course." He continued to chuckle as he used the same handkerchief to clean his eyeglasses.

"The jury convicted McCain of multiple counts of fraud in relation to that test data. Ida McCain says your father inserted you into the Engineering School to spy on Quentin McCain, and when you couldn't find any evidence of wrongdoing, you made some up."

"Oh, Ida," Wexler sighed, still amused. He finished cleaning his glasses and repositioned them on his nose. "What she suggests doesn't hold water. I was a terrible engineering student. Couldn't handle the math. I didn't know the difference between a sine and a cosine, let alone make up NASA test data." He laughed again, shaking his head. "I'm sure I can dig up my old college transcript if you want proof."

"Then why were you in the Engineering Office all the time?" Abbie asked.

"Is that what Ida said?"

"I think the word Mrs. McCain used was 'loitered'."

"Oh, that's rich." Wexler sniffed and tucked his handkerchief away. "I don't believe I was in that office as much as Ida thinks I was."

"You dispute this?"

"Of course." Now, he uncrossed his legs, and leaned on the table with his elbows. "What on earth does this have to do with your investigation?"

Abbie mimicked his action, so that their heads were a couple of feet apart, and their eyes even with each other. "See, that's where the newspaper article comes into play. I couldn't find a connection. But then I found out that Rosalie worked in that office, too. You remember seeing her there, don't you?"

"Yes," Wexler admitted. Abbie could imagine gears churning in his brain, as he considered which facts she could probably confirm without his comment.

"See, I got to talk to quite a few people who were with Rosalie that last night, people who confirmed that when she wasn't studying, she was working in that office. I think your father placed Rosalie in that office, not you, to spy on McCain. Rosalie brought a big stack of papers to the house that night. I think she brought them to your father, because I have witnesses who say she didn't have them when she left."

"And you think this was the evidence of McCain's complicity?"

Abbie nodded. "During the party, your father and McCain had a blowout fight, and McCain stormed off. This was the night of the school's triumph, remember? They should have been celebrating! But, instead, McCain and your father fight, and Rosalie was headed out of town."

"Oh?" Wexler arched one bushy eyebrow.

"She had a bus ticket in her purse dated July 25th." Abbie sensed, rather than saw, his interest, perhaps an instinct born of years of listening to him tell a story, and recognizing when she'd piqued the curiosity of her professor.

"And you think she was leaving Hunts Landing because, what, because she feared repercussions from McCain?" He pursed his lips in thought.

"It's an explanation," Abbie said. "One I can print."

Wexler nodded. "I would have to agree, Abbie. It's an explanation."

Abbie smiled, then flicked the recorder off on her phone. She stood. "Thank you for the coffee. And the comments. It's the best theory I have, the one we'll go to press with." She nodded and turned to leave, but at the last minute stopped to face him. "At least, it's better than my other theory."

For once, his manners overrode his pomposity, and he stood in turn. "Which is?"

She caught his gaze, and willed herself not to blink, lest she miss a fraction of his response. "That Rosalie DuFrayne was leaving town because she was pregnant."

Sunday, 2:04 p.m., the War Room

Loreen's family hangover recipe was wearing off, and the dull pulse of pain returned to Joss's skull with increasing intensity. He popped two more Advils and willed the headache away. It was better to focus on Harry Lawlor's news than his deadline, only five days away. Amazing, what the addition of one paltry word in his browser's search bar revealed.

Previous searches for hidden Civil War treasure had resulted in so much junk that he'd been forced to discount the bulk of it. Now, however, he had a magic word.

Tunnel.

Jackpot.

There was still the mix of conspiracy theory sites touting Civil War gold hidden in tunnels as far north as Michigan, but plenty of reputable sites maintained by historians. Adding *North Alabama* to the search bar yielded the results Joss was searching for.

Limestone County was aptly named, as much of the land sat upon relatively soft limestone deposits. Ice houses were often dug deep into the limestone to ensure a supply of the cold stuff during hot summer months. And some larger plantations had tunnels between important outbuildings.

It wasn't outside the realm of possibility that there could be tunnels leading from the Grover House, as Harry Lawlor had suggested.

Yet, he'd found nothing in the Grover basement to suggest openings to other spaces.

Yikes. The bomb shelter.

Abbie had a map of Hunts Landing in 1969 spread flat at the far end of the long dining room table. Joss used the magnifying app on his phone to zoom in on the corner of Jefferson and Elm Streets.

When he'd gone down into the bomb shelter, the stairs led steeply down back toward the house. He estimated that the lower landing was only five or six feet inward from the upper one, maybe twenty feet downward. The door to the shelter had lain to his right, to the northwest.

Which meant the steel pill-shaped structure was directly underneath the driveway. Pointing toward the Lawlor House.

The Chenoweths had stuck an atomic bomb shelter into the tunnel like a cork, a bomb shelter that had had no possible chance of saving the family from an atomic bomb.

Joss hung his head, his fists involuntarily clenching at his side. He was right, he could feel it, and so close he could taste it, but his suppositions would never impress Kenetsky. He banged his fists on the table, and the expletive he should never use when there were kids somewhere in the house escaped his lips.

He hadn't heard Abbie come in, and didn't even know she was in the house, until he heard her admonish him. "Hey, watch it!"

His weary eyes looked up at her, but he couldn't manage a "Sorry."

"What's wrong?"

It came out in a gush. "There's a tunnel, a *tunnel* under Grover House, and it's probably where old Dr. Grover hid the town valuables —at least it's the likeliest place, but those dingbats who owned the house plugged it with a freaking *bomb shelter*, a big, fat, heavy steel can that wouldn't have saved them if the Russians attacked because there's an open air shaft straight up into the garage, but what did the Chenoweths care, they're the freaking people who put aluminum siding on a two-hundred-year-old house, and I've only got five days, and crap, my head hurts . . ."

It wasn't exactly a look of pity she gave him. Concern? Probably not.

Abbie let her bag slide off her shoulder onto the floor, then walked to his whiteboard. She scrutinized his notes for a minute or so, then pushed her sleeves up to her elbows. "Your background on the Grovers seems a little thin," she said finally.

"Saving it for the full script. I'll only get a few minutes to pitch, can't waste it on background."

"I'm not so sure," Abbie said, and reached into her back pocket for her phone. She started working her thumbs. "Finding out more about the family might land you some good nuggets for the pitch."

"Well, when you look at it that way . . . who're you texting?"

"Whitney." Abbie's thumbs flew rapidly over her phone.

"But, it's Sunday."

She shrugged. "The lot of the intern." Abbie finished texting. "Now, have you eaten anything today?"

His stomach warned him with an uncomfortable growl. "No, no food, please."

"Well, I'll make you another cup of the Oliver family recipe. And, then, you're going to take a nap."

CHAPTER FOURTEEN

Sunday, 12:41 p.m., the War Room

A bbie had settled down at her laptop with a cup of chai when George descended the stairs with the energy of a teenager who'd slept through breakfast and lunch. "Hey, Mom, can we take the car?"

"Who's we?" Abbie blew on the steam of her tea.

"Me and Martha. She needs some stuff for her school project."

"Oh, gosh, I forgot her project!" Between Rosalie DuFrayne and Joss, it had completely slipped her mind. "Was she peeved?"

"A bit. Loretta's coming over, remember?"

"Good grief." Abbie's heart ached with the pang of what Loreen called Single Mom Guilt. She hated letting Martha down. She fished some cash out of her wallet. "Get yourselves something to eat as well."

A few minutes later, Abbie faced her whiteboard, Ida McCain and Frank Wexler heavy on her mind. She couldn't reconcile the woman's memories of Rosalie simply answering phones with Bernice Strong's recollections of Rosalie working late nights. And she couldn't give any credence to Ida's theory of Frank Wexler manufacturing false evidence. But she'd clearly startled Frank with the news that Rosalie might have been pregnant, his reaction too pronounced for a man who claimed only a passing acquaintance with the daughter of his family's cook. Abbie felt it in her bones that there was much more to the relationship between Frank and Rosalie than met the eye. Juicy stuff, as Loreen would say, but nothing she could print. She'd learned her lesson well with the Puckett fiasco.

The NASA scandal, however, was fair territory.

Her phone's incoming message tone sang.

Nick: Can we talk?

Abbie watched the font of the text change from the unread bold to the plain font meaning "read." Was she ready to talk to Nick? She didn't trust her mouth and the words that might pop out of it. She turned the phone over and placed it softly on the table. Pushing Nick Preston out of her head, she pulled up Newspapers.com to try another search. One search term and two clicks led her to the testimony of the NASA Inspector General from 1972. The falsified test data appeared authentic enough to pass the review process at several levels. Only a trained engineer could counterfeit those results. And there was no way McCain himself could remain unaware of the fraud. A chain of thoughts began crystalizing in her mind, growing stronger with each second. Abbie grabbed a dry erase marker and scribbled before the nebulous idea dissipated.

Theodore Wexler—>Rosalie (informer)—>Engr. Dept.—>Papers 2 party—>T. Wexler—>Fight w/McCain—>McCain leaves—>Rosalie leaves (no papers)—>Rosalie killed—>McCain no alibi. She circled the last link in the chain twice with a red marker.

Oh, good God. Abbie leaned back against the table, unaware of her uncapped whiteboard marker. It was a theory, for sure, and one the paper could probably print. What was it they always said in the movies? *You can't slander the dead.*

The second dose of the Oliver family hangover cure worked like a charm. Joss had skipped down the stairs, much like George had a few hours earlier, freshly showered and with no obvious lingering effects of Jethro's moonshine. "Gonna get stuff for dinner." Abbie accepted the fact that he was interested in food as a good sign.

Now he was bossing her around in her own kitchen.

"It's just tacos, Joss," she complained.

"It's Tacos à la Joss. You must pay attention." He diced tomatoes into precise cubes, and Abbie envied his knifework. "Tell me why you have a big red circle on your whiteboard."

At the stove, she browned ground sirloin. *When did Joss start paying attention to my whiteboard?* "I've got a theory." She brought Joss up to speed, then stopped to taste. *Needs something.* She twisted the pepper grinder a few times and then concluded her recap with, "If I'm right, McCain had the strongest motive. Rosalie's wounds were savage, a sign that her killer knew her and was angry."

"So, you've given up on Wexler being your bad guy?"

"I can't get around the fact that Cyrus Porter placed Frank on the Quad, not without dismissing Cyrus's other testimony. Gosh, Joss, I really wanted to nail him, but Frank couldn't have been in two places at the same time. And Frank had no motive to *kill* her, even if he was the alleged father of her alleged baby. Meat's done." Abbie turned off the burner. "I really don't think he did it. The night of the party, I think Rosalie handed Old Dr. Wexler proof of the fraud and McCain's complicity and, concerned about repercussions, planned to skip town."

"But wouldn't Wexler protect her?"

"On campus, perhaps, but off-campus, Cyrus told me it was still very much a white-versus-Black world." Abbie wiped her hands on a dish towel. "Besides, I don't think Rosalie would walk away from her education unless she thought she had no options."

"Well, it's a good theory. I think your editor is going to like it."

"I hope so," she said. "I can't prove Rosalie's papers came from the Engineering Department, I can't prove she gave them to Theodore Wexler, I can't prove McCain didn't go straight home like his wife insists."

Joss arranged bowls for a taco assembly line. "Why don't you contact the department? Maybe they kept records."

George rushed into the kitchen. "Food ready?" George possessed food-detecting sonar.

"Start without me!" Abbie said. She brought up the Hunts Landing College website, browsed to the School of Engineering. On the *Faculty & Staff* tab, she found the name of the current dean, Dr. Tyler Nesmith, and a link to his email. She clicked the link and started typing.

Dr. Nesmith. My name is Abbie Adams, and I am researching a story for *The Hunts Landing Times*, regarding the NASA grant scandal in the early seventies. Does the department maintain any archives? I'd like to look through the records, tomorrow if possible—I'm up against a deadline.

Sunday, 6:37 p.m., Under the Willow Tree

No one was paying any attention to Joss. *Good.* Abbie and three teenaged girls huddled around the kitchen island with poster boards, scissors, glue, and printouts of various countries in the European Union. He wouldn't be missed. He grabbed Benny's leash and led the dog out the front door.

Abbie barely looked up at him.

Had Jethro come? Was he out here, watching the house as promised?

Last night, the notion of an ex-cop watching Abbie Adams's house had seemed silly. Tonight, with sober clarity, Joss admitted it wasn't a bad idea. The old-fashioned streetlamps cast a dim yellow light, creating many shadows. Anybody could hide, unnoticed. Still, Joss saw no black SUV in any direction.

And he'd been watching for them, for any SUV that drove a little too slowly past the house. His eyes were on the windows more than anything else. Abbie had tried to explain that most people in Hunts Landing owned a pickup or an SUV. That factoid did little to settle his nerves.

He decided to walk Benny around the block and see if he could spot Jethro, though his gut told him he wouldn't find Jethro unless Jethro wanted to be found. Indeed, he'd barely gotten past the driveway when a bird sounded, low, lyrical. Benny's ears pricked, and the dog tugged the leash toward a weeping willow whose branches hung like a curtain to the ground, across the street from Abbie's front door.

After checking the street for cars, Joss unlatched the leash and let Benny go. The mutt galloped straight for the weeping willow.

The closest streetlamp cast an amber glow in front of the tree, making what was behind the branches all but invisible. Joss ducked under the leafy boughs, which spread like an umbrella, leaving space underneath.

He found Jethro near the trunk of the ancient tree, sitting in a lawn chair with a cooler at his side, scratching Benny's scruff.

"You survived last night," Jethro drawled.

"No permanent damage."

"I brought the moonshine, if you're wantin' any."

No way, not after last night. "Are you serious?"

"Gotcha." He patted the top of the cooler. "Have a Coke. You tell Abbie I'm here?"

"No, sir." Joss grabbed an icy soda can from the cooler, then sat on the lid. "She's got her hands full with teenagers."

Thankfully, Jethro didn't ask him to explain. "Better that way, at least for now. She's got a houseful of kids, that's what she should worry about tonight."

"You really think there's going to be trouble?"

Jethro shrugged. "A buddy at the station called earlier. Told me about Porter, how Abbie was the last known person to see him alive. Coincidence? I don't care too much for coincidences. Trouble? Two black SUVs have already driven by this house, but one had Georgia plates and a parking sticker from the college, and the other one was so muddied up I couldn't make out a plate."

Joss felt rather than saw Jethro's eyes peering at him. "Loverboy came and questioned her today." He related the details of Nick's visit.

Jethro swore under his breath. "Aw, dang it, anybody in town could tell that kid he was barking up the wrong tree. Why would Abbie go and shoot somebody she'd just met?"

"I don't think she did, but she did have a gun that matched the, what is it, caliber?"

"Shoot, Matt Adams was a gun collector. Historical pieces, mostly. There are more guns in that house than Preston realizes." Jethro drank from his own Coke. "Forensics will clear her. Waste of Preston's time, I suppose, but every out-of-towner's got to come to the realization that Hunts Landing's not like a big city on his own."

Benny ducked under Jethro's fingers and went to sniff the perimeter of the circle made by the willow's branches. The men sat quietly for a bit, watching the dog, making sure Benny didn't suddenly dart out of hiding.

It was like a cave, this space. Perfect for a stakeout. Joss could make out Abbie's front porch through the leaves.

Caves reminded Joss of his conversation with Harry Lawlor. "Hey, Jethro. You ever hear of tunnels between houses around here?"

Jethro thought for a moment. "Hear, yes. Seen with my own eyes? No." Headlights appeared on Westbrook Street. Men and dog's attention flipped up to high alert mode. None moved until the vehicle was out of sight.

Only when he heard Jethro's loud exhale did Joss realize he'd held his own breath.

"Never saw a tunnel," Jethro continued, as if no car had approached Abbie's house. "'Course, I saw quite a few sinkholes that'd bust open when the city started pavin' Hunts Landing proper. Stood traffic patrol then, when I was a rookie, more often than I care to remember, 'cause it would take the road crews a couple of weeks to do the repairs. But a tunnel? Nope. Never saw one."

Monday, 7:41 a.m., Hunts Landing Middle School

"Mom! The door!"

Abbie fumbled with the lock to the passenger door. Martha, carrying her poster board project, squirmed out of the car.

George flipped through flashcards, some last-minute studying for his physics test, and the quiet of the car was fine with her. Sleep had eluded her the previous night, troubled and broken by wisps of dream. Sometimes Cyrus Porter begged her to find justice for Rosalie. Sometimes Nick stood before her with her Beretta, chanting, "Just a robbery." Sometimes it was Rosalie in a maid's uniform at the party. Sometimes it was Zach, holding his flag, folded precisely thirteen times. Fits of clammy wakefulness separated the sleepy tendrils.

She crawled through the carpool lane on autopilot and headed toward the high school more by muscle memory than by intent. And when she dropped George off, she remembered his test. She wasn't sure George heard the "Good luck!" thrown at him last minute.

Instead of going straight back home, she headed for the Calvary Baptist Church. As she parked, her phone buzzed.

Nick: Call me, please.

One night's sleep hadn't eased her heart. *Not yet, Nick, not this morning.* This time, Abbie put Nick's number in do-not-disturb mode. She'd call him after lunch, maybe, or tonight, perhaps.

Rosalie's gravestone appeared brighter under the morning's gray skies. Thursday had been sunny, the big oak tree providing dark and cool shade over the grave. She read the inscription again. Cyrus's face swam before her. She felt her skin crawl, as if Cyrus were watching her, and not pleased with Abbie disturbing Rosalie as she slept.

Oh, for chrissake, Abigail! She shook her head to chase the ghost away.

She knelt in front of Rosalie's grave. "I guess Cyrus is up in Heaven with you. He wanted me to bring you justice. I don't know if I can, but I'm going to try. I promise, people in Hunts Landing are going to learn about the horrible way your life was cut short."

"Are you Abigail Adams?"

She turned around to face a short Black man, only five feet or so, wearing a black suit and tie. She didn't recognize him, but his voice was unmistakable. "Reverend Fisher?"

"I saw your car, took a chance. Is your research going well?"

"I'm making progress. Luckily, I found a few folks who remember Rosalie DuFrayne. Unfortunately," she paused, uncomfortable, "one of those same helpful people was killed this weekend."

The pastor's face saddened. "You must mean Cyrus. Terrible tragedy. His wife is, oh, I want to say, second cousin to Mrs. Leonard. The family is over at the Porter place."

"How horrible for Mrs. Leonard." Abbie had genuinely enjoyed meeting the woman only a few days ago, and her heart ached for her loss.

"She mentioned she had some information for you," Reverend Fisher said, touching his temple. "She told me the details, but I'm afraid I don't remember."

"It's nothing that can't wait," Abbie assured him. "Has the family finalized the arrangements?"

He nodded. "Here, tomorrow. Nine o'clock."

"I'll be here," she said. "I only met Cyrus once, but I really liked him."

Back at her car, Abbie checked her phone. There was a single message. Miss Adams, this is Dr. Nesmith's admin. He got your message, and it so happens his next meeting canceled. He can meet you now, if you like.

Monday, 8:29 a.m., Abbie's House

Joss answered the doorbell after its third insistent buzz.

Madeleine swept into the house, her orange sneakers brightening an otherwise plain outfit of jeans and blue cambric shirt. "What took you so long to answer the door? And why isn't Abbie answering her phone?" she demanded.

"Well, Miss Madeleine," Joss replied. "I had to hoof it from the back porch, problem was that Benny was on top of me at the time. As for Abbie, she texted something about a meeting on campus."

"Well, never mind. It's you I want to talk to." Without waiting for an invitation, Madeleine headed straight for the coffeepot and poured herself a cup. "I've learned something that's sure to interest you." She carried her cup out to the sunporch and made herself comfortable.

Dutifully, Joss followed. "I hope it's better than my non-tunnel tunnels."

"Huh? Oh, don't tell me. You need to hear this. I was at the club last night, and of course most of the chatter was about the Grover House auction this Saturday, and what with all the old biddies speculating about how much the family is going to get for the place, especially after they let it go to pot and all, there were plenty of

Grover stories to go around. But it was something that Fiona Lemon said that piqued my curiosity. Oh, my, this coffee is wonderful. Did you make it?"

Joss was scribbling the name Fiona Lemon into his mental note-book. "Yes, ma'am."

"You could teach some folk around here something about coffee, that's for certain. Well, last night, Fiona Lemon—normally I avoid the woman like the bubonic plague, she's as sour as her surname. Fiona's momma was a midwife in town before the war—that's the Second World War—and not one of the respectable ones, if you catch my meaning."

"You mean, she was one of those you went to if you got into trouble?"

"Precisely. Whether or not you wanted to keep the baby, Fiona's momma was the one the good girls in town consulted. Though known for her discretion, she blabbed all to her daughter. That is, according to Fiona, and you've got to take what that woman says with a fistful of salt." Madeleine placed her hands on her thighs and leaned forward, "Last night, Fiona swore that her momma delivered a Grover baby, out of wedlock, in the thirties."

"Sorry, Madeleine." Joss opened his hands, palm up. "I'm not following how this has to do with any Civil War treasure."

"Well then, you've got to let me *finish*, son." Madeleine began rooting around in her handbag, a modest cross-body bag that didn't match her orange sneakers. "Well, I couldn't remember anyone telling me that particular story before, so I got up good and early this morning and went down to the Historical Society to have a look. I really do need to get some help in there to help me organize those files. Anyway, turns out there were four Grover children of age in the thirties, three girls and a boy. Two of the girls married and moved away. The son, Ted Grover, stayed."

"Oh, I'm ahead of you now," Joss said. "Just a second." He retrieved the clippings from the war room and let her read them. "The Grover family fortunes seem to have gone downhill after Ted died."

"Mmm. Perhaps. The Depression hit this town hard, and even some of the most prominent families suffered. But Ted's not the most important Grover. It was the third daughter, Eudora. I found a picture of her from 1927. Look close."

Creases marred the black-and-white photograph, but the young woman looking up from the paper square with scalloped edges had sad eyes and a sadder mouth. "What am I looking for?"

"Look on her left cheek."

Joss squinted. "What, these two moles?"

"In my day they we called them 'beauty marks,'" Madeleine said. "Once Elizabeth Taylor came on the scene, all the girls wanted one. But Eudora had two. And I recognize those two beauty marks." Madeleine handed him a second photograph.

In this photo, an older Eudora posed portrait-style with a forced smile, the beauty marks prominent on her left cheek. Joss still couldn't guess the importance of this information. "Okay, I give."

"You see, sweet child, that picture isn't of Eudora Grover. No, that picture is of a matriarch of one of the most influential families this town has ever seen, a family who came from nowhere and whose fortunes sky-rocketed after World War II. That, my young Californian friend, is a photo of Eudora *Wexler*."

Monday, 9:08 a.m., the School of Engineering

Nesmith's admin directed Abbie to go to Ellesby Hall on the Quad instead of the New Campus. She parked behind the building, entered through the staff door, and headed straight for the elevators. Dr. Nesmith and staff occupied space on the fourth floor.

Mrs. Couch met her by the elevator. "It's such a maze up here. This will be home for a while, but not too long, I hope. You remember those storms a couple of weeks ago? Tore holes in the roof. The water made it all the way down to the basement." Indeed, the hall smelled of old, damp cardboard, of disuse and decay.

Mrs. Couch led them through a labyrinth of narrow halls lined with storage boxes. "They call it the New Campus, but those buildings are over forty years old." She stopped at an old-fashioned wooden door with a frosted glass window and a sign reading "School of Engineering" taped to the glass. "Here we are."

Dr. Tyler Nesmith stood up from behind a scarred wooden desk, a balding man with spectacles and an academic paunch. "Miss Adams. Please excuse the mess."

They shook hands. "Thank you for squeezing me in," she said.

"So, *The Times* wants to do a story on the grant scandal? Forty-year exposé or something?"

Abbie opened her notebook. "Not quite, no. The story I'm researching is about a 1969 murder. Rosalie DuFrayne."

"Rosalie!"

Surprised, she asked, "You knew her?"

He tilted his head. "Of course I knew her. She was a classmate."

She explained the scandal article in Caleb Jackson's file, and Cleta Blakebill's recollection of Rosalie dropping papers. "It's only theory, but I think Old Dr. Wexler installed Rosalie in the department as a spy, and she brought evidence regarding the falsified data to the party."

He frowned. "Are you implicating Quentin McCain in Rosalie's murder?"

"Not without direct evidence, no." *Tread carefully, Abbie.* "Witnesses that tell me Rosalie brought papers to Wexler House but didn't leave with them. Months later, Theodore Wexler testified against McCain. I'd like to confirm the theory, one way or another. That's what I'm here for, departmental records that might firm up those connections."

Tyler brought his fingertips together like a teepee. "Dr. McCain certainly took off in a hellfire snit that night."

Abbie's jaw dropped. "You were *there*?"

"At the party? Sure. Frank Wexler was one of my best friends. David Breckenridge and I attended the Wexler party as Frank's guests."

She pushed scandal questions aside. "Can you tell me about the party? I heard the perspective of the staff, but not of the guests."

His gaze focused on the college ring on his right ring finger, a ring he twirled with this thumb. "I haven't thought about this in years." He exhaled a deep breath. "Damn, we were young! Nineteen, twenty. Full of spit and vinegar. As undergrads, we didn't take part in the research that was about to make the school famous, but dammit, we didn't care, we walked around like we owned the place. Stupid, naïve kids. That night, the three of us celebrated like we had just came back from the Moon ourselves. Miss Nevelyn insisted on white dinner jackets, except David and I didn't own any, so we borrowed a couple of old ones from Dr. Wexler. Still, the three of us strutted like James Dean and Brando and Cary Grant, all wrapped up into one cocky mess. The girls came with us to the house, my girl Katie and David's girl, Valerie Rigsby. David loved teasing her, would sing *Eleanor Rigby* to her, except he sang *Valerie Rigsby*." He grinned, a lopsided grin that crinkled his eyes.

"What about Grace Wexler? Was she there?"

He had to think for a moment. "Yes, she was there, but she and Frank weren't an item then. She was Grace Volbracht, daughter of one of McCain's researchers."

"Then who was Frank Wexler with?"

Tyler shrugged. "If I remember right, Frank stagged it that night."

"That seems weird, going dateless to a party like that."

"Well, the thing with Frank was, being a Wexler, he was more of the chasee than the chaser, if you know what I mean?"

Try as she might, Abbie couldn't imagine Frank Wexler being a hot ticket. "So, what do you remember of the party?"

"Miss Nevelyn relegated us youngsters to the lower patio, not entitled to mingle with the up-and-ups of Hunts Landing society." His nose tilted up when he said the word *society*, and he winked. "We had a terrific view of the fireworks. I remember that's when McCain took off in a huff, during the fireworks, because he pushed through our group and went down the stairs to the Quad."

"Do you remember what time he left?"

"After forty-six years? You're lucky I recall any of this."

Perhaps he'd seen Rosalie leave? "Did you stay for the rest of the party?"

"No, after the pyrotechnics had finished, some guys from the other houses—we were Kappa Lambda's—started a bonfire down by the river. And it was getting close to the girls' curfew time. I guess we got to the river about twenty after eleven. It was a good shindig while it lasted. Lots of beer, some girls from town, a little pot. Lots of toasts to Neil and Buzz. I didn't find David and Frank at first, not until after the fight broke out. The party went from a typical frat thing to chaos in a minute. Frank got beat up pretty bad. David took him home."

Frank Wexler getting beat up? Abbie squelched the tiny tinge of satisfaction. "You didn't help them?"

"David had it handled." His smile was forced, tired, and clearly uncomfortable with the notion that he'd neglected his friends that night. "Now, back to Rosalie. As to her being Old Dr. Wexler's spy, well, you're correct, she worked a lot of hours in the office, but so did a lot of other people the semester before Apollo 11."

And Tyler would know, as he was in that office often. "Mrs. McCain remembers Rosalie answering phones and making coffee."

"That's not the way I remember it, but, then again, it's been over forty years."

"I need to confirm Rosalie's activities," Abbie said. "Do you think there might be anything in the department's files that can help?"

"Miss Adams, you passed all our existing records outside in the halls. Everything we salvaged from the storm is out there."

Her excitement fizzled.

Even if any documents remained from 1969, she didn't have the time to climb all over those boxes and search.

"Knock knock!" A petite woman with coiffed platinum gray hair, and wearing a navy suit, peered into the office. "Are you ready?"

"Almost, dear. Katie, meet Abigail Adams."

"Miss Adams." Katie Nesmith extended her hand.

"This young lady is on assignment for *The Times*, researching the NASA grant scandal from the '70s," Tyler offered as an introduction and explanation.

"Oh, that old nonsense?" Katie asked. "Can't *The Times* find a more interesting story to print?"

"The piece is about an unsolved murder from July 1969," Abbie explained.

"Yes, of course, the Black girl," Katie said. "Well, that is more interesting than some musty old grant scandal."

Abbie raised a brow. *Didn't she remember her name? Her husband did.* "I believe the scandal is connected to the murder," Abbie said. "Rosalie DuFrayne, the murder victim, worked in the office, and it's possible she discovered evidence of the falsified test results and turned them over to Old Dr. Wexler."

"How interesting!" Katie turned to her husband. "You simply must help this young lady out."

"Those records are such a mess." He cocked his head toward the door, beyond which the stacked boxes of the department's records blocked the hallway. "Besides, I'm not sure we want to connect the school to the scandal."

"Nonsense, didn't the courts clear the school of any institutional wrongdoing in the seventies?" Her smile revealed perfect white teeth. "Can't you recruit an undergrad to dig through some dusty boxes?"

Abbie liked Katie Nesmith—she was a woman used to taking charge.

"Of course," Tyler conceded. "Miss Adams, we'll do what we can. When do you need this by?"

"If I'm not too pushy, as soon as possible. My deadline is Wednesday."

"Then we should get cracking." Dr. Nesmith went to the outer office to give instructions to Mrs. Couch.

Katie Nesmith smiled at Abbie. "Wonderful work you're doing. Don't let anyone get in your way."

Monday, 11:11 u.m., Abbie's Kitchen

Abbie had barely tossed her car keys onto the kitchen counter when both Joss and Benny attacked.

Benny stood on hind legs, placed his paws on her thighs, and barked. He wanted outside.

Joss was only slightly less vociferous. "Abs, you gotta hear what we found out, you're never gonna believe—" The doorbell rang. "Flippin' Grand Central Station," he muttered as he went to answer it.

Abbie let Benny out the sunporch door. She heard Joss's, "Can I help you?"

A familiar woman's voice answered. "Abigail Adams, please."

"Sure. Who's calling?"

"Grace Wexler."

Abbie's hand froze, the sunporch door still ajar. She should have expected this. She had violated Frank Wexler's space yesterday. Of course he'd send Grace to violate hers. Abbie shuddered, then shook off the chill.

Grace couldn't help the monster she'd married.

Joss led the way to the sunporch. Grace paused in the dining/ war room briefly to take in the Rosalie DuFrayne wall. A tallish woman, she usually wore flats. Abbie recalled a photographer hired to photograph the Wexlers, and Mrs. Wexler insisting on sitting down so no one could tell she was the same height as her husband.

"Why are you here?" Abbie asked. She had no time for pleasantries.

"Oh, I think you know," Grace said. "Your ridiculous investigation."

Abbie bristled. "*The Times* doesn't find it ridiculous."

"Of course it is. The worst sort of yellow journalism. How could you?"

The need to defend overwhelmed Abbie. "I disagree. Rosalie DuFrayne's unsolved murder is a dark spot on our town's history."

"Rosalie's family are all dead. There are no recipients of justice for that girl. May I sit?" Grace took a seat when Abbie nodded. "What good are you doing?"

It was a question Abbie'd asked herself often in the past few days. "I'm bringing facts to light."

"What will those facts of yours do but disparage my family? What's going to happen to Nora and Gregory when their granddaddy's name pops up in connection with a murder? Or when Frank's name—"

Abbie's hands flew open, and she pointed her shaking fingers at Grace. "Do you honestly think I give a *damn* what happens to your husband? I hope he's uncomfortable, I dream of him squirming. I pray to God every night Frank Wexler loses sleep over what might be in the story. Because I hope he gets assigned to the worst cave in Hell and *rots* in it!" Abbie's breath heaved, and she gulped, unclenching teeth.

She paced to rid herself of the sudden nervous energy. "Do you have any idea what happens to a failed Ph.D. candidate? No one answered my calls. I was *published* for chrissake, in reviewed journals, and suddenly I was *nobody*. I had no work. No money came in. History majors don't have a future once their mentor trashes their research." She grabbed Grace's shoulders, hard. "I had to go to a food bank for baby formula." Her voice sank to a whisper, garbled with tears. "Have you ever begged for your baby's food?"

She let Grace's shoulders go; her own slumped.

"Abbie, surely your parents left you money."

How like someone who had money to assume everyone else did.

"They did," Abbie said, "and I put all of it into trust funds for the kids the week after Martha was born."

"Didn't you receive benefits from the Army?" Grace raised her eyebrows.

"Benefits?" Abbie wiped her eyes. "There was a mix-up at the VA. I kept my maiden name, but someone put Abigail Youngblood on his records. All my identification read Adams, not Youngblood. And the computer systems had a glitch with Canadian records. We'd gotten married in Quebec. Should have been easy to fix, but then again, we're talking the VA. It took a year. Oh, what the hell." Abbie wiped her eyes again and strode to the kitchen. "I'll fix us a drink."

She didn't care what time it was. A perverse sense of humor drove her to take the last of an old bottle of Woodford Reserve from the liquor cabinet and pour two glasses, neat. Abbie found her guest in the war room, staring at the Rosalie DuFrayne wall. Abbie inhaled, willing the sudden anger down to a simmer, because this was Grace Wexler, not Frank. She had to remind herself of that. "To Theodore Wexler." Abbie gulped half her drink, swallowed, and gulped the rest. "For what it's worth, everything I've found so far tells me that Theodore Wexler was a philanthropist and humanitarian. Rosalie DuFrayne gave him evidence implicating Quentin McCain in the NASA grant scandal. That's as far as the Wexler family goes in this story. I have no desire to besmirch the Wexler name just because I wish your husband would go to hell. Now, please go."

Grace Wexler held her drink up so that the tumbler was between her eyes and Abbie's. She held it there for a moment, then placed it, untouched, on the coffee table, and quietly let herself out. Abbie stared at the Rosalie wall, staring but not seeing. She felt a warm hand on her shoulder. Joss. She'd forgotten he was in the house. "I'm sorry you heard that."

His voice was soft behind her. "Abs, I had no idea."

"I don't exactly go around blubbering about my failures."

"Not failures. Setbacks, followed by recovery."

She smiled and wiped a last tear away with her finger when her phone buzzed in her back pocket of her jeans. Loreen.

Loreen: Why aren't you taking Nick's calls?

"It's called do-not-disturb, pal of mine," Abbie muttered, her thumbs rapidly tapping a response.

"Abs, listen," Joss tried.

"Just a second." The phone buzzed again.

Sylvia: Need an update.

Damn. Her heart skipped a beat. Nick and Loreen and Sylvia and Grace Wexler and Frank Wexler, she could handle one at a time. Not all of them in a single twenty-four-hour period. Not today.

"Abs—"

Benny was scratching at the outer door. *Even Benny . . .* Her breath started coming faster. It was harder to catch. She spun away from Joss, needing just a minute, just a few feet of space.

"Abbie, I've got to tell you something—"

"Dammit, Joss! Even my toddlers knew that there were just some times it wasn't a good idea to pester me."

His jaw dropped. "Are you calling me a baby?"

"Yes! I raised two of them. I *know* how a baby behaves!"

"This is important."

"*Everything* is important to you, Joss, especially things the rest of us don't think is. Only your ego is telling you that whatever you have to say is important. Your immature, self-indulgent, name-all-my-recipes-after-myself, I'm-a-TV-star-but-don't-have-any-adoring-fans-handy, pain-in-the-ass ego!" At that moment, she didn't care how bitchy she sounded. She grabbed her car keys.

"Where are you going?"

"Lunch."

Slamming the door behind her felt *good*.

CHAPTER FIFTEEN

Monday, 11:31 a.m., the Cottage District

A bbie changed her mind and left the keys in the car before stalking out through the garage door.

Hunts Landing was enjoying another spectacular March day, with the Garden District's azaleas coming into full bloom. The beauty of the shrubs barely registered. She stomped for five blocks before her temper cooled enough for her to notice she'd headed toward the New Campus.

She stopped for the light, grateful for the pause so she could decide where to head next.

Maybe she should have let Joss stay at the inn. Then he wouldn't be underfoot. He wouldn't be complaining about bomb shelters stuffed into imaginary tunnels. He wouldn't be pestering her for attention. He wouldn't be in her house, taking over her kitchen, and feeding everybody steak and who-knew-what-else à la Joss.

If his made-for-TV derrière were handy, she'd stuff her four-year-old Nike sneaker right into it. Nike à la Abbie.

Except . . .

The *Walk* sign blinked at her.

Except that this project was as important to Joss as Rosalie was to her. The only difference, so far, was that Joss's questions hadn't yielded any dead witnesses.

A robbery gone bad, Nick had said.

Do you really believe that, Abbie?

The *Walk* signal blinked again as she pecked out her text.

Abbie: Do you have time to meet me?

The reply came a moment later.

Jethro: Yup.

Abbie: Where?

Jethro: Stop walking. I'm a block behind you.

Abbie wasn't sure how long her jaw had been dropped open when Jethro pulled up next to her on the sidewalk in his pickup truck. She opened the passenger door and climbed in. "What are you doing on this side of town?"

Jethro grinned and cut the engine. "Just catching up with a friend. What's up, little girl?"

Something about his grin didn't sit right, but Abbie pushed the thought aside, just like she was pushing aside thoughts of Joss and Nick and Frank Wexler. "Did you hear about Cyrus Porter?"

"Read the paper. Looks like robbery."

"Nick came to tell me last night. He took Daddy's Beretta. Said the caliber was .32 ACP."

"Interestin'," he mused.

"I thought so, too." She shifted in her seat to face him better. "Unusual choice of caliber for a robber. The ATF website lists the top ten firearms used in crimes. All large caliber, lots of firepower, nothing in the .32 range. What do you think?"

Jethro sniffed. "You messin' with an active police investigation?"

She shrugged. "The choice of ammunition seems odd to me."

"I think your daddy taught you too much about firearms. You have another piece, right? One you can shoot in a pinch? Oh, don't you give me that Jethro-you're-a-moron-look. You keep that piece handy. Other than that, stay away from Preston's investigation."

"Don't you find the circumstances weird? I talk to Cyrus, and hours later he's killed?"

"Can't tell ya, but if Preston thought there was a connection, he'd have brought you in for a formal interview already. Besides, ballistics is going to clear you." He focused on the truck hood.

"It's just . . . I liked him. Cyrus."

"He was pleasant enough when I arrested him," Jethro remembered.

He'd spoken to the hood, not to her face. Was he deliberately averting his eyes? It was something the kids had done, when they were younger, and hiding who broke the TV remote from her. And he was telling her to keep a firearm 'handy'?

"Jethro, do the kids and me need to leave the house?"

He watched a couple of cars roll through the stop sign ahead before finally answering. "I find the circumstances odd. Joss told me about the black SUV. Made this cop's nose twitch, I can tell ya. I was watching your house last night, keepin' my eye on things."

Abbie's lips parted, and she placed her fingertips against them as she digested this news. "Joss never said anything."

"Asked him not to."

"But where?"

"Underneath that big willow."

As a child, she and Loreen had built secret clubhouses under that willow tree. Abbie had to admit, the tree was the place she'd pick if she were on a stakeout. "Y'all should have told me."

"I'm tellin' you now."

Abbie swallowed, sucked in some breath, and swallowed again. "Do I need to get us away from here? You're not a cop right now;

you're Daddy's friend. Do we need to leave? What are you *not* telling me?"

He held her eye for a moment. "There was a lot more traffic in your neighborhood than there should be on a Sunday night, your visitors not withstandin'. My nose is still twitchin'. Now I don't know if what happened to Porter has anything to do with you or your story, but I'm gonna err on the side of caution. You've got people coming in and out of your house all the time. That's good. Busy deters. In the meantime, I'll be there, under that very tree, every night, until Preston catches Porter's killer."

Monday, 12:36 p.m., Hunts Landing

Abbie walked into the kitchen, one hand waving a Kleenex. "Truce!"

Joss had fretted since she'd left. They'd bickered plenty in college, two history geeks who probably spent too much time with each other than was good for them. But now, as Martha would say, they were grown-ups. "Does this mean you forgive me for being a horse's ass?"

"Do you forgive me for being a sharp-tongued harpy?"

Joss laughed, and the chill between them dissipated.

She fetched a bottle of water from the fridge. "So, what was it you wanted to tell me before I turned into Mrs. Hyde?"

Oh, he finally had her attention! "Madeleine came by—oh, by the way, that notable lady does not like it when you don't answer your phone. But she brought some interesting news. It appears that your Frank Wexler is also, wait for it . . ." He closed his eyes to savor the moment. "Frank Wexler is also a Grover."

"Get outta town!"

Oh, her expression. It was a beautiful thing to catch Abbie Adams flat-footed with a historical tidbit.

"Tell all," she said, and he did, explaining the connection between the Wexler and Grover families.

"How did Maddie not know this before?"

"Shotgun wedding, no announcements in the paper." Joss led the way to the war room, where the map of Hunts Landing in 1969 occupied the end of the dining table. "So, that got me thinking. I'm fairly certain that the Chenoweths installed that bomb shelter in the tunnel between Grover House and the Lawlors' place. Harry Lawlor said his great great—wait, it might be three greats—anyway some great grandfather of his courted one of the Grover girls via that tunnel. But, I'm wondering, what if that wasn't the only tunnel?"

His finger traced a line from Grover House in the opposite direction from the Lawlors' home. The line ended at the northeast corner of Wexler House.

Abbie whistled low, using all her breath. He could imagine wheels turning in her head, as she immersed herself in the new puzzle before her.

"Well," she said finally, "you're going to need to confirm this." Her own finger traced a square, one that encompassed both Grover House and Wexler House. "If the theory is that this was all part of the Grover property in the nineteenth century, you're going to need survey records and deeds."

"Way ahead of you. Whitney is down at the courthouse as we speak."

"Mmmm." She continued to scrutinize the map, deep in thought. "We need to get you inside Wexler House."

Internally, Joss agreed. His mind had been playing with ideas of how to present his findings to Kenetsky. First, the tunnel to the Lawlors, which could then be dramatically disproved. Then the proposed tunnel to the Wexlers. It would be a good dramatic narrative. He absolutely did need to get into that house to see if the tunnel was there.

"I don't think either Frank Wexler or Grace Wexler will let me in," Joss said. "I mean, after . . . after . . ."

"After I told Grace off this morning and had multiple confrontations with Frank?" She shook her head. "No, they aren't going to let us into that house. But, there's another Wexler."

Monday, 3:09 p.m., the War Room

George: Aced it, Mom!!!
Abbie: Awesome!
George: And I need a ride home.
Abbie: On my way

Abbie stopped in the war room. "I'm going to get George."

Joss pushed his chair back. "Let me do that. I've got some excess energy."

"Are you sure?" *He couldn't possibly know what he was getting into.* "You've never been in a carpool lane before!"

"How bad can it be?" He snatched the car keys off the counter "Take the time to write something, will you?"

He *had* to remind her she had spent little quality time with her laptop in the past few days, and her deadline was looming.

Joss had so much energy because Nevelyn Wexler had invited them for coffee the next morning. Now, the ideas were pouring out of his head faster than he could type.

Abbie, however, was stuck, waiting to see if Tyler Nesmith could find anything useful in a mountain of storage boxes that had been subject to storm damage. Until and unless someone from the Engineering Department came through, what she had wasn't enough for a Sunday feature article in *The Times.*

Back in college, she and Joss had spent an exceptionally heated evening debating the presentation of history. Joss had argued that history should be presented via the lens of the Storyteller's Triangle, the interdependence between the story, the storyteller, and the audience. The historian as storyteller, sharing the history as a story, to an audience ready for it.

Abbie, on the other hand, contended that her audience, the body of her peers, was most concerned with the plausibility of her theories, the veracity of her facts and the thoroughness of her research.

Whether the story told was interesting to read was of little importance. At one time, she had cared about things like the makeup of a British soldier's diet in 1762—his rations included a pound of peas, a rasher of bacon, flour and salt and a pint of ale, each day, every day. Right now, she was immersed in history that was so much more interesting. People had grieved over the loss of Rosalie. Abbie'd heard it in their voices and, in Cyrus's case, saw it on his face. Forget peas and bacon. This was when history got under a person's skin, infiltrated the pores. She suddenly understood Joss's triangle. The storyteller had to love telling the story as much as the audience wanted to hear it. Footnotes be damned.

Words, phrases, sentences popped into her head like the fireworks in July 1969. The words flooded her brain, fast and furious. She pounded the keyboard, struggling to keep up with her thoughts. She didn't dare stop typing long enough to switch to dictation mode.

When someone knocked on the sunporch door, she cursed, appreciating Joss's description of her house as Grand Central Station.

Tyler Nesmith stood on her back porch.

Abbie hurried to open the door. "Dr. Nesmith!"

"Sorry to barge in on you like this, Miss Adams, but I am running late for a meeting with the contractors, and I wanted to bring this to you right away." He handed her an old interoffice envelope. "Mrs. Couch found this in a box labeled *Dr. Strunk*, Old Dr. Wexler's successor." She ran a hand over the envelope, darkened by age, with a string and button closure. An envelope, like the one Cleta Blakebill had described. She tingled with excitement.

The envelope contained pages covered with handwritten notes and carbon-copies still bearing blue ink smudges. Nesmith pointed to the first page. "It looks like Old Dr. Wexler's hand. This appears to be a draft of a letter Wexler sent to NASA detailing the evidence on the grant scandal."

There were six pages of handwritten text and nine pages of typewritten lists with entries like one Mrs. Couch highlighted. SOE-LJS-670217, Ref RD-103.

Nesmith's forefinger tapped the yellow-marked entry. "See this? We've been using the same system for decades. SOE is School of Engineering, LJS are the initials for Dr. Strunk, and the date, February 17, 1967. Mrs. Couch found this memo in another box. It's a memo from Strunk to McCain questioning the calibration of instruments used in a particular test. See the cross-reference, *Ref RD-103*." He ran his finger down the right column of similar numbers "About two-thirds of these begin with an *RD*—I'm sure that signifies Rosalie DuFrayne. The other numbers are SOE references."

Abbie flipped through the rest of the pages. "This is remarkable," Abbie said. "Wexler collected evidence beyond what Rosalie gave him."

"I think he used Rosalie's evidence as a starting point and conducted his own investigation before handing it all over," Nesmith said. "Theodore Wexler took an inventory of Rosalie's evidence, numbered the documents numerically. Then he followed the evidence and supplemented the inventory with department documents. Unfortunately, Mrs. Couch didn't find any documents labeled *RD*."

"Do you have any objections to me sending an intern from the paper over to go through boxes?"

"Not at all, and Mrs. Couch will be delighted to help. She's enjoyed playing the detective." Nesmith checked his watch. "I've got to run. If I'm late, the contractor might find a reason to delay repairs another week."

"Any ideas on where we might find the *RD* documents?" Abbie asked.

Nesmith thought for a moment. "Forty years now, the only person I can think of is the local NASA historian. Margo Temper. She's on their website."

Monday, 6:32 p.m., the War Room

Everybody in the house seemed content.

George was in his room, happily ignoring homework after acing his physics test.

Martha had sailed into the house after practice. Her coaches had invited her to step in for a varsity player who'd gotten injured.

Joss was quietly typing away at his keyboard, earbuds firmly fixed in place. Benny snored softly near the door, every so often sighing in his doggie dreams.

I should have a come-apart more often.

So why wasn't she content herself?

Perhaps because Cyrus Porter had firmly placed Frank Wexler on the Quad at the time of Rosalie DuFrayne's murder, and he'd been killed, and she couldn't question him again to delve further into what he'd seen?

Perhaps because her best theory, the McCain theory, was, as Joss would say, as sexy as a saltshaker, and likely to drive his fruitcake widow to complain like Mrs. Puckett had?

Perhaps because for the first time in years she'd been kissed, truly kissed, a feel-it-from-your-hair-to-your-toes kiss, and the next day the kisser had all but accused her of murder?

But it was probably because, deep down, she'd wanted to find Frank Wexler guilty of *something,* and all she could nail on him was his possible affair with a Black student who happened to be the daughter of his family's cook and the possibility of him fathering a child out of wedlock.

In 1969. With the influx of newcomers in Hunts Landing now, who but the oldest of the old guard would care? That part of her that sought vengeance against Frank Wexler, the part she hid from the rest of the world, was screaming for satisfaction.

Chirp chirp chirp, saved Abbie from her ruminations. It was Margo Temper, the NASA historian. She explained her project. "What I'm looking for is a copy of the evidence Dr. Wexler handed over to the Inspector General."

"I'm afraid there is no way to get that information to you, not in time," Margo said. "You'll need to make a Freedom of Information Act request. That can take up to four months, and the agency will charge you a dollar a page."

Abbie didn't know if the paper had a budget for FOIA requests. "I didn't know."

"FOIA made a lot of government documents available to the public, but it isn't perfect."

Abbie thanked Ms. Temper for her time and hung up the phone. "Nuts."

"What's wrong?" Joss had come into the kitchen and was strapping on her apron.

"I struck out with the NASA historian." Abbie took some garlic cloves and smashed the side of her knife down on them to make them easier to peel. "I'm at a dead end. I have a list of documents with all these *RD* references but can't prove they refer to Rosalie's evidence. The story is incomplete without that last link."

The doorbell rang.

"Is it ever quiet around here?" Joss asked, and motioned for her to hand over the knife.

Abbie headed toward the front door. "Not since you showed up."

Nick Preston stood on her front doorstep. He wasn't smiling. He looked tired, his brilliant blue eyes dimmer than Saturday night. But she didn't care. Her lips tightened. She wouldn't respond to his texts, so now he shows up at her front door? Abbie exhaled. She'd meant to call him back, she really had, but the day had gotten away from her. "Nick."

"Abbie, I need to talk to you."

She stepped back to allow him in. "What is it?"

He stared her dead in the eye. "There was an incident on campus involving Dr. Tyler Nesmith and his wife Katie."

That sinking feeling, the kind where you knew bad news was coming, though you didn't know exactly what it was, gushed down her throat and splashed down in her stomach. "What?"

"Dr. and Mrs. Nesmith were climbing the stairs in Ellesby Hall when the suspect rushed them from above. The guy tried for Mr. Nesmith, but Mrs. Nesmith swung her purse at him. He pushed. She fell, hard."

"Oh my god!" The stairs in Ellesby Hall were marble. And Mrs. Nesmith was so little.

At the sound of Abbie's raised voice, George bustled down the stairs.

"Get your mother some water," Joss said from behind her.

She took the interruption to breathe. She'd seen Tyler Nesmith, what, two, three hours ago? Now he'd been attacked, and his wife was hurt?

Nick closed the door behind him. "She's in a coma. Too soon to tell. Nesmith's secretary said he got a call from the contractor to meet him at the Engineering building. He had a lunch date with his wife, so I guess she was meeting him there. This was right after he met with you."

Her fingers trembled. She wrapped her arms around herself. George brought her some water, but she couldn't stop her hands from shaking. "Could it have been an accident? A construction guy in a hurry?"

"Nesmith says the guy came straight at him." Nick leaned closer, his voice softer. "Listen. Cyrus Porter meets with you and is killed that night. Tyler Nesmith meets with you and is what I would normally call mugged. And a strange car has been parked across the street from your house over the past few nights."

"No. Just a couple of nights . . ."

"Jethro Turner called me," Nick said. "Ford Explorer. Tennessee plates, covered in mud. Stayed a few minutes last night. Jethro said there were so many people here, the guy probably got spooked and took off."

She hugged herself tighter, trying to absorb all she was hearing.

Joss nodded to George. "Why don't you make sure your sister stays upstairs?"

With the boy gone, Joss asked the question. "Do you think Abbie's a target?"

"I don't know," Nick said. "We've treated Porter's homicide as a robbery. The Nesmiths' mugging, a random act of violence. Take those incidents together, however, both happening after talking to Abbie, both connected to an unsolved murder from over forty years ago, and the picture looks a little different. Abbie, what have you found?"

"To be honest," she confessed, "I'm sort of at a dead end."

"Talk me through it." He scrutinized the Rosalie wall.

She explained how she got from Rosalie to McCain. "After Rosalie's murder, Wexler conducted an internal investigation and handed over all the evidence. The courts convicted McCain of fraud. He died in prison in 1973."

"So your theory is that McCain killed Rosalie for turning him in to Wexler?"

She nodded. "Can't prove it, though."

"Your guy has a motive and opportunity, and no alibi."

"A dead man can't give me an alibi," she said. At least the shaking had stopped.

"Right." Nick turned back to the Rosalie wall. "Anybody else you talked to have a reason to go after Porter and Nesmith?"

"I can't imagine who . . ." Abbie gasped. "Ida McCain!" She described her interview with the elderly woman.

Nick pulled out his cop's pad. "What's her address?"

This was happening way too fast. "No, you can't possibly think she's a suspect. She's eighty years old." She paced the war room. "Listen to me. Ida is a crazy, angry old lady, but she's frail. She couldn't possibly try to mug somebody, let alone two people."

"Can she pull a trigger?" Nick asked. ".32 ACP is a light payload."

"No, she couldn't, and she's crazy mad at the Wexlers, not Cyrus, not Dr. Nesmith."

"Why are you so convinced she couldn't do it when she was the first person who came to your mind!"

"Because . . . oh dammit, I should've kept my mouth shut." How could her *first* thought have been of Ida McCain? No matter the bitterness, Abbie doubted Ida could hurt a proverbial fly. She was . . . grieving . . . mourning for a husband she'd lost decades ago. All Abbie had accomplished was to target a poor woman.

And what else had she accomplished but to endanger Cyrus Porter, to endanger the Nesmiths. She didn't believe in coincidences any more than Jethro, Jethro who was sitting under the tree across the street watching the house.

She heard a familiar creak. Her children had snuck down the stairs and were listening in, just out of view.

Those two snoops. Were they in danger, too?

She was looking at George and Martha, but it was Joss who spoke first. "Abs?"

"Right," she said. "First things first. Dinner. Joss, please take the kids to get a bucket at KFC."

"*KFC?*"

"KFC!" Abbie insisted. "You can wipe that look of gastronomical horror off your face. Good old greasy, eleven herbs and spices, KFC! I've got two days before my deadline. I want extra-crispy."

He surrendered and led the kids out to the garage.

She turned and faced Nick. "You want to bring Ida McCain in, go ahead. Waste of your time, if you ask me. But if you would, first take me to the hospital."

Monday, 6:67 p.m., Hunts Landing Medical Center

Abbie made her calls while Nick drove.

"Loreen? Need you . . . Pack a bag and come to the house . . . I'll explain when I get back . . . Going to the hospital . . . *I'll explain when I get back* . . . Park on LaFayette."

"Maddie, hey . . . It got crazy . . . I'm sorry . . . Listen . . . I'm *sorry* . . . I said, but please . . . Yes ma'am . . . Yes ma'am . . . Is it my turn to talk now? . . . Come be my guest for a couple of days . . . At my house . . . You can spoil my kids rotten and I won't get mad . . . See you later."

She swiped the call off and turned her eye on him. "What?"

He shrugged. "Just not sure what you're doing."

"I'm filling my house with as many adults as I can and putting as many cars as I can in my driveway." She pulled her purse strap up on her shoulder. "Good enough?"

"For now." Nick drove quietly for a couple of blocks. "That weird call you got the other night. They ever call back?"

"I don't know. I blocked the number."

"Check your blocked list."

They were getting close to the hospital. Abbie scrolled through her voicemail messages to the bottom and tapped *Blocked Messages.*

She sucked in a lungful of air.

"What?"

"There's over thirty of them."

Nick pulled into the parking lot near the front of the hospital. "Send me the number."

"Dr. Nesmith?" Abbie asked softly from the doorway.

Tyler Nesmith stopped stroking his wife's motionless hand and slowly turned to greet the visitors. "Hello, Abbie. Come in."

Abbie took the only other seat. Katie Nesmith, her bruised face partially obscured by tubes and other medical apparatus, breathed a slow and steady rhythm marked by the machine next to her bed.

Tyler turned back to his wife and resumed stroking her hand with his thumb, rocking slightly. *Stroke, rock, stroke, rock*, in time with Katie's ventilator.

"How is she?"

"Fine, other than four broken bones and a coma," he replied, then shook his head. "I apologize. Rudeness is never acceptable."

"I'm so sorry, Dr. Nesmith."

"I told you, it's Tyler. And what are you sorry for?"

"For Mrs. Nesmith . . . the story . . . dredging up these memories." Abbie ran out of words.

"Memories, hmm." He didn't take his eyes off of Katie. "You can't really dredge up memories that weren't ready to come back all on their own. You've got nothing to be sorry for, Abbie Adams." *Stroke, rock, stroke, rock.* "Katie had remembered something about that night, and she was sharing that with me. We were distracted. That's why I never saw the guy coming for us."

Stroke, rock, stroke, rock.

Abbie waited for him to continue.

He finally squeezed Katie's hand and faced her. "Katie was telling me what she and the girls did *after* we'd taken them back to their sorority house. She and Valerie, well they had a little adventure on their own."

"Valerie?" Abbie knew the name from somewhere but couldn't remember exactly.

"Valerie Rigsby. David's girlfriend. David Breckenridge."

"I remember you telling me. You and Frank and David, together that night."

"Strutting like James Dean." He lost himself for a moment, to his memories, perhaps, of a steamy summer night so long ago. Perhaps. "Katie wanted to talk to you herself, but there's no telling when she's going to wake up." He'd said *when* instead of *if,* and Abbie hoped it wasn't misplaced optimism. Katie's face, well, Katie didn't look good.

He pulled his phone from his pocket. "I hadn't spoken to Valerie in years, but she texts us both for Christmas and birthdays." He swiped with his thumb a few times. "I already texted her. She's expecting your call."

Tyler turned back toward his wife and resumed his stroking.

Abbie'd taken enough of his attention away from his wife. She stood to leave. "I hope Mrs. Nesmith wakes up soon." Her eye caught Katie's full name spelled out on a nurse's whiteboard. Katherine Cavanaugh Nesmith.

"Dr. Nesmith, your wife's maiden name is Cavanaugh?"

"Yes, it is."

"One of the first mill families in town?"

"Yes."

"And the owners of *The Hunts Landing Times*?"

Tyler exhaled. "As Katie would say, it's about time you figured that out, honey."

CHAPTER SIXTEEN

Monday, 7:37 p.m., the War Room

J oss had to admit, the KFC was good. But he shuddered to think
what the chicken fat, mashed potatoes and gravy were doing to
his arteries. On the other hand, the heavy meal kept him from
dwelling on his looming deadline.

Three days times twenty-four hours . . .

Still, he had to wait until morning for the visit to Miss Nevelyn
Wexler.

He'd absolutely loved Nick's face when Abbie'd left the shock
over the Nesmith news to turn into a drill sergeant in a matter of
moments. At his side, Benny laid a paw on Joss's lap. He scratched
the dog's scruff. "Boy, Nick doesn't know what he's in for, does he?"
Secretly, though, he was rooting for Nick. Hopefully, the idiot would
apologize and get back on Abbie's good side.

Joss preferred to ponder Abbie's love life. His own was in shambles.

His phone rang. Joss had barely said hello when Jethro's gruff
voice demanded, "What did Preston want with Abbie?"

"I thought you had your sources at the station."

"Don't you be flippy with me, boy."

Joss figured that the *boy* meant Jethro was worried, or pissed, or both. "Sorry." He explained what had happened to the Nesmiths.

"And Abbie talked to this professor this morning?"

"As far as I know. We haven't exactly crossed paths today."

"Well, I'll be watching. Uh oh, you're about to get invaded. Looks like Miss Loreen Oliver is in the driveway."

***

Monday, 9:03 p.m., the Back Patio

Abbie paced circles around Madeleine. They were on the back patio, because Abbie didn't dare raise her voice to Madeleine while the kids were in the house. "Why didn't you tell me Katie Nesmith is a Cavanaugh?" she demanded.

Madeleine threw both hands up in self-defense. "What difference does it make?"

"You didn't find it odd the owner of the paper picked this story to lead the series? Oh, golly, and she was a potential witness?" Abbie's pacing hadn't abated a bit.

"Of course I did, and I told Katie so."

Abbie scowled.

"Katie made it clear that the Wexlers were her target," Madeleine said, with the same soothing voice Abbie remembered from her childhood. "Why, well, she didn't tell me why. But, I've known that woman for close to fifty years, and she would never have willingly put you in danger, or herself, or Tyler."

Abbie's anger deflated as she thought of Katie Nesmith's bruised face, a ventilator tube taped to her mouth.

"No, of course not."

Madeleine plunked herself down onto a patio chair. "So, young lady, why exactly am I here? My eyes aren't as good as they used to be, but don't you tell anyone that, so I'll be pretty useless with one of your Daddy's little pistols."

"You're here because a black SUV has been watching my house. Jethro says the driver got spooked by all the cars parked out front last night. So, I'm parking a lot of cars. Which reminds me, gotta talk to Jethro."

Abbie entered the house and went straight to the kitchen. She grabbed two beers from the fridge and headed out the front door.

Years ago, when George-the-toddler had gotten out of the house and disappeared under the branches of the ancient willow tree, Abbie'd sworn to force her neighbor to cut it down. But the owner passed, and George had grown, and Abbie had forgotten that the tree was such an excellent hiding place. She parted the branches and peered through the gloom. "Jethro?"

"Over here."

He'd positioned himself so he could keep his eye on both Birch and LaFayette streets, sitting in a folding lawn chair with a cooler next to him. "Ahh, that's my girl," he said, accepting a beer. "All I brought was Mountain Dew." He jutted his chin at the house. "I saw Madeleine and Loreen pull up. They staying?"

"Yes. For a couple of days."

"I'll park my truck in your driveway tomorrow night. A squad car drives by every hour or so. We've got our eyes open."

She felt goosebumps erupt on her arms. "Do you think we're in danger?"

"Would have packed you up and brought y'all out to the farm if I thought that was the case," Jethro said. "But I'm watchin'."

Monday ,10:17 p.m., the Sunporch

On the sunporch, four adults sipped wine Loreen had brought by the light of a waning spring moon.

Although the sunporch faced the backyard and wasn't visible from either street, Abbie felt no need to shine a proverbial spotlight on them. So they sipped in the dark and argued softly.

"They can come stay with me at The Sommelier . . ."

"You only have one bedroom, Loreen . . ."

"There's my sister's summer cabin upriver . . ."

"The kids need Wi-Fi for their homework . . ."

They went in circles until Abbie felt a migraine building. "Enough, y'all, please. I'm not going to disrupt the kids' lives over an SUV." Benny jumped off the sofa next to her and headed for the outer door. Joss let him out.

"It's not just an SUV, Abs," he said. "There's also been a murder and a mugging."

Outside, Benny growled and headed straight for the back fence, and the hairs on the nape of Abbie's neck stood on end. With the moonlight, she could make out the dog's shape. Her own body was as alert as Benny's. After a minute or so sniffing at the fence line, he trotted back to the house. The silence behind her remained unbroken. No one had spoken since Benny's menacing growl.

"Look at us," Abbie said. "We're all spooked because Benny sniffed a possum."

"It could have been the killer," Loreen said. "You didn't get us all here because you think a possum is driving a black SUV around Hunts Landing."

"I'm texting Jethro," Joss said.

"Oh, please!" The dull ache in Abbie's head sharpened. "We don't know why Cyrus was killed or why the Nesmiths were attacked. We don't know for sure why that SUV has been hanging around."

"C'mon, Abbie," Loreen thumped the pillow in her lap. "All of this started after you got the Rosalie DuFrayne assignment. It has to be connected."

"I deal in *facts,*" Abbie said, a little more forcefully than intended. She softened her tone a bit. "My gut says you're right, but I don't have the facts to support my gut. *If* all of this truly has to do with the Rosalie DuFrayne murder, why not come after me instead of Cyrus and the Nesmiths? I've been walking and driving around town, asking questions, for days now."

Madeleine, who had not spoken in a while, now did so from the shadowed corner of the porch. "I agree with Abbie, let's deal with the facts. On Wednesday, Abbie gets the DuFrayne assignment. On Friday, Cyrus Porter was murdered, after speaking with Abbie. Today, the Nesmiths were attacked, after Tyler Nesmith spoke with Abbie. The facts are that key witnesses who could provide information to Abbie have been targeted. I ask, have any of the witnesses you've spoken to on the phone have been harmed?"

"No, ma'am, not as far as I know," Abbie said. "In person, I spoke to Jethro, Cyrus, Ida McCain, and Tyler Nesmith."

"The guy would be stupid to take on Jethro," Loreen said.

"And Ida McCain is too nutty, she didn't give me any useful information," Abbie said.

"Dear Joss, would you get me a refill?" Madeleine held up her glass. "Then, given these facts, I think we can draw a line, if not a conclusion. Witnesses have been attacked after interviews with Abbie. The killer is here, in Hunts Landing, and doesn't want this story to come out."

"But then, why is he circling Abbie?" Loreen asked. "Is he merely trying to scare her off the story?"

The realization came swift, hard, and almost took Abbie's breath away. "Because I'm just the reporter. Anything happens to me, the paper can find someone else to finish the story."

"Listen, I've known Katie since kindergarten. She'd never put anyone in danger. When you told me you'd been assigned to the story, I called her. She made it clear to me she wanted this story told," Madeleine said. "Damn that woman for not telling me her reasons why. I swear, I just might thrash her from here to next month when she gets out of that coma."

"So what do we do now?" Joss asked. "Nothing? Just let Jethro keep on watching from the tree across the street?"

Abbie crossed her arms. "My deadline is Wednesday. I should call—" *Chirp chirp chirp.* "Speak of the devil. It's Sylvia."

Abbie flipped on the yard flood lights and took her phone outside. "I was—"

"Will told me everything," Sylvia interrupted. "Abbie, you've got to believe me. I didn't know this was going to happen. I didn't know people could get hurt." Sylvia didn't sound like the tough-as-nails reporter Abbie knew.

"We don't know anything for certain, Sylvia, not until the police finish—"

"Fuck it, Abbie. Get that historian out of your head. Use the reporter gut that Will Irestone swore to me he saw in you. What do your instincts tell you?"

What had it been that had kept her from following her gut? Denial of the danger at hand? No, it was a little deeper than that. And it had to do with Frank Wexler, although she didn't really want to admit that to Sylvia. "My gut told me straight off that Frank Wexler had something to do with Rosalie's murder. And my gut was wrong. So how do I trust it now?"

"You trust it because you have to," Sylvia said. "You're going to be right sometimes. You're going to be wrong sometimes. You're going to be both right and wrong sometimes. Remember the Pucketts? Now, you dust yourself off and check your gut again."

Crap. This was one of those sometimes where Sylvia was right. "My gut says . . . well, my gut says if this guy's motive is to stop the Rosalie story from coming out, then he stops after you publish."

The editor was quiet on the other end for a few moments. "The board, without Mrs. Nesmith, agrees. At least that's what they told me fifteen minutes ago. Will you still be able to make your Wednesday deadline?"

"I don't have it. Yet. I don't have the full story."

"Submit what you have by Wednesday night. With this murder and the attack on the Nesmiths, we can flesh it out. But, don't stop digging. And don't forget, photos due Thursday."

The house was quiet. Kids were in their beds, Joss in the garage apartment, Loreen in the spare bedroom upstairs, and Abbie had given Madeleine her own bed. The sofa in the living room was old but extremely comfortable, as Abbie had proven many a night, falling asleep with a book under an old quilt.

Still, the tension in the house seeped from window to door, from floor to ceiling. Even Benny seemed to be aware of it, falling asleep in the main hallway, equidistant from all the humans inside the house. He didn't snore.

Her bedroom door opened, and Madeleine emerged in slippers and bathrobe. "I didn't think you'd be asleep."

Abbie pulled her knees up to make room on the sofa. "No, ma'am."

"I think I owe you an apology, Abigail."

It hadn't been that long ago when Abbie was chewing out Madeleine on the patio. It seemed like days, not hours. "No, ma'am, I don't believe you do."

"Yes, I do. I should have told you Katie Nesmith was Katie Cavanaugh."

Abbie swallowed. "Isn't there something in the reporter handbook about protecting sources?"

"Katie Nesmith isn't a source. She's a woman who's going to get the blistering part of my tongue once she wakes up."

"Oh, that's an image." Abbie tossed off the quilt. "Let's make some tea."

While waiting for the teakettle to whistle, Abbie spoke softly. "I wonder what else you've been holding back from me, though. I mean, sometimes it seems that the newspaper intern was able to find out things the historical society's archivist didn't know."

"I suppose I deserve that," Madeleine admitted. "Although, in my defense, I only took up the reins a couple of years ago."

"But your family has been here for, what—?"

"Since the age of the dinosaurs? Let me get this." Madeleine busied herself with pouring the hot water. "What was it you told me Cyrus said, something about the campus being a different world than the town?"

It was a quote Abbie remembered, as it was going into her article. "Off campus, we lived in a very white-against-Black world."

"Hunts Landing wasn't just Black-vs-white, Abbie," Madeleine said. "Your momma would have described the town in 1969 as an exercise in dichotomy. It was so many things versus so many things. It was Black versus white, it was young versus old, establishment versus Woodstock, and the 'right' side of society versus the 'wrong' side. My family was white, respectable, establishment, and the most rebellious thing I ever did, before becoming a reporter instead of a debutante, was to sneak shots of Apple Jack whiskey from my Daddy's liquor cabinet."

Abbie thought of Madeleine's orange sneakers. "I think you would have been a hoot at Woodstock."

"Blood, Sweat and Tears was my favorite band. But what I meant was, in 1969, I never would have spoken to Cyrus Porter, or Rosalie DuFrayne, for that matter. My family thought my dear Peter was a commie hooligan. Not that I'm saying that was right, by no means, I'm just saying that one didn't cross over certain lines. So, I knew nothing much outside my little sphere. Besides—" Madeleine blew on her tea—"those archives are a mess."

Abbie groaned. "So are the ones at the Engineering Department." She explained the storm damage. "Our intern was supposed to get over there to help, but I haven't heard from her."

"Well, it won't be the first time my hands got a little dusty. I'll go over tomorrow and lend Doris Couch a hand."

"You know Mrs. Couch?" But Abbie knew the answer already. Despite her protestations to the contrary, Madeleine knew *everybody*.

"She used to play a mean golf game before her husband passed."

Abbie hugged her knees close to her chest. "Hey Maddie, a side question. Were there any Black reporters at the paper when you started?"

"Not when I started, but my Peter did bring in Bob Murray from New York. Change takes time, Abbie. Bob wound up being your boss's predecessor."

Chirp chirp chirp. "Who can be calling me at this hour?" She recognized the number. "Oh, gosh, Maddie, I have to take this call."

Madeleine departed with a soft *good night* as Abbie swiped on the third ring. "Hello? Ms. Rigsby?"

"Ms. Adams? I'm sorry to call you back so late. But Tyler explained your deadline, so I took the chance."

Abbie fetched her notebook from the war room and returned to the outer porch. "Not a problem."

"I just got off the phone with Tyler," Valerie said. "I'm sick to my stomach. But you want to talk about July 1969, correct?"

"Yes, ma'am. It was something Dr. Nesmith said, that Mrs. Nesmith was telling him at the time they were attacked. You and she were having some adventure that night?" Abbie flipped to an empty page and propped her phone against her ear with her shoulder.

"That's one way to put it. Where should I start?" Valerie asked. "I guess I should say the 'adventure' started after the boys had brought us home to the sorority house."

"The boys being Tyler Nesmith and David Breckenridge."

"Yes, Tyler and David. My David." Valerie paused. "Did you ever have a true love, Ms. Adams?"

She'd gone through an entire day without thoughts of Zach pinging her heart. "Yes, ma'am."

"Well, David was mine. The only one for me, ever, and I have three divorces to prove it. But, yes, we'd gone to the party by the river with the boys. I remember pulling off the stockings Miss Nevelyn insisted we wear to Wexler House. Can you imagine, stockings in July? I tossed them into the water. After that, the party was *fun*. Good music, they don't make music like that anymore, and cold beer and a little grass down by the water where we could get rid of the evidence if we needed to in a hurry."

"So you and Katie, Tyler and David. And Frank Wexler?"

"He was there."

"Did he have a date?"

"No, Frank was always the fifth wheel that summer. Good for scoring the grass, though."

That was yet another little tidbit that made Abbie feel smug, yet could never go into the article. "Were y'all there for the brawl?"

"Not when it started. We had a curfew, Katie and me. Our housemother was a battle-axe of a woman, Mrs. Morris. She could *smell* when one of us was planning something. We had to get back. I guess this was where our adventure started. The music by the river was still playing, it was still a good party, and we wanted to go back. So Katie bribed one of the girls—I can't remember which one—with a pack of cigarettes and a bottle of brandy she'd swiped from Wexler

House to create a distraction. Mrs. Morris fell for it, and we snuck out the laundry room window."

Abbie visualized the map of the Old Campus. The sorority houses butted up against the woods of Meyers Plantation, with the path that Rosalie had taken to the river. Had Katie and Valerie been outside when Rosalie passed? "Do you remember what time that was?"

"After our curfew, before the brawl. We had to go through the trees to get to the river, so Mrs. Morris wouldn't spot us. We came out of the woods by the boys' frat house. By that time, all those boys were fighting hard, and cops were all over the place. I was so worried about David, I wanted to get closer, but Katie made me stay put. That's when we saw Dr. McCain."

"Are you sure you saw Quentin McCain on the Quad?" Abbie caught herself. "I'm sorry, but it's been a long time, and I need to be certain."

"Of course it was Dr. McCain. He was still wearing his tux from the party."

"Which way was he headed? Toward the river? Away from the river?"

"Neither. He was passed out cold, on a bench in front of Sigma house."

Abbie grasped at a straw. "Any chance he could have been faking being asleep?"

Valerie thought for a moment. "No, I don't think so. Deadbeat husband number two snored just like McCain when he was passed out."

Dammit. Sylvia had said to follow her gut, and Abbie's gut said Valerie Rigsby's recollection was accurate. "Do you remember anything else relevant?"

"Relevant to me, yes," Valerie said. "To you, not so sure. I was so worried for the boys. All those flashing lights. I didn't know if he was hurt or not. But then they came up the path from the river, Frank leaning heavily on David. They stopped in front of us—those boys beat up Frank pretty bad, but David only had a bloody nose. I can't tell you how relieved I was. David took care of Frank that night. What Frank's father did to them later was plain awful."

Abbie sat straight up. "How do you mean?"

"David and Frank's numbers came up in the fall. Wexler did nothing to keep them stateside."

"That's the second time in two days I've heard that story. I don't quite understand it, though. Old Dr. Wexler didn't help his own son?"

"He played poker with all the guys on the Draft Board, and didn't whisper a thing to help David. David was pretty sure that he helped Frank out, though, because Frank got a cushy desk job in Tokyo, while the Army shipped David all the way to Vietnam." Valerie sniffed. "My poor David—the noises in the jungle at night terrified him. He died in a chopper crash. I didn't get all his letters until after we'd buried him. He felt so betrayed by Dr. Wexler, felt Dr. Wexler owed him for taking care of Frank that night, and instead David died scared and far away from home."

This didn't seem to mesh with the other testimonials in Old Dr. Wexler's favor, letting that poor boy go off to war like that. At least when Zach was deployed, he had his buddies, and was in his base camp every night. "How awful."

"Theodore Wexler was evil, Miss Adams," Valerie said. "I wouldn't be surprised if he caused that girl's death."

Abbie knew she couldn't keep witnesses from coloring their recollections with their own emotions. It was something a historian trained to do, to see past the filters to the facts. Even Cyrus Porter hadn't been completely removed from the impact of his memories. Yet, on the memory clarity scale, Abbie was placing Valerie closer to the Ida McCain end than the Jethro Turner end.

Both had lost a man they'd loved, and they both blamed Theodore Wexler.

Was this all to the adventure Katie had intimated to her husband? "I'm wondering, Ms. Rigsby, do you have any idea what Katie might have meant about an adventure that night? I mean, other than witnessing the river brawl?"

"All I can think of . . . no . . . that couldn't be it."

Let me be the judge. "What couldn't be 'it'?"

"Well, it was when we were trying to sneak back into the house. We'd planned for the getting out, not the getting back in. We hid in the bushes behind the house, trying to figure out what to do, when suddenly the downstairs lights came on. We heard Mrs. Morris out front, shouting, something like, 'Hey you, young lady!' So we took the chance to climb back through the laundry window, but we didn't need to. Everybody was on the front porch watching Mrs. Morris in her curlers and bathroom shouting at the Quad. I asked one girl what was going on. And she said, 'Mrs. Morris is chasing some half-naked girl.'"

Tuesday, 8:37 a.m., the Cottage District

Joss and Abbie walked to Wexler House. For the first time in days, hope kindled in him, a wispy thread that he grabbed onto and refused to release. His body was finally on Hunts Landing time, and, with the lucidity of a rested brain, the hunch that Wexler House held secrets good enough to impress Kenetsky dominated his thoughts.

Aside from the SUVs. Abbie had explained that in Hunts Landing, people usually drove a pickup truck, or an SUV. Some shade of gray. Some level of dirt—it was spring, after all. She was doing her best to acclimate him.

Still, every passing SUV, muddy or not, caught his eye.

Abbie herself wasn't looking too good, he had to admit. Her eyes were puffy, and she was unusually quiet as they walked. At one point, her phone jingled with a text tone he hadn't heard before. *I shot the sheriff . . .* She ignored it.

"Let me guess. Nick."

"Yup."

"Still not talking to him?"

"I'm really not sure exactly what I'm doing with him, to be honest."

Joss himself had been on the tail end of Abbie's digging in her heels on more occasions than he cared to remember. Maybe he should get a message to Nick, give him a hint. Abbie did like flowers. Groveling was also a useful technique.

Abbie stopped. They'd reached the corner by Wexler House.

Joss took a quick look toward Grover House. Tall, overgrown hedgerows at the back of that property obscured most of the house except for the roof and the five chimneys. Given his unfamiliarity with Hunts Landing, he wasn't surprised that on his first trips to Grover House, he hadn't realized how close the two homes were to each other.

Abbie was staring at the Wexler driveway.

"Are you scoping the place out?" he asked, perhaps more brusquely than intended.

"I don't want to get ambushed." She checked the streets in all four directions before crossing.

It took Nevelyn Wexler a couple of minutes to answer the doorbell of her cottage on the northeast corner of the Wexler property. "Abbie! And your handsome friend. Come in, come in." Using a blinged-out walker, Nevelyn led them to the kitchen space in a room with a nicely appointed open floor plan.

Abbie tried to make introductions.

"Oh, I watch NMC TV. What a wonderful show you have, Mr. Freeman. Abbie, would you pour for us?"

Finally, a fan in Hunts Landing! There was hope for the town, after all. Abbie reached for the coffeepot while Joss beamed.

Nevelyn smiled. "Now you, young man, I understand you think there might be a tunnel underneath the big house?"

Joss explained his theory, and Nevelyn never broke her gaze with him. He was careful with his language when it came to the identity of Nevelyn's mother. "Fascinating," Nevelyn said at the end. "Well, you're absolutely right. Mother was a Grover. Theodore was born—how did they used to put it—oh, so very early. And without a wedding ring on her finger, at least not at delivery. An early ten-pound baby boy. Of course, Mother couldn't have him here in Hunts Landing. No, Theodore was born in Memphis. Far enough away to keep the tongues from waggling."

"I apologize if we're stepping too far into your family's privacy," Abbie said. "None of this is going into my story."

"Nonsense. I stopped worrying about such things a long time ago. Who cares these days, really? I don't, but there were plenty in the day, mind you, just waiting for any Wexler to fall off the pedestal. You've raised two children on your own, and they are delightful, from what I'm told, and you've had a single man *you aren't married to* living in your garage. *Who cares,* I ask you, but there was a time when people cared plenty. Mother was a product of her time, nothing more, although she paid more prices than most people would understand, nowadays. Grace might care. That's probably because of all the airs she took on when she married Frank."

Nevelyn chuckled, and Joss glimpsed the mischievous young woman she might have been.

"Oh, and the idea of the old Grover family treasure underneath Wexler House. Well, wouldn't that just push Grace off the deep end?" Nevelyn didn't elaborate on her comment, and Joss didn't get the chance to ask, because the older woman picked up her phone and tapped a number. "Of course I can't take you down there myself, but Consuelo, the cook, well, I hired her when she was a young thing . . .

Consuelo? Yes, dear, listen, I'm sending some friends over. Let them in by the side gate. And don't let Grace see them."

Nevelyn winked at them. "Don't forget to come back and tell me what you've found."

CHAPTER SEVENTEEN

Tuesday, 9:14 a.m., Around Wexler House

A bbie and Joss took a circuitous route around the block to avoid passing directly in front of Wexler House. Although none of the family cars were in the driveway, she wasn't tempting fate. They approached Wexler House from the west side, where the alley to the campus bordered the property.

"So," Joss asked, "what's the deal with Old Nevelyn and Grace?"

Abbie shrugged. "I couldn't tell you for sure, but I've always noticed some ice between them. Maybe because Nevelyn raised Frank. She thinks of him as more of her son than nephew, and a man's mother can be the harshest critic of a man's wife."

"Was Zach's mom like that?"

That Zach's mother had blamed Abbie for his desire to return for a second tour was something Abbie'd never spoken of, not to Loreen, not to her children.

But, somehow, it spilled out for Joss. "I think monster-in-law would have been more appropriate. But I shouldn't speak ill of the dead. She passed, oh, when Martha was in kindergarten." She stopped and held her finger to her lips. "We're here."

The ivied gate with the rusty lock appeared unopened in who knew how long. *How much noise is this sucker going to make?* She winced as she pushed, then gaped when the latch gave noiselessly and the gate swung inward with ease. She had to peek. On the garden side of the gate, the lock and hinges were rust-free and oiled.

The kitchen door was a few yards away. They walked in the grass, avoiding the flagstones. As quietly as possible, Abbie rapped on the door, which opened immediately.

Grace Wexler's cook, a small woman in a white chef's shirt and gray checked trousers, smiled. "Miss Nevelyn tells me to take you to the cellar. Please, come."

They followed her a few steps down a hall to a narrow wooden door painted white. "I'll stay up here," Consuelo said, handing them each a small utility flashlight from a shelf next to the door. "Go." She opened the door, revealing steep wooden stairs straight down. There was an old-fashioned electrical switch at the top of the stairs. Consuelo turned it on before closing the door behind them, and Abbie heard the latch click.

"Let's go!" Joss descended the stairs faster than Abbie thought prudent.

Abbie's own home didn't have a cellar, but she remembered well playing at Loreen's house. The Wexler cellar reminded her of that place, dim and chilly. Old, cracked brick lined the walls and served as support posts for the main floor above, almost cordoning off the space. Bare lightbulbs lit a faint path away from the stairs.

"Do you have any idea what we're looking for?" she asked.

"If my sense of direction is right, we're headed toward Grover House."

Abbie wasn't so sure of his sense of direction, but he seemed confident.

The utility flashlights did little to add to whatever light the grimy basement windows allowed in. Off to the sides of the space, Abbie spotted little chambers recessed into the wall, dirt-floored, but empty. "Do you want to check any of those out?"

"No. Those would have been used to store foodstuffs. Corn, sweet potatoes, the like. First place the Union troops would have looked."

As they ventured deeper into the cellar, the light from the basement windows decreased, blocked by shrubbery outside. Joss slowed his step, his flashlight beam feebly revealing dust-cloaked wooden crates.

At the farthest end, rusty metal shelving ran along each side wall and down the back. They each shined their lights on the shelves.

Old mason jars, their lids coated with grime and rust, lined most of the shelves on the back. To Abbie's eyes, they appeared to have been undisturbed for decades. Abbie had a dusty carton or two in her own garage.

Joss stuck his head into an open space, flashlight pointing this way and that.

The thought of spiders, or any other critters, lurking in those shelves was a sufficient deterrent. Abbie turned her own light to the side shelves.

There were banker's boxes along one wall, the kind she'd used for her own parents' archives. Boxes that were labeled in block letters by year. Familiar letters. Frank Wexler's letters.

Her heart skipped a beat as her flashlight shone on a box labeled 2002. The year of her failed defense of her doctoral thesis.

Her hand reached for the cardboard lid.

Beside her, Joss shook the shelves with the mason jars. Glass tinkled softly, but the shelves didn't budge. "There's got to be some trip catch here."

Abbie's hand rested on the box lid.

Open it, Abbie. There was that little voice in her head, telling her there was no way Frank Wexler would store precious, delicate historical documents in a cardboard box in a damp cellar. The idea defied reason. But her hand moved of its own volition. She raised the lid.

Sealed plastic envelopes lined the box, side by side, with a thin sheen of dust on the topmost edge. Over two dozen at least. She pulled one out. A yellowed label stuck to the plastic revealed a name she recognized, a fellow doctoral candidate who'd studied under Frank Wexler, one who had been awarded his PhD.

Inside the plastic, yellow sheets of legal-sized paper. She didn't need a stronger flashlight to read. She knew. Frank Wexler always captured his thoughts on yellow legal pads.

These were his notes on his students.

Abbie pulled out another envelope, then another. He hadn't troubled himself to alphabetize the envelopes, just tucked his notes away in a box in his cellar. A fourth envelope, a fifth. Her fingers scrambled to find one with her name.

Then she froze.

Frank Wexler had lost power over her that fateful day in 2002. She'd worked hard to recover. Now, reading his notes about her, caring about what he'd thought thirteen years ago, would topple all that, would cede the power back to him. *No.*

He'd belittled her work, then and now, mocking her attempts to discover the truth about what happened to Rosalie DuFrayne. There was nothing in that box that would help with her story. And writing a piece that she could be proud of, that had a historical basis, and that told the story, that was the best way to achieve any kind of satisfaction where Frank Wexler was concerned.

And yet, her fingers longed to open the envelope with her name on it.

Why? To resurrect her failed PhD aspirations? Abbie forced her hand away from the box. Frank Wexler's notes on her progress, all those years ago, of what use could they be now? Her academic ambitions were in the past. Her work of the present, and the future, was in telling stories like Rosalie DuFrayne's.

She replaced the envelopes she'd extracted from the box and covered it back up.

"Did you find anything?" she asked Joss.

"No. This thing won't budge. And the brick behind it is as old as the other walls down here."

Abbie cocked her head. "Then, let's go."

Tuesday, 10:19 a.m., Nevelyn Wexler's Cottage

Abbie inhaled the fresh coffee Nevelyn had made. "It's a shame you didn't find your tunnel, Mr. Freeman. I would have relished Grace's face if you'd emerged with an armful of Civil War treasure." She looked thoughtfully at Abbie. "Come, dear, let me show you something." She worked her walker to the wall with the curio and the pictures. "I thought you'd like to see this, Abbie."

Nevelyn stopped at a framed photograph, a black-and-white photo of people dressed in party garb on the Wexler patio.

"Is this . . ." Abbie stared at the picture, ". . . is this the night the astronauts . . ."

"Of course it is. There's Theodore in the middle, next to the mayor and Max Andrews from Boeing, and look at me. I used to have a figure."

"You were beautiful, ma'am," Abbie said.

"And you're a good fibber." Nevelyn's gnarled finger pointed out one guest after another. "And there's Frank and his friends."

That Frank Wexler could ever have been that young amazed Abbie. Joss spent enough time looking at the photograph to be polite, then wandered down the wall, checking the others out.

Nevelyn continued. "And here's Grace, over on the other side with her parents."

"I thought she and Frank didn't start dating until later?"

"They didn't. Grace's father was one of engineers on the NASA project, and we entertained them frequently. She sniffed after Frank for quite a while, I can tell you, but he wasn't interested, not before Vietnam, anyway."

Joss was now peering into the curio cabinet.

"Where is Dr. McCain?"

Nevelyn moved her finger again. "Here. And that's Ida next to him."

"I'm told Ida McCain blackballed Grace off the museum board," Abbie said.

Nevelyn *humphed*. "Ida McCain would blame us Wexlers for her arthritis if she could. Let's sit for a moment." She pushed on the walker. "Tell me, Abbie, how does your story go? Any progress? We were so disappointed, of course, when the ABI closed the case. Theodore especially. He adored the girl. Rosalie and Miss Etta, they were family."

Family? Abbie had to remind herself that Nevelyn Wexler was old school and probably didn't even realize that some of the things she said sounded patronizing. She explained the connection between Rosalie, the evidence of the grant scandal, and Quentin McCain.

"That's going to light a fire under Ida's fanny." Nevelyn said. "However, the idea that Theodore put Rosalie into the office to spy for him, well, the notion's a little hard to believe."

"Why is that?"

"Theodore wouldn't send a young girl to do his dirty work." Nevelyn shook her head with conviction.

Abbie placed her fingers on Nevelyn's hand. "Rosalie brought a bag full of papers to your house that night, but she didn't leave with them. The only thing that makes sense is that she was carrying the evidence to your brother. The Engineering School is searching the archives but, I wonder if, maybe, Theodore kept copies?" *Please-oh-please, let there be duplicates somewhere.*

"Oh, dear, Theodore's papers are all up in the loft. There're quite a few boxes up there. I can't handle those stairs these days, but you go on up. The stairway is down the hall."

Nevelyn winked at Joss. "Tell me, Mr. Freeman, what's it like to be on TV?"

Nevelyn's loft reminded Abbie of her own attic, with sloped ceilings and walls lined with boxes. Antiques saved from the big house sat covered in sheets. At the far end, stacked file boxes cluttered the space in front of an immense mahogany desk. She turned on the desk lamp and pulled a box onto the desk.

In the seventh box, she found the envelope.

The last name on the distribution list on the envelope was *Wexler*. Brown string wrapped around the closure button, frail with age, broke when she unwound it. The envelope itself seemed fragile, as if ready to burst. Thankfully, Nevelyn Wexler had stored the papers in the controlled climate of the loft. If the papers had been left in an attic, they might have deteriorated.

The first stapled sheets confirmed her find—a handwritten copy of the document inventory, with the *RD* references. Each document behind the inventory bore an *RD* reference in the upper right corner. She could hear her own heartbeat.

Abbie forced herself to inhale and exhale, slow breaths, a few times. With a practiced care for artifacts, she replaced all the boxes the way she'd found them, then hurried down the stairs.

"Did you find what you were looking for, dear?" Nevelyn asked. Even Joss seemed interested, not that he'd come upstairs to help her look.

She held up the precious envelope with both hands. "I found them. May I borrow them, please? I'll make copies."

"Oh, posh, keep them. What would I do with a bunch of Theodore's old papers? I really should arrange for someone from the school to pick them up, but I don't know if there are any personal documents up there."

Abbie bristled at the idea of some untrained stranger handling Theodore Wexler's papers. "Tell you what, Ms. Wexler. Next week, when I'm past these deadlines, I'll be happy to come over and sort things for you."

"You are a sweet girl." Nevelyn clasped Abbie's hands. "You know, I didn't agree with what Frank did to you. We knew your parents. Lovely people. I never understood why he did what he did."

Tuesday, 1:10 p.m., Abbie's Kitchen

That tunnel *had* to be somewhere in the Wexler basement. Joss was sure of it. As certain as he was that he was running out of time. *Two days times twenty-four hours . . .*

He rammed Abbie's kitchen mallet down onto the duck breasts on the cutting board. *Whack*. It had to be. He didn't easily get disoriented. The layout of that cellar pointed directly toward Grover House.

Whack.

In his imagination, the mallet became a sledgehammer, the duck breasts became mellow crumbly brick that stood between him and the Grover gold.

Whack.

"I'm pretty sure that bird never did anything to you," Loreen said from the kitchen doorway.

Joss's mallet stopped in midair. It took his mind a second to withdraw from his imaginary basement. "It's called tenderizing."

"Using sweet words might work easier." She hefted a cardboard winery box onto the counter. "Protection duty requires sustenance."

"That's not pinot noir, is it?"

"It's a *barolo*," Loreen sniffed. "Madeleine called with a menu warning. Seriously, you're a bigger wine snob than I am." She eyed the cutting board. "So, why are you mistreating poultry?"

Whack. Whack. "Because I couldn't find the tunnel."

"I doubt that was the duck's fault."

Joss let go of the mallet. He wasn't up to defending his actions against Daffy Duck. "The Wexler cellar is like an arrow. Aimed at Grover House."

"Perhaps you need to stop thinking so linearly," Loreen suggested. She carried a couple of bottles to tuck into the fridge. "I had an uncle Bucephalus, crazy old coot, didn't mind when us little ones called him Uncle Buck. Or was he Mother's second cousin? Anyway, Uncle Buck used to examine my crayon drawings, and he'd always tell me I had too many lines and I needed more circles. I didn't like circles, you see, I liked lines, but Uncle Buck said a circle was just a line with a big old hole in the middle."

Joss soaped his hands at the sink. "So, what's your point?"

"My point, sugar, is that you need more circles." She strode into the war room and picked up a marker from his whiteboard. "You see this red arrow here from the Wexlers to the Grovers. But, I see curves." She drew arcs from the corner of the Wexler property to the corner of the Grover property, curves that avoided the intersection of French Street and Drexel Street.

"Not curves." Joss flipped the kitchen towel onto his shoulder. "Angles." He took the marker out of Loreen's hands. "The bomb shelter at Grover House . . . the steps went down, farther than the Wexler cellar steps . . . and at the bottom there was a sharp turn . . ."

He drew a square-bracket shape connecting the two properties, erased it, drew another. The possibilities seemed . . . endless.

He'd been looking at the wrong wall in the Wexler cellar.

"You know what this means, Loreen?"

"You can't draw?"

He didn't take his gaze off his whiteboard. "I have to get back into the Wexler cellar."

Tuesday, 7:19 p.m., the War Room

Abbie spent her afternoon cross-referencing the documents she'd discovered in Nevelyn Wexler's loft against the inventory Tyler Nesmith had uncovered at the Engineering School. Theodore Wexler had been immaculate in his investigation. Paper-clipped to the documents marked with an *RD* for Rosalie DuFrayne were supporting documents—status reports, lab results, test findings—all bearing Dr. Quentin McCain's signature.

Most of the documents were photostats, the blurry gray and white results of early 1970s copiers. But some of the documents were original, yellowed, cracked, bearing the faint red ink of departmental timestamps. Abbie's own hands shook when the realization hit her that, decades ago, Rosalie DuFrayne had handled these very pages.

But was this what got her killed?

Her involvement in the exposure of the NASA scandal was interesting for sure, something that would entice old-time residents of Hunts Landing. But was it enough for a feature? Was it good enough for her first byline?

She still could not make that direct connection between the grant scandal and Rosalie's murder. According to Valerie Rigsby, her most likely suspect, Quentin McCain, was passed out on the Quad at the time of the murder. And who did she know who could back up Valerie's story? Katie Nesmith was in a coma, Cyrus Porter and David Breckenridge were dead, Frank Wexler wasn't talking, and she hadn't ever found a trace of Isaac Leon Moore. Who else?

Jethro.

Had *he* seen McCain? There was only one way to find out.

She fixed a plate of some leftover Duck à la Joss—which, she had to admit to herself, if not to Joss, was fabulous—and left through the front door, checking the street first. Other than a blue pickup she recognized as a neighbor's vehicle, the street was empty. She found Jethro sitting in his lawn chair, right where he'd been last night.

"What are you doin' out here?" he asked.

She offered him the plate. "Duck à la Joss for you, and perhaps an answer to a question for me."

He lifted the napkin and inhaled deeply. "Ah, I love the way you think, darlin'. Ask away."

While he chewed, she posed her question. "Do you remember talking to a Dr. McCain that night? He was a professor, drunk on the Quad."

"There were more drunks on the Quad than we could shake sticks at that night."

"You might remember this one. One of the sorority girls found him and ran over to a group of cops to get him help."

Jethro licked his lips. "Sure, I remember now. Funny how some things stand out. Passed out in his tuxedo, right?"

Abbie clasped her hands together. "Did the town cops take him home that night? Or the campus cops?"

"I doubt it. Campus PD didn't have patrol wagons in those days, and we townies were knee deep in those idiot boys down by the river."

She sank to a seat on Jethro's cooler. "McCain's got the best motive I can find for murdering Rosalie DuFrayne. He was within a couple of hundred yards before, during, and after the murder. My witness, and now you, put him down as dead drunk. So he has an alibi." She thought for a moment. "Or, does he? Could McCain have been faking it?"

Jethro shrugged. "No way to tell now, and not sure if it matters. You know, Preston stopped by to check on you. It might be a little easier on the fella if you answered his calls."

"Tonight, Nick Preston isn't the most important thing on my mind."

"Well, he had a thought, and I happen to agree. If what happened to Porter and the Nesmiths is related to your story on Rosalie DuFrayne, then McCain can't possibly be your killer." He grunted with satisfaction. "Now, get yourself inside, and you tell that California boy he makes a mighty fine duck."

Wednesday, 9:03 a.m., Calvary Baptist Church

Abbie took a seat in one of the back pews. The church was quite full, with more people streaming in. It would be standing room only. She watched mourners stopping to speak to a woman wearing a modest black hat and veil. Cyrus Porter's wife. The rest of the family squeezed into the front row of pews. She struggled to squash the memory of when she herself sat in the front pew, before her mother and father's matching caskets, before Zach's flag-draped coffin.

Abbie recalled a news story from the previous year, where the killer attended his victim's funeral wearing the same jacket he'd worn at the time of the murder. Was Cyrus's killer in the building now?

For a man with such a short frame, the Reverend Fisher's voice carried to the back of the church without the need of a microphone. His voice was the kind that a person heard in their heart, the kind that could whip his congregation into a frenzy every Sunday morning.

Cyrus's brother gave the eulogy, a heart-wrenching recollection of turkey fryer accidents and missed putts. Abbie's tears flowed unchecked as she heard Cyrus's last wish, to be cremated and his ashes spread over Augusta National Golf Club.

After the notes of the last song faded, Reverend Fisher announced refreshments would be served in the congregation hall. When the church was almost empty, Abbie got in line to pay her respects to Mrs. Porter. The widow was gracious in her grief. "You're the one writing the story about Rosalie DuFrayne? Thank you. Cyrus wanted some justice for her."

Abbie swallowed. *Who's going to get justice for Cyrus?*

She was signing the condolences book when a name near the top of the page jumped out at her. *Isaac Leon Moore!* Cyrus's buddy from the 1969 brawl. Abbie whirled around. There were dozens of men who could be his age, mid-sixties.

It wouldn't be appropriate, she supposed, to go up to each of them and ask their names.

She *could* ask Reverend Fisher, though. She found him by the refreshment table. "Lovely service, Reverend."

"Miss Adams. Your coming means a lot to the family."

Abbie nodded. "There is a friend here of Cyrus's I'd like to speak to. Isaac Leon Moore? Do you know him?"

"I'm sorry to say that I don't."

Abbie searched for the church secretary, Mrs. Leonard. She found her rocking a sobbing little girl, one of Cyrus's family perhaps, a granddaughter? The flash of memory, when her own little boy realized his daddy wasn't coming home and screeched his despair with that awful *No!* She couldn't intrude on the child's grief. You didn't do something like that in Hunts Landing.

The Hunts Landing Times's legal department didn't need a photo of Miss Etta's artwork to complete their review.

Tomorrow was soon enough to catch up with Mrs. Leonard.

Wednesday, 9:41 a.m., Wexler House Cellar

Joss approached Nevelyn Wexler's garden gate only after making sure the driveway next to the big house was clear of cars. Rain threatened again. He knew this not because of the lack of sunshine but because he could smell it, an earthy smell, as if all the garden plots in Hunts Landing had opened their pores to soak in the coming drops. The smell was heavy in the air. Like that old man at the hardware store had said.

In the Wexler cellar, light from the basement windows would be dimmer than yesterday.

He'd come prepared, though, with a powerful flashlight swiped from Abbie's garage, George's old boy scout compass, and a can of WD-40 tucked into his knapsack. With a baseball cap on, he hoped he looked like any other student headed toward campus. No one looked at him as he crossed the street and entered Nevelyn's garden.

Nevelyn Wexler did not answer the door. He gave her three minutes.

Shit, should have gotten her number from Abbie.

He had to get into the cellar.

Joss retraced the route he and Abbie had taken the day before to the far side of the Wexler property, to the rusty iron gate that looked as if it hadn't been touched in years. It swung open as silently as it did yesterday.

Here goes nothing.

Joss knocked softly on the kitchen door. He listened for sounds of someone, anyone, approaching from inside, but there were none.

Where were they all today?

His hand rested on the doorknob, and only a smidgen of guilt, of perhaps taking advantage of Nevelyn's obvious fondness for Abbie, stopped him from turning the knob. It wasn't really breaking and entering, after all, if he didn't break anything.

The latch opened with a soft click.

Joss quickly stepped inside, closing the door quietly behind him. He halted, listening for sounds.

The house was quiet.

His trainers made no sound on the faded carpeted runner from the back door to the cellar door. He popped inside but didn't turn on the light switch he knew was there. Instead, he stepped gingerly down the steps, toward the very faint light at the bottom, dim light from the basement windows.

After a few moments, his eyes adjusted to the gloom.

The light was enough for him to traverse the length of the basement without resorting to the flashlight. Today, he passed the storage alcoves on either side of the main cellar without further inspection and headed straight for the end farthest from the stairs.

He dropped his knapsack to the dirt floor and considered the metal shelving with the mason jars before him. Just to be sure, he grabbed vertical supports and pulled. Those shelves didn't give.

Joss examined the rusted metal shelves on either side of him, and checked his compass. The wall on his left was the northern wall, the one on his right, the southern wall. Grover House lay to the northeast. He tried his luck on his left.

He pulled dozens of paint cans off the shelves. *How many times did these people redecorate?* From the color of some of the labels, some of these cans had to be as old as the Grover's bomb shelter. He tugged on the shelves, aimed his flashlight at every nook and cranny, felt for hidden latches. Nothing.

All that remained were the shelves on the right, the ones with the dusty boxes that Abbie had examined yesterday. He didn't recall that she'd removed that many boxes.

Maybe?

Joss wrapped his fingers around the closest vertical support and tugged slowly.

The shelving moved.

Above him, he heard footsteps. Someone was home.

As quickly and quietly as he dared, he pulled boxes down from the shelves and stacked them off to the side. Urgency flooded him, he had to get down into the tunnel before whoever was upstairs decided to check out the basement and catch him red-handed. When the shelves were empty, he tugged them away from the wall again. Bare metal scratched the dirt floor, but otherwise made only a muffled sound. He slid the shelf unit free and risked his flashlight.

The beam of light rested on a wooden door made of planks blackened with age and held in place with old-fashioned hardware.

Bingo.

He sprayed some WD 40 on the latches and gave it a second to soak in. The slide bolt gave with a scratchy clang, revealing a gaping blackness, blackness like the one he'd experienced in the Grover bomb shelter.

Weathered tips of a wooden ladder were all he could see from his position. Joss dropped to the floor and stuck his torso into the hole.

The ladder went straight down at a steep angle. He could see nothing but the bottom landing.

He hesitated for a moment, listening for sounds of the person in the house above, before slinging his pack onto his shoulders and poking his legs into the hole. He held the flashlight in one hand, his feet blindly searching for the wooden rungs. Cold, colder than he'd expected, enveloped him as he descended.

Each rung of the ladder creaked. After eight or nine steps down, the flashlight flickered. *Shit, shit, shit.* Why hadn't he checked the batteries? Four more steps, five, six. His foot touched solid earth.

He shone the light around. It flickered again. Joss pressed his back against the ladder.

The last thing he saw before the light flickered out was an empty wooden crate. *Very Old Fitzgerald. 1952.*

The flashlight app on his phone was next to useless against the darkness. He would need to go back up and see if there were any lights to be had in the cellar.

His foot planted itself on the sixth rung up the ladder when the rung snapped. He grasped for the ladder with one hand as he fell downwards, bracing himself for impact with the other hand. His wrist collapsed beneath him with a sickening *crunch*.

CHAPTER EIGHTEEN

Wednesday, 12:17 p.m., Wexler House Cellar

He'd bumped his head on the way down. At least, that was what the lump on his forehead and the ache in his temple told him.

Joss's phone was only a couple of feet away in the dirt, the glow from his flashlight app still beaming up toward the wooden ceiling. His right hand was sore and swollen. *Yup, broke for sure.*

That's how they would say it in Hunts Landing.

He tucked his hurt hand against his chest and used his good one to reach for the phone. No signal. Battery down to almost nothing.

Shining the light onto the ladder, he saw the series of broken rungs, snapped like kindling. Pieces lay strewn on the floor at the foot of the ladder. The WD-40 can lay next to his pack, a few feet away.

Okay, buddy, how are we going to get out of here?

Abbie would worry, right? After he didn't show up, she'd send out a search party. Right? She'd drive around town, looking for his car . . .

Shit. He'd walked to Wexler House.

Okay, maybe she'd get Nick to do a trace on his phone.

Except she wasn't really talking to Nick.

And his phone had no signal, twenty feet below ground.

Oooh, oooh, oooh. She could use Benny's bloodhound nose to trace him. All of his laundry was there above the garage, waiting for one good sniff . . .

Joss had no idea if Benny had any tracking skills in him.

Okay. His head hurt. *On my own.*

He panned the light around. There was the old crate, grey with age. *Very Old Fitzgerald.* Maybe he could use it to bang against something. Anything, to make noise.

He kneed himself over to the crate. On the ground next to the overturned crate, grubby white wax candlestubs were strewn.

Why did I ever quit smoking? Would have matches in my pocket right now.

He panned the light some more. The tunnel was supported by wooden beams, which wouldn't make any good sounds. Not good enough to get above ground.

He needed to be able to make enough noise . . . oh, wait. If his theory was right, at the other end of this tunnel was a steel bomb shelter. He had a can of WD-40, and he had a dead flashlight. Both of which he could bang against that bomb shelter.

He just needed enough light to get to the other end.

Wednesday, 2:21 p.m., Abbie's House

Abbie was late returning to the house from Cyrus Porter's funeral.

She'd driven down to the boat launch where she'd first met up with Jethro, only a week ago. It seemed so much longer. The river was choppy ahead of the coming storms. Springtime in the Tennessee Valley was always a volatile mix of sun and rain. On the campus side of the bridge, benches dotted the river path, but on this side, there was no place to sit. So she stood watching the water, ambivalent toward the increasing breeze.

Last week, her purpose had been clear, the goal plain. Research and write a story on the unsolved murder of Rosalie DuFrayne.

And she'd allowed herself to be distracted.

Yes, she'd made the connection between Rosalie and an institutional scandal. Yes, she'd found evidence of the connection. Yes, it was an interesting piece of the history of Hunts Landing.

But Quentin McCain's doctoring of test data had nothing to do with Rosalie's murder. She didn't believe the alibi Ida McCain had attempted to provide for her husband, but she believed Valerie Rigsby, or at least her gut told her to believe Valerie Rigsby, and Sylvia had urged Abbie to follow her gut.

Her gut told her that Jethro (and by extension, Nick, whose idea it was) was right, that if the attacks on Cyrus Porter and the Nesmiths were connected, neither Quentin McCain, who was long dead, nor Ida McCain, who couldn't possibly have taken on men so much younger and stronger than she, could have done it. Whoever attacked Cyrus and put Katie into a coma was still out there.

She'd love to blame it all on Frank Wexler, but if she was honest with herself, she'd already spent too much of her life blaming her former mentor for her woes. She needed to salvage what she could. Today was deadline day. It was time to go home, put the last dob of polish on the piece, and send it off.

So when she returned home, it didn't immediately register how quiet the house was. Only Benny was there, demanding to be let out. She went to the backyard with him, thinking about the last of the items on her to-do list for the article, pondering how she could turn her lack of success into an interesting piece on a still unsolved-murder.

Benny yelped and trotted along the fence line behind her yellow roses. From the porch, Abbie could see over the hedge. Students often took the shortcut behind the house, but at the moment, no one was there.

She whistled softly. Benny glanced back at the fence before galloping to her side. Only when she was back inside the house did she fully realize that Joss wasn't there. And there was no note on the whiteboard. That was odd. He'd picked up the kids' habit of leaving her notes in erasable marker.

Abbie tried his cell. The call went directly to voicemail. Her thumb hovered over the green phone button. Should she try again? She wasn't his mother, after all.

But the same instincts that had, years ago, known George was about to fall out of his high chair seconds before he toppled, told her something was wrong.

Abbie worked her phone list quickly. Madeleine had not seen him since breakfast. Loreen had a customer, but promised to call right back. Abbie hesitated before dialing Jethro's number—the man had been guarding her house all night long, after all—but she reasoned that after their moonshine/bourbon male bonding incident, Jethro would want to know. Jethro hadn't heard from Joss, either.

Joss didn't really know anyone else in Hunts Landing.

Pop. Pop. Pop. Abbie's thumb swiped to answer the call. "Loreen. Have you seen Joss?"

"Not since last night." Loreen had left the house early, as tonight was Wine Down Wednesday at The Sommelier.

"Nobody's seen him. And he's not answering his phone."

"Oh, gosh, Abbie, I don't know . . . wait . . . last night, he was talking about going back to the Wexler's cellar. I didn't think he'd go without you."

Joss was foolhardy enough to do exactly that. "I've got to call Nevelyn Wexler."

Somewhere outside, she heard sirens.

Wednesday, 3:03 p.m., Wexler House Driveway

"He was trespassing!" Grace Wexler shrieked, her perfectly manicured finger pointed at Joss. Seated in the back of the ambulance that was parked at an angle in the Wexler driveway, Joss shifted so that the EMT wrapping his wrist was between himself and Grace.

"Oh, posh, dear," Nevelyn Wexler replied calmly. She wore a slicker against the impending rain, and she braced herself on what he guessed was the outdoor version of her walker. "He had my permission to continue his investigation."

"He didn't have *my* permission to crawl around underneath my house!"

"Technically, dear, it's still my house."

Grace grunted and glared in his direction.

"Oh, Nevelyn, how could you?" She looked so distressed, Joss *almost* felt sorry for her.

And guilty for crawling under her house.

Fat raindrops splashed on the driveway gravel. Next to him, Abbie crossed her arms, as if protecting herself from the elements.

"We need to take him for an X-ray," the EMT said. The tag on his jacket said *Charles*. "And get him checked for a possible concussion."

"I'll follow," Abbie said. "The sooner we get out of here—"

"Abigail Adams!" Grace Wexler stomped toward them, each step in the gravel heard with a loud crunch.

Joss didn't miss Abbie's barely disguised wince. But Abbie turned and faced the woman anyway.

"How dare you send a spy into our home?" The woman was practically spitting her words, but the increased breeze was in her face.

No noxious droplets reached Abbie. "Frank told you that there would be no comment from this family."

"Grace, I didn't send a spy." Abbie settled her crossed arms, her shoulder pulled back. "Joss Freeman is a world-renowned documentarian, and he's following his own story in Hunts Landing."

"Under my home? I don't believe you." Grace's arms, at her side, were pulled back a little.

Joss had the sudden image of two momma bears facing off.

"You know something, Grace? I really don't care what you believe and what you don't. We got permission from the owner of the house, Miss Nevelyn, who is, by the way, a genuine lady."

Grace recoiled, her jaw opened in disbelief.

Touché, Abs.

Gravel crunched behind him. Joss peered over his shoulder. Nick Preston.

"And what are you, Abigail Adams?" Grace retorted back. "You're nothing but a failed academic, a cheap writer for the local rag who does nothing but try to ruin the reputation of good people."

Nick stepped forward, but Joss held him back with his good hand. "I wouldn't get in there if I were you."

The cop ignored him. "Ladies, let's calm this down."

The two women glared at him so fiercely that Nick involuntarily took a step back.

Off to the side, Nevelyn Wexler stood, a ghost of a smile twitching her lips. She must have been quite a pip back in her day, the kind of woman Joss might have tried to date in college.

Abbie was glaring back and forth between Nick and Grace. *At least I'm not in trouble.* The thought was premature, because Abbie's gaze fixed on him. Joss knew that look.

She wanted to speak her mind, to all three of them, he supposed, but was restraining herself. Admirably restraining herself, he had to admit.

Abbie turned her back on both Nick and Grace. "I'll meet you at the hospital," she told Charles, the EMT.

Nick followed her. All Joss could hear was, "Hey, Abbie," before Charles shut the ambulance doors.

Wednesday, 6:11 p.m., Under the Willow Tree

Loreen brought pizzas from Mario's off the Square, the kind where the customer had to arrange the toppings before baking. George and Martha carefully placed slices of pepperoni and chunks of sausage under Joss's one-handed supervision.

Abbie carried a few slices out to Jethro, fresh out of the oven.

"Stakeout food." He smiled. "Perfect."

"Well, Joss couldn't cook tonight one-handed."

Jethro tasted a slice and sighed with contentment. "I need to do something nice for that boy before he leaves. When is he leaving, anyway?"

"Tomorrow. He pitches to the network on Friday."

"And your deadline?"

"Sylvia's got the full piece for the Sunday edition, and she wants to post a teaser tomorrow. Which should hopefully end all this craziness."

He swallowed his mouthful and washed it down with some beer. "What makes you think this is all going to end tomorrow?"

"Because if somebody is after me because of the story, tomorrow will be too late."

He licked his fingers. "Darlin', I hope you're right. In the meantime, I'll be watchin'."

Wednesday, 7:51 p.m., the War Room

The kids were in their rooms studying. Loreen had dragged Joss, cleared by the ER doctor of any signs of concussion, down to the shop for Wine Down Wednesday. It had been the auctioneer Wayne Harmon who'd heard Joss banging on the bomb shelter from the Wexler side of the tunnel and called the police. Loreen had decided to hold Wine Down Wednesday in Wayne's honor, and dragged Joss with her so he could regale anyone with his exploits in the tunnels; after all, he had the cast to prove his bravery.

Now, it was just Madeleine and herself.

"Deadline met?" Madeleine slid into an empty chair in the war room.

"As of six o'clock."

"And are you satisfied with your work?"

Abbie wished she could answer the question in the affirmative. "I can make a clear trail from Rosalie through to the grant scandal, and Quentin McCain's alibi is less than airtight. Ida McCain's likely to have a hissy fit."

"Hissy fits are the only kind that Ida McCain knows how to have. There's a 'but' in your voice."

"But . . . I believe Valerie Rigsby. McCain was too drunk. And he was still in his tux from the party. Valerie didn't see any blood. The story's not . . . finished."

The crash of patio furniture roused them. "What on earth?" Abbie ran to the sunporch and flicked on the outside lights.

Nick Preston wrestled with a large Black man who yelled, "Get off me, man!" Arms and legs were flailing. Nick wasn't having an easy time.

George tried to rush past Abbie, but she held him back. "Stay inside!" She pushed open the screen door and ventured out to the patio.

Nick and the stranger gripped each other's upper arms in a macabre dance that neither was winning. Nick had finally gotten his knee into the stranger's back and snapped cuffs on his wrists.

The man struggled and almost pushed Nick off. "I gotta talk to Abbie Adams."

"Visitors use the front door!" Nick got off the man and pulled him up by his arms.

"I didn't want anybody to see me."

"Why are you stalking Abbie Adams?"

"I ain't been stalking her! I've been watching the house is all!"

"Why?"

"Nick, wait!" Abbie stepped closer. The man had salt and pepper hair yet still was able to hold his own against a much younger man. She took a stab. "Are you Leon Moore? Isaac Leon Moore?"

Leon nodded.

"He's okay," she told Nick. "Let's go inside."

She sent the kids up for their showers while Madeleine made coffee. Leon rubbed his wrists after Nick unlocked the handcuffs, never taking his eye off the cop. Nick had a darkening bruise on his cheek. She put some ice cubes in a paper towel and handed him the makeshift ice pack. "What happened?"

"Jethro called me a little while ago," Nick said. "Jethro told me what you told him, how tomorrow all this should be all over. He figured if that's true, something might happen tonight, and he couldn't keep his eyes on both the front of the house and the back. I decided to take the back, and I wasn't here more than ten minutes when this guy comes out from behind the garage and starts running straight for your back door."

She turned to their visitor, who rubbed his wrists. "Mr. Moore? What were you doing?"

"It ain't what it looks like, Ms. Adams. I *been* watchin' your house, but I ain't the only one."

"You better start explaining," Nick said.

Leon directed his comments to Abbie. "Cyrus called Friday afternoon, right after he met you. He was askin' me all these questions about that big fight down by the river. He couldn't remember, you see, wasn't sure about some of the details."

Guilt slammed into her. "What kind of questions?"

"Things like what did I see after the fight started. What did I see? I saw a big old boy's fist smashin' in my face, that's what I saw. And I told him so."

"You didn't notice anything unusual?" Nick asked.

"Other than boys beatin' the crap out of each other? I didn't remember at first. He kept at it, though, 'cause somethin' bothered him. Kept sayin' somethin' was outta place. Like that lady runnin' around wearin' nothin' but her drawers. Then, it come to me." Abbie noted that his big hands shook a little. "The two white boys, you see. They was all bloodied up, like they was in the fight, but they wasn't, 'cause they was comin' out of the woods."

Abbie caught Nick's look. "Two white boys came *out* of the woods, looking like they'd been in the fight?"

"Yes, ma'am."

"Jethro should hear this," she said to Nick.

"I'll get him," Nick said.

Abbie turned back to Leon. "And you told this all to Cyrus? What you remembered?"

"Yes, ma'am." He accepted a cup of coffee from Madeleine. "Cyrus got all quiet on me. Took his time before he talked again. Said he had somebody to talk to, right away."

Abbie reconstructed events in her mind.

Cyrus met with her, called Leon, then rushed off to see someone. "Any idea whom?"

"No, ma'am."

"Did he say anything else?"

"Yes, ma'am," Leon said. "Cyrus told me you was stirrin' up a hornet's nest. And his words bothered me, you see. I called him Friday night, but he didn't answer. Then the news come on Sunday he got killed. I kept on thinkin' 'bout what he said. Thought 'bout it all afternoon. I kept thinkin', Cyrus got clocked, 'cause of somethin' that happened in '69. I said to myself, 'Leon, you gotta go talk to that girl.' So I walk over here, up the back path behind your house. But you was havin' a party or somethin'. I stayed in the corner over by your garage, where it's real dark. I get this funny feelin', standin' there, like I wasn't alone. Then the cop comes to your house. When he left, he crosses the street and walks right into that big old willow tree. He comes out a few minutes later. I figure, cop's got somebody watchin' the front of the house, it's a good thing I stuck to the back. I wait a little longer, but it didn't seem like anybody was leavin' anytime soon, so I figure tomorrow's soon enough, and I head back down the path toward home. Then I saw him. Some fella standin' behind your camellias, he heard me comin', and he took off."

Abbie shuddered to think of how close that corner of the yard was to George's room.

"Did you catch a good look at him?"

"No, ma'am. Too dark."

"Why didn't you go to the police?" Madeleine asked.

"And tell them what, ma'am? I was standin' behind your house and maybe some fella was there too? They'd lock me up in a moon-shine minute. I kept thinkin' 'bout what Cyrus said, 'bout you and the hornets. So last night, I come back after dark. I stayed real still, and I wait. A little while later, you let your dog out, and I freeze, but he goes trottin' around the yard doin' his thing, you see. I figure he's the worst guard dog I ever seen. I'm only twenty feet away from him, and he doesn't catch my scent? Damnedest thing, though, he comes right up to me. I let him sniff my hand, and he seemed satisfied, 'cause off he trots, to the other corner of the yard. He stopped and snarled, and

I knew the fella was hidin' in the dark like me. Your dog growls a couple of more times, and the fella takes off. Not runnin', but walkin' real fast."

Abbie looked down at the mutt, snoozing near Leon's chair. Benny snored and rolled over.

Leon continued. "I figure the fella didn't know I was here last night, so I could do the same thing tonight, try and catch him. And he was here, Ms. Adams. I saw some guy walkin' toward your back door, and I start to go after him when the cop tackles me."

"Good lord! You've got to tell this to Nick." He should have been back with Jethro already. Abbie whirled around only to see the flashing lights dancing over the living room wall and raced out the front door.

Three squad cars and an ambulance crowded the street. Paramedics were loading someone into the ambulance. Abbie ran to the gurney, searched his pale face beneath an oxygen mask. "Jethro . . ."

"We've got to take him, miss." The paramedics lifted the gurney into the rig.

"I think he's going to be okay," Nick said from her side as the ambulance pulled away. "He was unconscious when I found him, but I called for an ambulance and started CPR. He came to. Got hit in the back of the head."

Oh God, just like Rosalie. She wanted to go to the hospital, be with Jethro, but the idea of leaving the kids in the house . . . she looked up and down the street at nothing and everything at the same time, every car, every shadow made by the streetlamps. "I think I want to go to the hospital. But . . ."

Nick's nod was firm. "But we're going to handle things here first."

Nick listened to Isaac Leon Moore retell his story and took notes. "You should have reported this, Mr. Moore," Nick scolded, but not too harshly. Abbie was glad for it. "I'll call for a squad car to take you home."

"No disrespect meant, but I don't need to be showin' up at my front door in a police car. I can walk." Leon stood to leave. "Sorry for the trouble, Ms. Adams."

Abbie asked him for his cell phone number before he left, just in case.

Nick got on his phone to make arrangements while she checked on the kids. They were in Martha's room, watching the police cars out in the street.

George turned away from the window to face her. "What happened, Mom?"

"Somebody tried to mug Jethro," she lied. "He's going to be okay, though."

George didn't believe her—his arched eyebrows said so. Martha seemed uneasy. "Can Benny sleep with me tonight, Mom?"

Abbie squeezed her shoulders. "Of course. I'm going to the hospital with Nick. Joss and Loreen are back from the shop, and Madeleine's here too. Is that alright with you?"

"You gotta take care of Mr. Jethro," Martha insisted.

Back in the kitchen, Nick was explaining the arrangements.

"We're leaving patrol cars out front and around the corner, and I'd like to position an officer on your sunporch where he can monitor the back. Tomorrow is soon enough to plan other arrangements."

She agreed. "Can we go to the hospital now?"

"Yes," Nick said.

Wednesday, 9:13 p.m., Hunts Landing Medical Center

"How long do you think before a doctor sees him?" Abbie asked Nick.

"Retired Hunts Landing PD? They'll be treating him now." Nick flashed his badge to the nurse at the desk, who buzzed them through the security door. A uniformed officer down the hall guarded a closed-door room. He spoke in a low voice to the cop, then nodded.

"They took him up for a CAT scan. Now we wait."

Wait they did, in silence, Abbie lost in her thoughts, Nick perhaps wise enough not to speak. Somebody had approached her house. Somebody had attacked Jethro. The violence seemed to be escalating. Abbie wondered if Sylvia's promised teaser would be enough to stop it.

An orderly pushing a gurney emerged from the elevator, and Abbie leaped to her feet. "Jethro!" The doctors had shaved part of his head, and a four-inch bandage covered it.

He opened his eyes, smiling wanly. "Hey, darlin'."

"Jethro . . ."

He swallowed. "I'm fine. A knock on the head, a few stitches, that's all."

This didn't look like a simple knock on the head to Abbie.

"You should go home, rest some," he said.

She didn't want to leave him alone. "Someone should stay with you."

"My daughter's driving down from Memphis. You go home and take care of your babies. They're probably more scared than you know."

———

Before leaving for the night, Nick handed Abbie her Beretta. "It came out clean."

Abbie took the pistol. "Any word on the make of the gun that shot Cyrus?"

"It was a Walther PPK, the same model gun—"

"—that Hitler used to kill himself in the bunker. Don't look so surprised. Daddy was a collector. The PPK was a favorite souvenir for the GIs coming back from Europe."

"So I've been told." Nick sighed. "Well, I don't think you're going to need your gun tonight, and you've got a bunch of eyes watching you. I'll be in Jethro's tree. But keep it close."

He obviously didn't know she slept with a Glock handy. "Who's watching Isabella?"

"She's camped out at Dora's house. I would have put Martha there too if I'd thought about it in time."

Abbie shook her head. "I don't want Martha alarmed any more than she is. This will be over tomorrow. Sylvia's posting a teaser tonight. The killer will know they can't stop the story."

"You'd better hope so. I'm this close to putting you into protective custody."

On impulse, Abbie kissed his cheek. "We'll be fine. Lots of grownups in here."

Nick's exhausted eyes bored into hers. Was it exhaustion? She didn't know, and she didn't care.

He paused. "I wasn't going to tell you, but that phone number, it's a burner phone, bought in Decatur. But all the calls came from the Quad, not too far from your house. So, don't go anywhere alone. Agreed?"

She nodded slowly, eyes never leaving his. *I understand. You're keeping us safe. I won't do anything stupid.*

"Get some rest."

After he left and she locked the door, Abbie put the gun in her bag.

CHAPTER NINETEEN

Thursday, Dawn, the War Room

Abbie poured three cups of coffee. The uniformed cop accepted a mug with a salute of thanks and resumed his surveillance of her backyard. The eastern sky was brightening, with splashes of peach and purple lighting the horizon.

Handing the second cup to Joss, Abbie sank into her chair and looked over the Rosalie whiteboard. The loose ends list seemed to pulse at her. Rosalie's headstone. She never heard from Mrs. Leonard about the payments for the headstone, but Abbie didn't feel right pestering the woman only one day after Cyrus's funeral, not when the family probably needed her. Rosalie's possible pregnancy she would keep out of the final piece; Abbie wasn't going to start her journalistic career with smears she couldn't prove. Someone had asked the reporter Caleb Jackson to stand down, possibly Old Dr. Wexler. Abbie wondered how well Theodore Wexler had known Caleb Jackson.

The article was written, but Sylvia liked lots of artwork to choose from. She checked the pictures taped to the whiteboard. Most of them would work, Rosalie's yearbook picture, the one of Rosalie with Bernice and Cleta, Rosalie's headstone. She'd forgotten to go back to the cemetery to retake that shot. Simple enough to go this morning.

While she was at it, she could retake a couple of other pictures. She didn't like any of the photos from the crime scene. She also needed something about the Wexler party.

Joss's eyes were red and his hair a tousled mess. They'd stayed up late after she'd gotten home from the hospital, Abbie trying to calm her shredded nerves enough to sleep, Joss both excited and disappointed at finding the tunnel, despite it being empty, despite it ending in the rounded steel wall of a 1950s bomb shelter. He'd taken his laptop to the garage apartment to write the non-discovery up, so there was no telling how little sleep he'd gotten.

"What time's your flight?" Abbie asked.

Joss slumped in his chair. "Three."

"Do you have enough for the pitch?"

"You mean, do I think finding an empty tunnel is going to save my job? No," he yawned. "Not that I think the competition found Custer's gold. Eddie Udell would have plastered it all over YouTube by now if he had." Joss scratched his hair, much the same way he scratched Benny's scruff. "What about you?"

"Cemetery first, then I think I'm going to head over to Nevelyn Wexler's."

"You'd be a brave woman to venture back to Wexler House."

"Nevelyn Wexler has a photo from the party. Maybe she'll loan it to me." She scribbled a list of new pictures she needed to take.

"She *did* promise I could film in the Wexler cellar if Kenetsky takes the pitch. But, as for going back down there today," he held up his bandaged wrist, "I think that's out of the question."

Abbie thumped a pen on the table. "I can take the temperature, figure out if it's a good idea to try to get back into the basement today."

Thursday, 8:33 a.m., the Cemetery at Calvary Baptist Church

Abbie made the drive in less than five minutes. She walked straight to Rosalie's tombstone. This morning, the cloudy skies yielded a more even light over the inscription.

Abbie snapped several pictures and checked them through the camera's LCD display.

"Miss Adams?"

Abbie jumped and whirled around. "Mrs. Leonard."

The church secretary touched her arm. "I wanted to thank you for coming to the service yesterday. The family appreciated you coming."

"I would have said 'hello,' but you had your hands full."

"Cyrus's granddaughter. The child adored her grandpa."

Abbie never found it easy to slip into condolences-mode, not since her parents. "It's terrible, what happened, but the police are working the case hard."

"Hopefully we'll see justice for Cyrus, if not for this girl." Mrs. Leonard crossed her arms and looked down at the grave. "Turns out the family cleared out my Gran's house when we moved her to assisted living. No artwork left, I'm afraid. But I did find some of the other information you asked me for. Dr. Theodore Wexler paid for the original headstone, and he paid for Miss Etta's too."

Abbie wasn't surprised. Theodore Wexler had paid for the girl's education. A little more for her stone didn't seem out of character. "Makes sense."

Mrs. Leonard touched Rosalie's stone with her fingertips. "And Dr. Frank Wexler paid for this replacement in 1978."

"That's not the original?"

"No. There was an accident with a backhoe. Thing dropped right on Rosalie's stone. Dr. Frank Wexler replaced it."

"Good golly, things happened to that girl even after she died." How many times could she cry for this woman? Abbie didn't know. She was so tired. Tears streamed unchecked. She didn't have the energy to stop them or wipe them away.

Mrs. Leonard was ready with a tissue. "She's in God's hands, Miss Adams. Headstones, they aren't for the dead, they're for the living."

Thursday, 9:11 a.m., Nevelyn Wexler's Cottage

Nevelyn Wexler opened the door with a smile. "Come in, dear. Tell me, how is young master Freeman?"

Abbie followed her into the house. "Appropriately subdued. And I must apologize for his behavior again."

"Posh, dear, I would have gone down there with him myself if I could." Nevelyn shuffled to the picture of the Wexler party. "I got this darned thing off the wall the other day, now I can't budge it."

Abbie pulled the frame away from the wall and peered behind it. "The hook is bent." She slid her hand behind the photograph and wiggled the wire loose. "Thank you for loaning this to me." She looked at the faces in the photo. So many of these people gone, or terribly unhappy. Abbie felt a pang of regret. Ida McCain was going to be so unhappy with the story. One of the loose ends came to her mind. "May I ask, did your brother know Caleb Jackson?"

"Caleb? Of course. He was one of Theodore's fishing buddies."

"I found a curious note in Caleb Jackson's file. Somebody asked him to stand down, not write the story. He wrote a pretty good article, but the paper never printed it."

"And you're wondering if that person was Theodore?" Nevelyn considered the possibility. "Maybe he did so for Miss Etta. She was such a wreck. Certainly didn't need to see her daughter's picture splashed all over the front page. It sounds like something Theodore would do."

"He paid for Rosalie's headstone."

"That, too, sounds like something Theodore would do."

Thursday, 10:17 a.m., the War Room

Joss chattered away as she connected the camera to her laptop. "If Kenetsky takes the pitch, I'll probably be back in a few weeks. But I'll get a room at the inn this time."

"Nonsense." Abbie selected the best of the headstone photos and hit Print. "The kids love having you here, and you're a halfway decent cook . . ." She stared at the photo inching its way out of the printer. "Huh?" Her head bobbed back and forth from her laptop screen to the printer. "This can't be right." How had she not seen this before?

"What can't be right?"

She turned her laptop around to face him. "What do you see?"

"A headstone," Joss said.

"Look harder."

She pulled the photo from the printer and held it up to the older photo of Rosalie's headstone taped to her whiteboard. Through a funky chance of light from last week, sunlight illuminated the inscription on Rosalie's stone but kept the rest in shadow, creating an optical illusion. The headstone looked like a single person headstone.

Today's picture, the one taken under gray skies with even light, revealed more clearly what she hadn't noticed before—Rosalie's inscription, neatly centered, in the right half of the marker. The left half was empty.

Realization must have dawned on Joss. "This is a married couple's stone. But Rosalie wasn't married, was she?"

Abbie took a marker and drew new lines on her whiteboard. Oh gosh, it made sense. She unplugged the camera from her laptop and placed it in her bag, along with a copy of the Wexler party picture. "I'll be back in half an hour."

She made her call as she pulled out of her driveway. Isaac Leon Moore was at work, only a couple of minutes away.

Abbie pulled into the parking lot in front of Hunts Landing Auto Supplies and hurried inside. She spotted Isaac Leon Moore at a counter standing next to bins of oil filters.

He wiped his hands clean with a blue garage rag. "Mornin', Ms. Adams."

"Good morning. Thanks for seeing me." She reached inside her purse for the Wexler party picture.

"Boss isn't here, it's alright."

"Would you look at this picture for me? Those two white boys you saw coming out of the woods, do you recognize them?"

After a long minute, he pointed to two young men in the back row. "That's them."

"You sure?"

"Yes, ma'am. As sure as I can be after forty somethin' years."

"Oh gosh, *thank you*, Mr. Moore."

"Her too."

"Which one?"

He pointed to another face. "That's the gal that was running around in her drawers."

Thursday, Noon, Abbie's House

Joss brought down his meager luggage from the garage apartment and then sat to wait.

He'd be home tonight, if he still wanted to call it home, a place without Harriet or Lincoln, if only for a few hours before heading to New York for the pitch. He hadn't given her much thought in the past couple of days, in fact, not since the one phone call when she announced she was moving to Baja. Nope, he didn't miss her one bit. Lincoln was a separate matter.

You didn't mess with a man's cat.

Benny yelped just before someone's fist banged loudly on the front door.

Nick didn't say hello, just strode inside. "Where is she?"

"She went to get some new pictures for the article."

"She's not answering her phone. Did she say where she was going?"

"Nope. But she wrote some stuff on her wall, then grabbed some pictures off the printer and took off. Said she'd be back soon."

Nick studied the Rosalie DuFrayne wall. "Look at this, tell me what's new."

Joss examined the board. There were so many damned lines crisscrossing all over the whiteboard. "I'm not sure . . ."

"Did she mention the Wexlers at all?"

Joss shook his head slowly. "No, why?"

"Because I just watched surveillance footage of Cyrus Porter headed to Wexler House the afternoon he was killed."

Thursday, 1:01 p.m., Walker's Boat Launch

The path proved easier to find the third time around. Spring green leaves rustled overhead. The wind picked up. The long boughs of the canopy swayed, rubbed against each other. It was early in the season for spring storms, but one was coming.

She hurried past the brush, bag over one shoulder, camera in hand. Darkening clouds overhead cast deep shadows in the brush. She only had minutes before the skies opened up.

She pictured the exact shot she needed. The log next to where Rosalie died, taken from the northeast part of the clearing. She dropped her bag on a rock and pulled off the lens cap, positioned herself, aimed and focused.

Her finger snapped the picture before she realized what she saw. She lowered the camera.

A fresh yellow lily rested on the log.

"Abbie," the oh-so-familiar voice said. "I waited for you."

It felt like slow motion, like when the internet slowed down, and her Netflix stream sputtered with a slow, jerky speed. Sounds of the river ceased—the pulsing beat of her own heart filled her ears. Brush around her blurred as she turned, individual leaves morphing into indistinguishable greenish blobs.

Frank Wexler stood at the pathway to the clearing, a revolver trained on her.

Thursday, 1:07 p.m., the War Room

"Madeleine hasn't seen her," Nick said, swiping his phone off.

"Neither has Loreen," Joss replied.

"She was going to take some pictures?"

"Some of the shots she took before didn't come out."

"Which shots?"

Joss scanned the board. "She'd already gone back to the cemetery. Here's the new one of the headstone." Joss pulled the sheet off the printer. "All these other pictures are of the campus, and the crime scene."

Nick called the station. "I need an APB on Abigail Adams, thirty-seven-year-old white female driving a dark green Nissan Pathfinder. APB on Dr. Frank Wexler, male in his sixties, vehicle unknown, lives on Washington Street. Send a car to the house and call campus PD to check out his office." He dropped the phone into his pocket. "I'll let you know—"

"The hell you will. I'm coming with you."

"I can't bring a civilian to a possible situation."

Joss was already headed to the front door. "Then you'd better deputize me."

Thursday, 1:11 p.m., the Clearing

Wexler extended a hand to a rock opposite the one where Rosalie had fallen. "Take a seat."

Abbie sidestepped to the rock, her eyes glued to the revolver. Every step took her farther and farther away from her own firearm. "What are you going to do, Dr. Wexler?" Her voice trembled slightly; she had difficulty coordinating her lips and jaw.

"I haven't decided yet. From the moment you told me about your *assignment*, I wondered how long it would take you to get to me. I watched you leave Aunt Nevelyn's cottage this morning. Today's the day, right? I had time to prepare, but I'm still not sure what I'm going to do about you." He tilted his head, a gesture she'd seen hundreds of times before, when he was her professor and she his student. "Go ahead. Impress me."

Start with the things you know, the facts. "Rosalie was your lover."

Shadows hooded his narrowed eyes, but she couldn't mistake his despair. "Yes. She was my lover. She was my best friend. Since we were twelve and the first time she came to help Miss Etta out in the kitchen. Rosalie could sass a smile out of me faster than butter melts on a hot biscuit. I loved her."

She needed time. Images of George, of Martha, Momma and Daddy, even Joss tried to elbow their way into her consciousness. She tamped them down flat. Facts, things Frank Wexler couldn't dispute, that's all she could allow in the front of her head. "Rosalie left your house after the party and headed here to meet you, right? This was your secret place?"

"Excellent conclusion." He smiled, a smile Abbie recognized, when a student answered a tough question correctly. "Yes, this was our place, where we could see each other with some privacy. I met her here. As soon as I saw her, my Rosalie, so beautiful, approaching me across the clearing, I must have snapped, and lights exploded in my head." He ran his shirtsleeve across his face. "I passed out. I don't really remember. David found me, a few feet over there. Rosalie, my sweet, sweet Rosalie, she was gone . . . her eyes . . . were . . . open, and she looked up at me, but she didn't see me, couldn't see me anymore."

The incredible sensation of being sucked into another's pain, one she first experienced with Cyrus Porter, consumed her—Abbie's chest heaved with his sobs.

Frank Wexler's voice broke. "I closed her eyes. I kissed her. David pulled me away, told me we had to get away. We headed up the northern path, but then we heard the fight, so we went east to blend in with the fighters, to explain away the blood. Her blood. It covered my clothes. I threw up. David practically carried me back to the Quad."

Another fact. "David got you home."

"Yes, he got me home, where my father waited."

From all she'd learned, Frank was a fraction of the man his father was, and she had firsthand knowledge of what coming up against a Wexler was like. Nineteen-year-old Frank must have felt so small. "Did you tell him?"

"Only a stupid boy would confess that kind of sin to Theodore Wexler." Frank's lower jaw jutted forward, quivered. "David put me to bed, told him about the fight at the river. My alibi was complete. Next day, the police came. I listened from upstairs. Miss Etta, she collapsed right there in the front hall. Father and Aunt Nevelyn knelt on either side of her, and sobs that came out of that little woman echoed throughout the house. I must've made a noise, because Father looked up and saw my face, and I knew in that instant, he realized what I'd done."

Frank had looked at his father and their relationship forever changed. "Your aunt said you and he argued that day."

"Yes," he sighed. "After Miss Etta's friends came to take her to the church, Father came into my room. He insisted on hearing every detail. I told him."

And what Frank said was enough for his father to turn away from him forever. "That's why he disinherited you, wasn't it?"

"Oh, you discovered that too?" Frank didn't look all that surprised. "He didn't just disinherit me. He refused to help me, his own son, when the Draft Board pulled my number. I even wondered if he bribed them. I don't care. He hated me from that moment on, and I hated him." He exhaled. "If my father had been a reasonable man, Rosalie and I could have had some kind of life together. But he couldn't see past what he expected me to be, and how much of a *disappointment* I was to him."

"You never told him that you and Rosalie loved each other?"

"What was the point? He would never have allowed it. I was Theodore Wexler's *son*. Family, honor, duty. Marry a suitable woman, any suitable woman, from the list that the matrons of Hunts Landing produced."

Her heart raced with the queer combination of fear and the exhilaration of the revelation. "You loved Rosalie. You replaced her headstone with one for a husband and wife. You're planning on being buried next to her. You leave her flowers. *Why* did you kill her?"

"You've figured it all out. Why do *you* think I killed her?"

"Because she was pregnant?" Abbie asked.

"You think I'd kill the woman I loved because she carried my baby? Disappointing, Abbie. I killed her because she was pregnant and *she was going to leave me!* She told me so before the party. I begged her to stay, told her we would make it work, but Rosalie . . . she refused, said things would be bad enough in Hunts Landing for her without a mixed-race marriage on top of it. *She was going to leave me!* I convinced her to meet me here after the party. I wanted to reason with her again. Part of me wanted to leave with her. But when I saw her, I must have snapped and killed her."

The last remnants of hate Abbie'd carried for all those years seeped away with his anguish. "That's not how this happened." She stood, and without meaning to, took a step toward him.

Wexler's hand shook as he aimed the gun at her head. "You calling me a liar? After all this?"

Another step closer. "I'm saying you can't be Rosalie DuFrayne's killer. Remember how sick you were the next day? How nauseous? I think that was because you had a concussion."

"You can't possibly know that."

"When we took Joss Freeman to the ER, they told me the signs to watch. Headache, nausea. Cyrus told me how hurt you were." Her lip quivered with the thought of Cyrus. "There's no way that petite little Rosalie could have hit you so hard during a fight as to give you a concussion. And I don't believe you could have done the damage to her that the killer did. Remember? You told me. You closed her eyes, *you kissed her*, but her killer stuffed her face into the sand." Five steps away from him and the gun, now four. "You didn't kill Cyrus Porter, not with that gun." Three. "And I know you didn't kill Rosalie, because you weren't running around the Quad in your underwear."

They found Abbie's car at the boat launch. Joss pointed to a black SUV parked next to it. "He's here."

"Okay, we go in quiet now. If he's in there with her, we've got to assess the situation before we make a move."

Joss swallowed and followed Nick onto the leafy path.

———————

"You're right, Abbie. It wasn't Frank running around the Quad in underwear that night."

Abbie whirled toward the voice.

"It was me." Grace Wexler stepped into the clearing from the path behind Abbie. She pointed a Walther pistol at her husband.

"There was so much blood." She motioned with the gun for Abbie to step away from Frank.

Abbie gingerly stepped backward. "You had to get rid of your clothes."

"Couldn't exactly stroll through the Quad covered in Rosalie's blood, now could I?" Grace tossed her head back a little, the movement shaking her otherwise perfectly coiffed hair. "I threw my dress and my slip in the river and went back out through the trees. The path opened up onto the Quad. I acted drunk. No one noticed me. The Quad was full of drunks."

Abbie kept her eyes on Grace's gun. "Cyrus Porter noticed you."

"Yes. The fool came to *my* house and told me what he remembered. I followed him down here. I guess he wanted to jog his memory. When he got back to his car, I was ready." Grace smiled.

Fat tears streamed down Frank's cheeks as he turned his gun on his wife. "*Why?*"

Grace pointed the Walther at Frank, but kept her eyes on Abbie. "You were *mine*, Frank, you were meant for *me*, not that filthy *whore*! I was going to be Mrs. Frank Wexler. That slut wasn't going to take that away from me! I followed you here and found you pleading with her, pleading on your *knees!* I grabbed the biggest rock I could find and brought it down on your head. Rosalie tried to get away, but I caught her, and I *bashed* her on her head, I bashed her *over and over*, even when I knew she had to be dead. I . . . knew . . . she . . . was . . . dead. *And I bashed her again!"*

Abbie had instinctively taken a step back, and Grace swung the pistol on her, now gazing at Frank. "I was in the trees when David found you. I *saw* you, saw how you kissed her. And when you'd left I grabbed her arm and dragged her over there and *stuffed those lips you kissed into the dirt."*

Frank's scream, wretched, visceral, unholy, erupted from his throat, and he charged at his wife, but missed. Grace brought both hands to her pistol grip and fired twice, hitting him in the side with the second shot. He fell to his knees.

She covered the distance to her husband in two strides of her long legs and wielded the pistol as a club, striking his head, his face, his head again. His feeble attempts to defend himself were useless. Each blow resulted in a fresh spray of blood.

Abbie stood frozen in place, unable to stop the assault, the image of a young Grace pounding Rosalie DuFrayne's body alternating with the vicious attack she witnessed now. Grace caught Frank on his high cheekbone. The crunch of breaking bone shattered her paralysis. Before she could think twice, she rushed to grab the pistol from Grace.

Abbie couldn't grip on the Walther's barrel, slick with Frank's blood. She wiggled a finger under Grace's watchband and pulled.

Grace turned her furious gaze on Abbie, who lost the advantage when the bigger woman rose and twisted her right wrist. Abbie's finger remained caught in the watchband; she had no leverage. Grace twisted her right arm, twisted more.

Her feet slipped in the sand; *pop!,* and white-hot pain seared her right shoulder.

Abbie dropped to her side and tasted sand, not taking the eyes off the Walther.

"Drop your weapon!" Nick stepped into the clearing, pistol drawn. "Drop it now!"

From somewhere behind Grace, Joss ran out from the trees, throwing his arms around her torso in a sloppy tackle. Grace shot wildly, three or four times, Abbie lost count of the shots. She shut her eyes tight until the echoes of the last blast faded.

Moments later—*seconds? minutes?*—she raised her head.

Help was coming, she heard the shouts, distant voices punching through the ringing in her ears. She'd fallen close to Frank. He lay on his back, face and neck bloodied almost beyond recognition, but he was breathing, his chest barely lifting. She used her left arm to crawl closer.

His lips moved, the sounds gurgled from the blood in his throat. "Rosalie . . ."

Frank lay next to the log with the lily. *Sweet Jesus, right where Rosalie died.* She pulled herself to her knees. The yellow lily, unscathed, lay on the log. She pressed the bloom into his hand.

His fingers closed over hers, a slight flutter of pressure. "Thank you . . . Abbie . . ."

Frank's eyes fluttered closed as the first fat raindrops fell.

CHAPTER TWENTY

Thursday, Sometime in the Afternoon, Hunts Landing Medical Center

"**T**his immobilizer will keep you from trying to work your shoulder," Dr. Esterhaus instructed. He wore purple scrubs with neon yellow shoelaces on his Nikes. Martha had shorts the same color . . .

"There are some additional instructions for tonight," he said to Madeleine.

Abbie paid little attention. His shoelaces fascinated her.

A door whooshed open. She felt a small hand on her back. "Abbie?"

The last vestiges of fog lifted. "Dr. Nesmith."

"I think, after all this, you should call me Tyler. Are you up for a visit? Katie's awake."

Katie was still pale, but Abbie figured her own pallor wasn't any rosier. Gauze taped to her hairline above her eye protected sutures, and the plaster casts on an ankle and an arm were proof of the long recovery ahead. "The damage that woman did," Abbie muttered.

"You're right," she said. "I'm sorry for putting you through this."

"Why did you?"

Katie swallowed. "Rosie and I did English Lit together, you know? For two semesters. Smart, classy lady. Would have been the first African American female engineer to graduate from Hunts Landing College."

"You thought Frank killed her."

She fought welling tears. "Back in school, I figured maybe they were a secret couple. He acted so different after she died, so unfeeling. Yes, I thought he killed her, and I thought Theodore Wexler covered it up."

"But, why me, why now?"

"After forty-six years, you mean? Because a friend asked me. Don't ask me who. Now that you have your first byline, you should remember that a good journalist never reveals her sources, right?" Katie frowned. "Please, forgive me. I never dreamed it would come to violence. I should have killed the story days ago."

The door opened, and to Abbie's surprise, Whitney the intern stepped in. "Miss Abbie? How are you feeling?" In the same room, the resemblance to Katie was unmistakeable.

Katie reached for her daughter's hand. "I sent you a little help, Abbie. Forgive the deception, please."

Abbie saw Madeleine's concerned face through the small rectangle of glass in the door. "I have to go."

"Thank you, Abbie. For Rosalie."

Outside in the hall, Will Irestone waited, dressed in a robe and slippers and seated in a wheelchair. "Care to give me a quote?"

"You've got to be kidding."

"Nope. You're going to be on the front page in the morning. *Local reporter solves decades-old cold case and nabs the killer.* I'll give it the good old Irestone panache, of course."

"I've gotta get home, Will."

"One quote."

Her mind didn't want to think. She just wanted to get home and hug her kids. She said the first thing that popped into her head. "Rosalie DuFrayne touched many hearts. She touched mine."

Thursday, 7:21 p.m., the Back Patio

Abbie and Joss stretched out on lounge chairs on the back patio. Madeleine had strapped gallon-sized Ziploc bags of ice to Abbie's shoulder with an elastic bandage. For Joss, she'd slipped crushed ice into the fingers of a surgical glove. The glove rested on his forehead, two fingers on each side of his broken nose.

"Was Ursula furious you missed your flight?" Abbie asked.

"I didn't have the chance to tell you. Our little stroll in the woods today made CNN. Ursula took it straight to the channel. Kenetsky is out of the picture. Ursula's going to pitch a new show in the morning. *America's Mysteries*." The stuffiness in Joss's voice from the swollen nose made the word *pitch* sound like *pitz*.

Madeleine came outside with a tray. "I brought decaf."

Abbie shifted so that she could take a mug of coffee without putting pressure on her bad shoulder. "Maddie, we're safe now, you can sleep in your own bed—"

"I'm going to pretend you did not just say that to me, Abigail Adams." The older woman settled in a chair opposite her two patients. "Now, are all deadlines met?"

"Yes, ma'am," both Abbie and Joss said.

"So the two of you can rest."

Joss tried to sip his coffee with the ice-glove balanced on his nose and failed. The glove slipped onto his lap, spilling the crushed ice.

"Damn. I didn't used to be so clumsy."

"You didn't used to be on Percocet." She laughed, then groaned. Laughing hurt.

Her phone buzzed.

Nick: How do you feel?

At least smiling didn't hurt. Replying to his text was slow going. She had to use her left hand.

"Tell Loverboy 'thanks' for a helluva time today," Joss murmured as he replaced his glove.

Abbie: Sore. Loopy. Got good drugs.

Nick: Me too, but I'm busting out of this joint tomorrow. Wanna take a special lady out to dinner.

Abbie: Oh yeah? Some place good?

Nick: Classy place. Middle school concession stand.

Abbie: Meet you there.

"Does that smile mean you've forgiven him?" Joss asked.

Had she? Sure, he'd come to her rescue, fired the shot that ultimately killed Grace Wexler, and took a bullet to his own leg in the process. "I honestly don't know. But, the guy took a bullet for me. The least I can do is treat him to a hot dog."

"Surely a bullet rates nachos?" Joss asked.

Abbie tried to stretch her good arm. "She only grazed him. Maybe a chili dog."

Friday, 8:11 a.m., Abbie's House

Abbie'd slept little despite the painkillers. Every time she closed her eyes, she dreamed of Cyrus or Frank or Rosalie. Her pillow was damp from her tears. After the sounds of breakfast and getting ready for school faded, she gave up on sleeping altogether.

With a fresh mug of tea, she headed out to the patio in time to see a strange car pull into the driveway. A young man wearing a black suit exited the driver's side, walked around to the passenger side door, and opened it. Nevelyn Wexler emerged from the car and waited for her companion to help her through the garden gate.

Simply dressed in mourning black, Nevelyn used a cane instead of her blinged-out walker. Abbie felt ashamed at still being in her bathrobe.

She rose. "Miss Nevelyn?"

"Don't get up for me, dear. Meet my grandnephew, Gregory."

The resemblance—the same nose, the same firm jaw, with Grace's blonde hair—floored her. Is this what a young Frank Wexler looked like? His sad smile, creases bracketing his mouth. He grieved, and she searched for blame in his eyes, but found none.

"Gregory, please excuse us."

Nevelyn waited for him to return to the car. "If you don't mind my saying so, dear, you look terrible."

Abbie had avoided the mirrors this morning. "It wasn't an easy night."

"No, I wouldn't think so." She eyed Abbie with a tilt of her head. "So, you discovered what happened to Rosalie."

She nodded. "Yes, ma'am."

"I spoke to Katie Nesmith a little while ago. She told me everything. All these years, Frank believed he had killed that poor girl. And Theodore, he died thinking his son was a killer. How terrible."

Oh, when were the waterworks going to stop? Fresh tears spilled. "Frank . . . he heard the truth. At the end."

Nevelyn leaned forward and grasped Abbie's hand. "We knew about Frank and Rosalie, of course. They thought they hid it so well, but they were terrible liars. We had us an impossible situation. We couldn't allow it."

"A mixed-race marriage would have been difficult," Abbie agreed.

"No, dear. Had nothing to do with that." Nevelyn caught Abbie's eye and held it with a steady gaze. "We couldn't allow it because Rosalie was Frank's half-sister."

Abbie gasped. "Oh, good God!"

"We never told them," Nevelyn said. "Theodore was devastated by his wife's death. He and Miss Etta had an affair. He did right by them, brought them both here to live from New Orleans. I think, for a time, they continued their relationship here in Hunts Landing, but I don't know this as a certainty. Theodore never remarried, never saw another woman after that, and, as you know, Etta never married. She was always here, and Rosalie practically grew up with Frank. Rosalie and Miss Etta were a part of our *family*, you understand? Family."

Nevelyn touched Abbie's arm gently and yet firmly, demanding attention the way only Wexlers can. "You have a job to do. I would appreciate any effort you took to help me protect their memory. I'm sure Katie Nesmith will agree."

Abbie's eyes widened. "It was you who put me up for this story? Why?"

Nevelyn ignored the question. "I was quite mobile before I hurt my hip, dear." She folded her hands in her lap. "It was right around Theodore's birthday, and I was remembering his fondness for Very Old Fitzgerald, and I suddenly remembered that he used to keep a stash of it, in the cellar. I knew where, of course; we'd been in and out of that cellar like monkeys when we were children. So, on a lark, I decided to take a peek, see if any of the Fitzgerald was left."

Nevelyn smiled with the memory. "That ladder, the same one Master Freeman fell down the other day, I climbed down that thing and with each step, I felt myself getting younger and younger, like the steps were chopping the years off. Can you imagine? This old body climbing down into a cellar. But I did it. The first thing I saw was an old crate with *Very Old Fitzgerald* burnt into the side. With the stub of a candle on it. Oh, hello young man."

Joss had come outside, his nose purple and swollen.

"I was telling Abbie of my own adventure in the tunnel," Nevelyn continued. "Well, that crate was empty, but there was another, with my mother's silk shawl draped over it, and more candle stubs, and photos. There was one of my mother, and one of Rosalie and Frank as toddlers, that Theodore took after Frank's mother had died, on a hot August afternoon when we took the children down to the river to cool off."

Nevelyn clenched her fist, and the *pops* from her arthritic joints were painful for Abbie to hear.

"We'd known about them, like I said, Theodore and Miss Etta and myself. We thought they'd grow out of it, would realize maybe that their worlds were too different to overlap. We couldn't tell them, or maybe *wouldn't* tell them, but it seemed to me that when Frank came back from Vietnam, when he so completely disconnected from the rest of us, he was still mourning Rosalie."

Abbie closed her eyes against threatening tears. How well she knew mourning, how well she knew how much of a shrine a single photo could be. She felt Joss's good arm snake around her shoulders.

"There was one other thing that was important in that cellar. Rosalie's scarf. Theodore had gifted it to her for her birthday. She always had it in her purse. The police never found it. But I did. In the cellar. And, though it had been over forty years, I thought I could still smell her scent on it. Lilies." Nevelyn's breath shuddered. "Amazing how the mind can trick you into impossible truths. Well, I collected those photos, and those papers, Frank's papers. The scarf. And the candle stubs. I took everything from that cellar until only the crate of Very Old Fitzgerald was left. And I waited."

Abbie sucked up sniffles. "You waited for Frank."

"Sure enough, got drunk enough one night, went to pay his homage to the cellar, and it was empty. He only drank like that when Grace was out of the house, you understand. I could hear him rant and rave, he broke most of the crystal in the library. I heard enough, though, to convince me of his guilt."

"And you thought he killed Rosalie."

Nevelyn's eyes lost their sharp brilliance for a moment, clouded with memory. "Rosalie . . . was . . . a *good* girl . . . all her life. Her momma, Miss Etta, well, I can't tell you how many nights we spent taking care of one sick child or another, or Theodore when he had his heart palpitations. There's still people in this town who'd have a come apart if I said out loud *I loved that woman like my sister.* Well, I'm not responsible for the narrowmindedness of others, just my own heart. And I loved Miss Etta, and I loved that dear girl. And, that sweet girl, with so much promise, was killed, and Miss Etta was never the same, and *my* life was never the same after that. There had to be some justice."

Abbie's hands trembled, and Nevelyn placed her own fingers on Abbie's arm. "To answer your earlier question, I didn't put *you* up for the story. Why would I, with your history with Frank?"

"I questioned my own objectivity," Abbie admitted.

"I would have too, if I'd known in advance. I'd asked Katie for help. Katie gave instructions to her editor, who assigned the story to Will. But then Will crashed his Jeep, and Sylvia, on a deadline and probably eager to impress her boss, assigned the story to you. Katie didn't know for a day or two, and by then, what could either of us do?"

Nevelyn reached for her purse and pulled out envelopes. "I'm keeping the documents I found in the cellar, Abbie. I'll let Frank's children decide what to do with them. But these, these he left on his desk yesterday. Addressed to you. I suppose he knew he wouldn't be coming back."

The first one, a protective plastic sleeve, felt alien to Abbie's fingertips. Inside, yellowed and creased sheets of unlined paper. She knew without looking what they were. For years she had longed to see these pages. Now she had no interest in even peeking inside.

There were two modern envelopes, unsealed, with Frank's handwriting on them. One of the unsealed envelopes was a memo directed to the university president, explaining the 2009 discovery of artifacts proving theories presented in Abigail Adams' doctoral thesis.

The other was a curt note addressed to Abbie herself. *Dr. Carlton at Cambridge sent this to me. I was wrong to keep it from you. Forgive me.*

Silent tears streamed down her face. Tears she'd held back for so long. Joss squeezed shoulder. "Abs."

Her hatred and anger against Frank Wexler flipped upside-down. She wanted to tell him, she wanted to go to his office and tell him she forgave him, but it was too late. Hours too late.

Nevelyn Wexler waited patiently for Abbie to compose herself before handing her a linen handkerchief. "Now, young man, I bring a gift for you too." From her purse, Nevelyn withdrew a silver spoon. "This is the last of the Grover treasure."

Friday, 1:17 p.m., Abbie's Bedroom

Abbie awoke to sunlight streaming through the slats of her bedroom window. At her feet, Benny wagged his tail. Funny, how'd he seemed to guard everyone else this past week, but now wouldn't leave her. "C'mere." She stretched out her hand.

The mutt crawled up into the crook of her good arm and she hugged him. "Good boy. Good job. Never let me tell you otherwise again."

Other than Benny, the house was empty. There were plenty of texts on her phone, though. Loreen would be back later with some new wine, Madeleine was bringing supper. George would meet them all at the high school at four. Abbie smirked. It took getting into a physical fight with Grace Wexler to compel George to come watch one of his sister's volleyball matches.

Joss's text was more mysterious. Have news. What news? She already knew he'd found the last of the Grover treasure, one remaining and tarnished silver spoon, the last piece from the small hoard that had been hidden away from the looting Union troops. Nevelyn Wexler, always gracious, had come clean about her uncle Harold selling most of the hoard to keep the family going through the Depression, some of the hoard sold to Abbie's old nemesis, the Puckett family. Well, perhaps not totally clean. Rumor had it Nevelyn had had her own run-ins with the Pucketts over the years.

So, what news?

Abbie had cleaned up, ready for the volleyball match, when Joss returned. The black-eye from his broken nose was now the color of Loreen's malbec. "I should take a photo of that for your social media."

"You're too late," Joss said. "Somebody snapped a shot at the hospital last night. It's on Twitter."

Joss of a week ago would have been horrified at the thought of his bruised face on the Internet. This Joss seemed, well, amused. "So, what's your news?"

"Well, I'm catching a flight to LA tomorrow. Gonna go to Baja."

What a terrible idea. "You're going to patch things up with Harriet?"

"I'm going to go get my cat."

"Good." The word popped from her lips before she could stop herself. "I never could stand that woman."

"I know."

"Fetching Lincoln isn't really news, though, is it?" Abbie asked. "I expected you to go after him."

Joss nodded. "After I get Lincoln, I'm going to pack up the condo. It's time for something new."

"That *is* news. Did you tell Loreen? She might bring over some champagne tonight."

"That's not the news."

It was as if they were back at Northwestern, Joss exasperating her and making her laugh at the same time. She wanted to throw a pillow at him, but her throwing arm was in the sling. "What, then? Spill it."

"You see, I've got this idea, now that the network is open to the new show. I want to start with this great mystery." His hands squared, as if he were framing a scene. "Picture it. It's 1763. The Ottawa plot an attack on British forts, but somebody informs Fort Detroit's commander about the conspiracy."

"No!" She really wanted to throw something at him. "You can't."

"I did. I pitched *The Identity of Henry Gladwin's Informant* to Ursula this morning. She loves it. We both think you're going to look fantastic on camera."

"Me? On camera?"

"You're the expert. And now you've got the proof you needed."

Thanks to Nevelyn Wexler, or rather, Dr. Frank Wexler, Abbie now possessed those letters that had eluded her for so long. She'd thought to write up the finding, perhaps post it on some Wiki page, so that the facts became known.

No, she'd moved past that part of her life. Abbie Adams, historian, was gone. "Joss, I can't do it."

"See, I figured you'd say that."

"So, why'd you bother asking?"

He smiled, and through the bruises Abbie glimpsed the TV star persona. "I also figured the best way to convince you that your thesis would make a great documentary is to come back here and argue with you until give up."

"You're coming back here."

"Me and Lincoln. Next week."

"For how long?"

"The foreseeable future."

"You, in Hunts Landing? You're a city boy."

"This town, it's growing on me." Joss inhaled with a satisfied smirk. "You know, I can smell the rain now. And those purple thingies, the lilacs, I can smell those too."

The impulsiveness of up and selling his condo and moving across the country, for a documentary? "You're going to do that, just to talk me into doing a show?"

"Well, first we've got to film the Grover Treasure episode. But, yeah, you're basically right."

Oh, golly, she was just getting her arms wrapped around the idea of having her house back, of some peace and quiet. Was he expecting to stay here? "Joss, I can have you as a house guest, but—"

"Ah, Miz Adams, I've got it all worked out. This is the actual news. Ready?"

"Joss, enough!" Abbie was ready to yank some of her hair out with her good hand.

"Just a moment." He stepped to the garage door and reached for something out of Abbie's sight. He carried a large parcel inside, wrapped in brown paper and string. "What you said last night got me thinking. So I took a chance at Amos's place." He pulled the string loose and unwrapped the parcel.

There were two paintings in the parcel. Joss pulled out the first one, an oil on canvas, as far as Abbie could tell, she knew next to nothing about art. One was of the bridge over the Tennessee River, painted at dawn, it seemed, because of the mist on the water and the color of the eastern sky. The artist had stood on the riverbank, behind some crooked branches. Abbie gasped as her gaze landed on the artist's signature.

EdF. Etta DuFrayne.

"Amos had this?"

"And a few more. Had no idea who the artist was until I enlightened him this morning. He let me have these at the labeled price because he can mark up the others. Ready for number two?"

She nodded.

He flipped it over, and Abbie felt like she couldn't breathe.

Rosalie DuFrayne's eyes looked up at her. Her face was much like the graduation photo that had been taped to Abbie's whiteboard for over a week now, except these eyes were sad, not sparkling, and the corners of Rosalie's mouth were slightly turned down into an almost-frown.

This must have been painted after Rosalie's death. How had Miss Etta kept her brush steady, when surely the tears must have been pouring out of her eyes?

"Pick one," Joss said.

"Huh?"

"One for you and one for me."

"Why do you get to keep one?"

"Because I need it. For decoration. Because—" he tucked one arm behind his back, the other across his abdomen, and gave her a small bow—"I bought Grover House."

Friday, 4:36 p.m., Hunts Landing Sports Complex

"C'mon, girls! Side out!"

Ace bandages might swathe his leg, butterfly sutures might criss-cross his face, but Abbie supposed that Nick's cheering voice worked just fine. Together, they made quite the pair of walking wounded. At least the parade of curious well-wishers had ceased, and they could both enjoy watching their daughters on the court. Well, maybe *endure* was the better word. The lead flipped so many times in the match, each side out either agonized or exhilarated.

The referee blew her whistle. Time out.

"So, is Joss on his way home?"

"He leaves tomorrow." Abbie wasn't sure if she cared for the hopefulness in Nick's voice. "But, he'll be back in a week."

"What?"

Abbie kept her eyes on the girls on the gym floor, in a huddle, their arms wrapped around each other's shoulders as they leaned in to listen to their coach. Martha was on the far side of the huddle; if she looked up, she'd be able to see her mother. "Yes, it seems that Joss is making a move to Hunts Landing. For the time being."

"Hmmm." He clasped his hands together. "Your kids will like that."

"It won't be boring, that's for sure."

The whistle blew. The huddles on the floor erupted with the teams' get-psyched chants.

"And are you going to like Joss being in town?"

As usual, Joss had given her little choice in the matter, so Abbie hadn't wasted a lot of mental energy considering the question. "He's an old friend."

Nick sighed and leaned back against the bleachers. "You don't make it easy on a guy, do you?"

"You thought I was a suspect."

"Only for about five, six minutes." He flashed her a smile.

She hadn't really had time to process from their date to his questioning her about Cyrus Porter to yesterday's confrontation in the clearing by the river. "We've only been on one date. Charm doesn't trump interrogation."

"Technically, we're on our second date."

Both teams returned to the court. Hunts Landing in white shirts led by one point, twenty-nine to twenty-eight. The referee waited for the girls to take their positions and blew her whistle. Isabella tossed the ball high and smacked a low, fast serve that barely cleared the net. Blue-shirted girls on the other side performed the intricate dance of getting the setters in position. One set, second set, spike! Martha dove low to her left, digging the ball up. Another set, followed by a pass back over the net. Blue shirts set once, set again, spike! Martha and another girl jumped, arms high over the net, blocking the spike. The ball swerved right and down, mere inches inside the line.

"Oh, thank God!" He stopped breathing during the volley. "I don't know which is harder, guarding you or watching a close game."

The Hunts Landing girls were hugging each other and their coaches. Abbie grinned and winked at him. "Oh, without question. It's guarding me."

EPILOGUE

July 24, 1969, 11:42 p.m., the Clearing

Rosalie DuFrayne crossed Washington Street, keeping to the shadows between two dim yellow circles of streetlamp light. She could smell the fireworks over the river as surely as she could smell the coming rain, off to the west, where the stars had all but disappeared behind black clouds. It was too hot for twisters, but not too hot for storms to crash through the valley, storms that could bring enough wind and rain to smash trees into kindling.

Fireworks and storms. A most proper end to the most improper of nights.

She turned toward the storm, her low heels clacking on the sidewalk as she sought the white hydrangea marking the start of the path. The shrub was on college property, but no one ever pruned it, it grew as wild and reckless as the mimosas on the river. There was no one to see her push aside branches bearing the last of this summer's blossoms. Anyone who would notice her was down at the party by the river.

Just past the hydrangea, at the start of the path, she paused to sniff at one of those lingering blooms, her shoes cushioned by so many discarded petals that the ground looked like the coat of confetti on Clinton Street during this afternoon's parade. She might never smell them again, not these flowers, not mixed with the summertime perfume wafting off the Tennessee. She might as well say goodnight to this guardian of her path—for she thought of it as her path, hers and Frank's, a passageway to their few precious moments of bliss.

Tonight was a night for goodbyes.

It was all Rosalie could do to keep her steps moving southward, along familiar curves in the underbrush dappled with splotchy moonlight. Her legs slowed of their own volition, but she couldn't urge them faster, not when they carried her to her last moments of happiness.

Tonight was also a night for broken hearts, and hers had been breaking for days now, weeks even, ever since that horrible afternoon at Midsummer. *Momma'd mopped her brow with a soft, wet washcloth while she'd heaved her breakfast into the toilet. Momma'd known. Momma'd understood. Momma'd called her sister Eugenia in St. Louis.*

Momma would follow as soon as she could settle things here in Hunts Landing.

The wind picked up a bit as the path skirted close to the tree line behind the sororities, a little too close for Rosalie's comfort. Faint traces of wood-smoke cleared the last remnants of catfish from her nostrils, and she inhaled the pungent fumes, so much like the smudge sticks Momma burned in the kitchen to help with the nausea. If nothing else, stopping to smell the smoke gave her a good reason to dillydally, to hold off, to postpone until the last possible moment the breaking of another's heart.

No matter how many times she'd practiced saying the words, now they seemed cruelly hollow in her mind. *I don't love you anymore, Frank. It's best for me to go.*

Except she'd never been able to lie to him, not even when they were children, and lying could be as easy as spitting downwind. Frank had never been fooled, had always known when she was hiding a cookie or a piece of licorice whip behind her back.

Rosalie was mere yards away from their clearing. She could see the open space ahead, bright with the overhead moon. She schooled her face, her cheeks, her lips, her eyes, to say those simple words and wound Frank as surely as if she were thrusting Momma's kitchen knife into his heart.

Ten feet, five.

I don't love you anymore, Frank . . .

Lying had come so easily with Dr. McCain. Lying to play dumb, lying to see everything while seeming to notice nothing. McCain had looked at her once and summed her up simply: young, female, Black, insignificant. If he'd ever suspected she'd been in his office spying for Dr. Wexler, he'd been too foolish, or arrogant, perhaps, to trouble himself with covering his tracks.

Lying to McCain had been easy. Lying to Frank would be near impossible.

But lie she must, because the truth would crush him more than the lie would. And Rosalie could never do that to him, not to her Frank.

Rosalie hovered at the edge of the clearing, drinking in the sand's smoothness, the silky light bathing the fallen tree trunks, the symphony of frog song and crickets. The pending loss of this magical place shredded her last reserves of composure.

Frank appeared on the other side of the clearing, emerging from the path toward the party at the water's edge, and she sucked in her breath, still hidden in the foliage's darkness. Only a minute, she promised herself, to look her fill, to etch his image on her memory, like a photograph. A photograph that would have to last her lifetime and never fade.

Oh, he was so handsome, this man of hers.

There was a time, when they were little, when she'd thought him overly noisy and stinky, with ears that were too big and a nose that wasn't. The memory brought a faint, unbidden smile to her lips. She hadn't thought of Frank as noisy or stinky since they were thirteen.

She stepped into the clearing, and his face cracked into a wide smile, a breathtaking smile. It would have to last.

For then she told him. This lie didn't come easy. His smile disappeared and he sank to his knees, pleading. And then, suddenly, his head lolled to the side and he pitched forward into the sand. She heard herself scream his name, twice, three times, but the screams were hoarse, rough, erupting from a place in her throat she didn't recognize. Rosalie threw down her purse and ran, hobbled by low heels in soft sand. One shoe slipped off before she reached him, and she collapsed at his side, whimpering his name in that strange voice that was hers but wasn't.

She wasn't sure if he breathed. His hand cupped her neck, grasping at her scarf. She pressed her ear close to his lips, to listen for the faintest sound, as the pressure on her neck lessened, and her scarf slipped free. There. Just the slightest hiss caressing her earlobe.

Bright yellow light shot through her eyes, exploding in bursts tinged with electric blue and green, like the fireworks earlier. *Pop! Pop!* Her arm folded, her body collapsed on her elbow. She didn't smell the fireworks any longer, didn't smell the wood-smoke, only smelled the rain, the coming rain, the storm coming to wash everything away. Another burst, this one brilliant red with sparks that arched into the sky and faded.

ACKNOWLEDGMENTS

It's impossible to take a novel from manuscript to finished book without the dedicated efforts of a team. Firstly, I need to thank my editor Helga Schier, who always believed in this story, even when I didn't. Many thanks to the other editors at CamCat, Elana Gibson and Bridget McFadden, whose numerous reads and thoughtful comments helped polish my words and ideas. And the rest of the CamCat team: Laura Wooffitt, Bill Lehto, Abigail Miles, Gabe Schier, Kayla Webb, Maryann Appel, Meredith Lyons and Jessica Homami—your efforts brought this book to fruition.

Thanks also to Cassandra Farrin and Renee Harleston and all the others who read with sharp and thoughtful eyes. Dr. McConnell who provided the inspiration for one of the main characters (and I'll never forget the many office hours we spent arguing Colonial history). Mom and Dad, for always believing in me. And, finally, the librarians at the Huntsville Public Library, for all their help in digging up old maps and newspapers from Madison and Limestone Counties.

ABOUT THE AUTHOR

S. K. Waters grew up in New Jersey and still misses it. In previous lives, she was a technical writer, a database administrator, and a championship quilter. When she's not reading, writing, following up on clues, or searching the skies for dragons, S. K. works as a small business consultant. She's also addicted to creating dioramas of her favorite scenes from some of her favorite books.

If you enjoyed S. K. Waters's

The Dead Won't Tell,

you'll enjoy

J. L. Delozier's *The Photo Thief.*

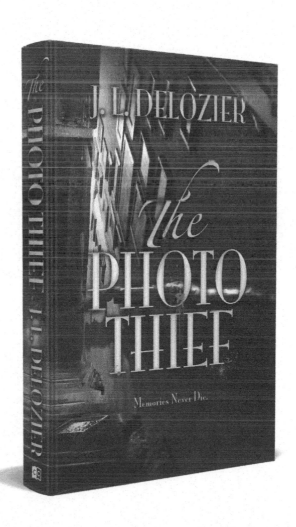

CHAPTER ONE

November, 2
First Journal Entry

A single black-and-white photo can damage a man's mind if the image is powerful enough. A thousand can shred it beyond repair. That's what happened to Pap, I suppose—why he simply stopped locking the photo room as if it no longer mattered. The damage to him was done. Mine was about to begin.

I didn't know that, of course, on that day six years ago when I first entered the photo room. Didn't know the images held the power to ruin me, too, if I failed to answer the questions they posed—mysteries from years before I was born, pictures of grisly crimes still unsolved despite today's modern methods of investigation. I needed—still need—to quiet their voices. But the questions they ask are difficult. I promised one I'd tell her story. I did. So far, no one's believed me. That's why I'm telling you.

I was more child than teen then—twelve, sheltered by wealth and religion and just beginning to rebel against my pap's strict Catholic dogma. The photo room's dangling padlock triggered an exhilarating surge of defiance. Heart pounding, I removed the skeleton key and crept inside with no idea what I might find. I honestly didn't care. Just knowing I wasn't supposed to be there was adventure enough. Even speaking of the photo room was a punishable offense in my house back then. I never saw anyone but Pap enter or leave. That's one of the reasons the first voice frightened me so.

"I killed a man, and I'm not sorry. Everyone has to eat." Delicate yet defiant, the female voice held a hint of sly amusement, as if its owner knew my reaction in advance. I later learned her name was Ruth.

Her voice echoed from nowhere and everywhere—from within the plaster walls, the floorboards, the ceiling. A chorus of others chimed in, clamoring inside my head. Their jumbled words swelled in intensity, pounding at my skull as if trying to crack it open and set themselves free. The brass chandelier flickered and dimmed; a faint odor like that of a candle wick violently snuffed into smoke stung my nose.

I stumbled toward the door I'd closed quietly behind me, only to awaken on the room's parquet floor sometime later, lying in a puddle of lukewarm urine with no memory of how I'd gotten there. My stiff, cold muscles implied hours had passed. Golden rays from the setting sun streamed through the lead-glass windows, highlighting the fine layer of dust swirling in the air. Dozens of eyes stared blankly at me from the crinkly black-and-white photos pinned to the wall. Whole families, most of them dressed in their Sunday best, bore witness to my fear and shame. The voices were gone. The padlock was set—on the inside. I gawked at it, my confused state not allowing me to wrap my brain around what had transpired and why or how someone would lock me alone in the photo room.

My pap pounded outside the door until the padlock swayed. I blinked, struggling to clear my foggy mind and focus on something other than my wet undies and the heavy object resting in my right palm. He repeated my name, his gruff voice growing frantic and hoarse. Even when he bellowed my scarcely used given name, I lay frozen in place—confused but calm, caged but not captive. For I knew something my pap didn't. In my right hand, I held the key.

CHAPTER TWO

Detective Dan Brennan paced the pavement outside the Independence Library of Philadelphia. Vibrations from a passing city bus triggered the building's revolving door to slowly spin as if pushed by a ghostly patron. Sunlight bounced off its shiny glass surface, rendering him temporarily blind. A dark cloud extinguished the glare.

He stepped toward the door, turned away, and then spun around again, nearly dropping the stack of picture books cradled in his arms. Get yourself together, man. Just get it done. He took a deep breath and hurtled through the door, lurching to a halt in front of the main circulation desk.

The librarian looked up from her computer. Her ready smile froze; her eyes flashed with recognition. The smile slowly disappeared. Brennan's frenzy fizzled into an awkward silence. He dropped the colorful pile onto the desk and backed away. The librarian stood and swept the books off the desk, tossing them into the return bin as if the mere sight of their childish covers was painful. "You didn't have to bring them back. Not so soon anyway. I . . . I know how difficult this must be—"

"They were overdue. Besides, she would've wanted me to, so some other kid can enjoy them. You know how much she loved it here. Best little library in the city." He glanced over her shoulder at the far corner, where a cozy alcove had been turned into a fantasyland for children, complete with beanbag chairs, painted unicorns, and grinning winged dragons. He had a photograph of Elle in her purple dress, the one with the polka dots she'd deemed "fa-boo-us," standing in front of a life-sized elf, if there was such a thing.

He cleared his suddenly thick throat. "I imagine I won't be back for a while. Thanks for . . . for everything." He spun on his heel, sensing too late the petite figure passing behind his back. They collided, and a flurry of papers floated to the floor. He cursed aloud. The librarian's eyebrows shot skyward.

"Sorry." Brennan cursed again, silently this time, and reflexively reached to steady the shoulders of a young woman he'd seen here before. She scowled and shirked away. Her scowl vanished at his despondent expression. She looked around the room as if searching for someone. The lump reappeared in his throat, and he crouched to gather the scattered copies of vintage newspaper articles and their photos. His eyes narrowed as he examined the morbid images. Her research had drawn his attention before.

Months ago, when chemo had cost his little girl her hair, this same young woman had been sitting at a corner table, its surface buried under mounds of similar papers. His bald daughter, entranced by the woman's long red hair, had dashed from his lap and, stretched to the max on tiny tippy toes, fingered the woman's auburn locks. Elle and the woman had exchanged smiles before he'd led his daughter away with a mumbled apology for the intrusion. He'd noticed the young woman at the corner table several times since, but that was the only time he'd seen her smile. After observing the nature of her research, he understood why. The content never varied. A gruesome murder conveyed in the stark black-and-white print of a 1930's Philadelphia Inquirer. A cautionary tale of a life gone wrong. An investigation closed too soon due to the lingering Depression, and after that, a looming world war. Heavy stuff for someone who appeared to still be in her late teens.

A subtle "ahem" interrupted his reflection. The young woman reached for the papers. "May I have those back, please?"

"Oh. Sure." Brennan thrust the stack into her outstretched hands. He studied her solemn expression, curious about her grisly research despite his grief, despite being on the clock, despite everything including himself. A retired colleague once told him the difference between a good detective and a great detective was the energy to question everything. Once that energy waned, it was time to turn in your badge.

The last six months of dealing with his daughter's illness had sapped his energy. Summer and autumn had disappeared in a rerun of hospitals visits. Everyday activities, even getting out of bed in the morning, felt like a slog through dense fog. The days were getting darker and colder. Or maybe it was just him.

His marriage was technically the first victim, cancer's collateral damage. His work had suffered as well, and he knew it. A few times, he'd thought about transferring to a desk job. He'd even considered retiring early—really early, especially after he overheard a conversation about his "soft" emotions between two long-term colleagues in the break room. After Elle died, their wives brought him meatloaf, chicken casseroles. He thought they understood.

Police work could be brutal sometimes, and no one was immune to the rough patches.

The young woman, with her armful of vintage papers, sparked his curiosity back to life. He'd dealt with a lot of young adults during his career and thought of them as clueless at best and surly at worst. Then again, in his line of work, he didn't usually deal with the salt-of-the-earth types, either.

But this girl oozed of finishing school and Main Line money, from her formal, polite mannerisms to the tips of her retro Mary Janes. She should be sipping lattes at a Starbucks on an Ivy League campus somewhere, not researching grisly murders at the local community library, even if it was in the best part of town.

On impulse, he stuck out his hand. "Detective Dan Brennan, Philly PD."

She hesitated and took a step back. He sensed her sizing him up much the same way the local hoods did when he approached their corners. He didn't blame her. He must've passed the sleaze test because she shifted the stack of papers to the crook of her left arm and shook his hand.

"Cassie."

"Cassie . . .?"

"Just Cassie." The scowl returned. She brushed by him to check out her items at the circulation desk.

He loitered until she finished and walked with her to the revolving door. "I couldn't help but notice on a couple of occasions that your research seems a little . . . dark for someone your age."

She shrugged. "School project."

"You can do better than that."

"Excuse me?"

"Your lie." He smiled to lessen the sting. "I'm a detective. Worked homicide for most of my career. I notice things for a living, which means I'm also an expert at detecting bullshit. You've been coming here at least once a week on varying days but during school hours and for a period longer than a standard school semester. You take notes in a leather-bound journal which looks like it cost more than my gun. Whatever research you're doing, it's not for school. It's personal."

"Exactly. 'Personal' means it's none of your business, just like your daughter's cancer was none of mine."

Brennan winced. He'd heard the word "cancer" a thousand times over the last year, but it still hit him like a punch in the gut every damned time.

She bit her lip. "Sorry. That was rude. Please excuse me." She ducked between the glass panels and pushed the revolving door into motion. "I should get home. It's supposed to rain."

He caught up with her on the sidewalk. "Elle. My daughter's name was Elle. She thought you were a princess and the library was your castle. She loved your hair and hoped . . ." He coughed. ". . . And hoped hers would grow out red and curly like yours."

Cassie flushed and averted her eyes. "Your daughter's hair was black."

"I know." His lips curved into a sad smile. "And straight as a soldier's spine. She was young enough to believe you could wish things true."

They stood in silence until a crack of thunder made them jump. The sunshine vanished behind a veil of black clouds.

"Whaddaya know? A thunderstorm in November." Brennan frowned. "You'll have to run to beat the rain. You want me to hail you a cab or call an Uber or somethin'?" His phone jangled, and he glanced at the number. When he looked up, Cassie had rounded the corner and quickly vanished from sight. "I guess not."

The first drops of rain fell, and he ducked under the library's eaves to answer the call. "Brennan." He rolled his eyes at the curt voice on the other end. "I'm about ten blocks away. Text me the exact address. I'll be there in a few."

When gifting a shitty assignment, his boss liked to call him herself. All his assignments had been shitty lately. His old partner, Tom, retired early spring, and Elle was diagnosed with can . . . had gotten sick shortly thereafter. Her treatments were copious and lengthy, and he'd missed a lot of work. The captain hadn't bothered to assign him a new partner yet, and he hadn't bothered to ask. It was low on his priority list.

The raindrops became a torrent. He turned up his collar and dashed to his car. His phone burbled the address. He wiped the rain off its screen and whistled. Locust and Third marked the border between Society Hill and Old City, two of Philly's swankiest neighborhoods. Maybe this assignment wouldn't be so bad after all. He could go for a simple Jag-jacking right about now—ease himself back into the workflow before handling something grittier. Grit usually meant blood. Blood meant death. He'd had enough of that to last for a long while.

He sped west past Washington Square and floored it. The short trip took forever, thanks to the oil-and-rain-slick streets and the sudden proliferation of taxis as harried tourists scurried to escape the downpour. He cursed with each sudden stop, his language growing more colorful block after congested block. He'd tried to quit swearing once, back when Elle was learning to speak. No reason to worry about that now. His vision blurred, and he cranked the wipers to high.

When he reached Third, he eased the car to the curb and lowered his rain-streaked window. The neighborhood was old—old enough that the cobblestone roads and alleys bore weathered tracks for horse-drawn trolleys. Most were too narrow for two-way traffic and many remained pedestrian-only. Franklin street lamps, rewired for electricity, lined the curbs and guarded the historic, three-story row houses which ran the length of several city blocks.

The real estate in this part of town cost more than he would earn in a lifetime—hell, in three lifetimes. The thought set his teeth on edge. Old families with old money made for the worst cases. Way too many secrets and a reluctance to share. Way too much to lose. Family legacies to preserve. The layers of bullshit never ended.

The house in question sat on an elite corner lot that intersected with one of the pedestrian-only alleys. The strobing red lights from a pair of police cruisers indicated the street was cordoned off ahead. He sighed and fumbled under his seat for an umbrella. He was hoofing it from here.

He approached and flashed his badge. The junior officer performing crowd control nodded, sending a stream of water flowing off his hat. "Everyone else is inside."

Brennan grinned. "Of course they are. Everyone except for you. Who'd you piss off?"

"No one. At least, I don't think so. I'm new on the force. Paying my dues."

"Let me guess—your partner fed you that line."

The officer nodded again. Brennan shook his head and climbed the wide, stone steps leading to the front door. Above it, a stained-glass transom glowed in shades of green and gold, lit from within by the brass chandelier hanging in the foyer. Security cameras mounted underneath the steep eaves swept in perfectly synchronized arcs. The tiny red light underneath each lens suggested they were functioning normally.

He gave a perfunctory knock, walked in, and stopped underneath the enormous chandelier to gape. It was as if he'd stepped back in time. To his right, a seven-foot-tall grandfather clock ticked the time as it had for the past hundred years. Through the mahogany pocket doors to his left, empty leather chairs faced a fireplace flanked by built-in shelves overflowing with books. The hush, broken only by the ticking of the clock, felt heavy, as if the windows, protected by thick iron bars as was typical for the neighborhood, refused to permit the slightest breeze or whisper to enter. Three generations of eyes glared at him from the oil paintings lining the papered wall of the foyer. The hairs on his arms stood on end. He was alone.

A burst of chatter from a police radio echoed down the elaborately carved grand staircase, shattering the spell. He exhaled and strode forward, breaking into an awkward jig as his wet soles slipped on the marble tile. The sturdy bottom newel kept him from hitting the ground. He grabbed the banister for support and placed his free hand on his gun. Even the house was out to get him. He hated this case already.

He tilted his head and stared up three steep stories. Thirteen steps took him to the first ninety-degree landing. He rounded the corner and stopped. Long, slender fingers dangled over the second-floor landing. Another step and the contorted body of a woman came into view. She lay face-up in a pool of congealed blood—so much blood, it had streamed onto the tread below. A pair of CSI circled her, snapping pictures like the paparazzi.

Brennan placed his foot on the next step. It creaked, announcing his presence. The younger of the two investigators crouched by the woman's head and focused his lens on the victim's battered skull. He paused his grisly duties long enough to cock his thumb toward the third flight of stairs. "Yo, Dan. It's been a while. I was hoping you'd get this case. Senior officer's up there interviewing the only witness. Officer Cortez, I think. Watch your step—they might be a little slick, as you can tell." His thick glasses slid down the bridge of his nose, and he pushed them in place with a shrug of his shoulder. "Welcome back, by the way. I missed our daily swim break."

"Me too, Jim. Thanks. It's good to be back." Liar, liar, pants on fire. Elle's childish chant echoed in his ears. Brennan climbed the remaining stairs. Pressing his back against the banister, he awkwardly skirted along the edge of the crowded landing. "What's the story?"

He studied the woman's delicate features. Mid-forties, he guessed, with green eyes and auburn hair. She was lovely even in death, if you could ignore the God-awful mess.

MORE SUSPENSE FROM CAMCAT BOOKS

CamCat
Books

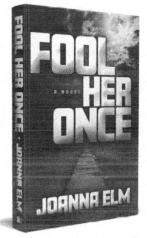

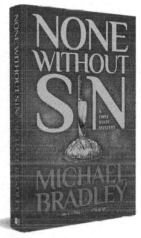

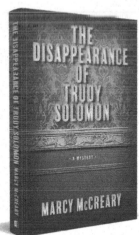

Available now, wherever books are sold.